713 200

P9-CQS-952

The Floating Islands

The Floating Islands

Rachel Neumeier

Alfred A. Knopf   New York

THIS IS A BORZOI BOOK PUBLISHED BY ALFRED A. KNOPF

Visit us on the Web! www.randomhouse.com/teens

Educators and librarians, for a variety of teaching tools, visit us at www.randomhouse.com/teachers

Library of Congress Cataloging-in-Publication Data
Neumeier, Rachel.
The Floating Islands / by Rachel Neumeier. — 1st ed.
p. cm.
Summary: The adventures of two teenaged cousins who live in a place called The Floating Islands, one of whom is studying to become a mage and the other one of the legendary island flyers.
ISBN 978-0-375-84705-9 (trade) — ISBN 978-0-375-94705-6 (lib. bdg.) — ISBN 978-0-375-89782-5 (ebook)
[1. Fantasy. 2. Magic—Fiction. 3. Flight—Fiction. 4. Cousins—Fiction.]
I. Title.
PZ7.N4448Fl 2011
[Fic]—dc22
2010012772

The text of this book is set in 11.5-point Hoefler Text.

Printed in the United States of America
February 2011
10 9 8 7 6 5 4 3 2 1

First Edition

This one's for Margaret Brown—my aunt and one-woman

PR department. Thanks for all your enthusiasm!

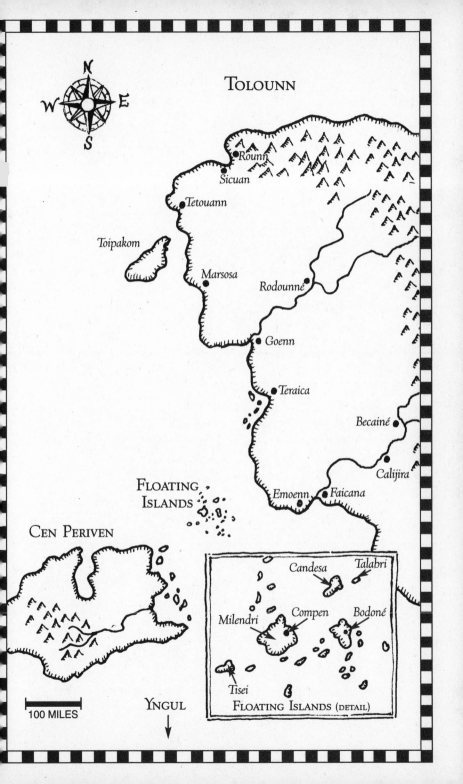

TOLOUNN

Rounn
Sicuan
Tetouann
Toipakom
Marsosa
Rodounné
Goenn
Teraica
Becainé
Calijira
FLOATING
ISLANDS
Emoenn   Faicana
CEN PERIVEN

FLOATING ISLANDS (DETAIL)

Candesa   Talabri
Milendri   Compen   Bodoné
Tisei

100 MILES

YNGUL

I

Trei was fourteen the first time he saw the Floating Islands. He had made the whole long voyage south from Rounn in a haze of loss and misery, not really noticing the harbors in which the ship sometimes anchored or the sea between. But here, where both sea and sky lay pearl-gray in the dawn, the wonder of the Floating Islands broke at last into that haze.

A boy high in the rigging called out in a shrill voice, pointing, and then the deeper voice of an officer rang out and the ship smoothly adjusted its heading. Before them, the Islands rose shimmering out of the dawn mist. They stood high above the sea—too high, even in that first mist-shrouded glimpse. Then the early sun, rising, turned the air to gold and the sea to sapphire and picked the Islands out of the mist like jewels. In that light, they seemed too beautiful to hold terror or despair or anguish. Trei could hardly bear to look at them, yet could not bring himself to look away. He gripped the railing hard and bit his lip almost till it bled.

Each of the Floating Islands was broad on top, narrowing to points of jagged rock below. Trei found a place to sit among coiled ropes, near the bow of the ship, out of the way of the busy sailors. He propped his chin in his hands and watched the Islands grow larger as the morning passed. They only seemed more astonishing as the ship approached them. Trei could have believed that someone had painted them on a backdrop and the ship would eventually tear through the canvas to find, waiting, a far less magical scene.

The Islands proved to be farther away than Trei had first thought. All morning, while the dawn cool gave way to the heavy southern heat, the ship sailed toward the nearest of the Islands, drawing close at last only as the sun crested in the sky. Pastures scattered with grazing sheep were visible upon its heights as they approached it, and the fluted pillars of a temple. Trei found his eye persistently trying to fill in the slopes of a mountain below the floating stone, but no matter how he stared, the red rock ran out into nothing but empty air where the gulls wheeled.

Trei craned his neck back and stared upward as they passed under the Island. Drifting mist, contorted trees growing directly out of the rock, gulls' nests, and the odd vein of white marble, all so high above there would have been room below for masts five times the height. Barely audible beyond the shrill cries of the gulls came the delicate thread of some unearthly melody.

"That's only Talabri," Mana said, stopping beside Trei. The burly sailor's tone was dismissive; Trei looked at him with mute amazement that anyone could sound like that while sailing hardly a long stone's throw from such a miracle.

2

"Sheep and shepherds, orchards and vineyards, temples and priests." Mana waved Talabri away with scorn. He enjoyed talking and never minded Trei's silence. Despite his own distracted indifference, Trei had come to like the sailor's friendly one-sided conversation. "It's peaceful, aye, but there's nothing on Talabri to interest a man. Candera, now—where's your family, lad, Candera?"

Trei closed his eyes briefly, wishing desperately that his family was on Candera, was anywhere at all in the living world. It took him a moment to manage anything like a normal tone. "Milendri. My uncle's family."

"Oh, Milendri! That's lucky for you, lad, supposing you want to live on an island held up in the air by nothing but sky magic. But Milendri's the greatest of all the Floating Islands, they say. Your uncle's family lives in Canpra, I suppose, the king's capital city, what's his name—some up-and-down Island name, nothing but vowels from start to finish."

The king of the Floating Islands was Terinai Naterensei, but Trei said nothing. His uncle's family did indeed live in a city called Canpra, but Trei hadn't really understood that this was anything special.

Mana, never deterred by Trei's silence, went on cheerfully, "I hear Canpra's a splendid city. Not that they let ships' crews up, but they say the old king, three back, built it to rival even Rodounnè. Not that I believe it. But it's true the bit you can see from the sea looks splendid enough."

Trei wondered how a city would look if it was deliberately built to be splendid. In Tolounn, all the towns had just sort of grown up where people had once decided to settle, like the town of Rounn growing up around the Rounn River, where, according to family legend, Great-grandfather Meraunn had once made his fortune backing the new steamboats over ox-drawn keelboats. He found he was curious about this new city, but didn't know exactly what to ask.

"We won't see Milendri before tomorrow afternoon," Mana rattled on. "We'll be passing islands all day, of course. . . ."

But Trei was no longer listening. He had just caught sight of his first winged Island fliers, and had attention to spare for nothing else.

There were a dozen of them—no, Trei saw as they approached: fourteen. Fifteen. They flew as geese fly in the fall, in a formation like a spear point. At first the shape the winged men made was stark as a rune against the empty sky, but as they approached the ship, they broke their formation, wheeled, and circled low. The morning light caught in the feathers of their glorious wings, crimson as blood, except for one man whose wings were black as grief.

As the fliers passed above the ship, Trei saw how each man wore his wings like a strange kind of cloak. Crimson bands crossed the fliers' arms and bodies. Though the wings looked like real wings, he saw clearly that the men were flying by some understandable kind of magic and were not actually winged people. He held his breath, staring up at them.

Then all the fliers tilted their wings and lifted up and up, spiraling back into the sky and away toward Talabri. Trei let out his breath, only then aware that he had been holding it.

"Show-away Island wingmen," Mana muttered.

"How do they *do* that?" Trei breathed.

The sailor lowered his voice even further. "Don't they tell stories about the Island wingmen, then, way up in the north? They don't fly with good solid human magic, but some gauzy dragon stuff. It's not right for men, is what I say. They like to come down low over foreign ships, especially Tolounnese ships. Impress the mainlanders. Like Tolounn isn't a thousand times the size of all the Floating Islands put together, and a hundred times richer besides, but Islanders don't know their place." He spat over the railing and added, "Clannish sorts, and the wingmen are the worst. Stick to men who walk on solid ground, lad, not those crystal-eyed ride-on-air dragon-loving wingmen."

Trei said nothing. He already knew that if he couldn't learn to ride the wind on great crimson wings, he would die.

Milendri was much larger even than Talabri, hard though this was to believe: thirty miles long, Mana said, and nearly as wide. The graceful towers of Canpra, blinding white upon the edge of the Island, were visible while the ship was still distant. The towers drew the eye insistently, yet as they approached, Trei found himself staring at the broken rock that fell away below that edge. At last, strange regularities descending below the towers resolved themselves into great structures that had been carved into the red stone above the sea. He stared in awe, understanding that Canpra's builders had carved their city down into the stone as well as flinging it up toward the sky.

Bridges and airy colonnades were strung between the white towers or out over the waves, but intricate stairways carved into the stone led down and down, to wide galleries almost low enough to feel the spray from high waves. Some of the stairways . . . Trei stared. But as they approached, he saw it was true: some of the stairways mounted straight through the air, broad steps following one after another, suspended from nothing. Most were carved of red stone, some of blinding white marble. Nothing but air was visible between each stair step and the next. The spray broke over the lowest ones—if they were the lowest: it seemed to Trei that those steps might go down and down into the sea, just as they mounted into the sky. But who might follow them down into the depths, if so?

And how was one supposed to climb those stairs, if one did not have wings?

Once Trei stood on the lowest of the stones, however, he found himself grasped firmly, as though the air itself held him in place. Even though the breeze pressed at him, once he was on it, the stair step felt wide and perfectly secure. And the floating step carried him somehow upward, though he felt no sense of motion; every time he looked down, he found himself farther from the rippling sea and the increasingly tiny ship below—already departing. So there was no way back, even if he could make his way down stairs that seemed bent on carrying him upward. Trei sat down in the center of the stair, next to the small pack of his pitifully few belongings, and waited to reach the surface of Milendri.

Canpra proved to be enormous, filled with brilliant light, shattering noise, chaotic movement, and crowds of people. Perhaps it *was* splendid, but nothing about the city made sense to Trei. He found it impossible to imagine that it ever could, not if he lived here a hundred years. Now that he stood surrounded by the clamor of the Island city, he was suddenly and fiercely homesick for the gentle hills of Rounn. But Rounn was gone. There was no way back home.

Trei blinked hard and used almost the last of his coins to hire a boy to guide him. When he followed his guide, he lowered his head, trying not to look at anything.

"Fourteen-three-forty," announced the boy at last, turning to look with curiosity at Trei. "Avenue of Flameberry Trees, Fourth Quarter of the Second City. You all right?"

Trei did not know. He was almost sure the *address* was right, but now that he had come here, he was not at all sure of his welcome. His other uncle had not wanted him. . . . He had never met his mother's brother, and if this uncle also refused him, he had no idea at all where he might go. He was seized with a conviction that he would find himself stranded, lost and with hardly a coin to his name, in a city and a country he did not know.

Slowly, Trei reached out and touched the brass clapper. The distant reverberation of the clapper's alert sounded from inside the house. There was a long pause. Trei held his breath. The boy shifted his feet, sighed, and glanced over at Trei, opening his mouth to make some comment or suggestion. But the door opened at last.

It was not Trei's uncle who peered out at them, but a thin, narrow-faced girl in a plain dress of undyed linen. The girl had a small mouth, a strong chin, and chestnut-colored hair as shiny and crisp as the feathers of a thrush—exactly the same shade as Trei's mother's. Her eyes were dark, determined, and notably fierce. Trei's sister had had eyes like those.

The girl glanced at the boy and then looked at Trei. Chestnut eyebrows rose over dark eyes. "Yes?"

"I'm looking . . . I'm looking for Serfei Naseida?" said Trei. He tried not to sound frightened, and thought he probably sounded stiff.

The girl tilted her head curiously and stepped back so he could enter. "Please be welcome to our house," she said. "I shall bring my father to speak with you."

"All right, then," said Trei's guide. He gave Trei a casual flip of his hand, accepted another coin with a grin, and jogged away down the street.

Uncle Serfei proved to be a tall, angular man with sharp cheekbones and smiling, quizzical eyes. He looked nothing like Trei's mother. But he recognized Trei at once. The smile disappeared from his eyes, and he stepped forward to take Trei by the shoulders, looking down into his face. "Your mother?" he asked him. "Your family?"

The kindness in his tone brought grief rising unexpectedly into Trei's throat so that he could not answer. He was unutterably relieved to find himself recognized.

Uncle Serfei's look became grieved and pitying. Trei looked away. He found the girl . . . his cousin . . . gazing at him from the doorway. She didn't look exactly unfriendly. But she didn't look friendly, either. She said abruptly, "I'll tell Mother," and vanished into the house.

"Come." Uncle Serfei gently drew him further in. "You're exhausted, I'm sure. And starving. The kitchen is through here—this is the servants' half day, so we must fend for ourselves," Uncle Serfei explained apologetically. "But Araenè does very well for us in the kitchen. There's pigeon pie, and I'm sure there are figs. Let me pour you some wine." He topped the cup up with water and handed it to Trei. "You

8

needn't—that is, even here we've heard what happened at Rounn. We were sure you must all—" He stopped.

"Is it true the whole town was covered by ash?" Araenè asked, following her mother into the kitchen. Trei's aunt, Edona, was a comfortable, softly rounded woman. She gave her daughter a small frown and Trei a welcoming smile.

"Trei, my dear," she said warmly. "I'm so happy to see you, and so sorry to see you here alone. You needn't talk about it if you don't wish to—"

"It doesn't matter," Trei said. He looked at the cup his uncle had put in his hand, then gulped the watered wine. It wasn't nearly as strong as he'd have liked. He looked straight at his cousin and said in the flattest tone he could manage, "It was all buried. Mount Ghaonnè took everything. The provincar's mansion was the only building tall enough to stick out, and it was four stories tall and had a bell tower on the top. But it wasn't the ash that killed everybody. They say poisonous air came out of the earth right into the middle of the city, where the baths were, over the hot springs. They say a lot of poison came out suddenly and just filled up the valley. So everyone died from that, before the mountain even exploded. And we—we couldn't even go down, afterward—"

Trei had to stop. His cousin, he was satisfied to see, was looking rather ill. So was his aunt Edona. Trei was sorry for that. He said quickly, "They say it would have been fast." He had not known whether to believe this assurance. How would anybody know?

"We are so glad you escaped, at least!" Aunt Edona exclaimed, coming to press Trei's hands. "And we thank the Gods you came to us. How difficult a journey this must have been for you, my dear! Please don't speak of such terrible things."

"You are safe now, nephew, and among family once more," added Uncle Serfei.

Trei put his cup down abruptly and left the kitchen. Then, ashamed, he hesitated at the base of a narrow stair, knowing he should go back.

"I'm sorry." Araenè turned up, leaning in a doorway. She did look sorry. "I don't . . . I don't think I really believed that, about Rounn, until you said that. She sent us stones one time. Your mother. Fossils from the river, the kind that coil around, you know? My father loved them. And she sent me some really good recipes for salt-cured fish. I'm sorry she—they all—"

Trei made himself nod.

"Why'd you come here, though? Didn't your father have family in other parts of Tolounn?"

Her tone wasn't exactly hostile, but it was hard to see that kind of question as friendly, either. Trei's other uncle, his father's brother in Sicuon, had made it clear that summers were one thing, or had been when his father was alive, but as for taking an Island half blood into a good Tolounnese family— and, worse, paying the tax to register a half blood as a Tolounnese citizen—well, that was something else. Trei wasn't going to tell her how he'd always thought his Tolounnese uncle and aunt liked him. But when he'd begged to stay in Sicuon, in terms he was ashamed to remember, his uncle had only given him some money and sent him away. Trei wasn't going to tell this girl about that. He said nothing.

"Well . . . let me . . . Shall I show you the house, then? Your room? You can get something to eat later. Or I can bring you something. But if you're tired now, that's all right. Father says we'll make the low attic over, but you can have my room for now and I'll go in with Mother."

Trei nodded again, warily. He could see how his cousin hated this disarrangement, but what could he do about it? He resolved to be very happy with the attic, as soon as possible.

Araenè led him up the stairs. One wall of the stairwell was pierced every few feet by a narrow window, each letting in a measure of light and air; Trei was surprised to see that it was now nearly dusk.

In the last light of the sun, high over the rooftops of Canpra, men with crimson wings drifted in a high, endless spiral. Trei pressed his palms on the windowsill and leaned out, staring up at them.

"What?" Araenè came back and glanced out the window. "Oh—you don't have kajuraihi in Tolounn, do you?" She sounded pleased about this.

Trei ignored her tone. He leaned out farther, watching the fliers—the kajuraihi—until their slow, spiraling flight took them at last out of sight. He said, barely aware he spoke aloud, a sigh of yearning, "Oh, I have to learn that. I have to learn how to fly."

Araenè stared at him in surprise. "Well, you can't. A Tolounnese boy, join the kajuraihi? That's Island magic."

Trei pulled himself back inside, returned his cousin's stare, and said nothing.

"Well, you might," Uncle Serfei said judiciously the next morning when Trei asked him over breakfast. The breakfast was warm wheat bread with figs and honey, not the beef and eggs and sweetened buckwheat porridge of northern Tolounn. Aunt Edona had taken Araenè and gone somewhere, so it was just Trei and Uncle Serfei at the table.

Trei dipped a fig in honey and ate it slowly. He could see his uncle was glad that Trei had asked about the Island's fliers, that he was anxious Trei should find a good place in Canpra and be happy here. Trei could not imagine being happy—but he longed to fly.

"You're fourteen, isn't that so? So you're the right age for it." Uncle Serfei spread honey on a slice of bread, regarding Trei thoughtfully. "It's true we don't want the Tolounnese getting a feel for dragon magic—especially now they've got Toipakom pacified; the Little Emperor is getting restless for another conquest, so it's said, and there's no obvious direction for him to turn but toward us. But then, you're not Tolounnese anymore. In fact, you never were, really, were you? Your father couldn't have registered you as a Tolounnese citizen until your majority, isn't that the law in Tolounn?"

Trei nodded, although, distracted by his uncle's comment about conquest, he'd only half heard the question. Trei had been very young when Tolounn had conquered Toipakom, but his tutor had made him study that conquest. Trei's tutor had approved of the subjugation of Toipakom because, he said, it wasn't right for a little island like that to take on the airs of a real nation. Trei's father had shaken his head and said who cared what airs some minor country put on? But he had added that the Great Emperor was wise to allow the Little Emperor to conquer all the world, as trade could only benefit from uniformity of law and an absence of tariffs. Trei remembered that, because his mother had rolled her eyes and said something biting about Tolounnese aggression.

But Trei hadn't quite put those comments together as suggesting a possible attempt to conquer the Floating Islands. He said, "You don't really think . . . ," but then did not know how to complete that question.

"Oh, well." Uncle Serfei gave Trei a wry smile. "It's something we think about here. Don't worry; I'm sure nothing will happen. Tolounn hasn't ever tried seriously to conquer us. Anyway, how could they?" He waved his bread in the air above the table, miming the height of the Floating Islands above the sea. "It's just, we can't help but be aware. . . . Not even the Emperors of Tolounn would provoke Yngul, but the Little Emperor is an aggressive man. If not Yngul, I'm sure he's considering what less formidable nation he might conquer. Cen Periven, for example. Small enough to control, rich enough to pay for the effort ten times over—conquering Cen Periven would secure his place in history far better than merely taking little Toipakom! But if he wants Cen Periven, he'd need to take us first, unless he wanted to risk having us behind him while he attacked it, which I doubt."

"But . . . ," Trei began, but stopped. If Tolounn *did* attack the Islands—but his uncle was right: he wasn't Tolounnese anymore. Except he didn't at all feel like an Islander, could hardly imagine feeling at home here. If he wasn't an Islander, yet wasn't really Tolounnese . . .

Uncle Serfei broke into Trei's confusion, his casual wave and matter-of-fact tone dismissing it. "Anyway, none of that's to say you couldn't try for a place in the next kajurai auditions. Kajuraihi . . . ah. I meant to say, kajuraihi embody the spirit of the Islands, but that sounds pretentious, doesn't it? Though it's true, in a way. Even nowadays." He made a little self-deprecating gesture, absently layered more honey on the bread until it dripped off the edges, and ate it in a couple of bites.

Then he said, "Kajuraihi have been soldiers, Trei, a first line of defense for the Islands, but not for a long time. Now they're more often couriers. Discreet couriers at the highest level, but still, fundamentally messengers. Does that sound like something you'd like to do?"

Trei didn't answer. If the question had been just that—do you want to be a courier?—then the answer would have been *no*. But if the question was, are you willing to become a courier if it means you can fly?—in that case, he thought, the answer would be *yes*. Because when he imagined walking in the streets of the city, watching winged men soar overhead and knowing he would never be among them . . . the thought was almost a physical ache within him.

Uncle Serfei seemed to see something of this in Trei's face. He added kindly, "Not *all* kajuraihi are couriers, of course. Some are attached to ambassadors' staffs; some are ambassadors themselves. It's sometimes expedient for the king to have a man with broad authority who can be in Cen Periven or Tolounn, or even Yngul, *fast*. Kajuraihi can fly faster than even the fastest ship can sail—it's said kajuraihi can bend even the fiercest winds to their will." He paused, and then said, "I don't know whether that's true."

Trei made a noncommittal sound. He tried to imagine being an ambassador. It was not a position he'd ever felt any desire for, before. He said after a moment, doubtfully, "But my father *was* Tolounnese. I don't . . . Your king surely wouldn't want me to speak with his voice?"

Uncle Serfei waved a second piece of bread at Trei. "*Your* king, too! *You're* not Tolounnese! You're my nephew, Alana's son, and as eligible to audition as anybody's son. Anyway, that's what I'll argue when I petition for a place for you in the auditions."

Trei nodded uncertainly.

"Mind, now, every boy dreams of the kajuraihi when he's your age. Most don't ever win their wings: it's a hard path to follow, the one that mounts to the clouds. Best not to fix all your dreams on the sky, eh? I'm sure Alana's son is clever enough for the ministry. Or you might even find yourself with a gift for magery, who knows?" Uncle Serfei looked wistful. "The odd mage used to emerge from the Naseida family from time to time, though we haven't had one for the past few generations."

Trei could hardly say anything to this. He certainly couldn't tell Uncle Serfei that he didn't want to be a minister of anything, or that magecraft would be even worse. Until he'd seen the winged men, Trei had assumed that he would someday be a merchant captain. Now . . . he just knew he wanted to fly. Trei looked up at his uncle. "I don't care how hard it is. Please. I want to fly. I need . . ." His voice trailed off, and he opened his hands in inarticulate longing.

"Well, then, I'll petition for a place for you," promised Uncle Serfei, reaching to pat his shoulder reassuringly. "More figs? Bread? After breakfast, we'll see about making a good, respectable Island boy out of you. Clothing, new shoes, what else? Let me see. We can register you at the library for the coming quarter. . . ."

It emerged that the library was where Island boys went to school. A common school. Trei's heart sank at the thought: dozens of boys together in a large room, sharing their books and their teachers with the rest instead of having a private tutor—even the wealthiest boys.

"These are mostly boys from ministry families," Uncle Serfei explained. "And the sons of magistrates, scholars, famous physicians, men like that . . . important men, you know."

"Mages?"

"No, no." Uncle Serfei gestured extravagantly. "The mages have their own school somewhere. No one knows where. Maybe in Canpra, maybe somewhere not exactly on Milendri at all. It's said a boy with the gift will find it himself when he's ready. No, the boys at the library aren't likely to be mages. But plenty of those boys will have posts in the ministries someday, so it's important they know one another. Now. The quarter changes in just a few days, I believe, so you can start at the library then. If you apprentice with the kajuraihi later, that's fine, but a little while in library classes will do nothing but help you."

"Does Araenè go to the library for classes, too?" Trei asked. He did not want to attend classes with ministers' sons—and he didn't think he liked his cousin anyway—but at least she would be someone he knew.

Uncle Serfei gave him a startled look, then smiled. "Girls do sometimes, in Tolounn, don't they? No, Trei. Island girls have private tutors sometimes. A few write tolerable poetry, I suppose, but it's not as though they are going to be scholars or ministers or magistrates, is it?"

Trei thought of how his sister would have responded to this comment, but he said nothing.

Island clothing was lighter, cooler, and far more brightly colored than anything worn in northern Tolounn. Trei put on a sleeveless green shirt, which he belted with a gold sash over sapphire-blue pants. He felt like he was dressing in a costume, not in real clothing. Trei knew he should go find his cousin and her parents. But he sat cross-legged on the bed, gazed out the window, and didn't move toward the door.

Outside his door, someone clapped. Araenè opened the door without waiting for his call—well, but it *was* her room, really, Trei supposed—and stepped in. She wore a dark green dress with a gold sash, and her hair was pinned up with a pearl comb. She looked far more elegant than she had the previous evening, but no more friendly. She looked Trei up and down. He felt his face warm, but said nothing.

However, his cousin made no comment about his change of clothing. "Do you like steamed fish?" she asked. "I used skin-on taki fillets and made silver sauce, only I used wine instead of lemon, and less sugar."

"Oh?" Trei wondered what he was supposed to say to this.

Araenè sighed and turned to go. She said over her shoulder, "Supper's always half past sixth bell, so we'd best move along."

The fish was delicious. You peeled the black skin away and drizzled the translucent sauce over the flaky fish. There were thin green-flecked pancakes to go with the fish. You tore off pieces and picked up bits of fish with them, then drizzled on more sauce and added some crunchy green vegetable he didn't recognize and ate the packets you'd made. Flavors then unfolded one after another in your mouth, complex and wonderful. Trei slowed down after the first bite to make his food last longer.

"Araenè is truly gifted," Aunt Edona said fondly, noting Trei's expression. "Her husband will be a lucky man."

"If she were a boy, she'd earn a place in the king's own kitchens," Uncle Serfei added, smiling proudly at his daughter. "She'd wind up a master of all the eight arts and five arts and be famous."

Araenè didn't look pleased by these compliments. Her mouth tightened, and she fixed her eyes on her plate. Trei said almost at random, to break the uncomfortable pause, "Eight arts and how many?"

"Sauces and creams, relishes and chutneys, mousses and whipped dishes, savory dishes with fruit, meat dishes, fish and seafood, vegetable dishes, and breads," Araenè recited to her plate. She looked up, frowning fiercely. "And the five confectionary arts: cream sweets, frozen sweets, grain sweets, sweets made with fruit, and pastries. People in Tolounn don't know how to cook."

"Now, Araenè—" Aunt Edona began.

Her daughter just looked stubborn. "Not really cook. Cen Periven has real chefs, but Tolounn? Just heating things until they're edible isn't really *cooking*." Her lip curled in disdain. Trei thought of how the food at his home had differed from the food made by his friends' servants, about the way only his mother, unlike the mothers of his friends, had sometimes taken over the cooking for his household. His mother's occasional tart comments about Tolounnese cooking, heard and disregarded all his life, fell suddenly into place. He asked Araenè, "Do you really know how to make all those things? Sauces and mousses and savory things and all those others?"

His cousin flushed and looked down again.

"She really does," Aunt Edona assured Trei.

Araenè looked at Trei and added grudgingly, "Not that Tolounn hasn't its own arts, I'm sure." She sounded like she didn't know of any and didn't think they'd count for much anyway.

"Araenè—" Aunt Edona said.

"Cen Periven prides itself on the eternal arts, and we on the ephemeral. Tolounn's only art is the art of war," Uncle Serfei said grimly.

His wife patted his hand. "Not at the table, love, I beg you."

Uncle Serfei looked embarrassed. He said to Trei, "Well, we do claim that our Island chefs are more skilled than any elsewhere. And Araenè truly is gifted."

"Pastries are hard to get right," Araenè muttered to her plate.

"You make wonderful pastries," Aunt Edona said firmly. "What did you make tonight, love?"

Araenè had made tiny crisp pastries filled with cream that was pink and delicately rose-scented. Each pastry was topped with a single candied rose petal.

"They're almost too pretty to eat," Trei said fervently, holding his third pastry up to admire it and trying to decide whether he had room left to eat it. His mother had never attempted anything like these.

His cousin smiled at last. "They're meant to be eaten. That's why it's an *ephemeral* art."

Trei ate the pastry in two bites and was sorry it was the last one. "You really ought to be cooking for the king!" he told his cousin.

Araenè lost her smile again, so that Trei understood that she did actually want to be a royal chef, and famous. Only she couldn't because, he supposed, she was a girl. From the way they acted, he thought that neither of her parents really understood this about their daughter, even though it was obvious. No wonder she was fierce. No one had ever tried to tell his sister she couldn't draw or paint, and someday Marrè probably *would* have been famous. He wanted suddenly to show Marrè's sketches to his cousin, to tell Araenè about his sister. He thought the two girls would have understood each other, that they would have been friends. His throat closed with the effort to restrain tears.

Uncle Serfei said to Trei, rescuing him from a public outcry of grief, "I checked this afternoon, and the next kajurai auditions will take place in forty-four days. That's a nice piece of luck; they only have auditions every few years. Tomorrow I'll petition for you to audition, and then while we wait for a response, you can attend proper Island classes. I hope you had a decent grounding off there in Rounn."

Trei recovered himself, stung. Rounn had hardly been some little cow-mire village. "Of course I did. But—" He started to say that he didn't want to attend library classes, but stopped himself. Uncle Serfei had already agreed to try to get a place for him with the Island fliers. It would be shameful—childish—ungrateful, even—to argue about the library.

But he wished Araenè could also attend the classes.

2

Araenè's Tolounnese cousin caused her much less trouble than she had feared. He kept out of her things—Araenè cleared out three of her drawers and half a wardrobe for him and covertly checked every day to be sure everything was exactly as she had left it in the rest of the drawers. *Especially* in the back of her most private wardrobe. As far as she could tell, her cousin never poked about. He seemed to understand he was intruding. Probably he was as eager to move into his own personal attic as she was to have him out of her room.

Araenè was surprised to find that the attic looked like it was becoming a fairly nice room, after everything was taken out and the walls dusted and the floor scrubbed. Mother bustled happily about the business of choosing the rugs and linens, delighting over a bed frame of twisted iron and matching iron lamps. Araenè thought the linens pale and insipid, the ornate bed frame and lamps overdone. But Trei, apparently reluctant to offend his uncle and aunt, agreed with Mother in all her choices. Araenè made no comment, so eager to have her own room back that she scrubbed and dusted with a will. Then, after Mother complimented her industry, she was a little ashamed—but still eager to have her cousin safely installed in his own room and out of hers.

Trei was a quiet boy. Really quiet. He was polite to Mother and Araenè thought he sincerely liked Father, but he didn't follow Araenè around, and he stayed out of the kitchen when she was concentrating. Nor did Trei often leave the house, except, as soon as his classes were arranged, to go to the library—though he was obviously, boy-like, completely sky-mad. Araenè thought that in his place, she would have been wild to explore Canpra. Her cousin could have roamed the whole city if he liked. A boy's freedom was wasted on Trei, Araenè decided. Absolutely *wasted*.

In general she was glad her cousin kept his distance from her, and was willing to let her keep her distance from him. The very last thing she wanted was a new shadow clinging to her heel. She was glad classes had been arranged for him; it was good to have some of her privacy back.

Now, at last, the Moon's Day after Trei's arrival, Araenè finally found an opportunity to put that privacy to real *use*. She folded back the shutters of her room. The late-morning heat rolled into the room at once, but she only leaned out and studied the narrow alley behind the house. No one was about: it would be too hot until dusk for anyone to willingly venture into the streets. There was a high, pale haze across the sky, blurring the brilliant sun, but this didn't mute the heavy, smothering heat.

Father was at the ministry, in the First City, at the edge of the Island; he would be gone until long past dusk. As was the custom on Moon's Day, Mother had gone to pay calls on other Second City matrons. By now she would be comfortably ensconced in the home of one of her friends, where she and other visitors would sip cooling ices and exchange all the Second City gossip. Trei, of course, was at the library. Even the servants were out: Araenè had given both of them permission to visit the market and take the afternoon off.

So Araenè was alone. That made it a perfect day. Wholly perfect.

Araenè stepped back into her room and turned to gaze at herself in her mirror. Dark green trousers and a dark red shirt, both from that carefully hidden stash in the back of her own wardrobe. A dusky purple sash, pinned on the right side. Her hair bound up and tucked under a hat with a broad, floppy brim—the hat was ridiculous, but conveniently popular among the sillier young men right now. Slender pins to hold the hat firmly in place. She had sewn pads into her shirt to broaden her shoulders and wore thick bracelets, foppish but very masculine, to disguise the fineness of her wrists.

Araenè glanced at herself in the mirror one last time. There was nothing she could do about her slender girl's throat, but no one had ever seemed to notice this flaw. Little more than the change of clothing was required: in a year or two she might have more difficulty, but Araenè did not yet take after her generously figured mother. If she was lucky, she'd take after her father's side of the family instead. She nodded, satisfied: it was not a girl who looked back at her from that mirror, but a boy. A vain boy, a boy who apparently thought too much of himself, yes. But a boy.

She made one more cautious inspection of the alley, then swung neatly out the window, hung by her fingertips for an instant, and dropped. It was several feet to the cobbles; Araenè bent her knees as she hit, put out her hands for balance, and straightened. She touched the brim of her boy's hat to make sure it was still in place and then walked quickly down the alley, turned the corner, and let her demure girl's step lengthen to a boy's free stride.

The avenues of the Second City radiated away from the white towers of the First City. These avenues were arranged in even, precise concentric arcs, cut through by long, straight streets that gave swift access to the First City. Araenè knew where to find the nearest open market, where the shops were that carried the most interesting Yngulin silks or the newest imports from Cen Periven, where the finest restaurants were, the high-class ones that well-bred women, if escorted, could patronize. Every Second City woman knew these things.

But Araenè also knew the three fastest ways to get from her house to the University. She knew her way around the University, too, and she doubted any other well-bred Second City woman knew *that*.

If one stayed on proper streets, then the University lay nearly a bell from Araenè's home. But she could cut more than half that time by crossing through two private gardens and climbing up and over the roof of a shop that sold secondhand clothing. Though it was important not to be spotted in the gardens, no one looked askance at boys taking the rooftop shortcut. Students, perennially late for one or another lecture or demonstration, used this shortcut as though it were one of

the official student pathways, and paid for the privilege by do-
nating clothing to the shop (if they were wealthy) or buying
clothing there (if they were poor). Long ago someone had
fixed hand- and footholds to make the climb even faster, and
now Araenè went up and over the shop almost as quickly as
she might have walked down a street.

The southeastern half of the University was First City,
all white marble and wrought iron. But gradually the University had pressed out into the Second City, and—in keeping with the decree of the ministry of stoneworks—as it
passed that traditional boundary, its architecture shifted
to the low style and red stone of the Second City. But the
University ran right up to and past the outer border of
the Second City, and so along its northwestern edge it dissolved into the congested, narrow, odd-angled Third City
streets.

This, of course, was where the used-clothing shop lay, and
this was also Araenè's favorite part of the University. She loved
the narrow crowded streets, the freedom, the noise, and the
unpredictable excitement of Third City. But she did not have
time to venture out into the maze of Third City, not if she was
to catch Master Petrei's long-awaited lecture—she'd been
sure, after her cousin's unexpected arrival, that she would miss
it, an outrageous disappointment.

But this perfect day had rescued her after all. Araenè did a
dance step or three in sheer delight at regaining the freedom
of the streets, and a passing older student shook his head at
her in mock disapproval and called, "Not so happy, youngster:
don't you know a show of joy makes the masters think we can
handle extra work?"

Araenè laughed. "I *can* handle extra work," she called back, boy-bold. "So I've no need of a sober face, though I thank you for your concern!"

The other student grinned and gave her the gesture that meant *And good luck to you,* with its implication that really you were riding too high and could expect a fall.

"Time enough to flinch when I'm falling," Araenè called over her shoulder, and ran on.

Once across the rooftop shortcut, she hurried past the main Classics hall on her left and one of the Rhetoric theaters on her right. After that, there was only a small courtyard before the Ephemeral Arts building where Master Petrei would be lecturing. A flight of stairs led down into the relative dimness of the thankfully cool lecture hall.

She made her way quietly along the back of the hall and found a place to stand, since there were few seats left.

"Hsst! Arei!" a voice whispered, and a discreet hand lifted in the very back row, beckoning Araenè to one of these few.

Gratefully, Araenè crept forward and slipped into the offered seat.

"You're always late! Even for Master Petrei!" murmured her benefactor, Hanaiki Cenfenisai, a boy a year or so older than Araenè. She had met Hanaiki two years ago. She remembered everything about that day vividly: Master Toranvei Hosidai had been visiting from Bodonè. Furious that she could not attend his lecture, agonized at the rules that constricted her life, amazed to find herself by chance with the entire day to herself, Araenè had hidden her hair under a hat for the very first time and made her way across Canpra to the University. She had timidly asked impatient passersby and older students, all of whom gave her confusing, complicated directions; she had been amazed at the size and complexity of the city and the University. Twice she had almost crept back home, but then she had found the hall at last and paid the fee for the right to slip inside.

Hanaiki—tall, sarcastic, and self-possessed—had borrowed a quill from her, broken it, and insisted on buying her supper after the lecture to make up for it. She'd barely dared speak to him, but he'd spent the meal dissecting Master Toranvei's fascinating lecture, until Araenè forgot her agonized shyness and started to enjoy herself. He'd been the first boy to ever treat Araenè—Arei—with the casual, uncomplicated acceptance one male offered another. His was a friendship Araenè cherished.

Now Araenè shrugged and whispered back, "I know!" She didn't apologize—a boy wouldn't apologize. She whispered instead, "Can I see—"

Hanaiki shifted his notes so that Araenè could see them.

The lecture was a good one, all about special Yngulin techniques that you could use to capture the essence of spices in hot oil for the last-minute finishing of a dish. Master Petrei was talking about finishing savory dishes, but Araenè instantly started thinking about using the same technique for finishing sweets. Grain-based sweets were the obvious extension: saffron and cardamom with rice, for example. But could the technique be used to flavor pastries? Or the creams one filled them with? What about using butter instead of oil? Well, but butter would burn at the high temperatures Master Petrei seemed to consider necessary for the technique. . . . Oil couldn't be substituted for butter in pastry, not if you wanted the pastry delicate and flaky, but, hmm . . . one might use clarified butter. . . .

"A good lecture," Hanaiki said afterward, walking with Araenè through the warren of Third City alleys. The afternoon sun pounded down upon the streets; the cobbles cast the heat back into the air and gave the thick afternoon air an almost physical body and weight. Hanaiki took off his own floppy hat and fanned himself with it. "Hot!" he complained. "And that lecture made me hungry. Want to run over to Cesera's? Everyone's going."

Araenè gave Hanaiki a playful—masculine—shove. "Everything makes you hungry. Yes, I would, but no, I can't."

"Your father's unreasonable," Hanaiki began.

"I grant you've the right of it, and indeed there's no possibility of denying it. But for all that, and for good and all, he's—"

"Still my dear, my honored, my own progenitor—and besides, he controls the family purse," they said together, finishing a quote from a play ragingly popular among the students.

"I'll need to run as it is," Araenè added.

"It's far too hot to run! Much better come to Cesera's," Hanaiki coaxed.

Araenè laughed and shook her head. "I truly can't! But you go, and start a contest of pastry-making—maybe you'll even win." She made the gesture that meant *And good luck to you*.

Hanaiki pulled a mock-sorrowful face and said, "Ah, that's why I want you to come! You never do fall!"

Araenè laughed again and heartlessly left her friend on his own. Yes, a good lecture. A wonderful day altogether. But a glance at the sun made her blink: she hadn't exaggerated as much as she'd thought when she'd said she needed to run. Thinking about the lecture, Araenè followed a couple of other students over the rooftop of the clothing shop without paying much attention to where she put her hands and feet, scrambled down the other side, turned automatically to the left, and strode into the Third City alleyways, heading for a familiar shortcut.

Some of Third City was red stone or red brick, but the rest was built of cheaper yellow brick or dingy plaster. Most of the buildings housed small shops below, selling handcrafts, cheap copper jewelry, dried herbs, old books—whatever could help support the families that lived above the shops. The buildings were crowded tightly together, sometimes leaning out over the narrow alleys so far that they roofed tunnels through which the alleys threaded. Children ran in noisy packs, weaving in and out among their elders, intent on business Araenè could not even imagine. She had never been able to decide whether she should envy them their freedom or pity them their poverty—both, maybe.

Monkeys ran along the rooftops: mostly the gold-flame marmosets and some of the larger brown ones with long white mustaches. Children fed them, even when their parents warned that no one was going to hand *them* a dinner free out of the air and did they think bread grew from the cobblestones? Sapphire-winged birds perched on clotheslines and hopped along the cobbles, independent and quick, finding their own crumbs in the streets. Araenè liked the birds best. She bought cumin bread from a cart to crumble for them, though she did eat a few bites of the fragrant, chewy bread herself. She could buy pastries on her way home, she decided: spicy lamb and lentil pastries. She knew a vendor who made good ones. That was the sort of thing she might have made if she'd spent the afternoon at home, and there were figs and pomegranates, so she could make a compote for dessert; that would be easy—she scattered the last of the bread crumbs, lengthened her stride, and looked up.

And stopped, so suddenly that a man behind her almost bumped into her and sheered aside with a growled comment about empty-minded boys who couldn't keep out of the way on public streets.

Araenè stared in confusion at the buildings around her. Where was she? She had turned left from the clothing shop—hadn't she? Yes, because she had passed Verenkei's bookshop on the corner. And then hadn't she turned right and cut through the alley after the cart selling roasted chickens? Or had she? She knew, with a sinking feeling all through her body, that she should have crossed into Second City by now, that she did not recognize the buildings around her, and that she was lost. And that the sun, never minding Araenè's urgent necessities, was still continuing its inexorable slide toward the west.

A woman at a pastry cart was happy to provide directions, along with a plum tart. The tart's crust was tough and its filling too sour. Araenè gave the pastry to a little boy in a ragged shirt and turned distractedly down the alley the vendor had indicated. Nothing looked familiar. All she found was more maze-like alleyways between crowded Third City buildings. She hurried down one and then another, but found nothing familiar. It might lack half a bell till dusk now, if that much. Araenè was filled with a growing conviction that she would not make it home before dark and that her parents would be waiting, appalled and worried, when she finally found her way back. Tears prickling at the backs of her eyes, she stopped in a doorway to catch her breath and try to recover her nerve.

"Here, now," a kind voice said near her. "You do look worried, youngster."

Araenè looked up, startled.

The speaker, a large, shapeless man of uncertain age, was sitting on the step in the next doorway over. He was holding a pewter mug, which he waved gently toward Araenè. "You know your own trouble best, no doubt, and I'm sure I'm just an interfering old fool, and a drunken fool at that. But I'm old enough to be forgiven for interfering, and so I'll just say, if you're in some little trouble, child, and you clearly are, you might ask over there." He gestured with his mug toward a doorway set in a red brick wall across the alleyway. Liquid sloshed over the edge of the mug and spilled across the stones of the doorstep with the yeasty smell of ale. There was something else mingled with that smell, though: a wilder, greener sort of herby scent that Araenè almost felt she knew, but to which she could not put a name.

Araenè sniffed and rubbed her sleeve across her eyes, but she thought she managed to keep her voice steady. "Who's over there?"

"Not a 'who,' exactly," the man said, with another vague wave of his mug. "Nor exactly a 'what.' You might say, a 'where.' But it's a good place to go if you've lost your way—not that I'm saying that's your trouble, hmm?"

The man *might* be drunk, but then the edges of his words

were clear, and Araenè hadn't seen him drink out of that mug yet. "Who *are* you?" she asked.

"Not a very interesting question," the shapeless man chided. "You might do better, hmm?" He climbed unsteadily to his feet, gripping the wall for support, and shambled through the door and out of sight.

For a moment, Araenè only stared at the swaying curtain that hung over the doorway through which the man had vanished. Then she got up, took a step toward that doorway, hesitated, turned, and ran across the street toward the door in the red brick wall. From up close, this door proved to be of heavy oak, each quarter of it carved with a different spiraling symbol, none of which Araenè recognized: a surprising door for any Third City shop or dwelling. The door had no clapper.

In fact, the building itself didn't really seem like a Third City building. The brick in which the door was set was a rich red, except that every now and then a straw-yellow brick was set among the red ones. Araenè got the impression that if she backed up again and really looked, she might find a pattern in the placement of the yellow bricks. But she didn't back up. She put her hand on the heavy door. It opened under her hand, swinging with well-oiled ease. Within was a dim hallway paneled in rich woods, where shadows fled reluctantly from the late sunlight Araenè had admitted. Down the hall, she just made out a curtained doorway, and she was almost certain she heard voices.

Araenè stepped through the heavy door, leaving it open behind her. But the moment she stepped through the door, it seemed somehow far behind her—not to the eye: when she looked nervously over her shoulder, it was still there, standing ajar to let through a bright beam of sunlight. But somehow, though only a step away, the door gave the impression of being remote. Unreachable. And the light that fell through the doorway seemed attenuated, as though in this hallway it lost all its hot power.

Afterward, Araenè couldn't understand why she didn't run back through the door into the ordinary Third City afternoon. But she did not run. She walked down the hallway, pulled the thick velvet curtain aside, and went into the room that had been hidden behind the curtain.

The room was large—more than large: looming. Araenè had a sense that the walls were farther away than they seemed to be, even a sense that maybe the room was changing size as she watched. Despite the numerous lamps, it did not seem well lit: the walls, or maybe just the air within the room, seemed to drink up the light. A single massive table took up almost all the available space. The table was cluttered with books and loose papers, spheres of polished stone and glass and metal that ranged from fist-sized to the size of a large melon, tall brass scales and thin copper plates.

Around the table stood five boys, the youngest perhaps Araenè's age and the oldest several years older. They looked around as she came in, but the man at the head of the table rapped his knuckles on the table and the boys all jumped guiltily and turned back to him.

The man was so dark-skinned that Araenè had at first completely missed him in the shadowed room. His eyes were all she could see clearly, and the shine of his white teeth, especially because he wasn't wearing the jewel-toned fabrics of the

34

Floating Islands, but a plain dark robe that fell without ornament from shoulder to ankle. Then, as her eyes adjusted to the strange light, she saw him better. Tall, lean rather than broad, with severe hawk features and a stern set to his mouth, this man was like no one Araenè had ever seen before. She had heard all her life of Yngul, but never expected to see a man from that country. Now she found that all her imagination had fallen short, and stood speechless.

"Come here, boy," the man said to her, brief and decisive. "Take this." He held out to Araenè a sphere of polished volcanic glass, large enough that he had to hold it with both hands.

Araenè opened her mouth, closed it again, walked forward, and took the sphere. It was heavy and cool, translucent as light slid across it. It tasted of cool anise and smoky cumin, with sparkly undertones of ginger and lemon. Araenè blinked and stared down at the glass sphere, but the tastes didn't fade or seem to be her imagination: anise and cumin, ginger and lemon. She looked wonderingly up at the face of the Yngulin man.

"Vision is always a useful gift," the man said to all the boys. His voice was smoky and mysterious as the sphere, his eyes hard to read. "Particularly in these tense times—but I believe you will find that all times are tense." He turned his attention to Araenè. "So, now, boy—shift the Dannè sphere toward a more open configuration."

A more open configuration? Araenè stared down at the sphere, turning it over in her hands and wondering what "more open" could possibly mean. The ginger undertone became more prominent, tingling across her fingers as well as her tongue—a strange sensation.

"Good," said the man, and took back the sphere. "You see," he said to the boys, holding it up. They returned an appreciative murmur, and he smiled. He said to Araenè, "And what would you expect to see within this particular sphere, given such a shift in orientation?"

Araenè stared at him. Spheres and spicy colors and a strange room that seemed suddenly far smaller, pressing in on her—she took a step back and stammered, "I have to, I—I have to go home—"

"If you must," said the Yngulin man. "But I shall assuredly see you again."

The statement had the force of a command, and Araenè found herself nodding.

"Bring this back to me," the man added, and handed her the sphere again. Araenè took it automatically and tucked it under her arm. She took another step back, then another, and found herself back in the hallway. Without thinking—she did not seem able to keep her mind focused on anything—she turned, walked back to the door, opened it, and stepped through.

She found herself not in the narrow alleyways of the Third City maze but in the infinitely more familiar and welcome alley behind her own home, looking up at her own window. When she turned, bewildered, to stare back the way she had come, there was no carved door behind her: only the other side of her own alley. It was just dusk: though the sun was below sight, faint glimmers of violet and peach still traced the banks of clouds in the west.

Araenè let out a breath she had not been aware of holding. Cimè and Ti might be back, though maybe not, but neither

Mother nor Father should have returned. Not quite yet—but soon. She took a step toward the house and then stopped, staring down at the sphere she still carried under her arm. Her brows drew together: the thing seemed even more strange and unsettling now, and her own response to it stranger still. The smoky taste of cumin tickled the back of her throat, and the sharper accents of lemon and ginger. The anise seemed almost missing, just a faint tickle on her tongue and across her palms.

Almost, Araenè dropped the sphere in the street and left it for the neighborhood children to find. But in the end she put it down her shirt so she would have her hands free, checked quickly for any unwelcome eyes that might be watching, and made the climb back to her window with extra care that she should not accidentally let the sphere strike the stones of the wall.

She had entirely forgotten that it was not, at the moment, her room.

Her cousin was sitting on her bed, reading some heavy, dull book from, Araenè presumed, one of his library classes. Araenè didn't see him until she was already halfway through the window, and then it was too late to retreat. Taken thoroughly aback, Trei stared. Since she could hardly pretend that she wasn't climbing through the window dressed in boys' clothing, Araenè raised her chin and stared back, daring him to say anything.

Her cousin's gaze shifted from Araenè's face to her hands, lingered for a moment on her masculine bracelets, lifted to take in her boy's hat, and moved back to her face. No fool, he let the book fall and spread his hands placatingly. "It's not my concern," he assured her. He asked after a moment, as though unable to help himself, "Do all Island girls, um . . . ?"

Araenè had never considered this question before. For all she knew, dressing up as a boy and slipping out of the confinement of the home was a universal stage through which all girls passed. When you were five, you loved to help the servants in the kitchens; when you were eight, you cried because your father wouldn't let you have a marmoset; when you were ten, you fretted desperately after some handsome young master of ephemera and thought you would die if he never noticed you; and when you were twelve, you dressed up in boys' clothing and ventured out into the world. But . . . "I doubt it," she concluded. It was impossible to imagine the girls she knew engaging in such a dramatic, dangerous rebellion. Though she wondered now if they would think the same about her, if anybody asked them.

"Umm . . ." Trei swallowed whatever he'd been about to say, picked up his book again, and pretended to be fascinated by whatever he'd been reading.

Araenè pulled the wardrobe doors open so that they would offer her privacy. Without really paying attention to what she was doing, she put the black sphere behind a false back she'd made to fit one of her drawers, checked to make sure her cousin was still looking at his book, and rapidly changed out of her boys' things back into a proper dress. A simple one that fastened up the front so she could reach the hooks without help. She asked around the edges of the doors, "Is Cimè back from the market? Ti?" She hesitated after asking after the servants, afraid to extend the query to include Mother and Father: what if they'd come back early?

"The servants were here when I got back from the library. Cimè asked me if I knew where you'd gone. She seemed a little worried," Trei told her, and added with unexpected perceptiveness, "But your parents are still away."

Araenè came around the doors and stared at her cousin, wondering what to tell him, how she could persuade him to say nothing about what he'd seen.

"You might have gone up to the attic and fallen asleep," Trei suggested. "I don't think Cimè or Ti have gone up there—not since I've been home. Maybe before, though," he added, ducking his head doubtfully.

"It's a good idea," Araenè admitted aloud. "It will work no matter what. If Cimè went up to the attic earlier, I'll pretend I hadn't gone up yet and she just happened to miss me." She hesitated. "You won't—that is, you'd be willing—"

"I won't contradict you," Trei promised.

Araenè felt driven to ask, though she was almost afraid of the answer she would get, "Why are you . . . I mean, why would you . . . ?" And what would he want from her in return?

Her cousin met her eyes, a level, honest look. He said in a low voice, "You're so . . . You remind me so much of my . . . of Marrè. My sister. You aren't . . . you aren't like her, really. But if she'd lived here, I think she might have been like you."

"Oh." Araenè had somehow not really thought of what her cousin might feel, losing his sister. His mother and father, yes, she'd been sorry for his loss, although she'd also found herself thinking how amazing it would be to travel all the tremendous distance from northern Tolounn to the Floating Islands by yourself. Though of course that journey wouldn't seem amazing at all if your whole family had just died.

But, truthfully, she hadn't spent much effort imagining how Trei actually *felt*. She'd been too busy resenting the disruption he'd brought to *her* family. Araenè felt heat creeping up her face. She crossed the room slowly, settling at the foot of the bed. "Would you tell me about her? Marrè?"

Her cousin sat up, laying the book aside. His eyes searched her face . . . not sure she was really interested, Araenè thought, not confident of kindness from her. Wondering, probably, whether she was trying to purchase his silence with a show of sympathy. She blushed again, ashamed he might think so.

But Trei must have decided she was sincere, because he got up and went to her desk. There was a large book she didn't recognize lying there, an expensive one, with gold letters on its dark leather binding. Trei took several loose pages from this book—oh, not pages from the actual book, Araenè saw, but sheets of heavy, cream-colored paper, expensive paper, too costly to be used even in a nice book like that one.

Her cousin held these for a moment, looking down at them, facing away from Araenè—she thought he was trying to make sure he'd be composed when he turned around, and didn't say a word to hurry him.

Coming back to the bed at last, Trei carefully laid one of these papers down on the bedspread so that Araenè could see it. The paper wavered a little as he put it down, but Trei's expression was calm. The calm broke a little when he said, "This was Marrè."

The drawing, a deceptively simple ink sketch, showed the upper body and face of a girl, not quite a woman, in quarter profile. The girl was elegant, serene, dignified; her hair was up on the side of her head in a young woman's figure-eight braid. Her hand rested gracefully on a delicate little table before her; a sheet of paper and a quill lay on the table next to her hand, and you could just see that the paper held the very sketch at which you were actually looking.

But that was not the only echo contained within the sketch: it also showed a mirror that stood beside the girl. In this mirror, you could see her reflected, this time in three-quarters profile. In the mirror, you could see that strands of hair had come loose from the braid to curl around her ear and down the back of her neck. Somehow, there was a different look in her eye in the mirror. Though her expression in the mirror seemed at first glance the same, this angle of view did not give an impression of serenity. In the mirror, there was a hint of mischief in the girl's eye, a wryness to her mouth, which suggested that her hair would never really be perfect—even that a casual imperfection was something she enjoyed and wanted you to enjoy. That she might be ready to step into womanhood, but not into any staid, demure womanhood. You could imagine this girl dressing up in boys' clothing and climbing out of windows: it was almost hard to imagine that she never had.

Araenè looked up, shaking her head. "Your sister drew this? This was her? This is amazing—"

Trei's mouth trembled, then tightened. He said after a moment, "Marrè would never have stayed here. In the Floating Islands, I mean. Or at least not in Canpra. Girls . . . girls stay at home here, don't they? Girls don't study or go out or . . . or anything. Do they?"

"Girls visit other girls. And then they sit around and

gossip about young men and do needlework, and go home and write letters to one another about young men and do more needlework." Araenè couldn't help her disdainful tone. "Is it really different in Tolounn?"

Trei offered a diffident shrug. "Marrè studied drawing and things with the best tutors, and she didn't have to dress up like a boy to do it. Her tutors—" Trei stopped, and then went on in a low voice, "Her tutors said she should do a showing. Mother was going to arrange it for next spring. Father said she should wait until after she got married, so her fame wouldn't drive her dowry up too high. But really he was so proud. He said once—he said she would be as famous someday as Kekuonn Terataan—" He stopped again.

Araenè said nothing. She had a terrible image in her mind of the girl in this drawing, sitting at the table pictured in this sketch, quill in hand and that mischievous look in her eyes, when the poisonous gas and hot ash poured out of the fire-mountain and came down upon Rounn. She didn't know what to say.

She was saved from needing to say anything, because at that moment her mother called.

Trei flinched and gathered up the sketch, taking it and the others back to the desk and putting them again into the large book.

Araenè got up and prepared to go down the stairs to Mother. But, lingering, she said to Trei, "May I see the other drawings sometime? Would you . . . You wouldn't mind showing them to me?"

Her cousin gave a small nod.

"And maybe you could tell me about her? Sometime? If you, I mean . . . if you wouldn't mind?"

42

"I'd like to," Trei said in a low voice.

Araenè nodded, and ran out as her mother called once more. The strange detour she'd taken to get home already seemed like a dream, and she refused to think about the glass sphere hidden in the back of her drawer.

3

As the kajurai auditions approached, Trei felt, to his surprise, almost at home in Canpra. Not like a true Islander. More as though there was a possibility that someday he might be able to feel that he was. He hadn't expected this. Nor had he expected Araenè to be responsible for the change. He hadn't guessed that his cousin would be so . . . so . . . *interesting.*

Of course his cousin knew all the respectable places to go in the First and Second Cities—Trei had expected that. "It's wonderful, Father wanting you to be familiar with Canpra," Araenè assured him, "or I'd never be permitted to explore like this. How splendid you are, cousin!" Her sarcasm didn't worry Trei; he understood perfectly well it wasn't directed at *him.*

She'd shown him the white towers of the First City and taught him how to walk on the airy bridges and floating stairways that linked them together. The people of Canpra loved to build between sea and sky. One hot afternoon, they'd bought a terribly expensive lunch from a restaurant on a wide balcony that overhung the waves. Araenè muttered comments about the food and tossed tidbits that displeased her over the railing to the gulls swooping below, but Trei spent the afternoon staring longingly out toward the men who soared above the sea on crimson or golden wings.

But the day before the kajurai auditions, when she saw Trei was fretting himself into a dither, Araenè finally insisted on taking him into the Third City and showing him the University. His cousin's boldness made Trei terribly nervous, but Araenè *would* change her gown and bangles for trousers and shirt and wide bracelets, pin her hair up under a wide-brimmed hat, and become a boy. She made a convincing boy. She even walked like a boy. Almost like a boy.

"Too feminine?" Araenè sounded skeptical when Trei ventured to suggest alterations to her manner. "Not likely! Mother always says I need to walk more softly and slowly. She says men like a woman to walk gracefully, speak gently, and show neither brains nor temper."

The sarcasm in her tone probably wasn't very correct for an Island girl, either. Trei grinned. But he also tried to explain, "It was something about how you turned. On your toe or something. Too graceful, you know. Maybe Aunt Edona thinks you're too boyish when you're a girl, but you still make a girlish boy. Don't look at me like that! You do!"

"Huh." Araenè didn't seem persuaded. "It's only because you know, that's all. Come on! If we hurry, we'll be right on time for Master Petrei's lecture. It's his fifth and last this season, and I've only made it to one other."

Probably she was right, Trei allowed. He gave up the point and said only, "A lecture? What an adventure!"

"*You* can say that. *You're* allowed to attend whatever lectures you like, go where you like, do anything you want to," Araenè snapped, and turned on her toe—it *was* a girl's move, too graceful by half for a boy—but she strode off at a pace that made Trei stretch to match. He didn't answer her sharp comment, and after a moment his cousin gave him an apologetic glance. "You're good to escort me."

"I don't mind. I want to. I—are you serious? We climb *over* this building?"

"It's the quickest way. Everybody does it. We can walk around Third City after the lecture, if it doesn't finish too late," Araenè offered. "Third City is wonderful—I'll show you my favorite places."

Trei shrugged and nodded. He didn't much care for what little he'd seen of Canpra's Third City so far. It seemed dangerous: crowded and disorganized and dirty. But Araenè seemed so . . . so . . . she seemed more alive, more expansive, even somehow more *herself*, dashing through Third City alleys dressed as a boy.

Later, waiting for the crowd of students to clear out of the lecture hall, he gave Araenè a sidelong look and said, keeping his tone bland, "Well, that was fascinating. No wonder you're willing to risk, um, to find out all about the subtle differences between rice from eastern Yngul, western Yngul, northern Yngul, northeastern Yngul, the southern half of the western third of some island off the coast of Yngul. . . ."

Araenè punched him on the shoulder, a good copy of the masculine gesture. But then she gave Trei an uncertain sidelong glance and asked seriously, "Are you scared about to-morrow?"

"No!" But then he met his cousin's eyes and felt his mouth tug reluctantly into a smile. "Maybe a little."

"You're an Islander now," Araenè assured him. "You'll do all right."

They had by this time passed back into the wider, quieter streets of the Second City, and Trei privately thought he'd seen enough of Third City squalor and crowding to last him. He said only, "Of course I will."

But he didn't really believe this. He didn't sleep well that night, only repeatedly dozed and jerked awake, sometimes with the feeling he was falling. He dreamed he needed desperately to see the wind, but there was no wind, only ash settling endlessly out of an empty sky, and Mount Ghaonnè with the huge jagged hole in its side where the fire had come out.

"You'll do splendidly, dear," Aunt Edona assured Trei over an early breakfast. Trei looked steadfastly at the uneaten slice of bread he held in one hand, and nodded.

"You will," Araenè said, but anxiously.

"You really will," Uncle Serfei told him one more time as they walked briskly through the Second City, heading for the First City tower where the kajurai auditions were held. It was a long way. They'd had to get up before dawn to make sure they had time for the walk. Uncle Serfei looked tired; he coughed once or twice and smiled apologetically at Trei. "Summer coughs! Let's hope you don't catch it, Trei. I'm sure you'll need proper rest after you pass your audition: apprentices always run hard."

Trei nodded. He wished that they'd already arrived; more than that, he wished the audition was already over. At the moment, he wished most of all that everyone would stop telling him how well he'd do. He said nothing.

"And if you aren't approved for kajurai training, you can still aim for the ministry examinations," his uncle went on. "Oh, I know that's not what you want, Trei, but plenty of boys have a much less enviable second choice—" Uncle Serfei took a more careful look at Trei's face and stopped. After a moment, he said gently, "It's hard to believe they'd be so foolish as to turn down a boy who wants it so badly, though."

Trei didn't say that aptitude probably counted for more than longing, or that, as he'd found out, fewer than a fifth of applicants were accepted for training, or that the wingmasters might very well decide, despite Uncle Serfei's assurances, that a boy with a Tolounnese father wasn't the best choice for making into a symbol of the Floating Islands.

"I'll leave you here," Uncle Serfei said once they'd reached the tower where the audition would take place. He rested a hand on Trei's shoulder. "Go on in. I know you'll do your best, Trei." He paused and then added, "Your mother always loved the dragons of these Islands, you know."

Trei tried to smile. Then he turned and walked into the tower, along with several other boys he did not know. He felt oddly bereft, even though he'd known Uncle Serfei fewer than fifty days. Or maybe that was just nervousness.

The tower seemed very large and, despite the other half dozen boys who'd just entered, very empty. They all glanced at one another, but nobody spoke. Their footsteps echoed. But the way they were supposed to go was obvious. Other than the door through which they'd entered, there was only one way to leave the room: a wide spiral stairway coiled its way down and down into dim shadows. Trei went down the stairs, neither the first boy nor the last. The treads were wide enough for at least three or four boys to walk down together, but they went down single file.

The stairway turned five times as it descended and then opened up to a large chamber, already occupied by several dozen other boys. Most were clearly from the Second or Third Cities, but one of the boys was clearly a First City noble. His air of assurance made him look older than most of the other boys, but after a careful second glance, Trei guessed he was actually only about fifteen, maybe sixteen. He wore white, with a violet ribbon threaded through his dark hair and a thin gold ring on one thumb.

"A *Feneirè* son," a thin, intense boy near Trei whispered to a stocky friend, with a glance at the one in white. "The third son, it must be. I don't suppose the kajuraihi would dare turn down—"

"They'll take who they take," the stocky boy murmured back with stolid calm. "Don't worry about him, Rekei."

Trei glanced at the Feneirè son—and what was the Feneirè family, that everyone would recognize their third son?—then gazed around the chamber. It was worth a second look, and a third. One whole wall was simply missing. On that side of the chamber, the tiles of the floor simply gave way to empty air. Far out in the sky, a small Island floated, its high, jagged peaks wreathed with streamers of cloud.

The small Island was connected to Milendri by a single

bridge. This bridge was nothing like the solid bridges of Tolounnese construction, however. It consisted simply of a pathway of floating stones that rose in a slow arc and eventually descended again as it reached the far side.

"I wonder when we're going to start?" Rekei wondered out loud.

One of the younger Third City boys gave the other boy a hostile glance. "Impatient, are you?"

"Oh, pardon me—" Rekei began hotly.

"Maybe we're supposed to just cross the bridge on our own," said the First City boy. His tone was merely thoughtful, but there was something about the way he turned his shoulder toward the incipient squabble that somehow rebuked both Rekei and the Third City boy.

Rekei's calm friend asked the Feneirè son, "How long do you think we should wait? I'm Kai Talana. My father is a minister of roadways and stoneworks."

"Ceirfei Feneirè," answered the other boy. He didn't give his father's name or position. Trei guessed he didn't have to. "I suppose the trick is to wait long enough, but not too long." He grinned suddenly, glancing around at the rest of them. "We can toss pebbles; shortest throw has to decide how long is long enough."

There was a slight pause. Then the oldest of the Third City boys said, "It's nearly second bell now. At half past, I say that's long enough." Although his tone was decisive, his glance at Ceirfei was deferential. Trei understood that the other boy was really asking whether Ceirfei thought that would be all right.

"That seems sensible to me. Kai?" asked Ceirfei, and not

just as though he was being polite. As though he really cared about the other boy's opinion. Trei was impressed that Ceirfei had so smoothly gotten all the nervous boys to settle down and stop snapping at one another.

"Probably if someone is coming, he'll be here before that," Kai said, giving the Third City boy an acknowledging nod. It was obvious all the Third City boys were happy to be taken seriously by the others, especially Ceirfei Feneirè.

As though hearing this thought, Ceirfei turned his head suddenly and looked straight into Trei's face. He was smiling, but the expression in his dark eyes was thoughtful. Yet Trei got no sense that the other boy was faking the smile. Both the friendliness and the restraint seemed real. In a moment, Trei knew, Ceirfei Feneirè was going to ask his name, and he tried to decide whether he should give his father's name or his uncle's.

Then, before either of them could speak, the rapid sound of boots on stone rang out, and four kajuraihi came into the chamber. None of them were wearing wings, but they were obviously kajuraihi. Their eyes were strange: what should have been the white part of their eyes glittered like crystal. This made their pupils look blacker than usual. They wore unrelieved black, except for steel studs at wrist and throat and for a single feather braided into each man's hair. Three of them had red feathers, but the one in front had a feather black as coal; Trei knew that this meant he was a wingmaster.

The men halted and just stood there for a long moment, regarding the boys, who drew together in a tight group in response. Trei noticed, a little amused, that they all gathered around Ceirfei Feneirè—that was even his own impulse.

The wingmaster had a strong, austere face and an air of chilly reserve. Two of his companions were young men in their twenties, probably not long out of the novitiate themselves. But the remaining man was older than the wingmaster, with iron-gray hair and a mouth set in what seemed a permanent expression of stern disapproval. Trei wondered whether it was his imagination that this man seemed to be staring directly at him.

"I'm Taimenai Cenfenisai," the wingmaster said abruptly. "This is Anerii Pencara, master of novices, and Rei Kensenè and Linai Terinisai, second-ranked kajuraihi. All your names and connections are known to me." He paused.

The boys gazed back at the wingmaster in uncertain silence.

"You will cross the floating bridge to the island you see," said the wingmaster, still speaking with that alarmingly brusque manner. "That is Kotipa, the Island of Dragons, which we also call the Island of the Test. No one ever sees it clearly, save kajuraihi. There you will do what you find to do. You will return as novice kajuraihi, or else not. There is some risk in this endeavor: from time to time a boy does not return at all. You accept this risk when you set foot on the first stone of the bridge." He paused.

None of the boys said anything, not even Rekei or the hot-tempered Third City boy who'd tried to start a fight earlier. Some of them, including Rekei, looked nervous; others seemed more excited, a few eager. Ceirfei Feneirè looked merely politely attentive. Trei tried not to show anything but a bland calm.

Wingmaster Taimenai surveyed them all. His stern mouth

curved in a smile more sardonic than encouraging. "You will go one after another, a tenth-bell between you," he concluded. "Remember: Do what you find to do. I can tell you nothing more specific than that."

"What if we meet each other over there?" one of the other Second City boys asked nervously.

"If you do, act as you see fit," answered the wingmaster. His tone was flat. No one else asked any questions. After a moment of silence, the wingmaster said to Ceirfei Feneirè, "You will cross first."

. "The benefit of rank," Rekei muttered under his breath. His friend Kai gave him a quelling glance. Ceirfei himself merely inclined his head to the wingmaster and walked toward the floating pathway of stepping-stones. He paused for an instant when he stepped onto the first one, however, looking startled. But then he drew a visible breath, lifted his hands a little out from his sides, and took the long step from the first stone to the next.

"I don't think there's a steadying magic on that bridge," a boy nearby whispered to a friend. Trei had reached the same conclusion. He felt slightly ill. Maybe there were boats below the bridge, ready to rescue anyone who fell? But then, the wingmaster had said that about risk. Trei wanted to go to the edge and look over, see if there were boats down there. But that would let everyone see he was frightened. He didn't move.

"Rekei Horirè," said the wingmaster, and Rekei twitched, hesitated, gave a sharp nod, clapped his friend Kai on the arm, and walked toward the bridge. Ceirfei had only reached the middle of the span.

"Tenarii Hanerè," the wingmaster said, and one of the other Second City boys stiffened, looked once quickly to either side, received an encouraging shove from a friend, and went toward the bridge. Far out over the sea, Ceirfei was hardly visible.

After that, Wingmaster Taimenai called Kai's name, and then that of another Second City boy, and then the names of the rest of the boys one after another, Third City after Second City. He did not call Trei's name. After the first Third City boy was called, Trei understood that he would be called last—if at all. He knew he flushed when he realized this, but his hands felt cold. He fixed his gaze on the first stone of the bridge and said nothing. It took a long time for all the other boys to cross the bridge. Third bell rang, and later fourth. Trei wanted to sit down. Pride, or maybe vanity, kept him on his feet. More than just on his feet: immobile, and blank-faced. His eyes burned. But he wouldn't show that to these men.

"Trei enna Shiberren," the wingmaster said at last.

Trei did not move toward the bridge. He lifted his gaze to the wingmaster's face and waited.

"Or Trei Naseida?" asked the wingmaster. His crystalline kajurai eyes held Trei's. His expression, perhaps because of those strange eyes, was unreadable.

Trei opened his mouth, closed it again, and swallowed. He said at last, "Both. Sir."

"You think you can claim both names?"

But the wingmaster's tone, Trei thought, held neither anger nor disbelief; really nothing worse than dry curiosity. "Yes," he said. "Sir."

"Tolounnese boys don't need wings," the master of

novices, Anerii Pencara, said abruptly. *His* tone was harsh, decisive. "Or eyes that can see the wind." He advanced the few steps required, reaching out to grasp Trei's chin and force his face upward, staring down into his eyes. "From Rounn, are you?"

Trei had fought not to flinch from the novice-master's unfriendly grip, but now he deliberately jerked himself loose and backed up. He bit his lip with the effort not to stumble, stiff after making himself stand still so long. He didn't try to argue with the man's all-too-obvious opinion, but only repeated, "Yes, sir."

One of the younger kajuraihi, Rei Kensenè, said mildly, "If he's not Islander enough, I think we'll find out." He gave the distant Island a meaningful glance.

The master of novices gave the young flier an annoyed stare. Rei Kensenè returned his look with perfect equanimity and said to Trei, "Your father gave you an Island name, did he?"

"My parents named me after my mother's grandfather. My father always said I took after my mother," Trei said firmly.

"We were all grieved to hear about the Rounn disaster," the young kajurai murmured. "But did you have no other relatives to go to, youngster? Tolounnese relatives?"

Trei met his eyes, then turned his head to stare at the master of novices. He made his tone flat and cold. "I went to them. *They* thought I wasn't Tolounnese enough."

Wingmaster Taimenai held up one hand, halting Anerii Pencara's forceful response to this before the novice-master could fairly begin it. "And so you came to your mother's kin here. Understandable. But why do you want wings?" the wingmaster asked, neutral as ever.

"I . . ." Trei swallowed. "I knew the first time I saw kaju-raihi, sir. They came down and looked at the ship I was on. I knew then. They say here I'm sky-mad, wind-mad. There wouldn't be terms for it, would there, if boys didn't sometimes feel this way?"

"Not Tolounnese boys," Anerii Pencara said harshly.

The wingmaster held up a hand again, glancing sternly at the other man. He said to Trei, "It's a long way across the bridge, and as Rei points out, you may find something to do on the other island. And you'll need to be finished with it by dusk. So you'd best go quickly."

Finished by dusk. That was the first time anybody had said so. And the wingmaster had kept him here till last, and then kept him back for . . . for nothing, really, for no reason except maybe to delay him. It had to be almost fifth bell by now—Trei turned, walked to the bridge, and stepped across to the first stone without letting himself look down. Anger and offended pride carried him across the first half dozen stones before he even realized that, indeed, there was no magic holding him on the bridge. He stopped involuntarily, wobbling. The sea breeze felt much stronger out here than if he'd stood on a balcony with a railing.

No one else had fallen, though. Or even hesitated, much. He was angry with himself for stopping—for letting all those kajuraihi see him stop. Why should he fall? Of course he wouldn't. The stones were more than wide enough. Anyone could walk this bridge. A child could walk it. Trei made himself walk forward, not running, but walking fast, jumping over the gaps.

The bridge was wider than some of the pedestrian walks

laid out in Rounn streets so people could keep their feet clean, and a lot smoother than parts of the mountain road between Rounn and Sicuon. If one simply didn't look down . . . and didn't think too much about the breeze, which out here seemed to gust harder . . .

He found the rhythm of it at last. The stones were mostly near enough the same size. You came down on the edge of a stone, took two small steps, and jumped across to the next stone. He went even faster, until he nearly *was* running, taking just one big stride per stone. The climb steepened, and he found himself panting. He wanted to stop and rest, but he wanted a lot more to have the bridge behind him, and all the time he was aware that minutes were passing. Finally he reached the crest of the bridge and found himself on the long downhill side, halfway across.

Then he unexpectedly found himself stepping into a gap wider than the rest. Before he could stop himself, his foot plunged into empty air. Trei flung himself forward, breath hissing out in a sharp gasp, clutching for handholds on the farther stone. His chest struck the edge of the step hard, but his hands found no purchase on the smooth stone, and he slid backward—he knew he was going to fall—his flailing left hand finally found the edge of the step, and with that hold and his right palm flat against the stone, he managed to stop his backward skid. Then he managed to drag himself forward and, with an effort that felt like it tore all the muscles of his shoulders, haul himself up on the flat surface of the stone.

He knelt there for a long moment, trembling. Eventually he crawled to the edge of the step and looked over, wondering whether there were really boats down there in case someone fell. But there was too much haze now to even see the waves below. Somehow this made him feel that he was even higher up, so high that he'd climbed out of the world entirely, and if he fell, he'd fall forever through the empty sky.

The sun, too, was hidden in the hazy overcast, but Trei was sure that fifth bell must have come and gone. Maybe it was even sixth bell. And what was he supposed to do, besides go forward? Back was just as bad as forward. He could hardly sit forever right here in the middle of the bridge, yet he could not make himself move. He would fail this test . . . he would never have his own wings, never fly. . . .

That terrible thought was the one that allowed Trei to climb, still shaking, to his feet. To edge his way toward the edge of the stepping-stone—this stone *was* significantly narrower than most of the others; no wonder he'd missed his step—and take a broad, cautious leap to the next. The jump was easy—he'd known perfectly well it would be, he could *see* how easy a jump it was—but still, for the instant in which he was in the air between the stones, he was sure he'd miss and fall. But he landed safely. Looking ahead, Trei tried to guess how many stones were left, but the end of the bridge was lost in the haze. He found it easy to imagine that these floating stones were all that was left in the world, that everything else had vanished, or even that nothing else had ever existed. Trei leaped to the next stone in line and then the next, concentrating on nothing but each stone as he came to it.

He could have cried with relief when the small island finally came into sight, closer than he'd expected, half veiled by streamers of mist and cloud. Even so, he didn't let himself hurry, but took one stepping-stone at a time until at last he could make the final leap off the floating bridge onto solid ground.

No one else was in sight. The bridge had brought Trei down into a paved courtyard. Around the courtyard, sharp-edged rock rose precipitously. Except behind him, where it fell away in cliffs just as steep; Trei had had enough of heights and kept well away from those cliffs.

The bridge had come down on the western edge of the courtyard. On the far side Trei could see a rugged path leading up to the mountain heights, though those heights were hidden in mist and cloud. The path looked difficult. Even standing at its foot, Trei couldn't see very far along it—it twisted around too many turns and there was too much mist. Trei looked around the courtyard once more in case he was missing something. Then he turned back to the path, took a slow breath, and took the first step to follow it.

The path was steep, sometimes more a vertical climb than a footpath. Trei used his hands almost as much as his feet to climb, but he quickly learned that the rocks could be sharp-edged as knives. He shook blood off his hand, sucked the cut for a moment, and finally sliced a strip off his shirt on that same edge of stone in order to bandage his hand. His palm hurt for a while, but so much of his attention was taken by the other perils of the path that he soon forgot the pain.

Occasional twisted trees, dwarfed by wind and scant soil, thrust almost horizontally out of the broken stone face of the mountain. Their roots could be seen, gripping hard along the stone before disappearing into whatever crevices of soil they'd found. They made good handholds, but almost more importantly, they served as reminders that life existed even here in this improbable place.

Mist wreathed the path, which sometimes took sharp turns back on itself. The switchbacks and the mist together meant that Trei could seldom see very far ahead. Each time he made his way around a turn or through a streamer of mist, he found something that seemed more dangerous than whatever obstacle he'd just negotiated. A narrow trail of broken footing above a precipice, for example. Or a long gap in the path across a sheer cliff, bridged only by a pair of thick ropes. He crossed that gap by sliding his feet along the lower rope, gripping the upper one tightly in his hands.

Trei was always conscious of time passing. He tried not to worry about it. He reminded himself how foolish he'd feel if he tried to rush and fell over a cliff. And he wondered, when he had a moment, where the other boys were: had they all moved so much faster that they were already finished and only he was left struggling up this mountainside?

Then at last he caught hold of one more stunted tree, hauled himself up and around a leaning shelf of stone, and found himself on a path that had suddenly become smooth and level. For a long moment he just stood, bent and gasping with effort, hands braced on his knees, gazing along the last short length of the path to the slender white tree that commanded this height. The tree bore silvery leaves, and both white flowers and small golden fruits. Under the tree was a small pool bordered by round white stones.

Trei made his way cautiously toward the tree. The whole mountaintop seemed to him like the sort of place that was probably dedicated to one of the Three Gods—to the Silent

God, most likely, because it was very silent here. A cup of white stone stood beside the pool. Trei found he was terribly thirsty. He made the sign of the Silent God, dipped the cup in the pool, and drank.

The water was very cold, so cold Trei was amazed it wasn't ice. It tasted of clouds and snow and high winds and of something else, something wild and unfamiliar. Trei spilled a few drops of water on the ground for the God.

The silvery leaves of the tree fluttered, though Trei could feel no breeze. He stepped over to the tree and laid a hand on its smooth bark, looking up into its branches. Its golden fruits were shaped like teardrops. They were gleaming and translucent, like polished gems placed on the tree by a master jeweler.

Wondering if this was right, feeling that it was, not seeing anything else to do, Trei plucked a single fruit from the tree and ate it. It was not like any other fruit he'd ever eaten. It was sweet and crisp, but it tasted, behind the sweetness, of the same vivid wildness as the freezing water of the pool. The wildness lingered on his tongue longer than the sweetness. It was not meant for men at all; he somehow knew that. He was immediately afraid that he might have made a mistake, that maybe he should have resisted the impulse to eat it, that he might have ruined his one chance to fly. The fear of this made him tremble, where the cold of the water had not. But he had chosen to eat the fruit, and it was too late now to choose again. . . .

The fruit had one seed, a little larger than an apple seed, white and faceted like a jewel. Trei spat the seed out into his palm and gazed at it for a moment. Then, acting on a sharp, inexplicable impulse too powerful to even consider, he put the seed back in his mouth and swallowed it whole. It felt cold and sharp going down his throat, and the cold of it spread from his tongue down his throat and through his blood. Trei put a hand on the tree's trunk again, steadying himself against a sudden wave of dizzy confusion; he found himself sitting on the ground, leaning against the tree's twisted trunk, with no memory of either deciding to sit or falling. He dipped a shaking hand in the pool and splashed the cold water across his face. A fragrance like snow and apples and crisp pine rose around him, and he shut his eyes and fell into a crystal wind as cold as ice.

4

On the day her cousin was due for his kajurai audition, Araenè rose early so she could make the breakfast bread herself. While the bread baked, she sent Cimè to buy the very freshest figs and made a sweet rice custard scented with cardamom and vanilla.

Naturally, after all that, no one had much appetite for breakfast. Trei remembered to taste everything and tell Araenè how wonderful it all was, which was, as Araenè thought, just like him. But really he only crumbled his slice of bread, and he only ate three figs—Araenè counted.

"You ought to eat more," she told him. "Who knows if they'll give you something later?"

Mother glanced up at this, registered how little Trei had eaten, and earnestly seconded this advice, throwing in all sorts of maternal fussing for good measure. "You'll do splendidly, dear," she promised him at last.

Trei dutifully ate a bite of the custard.

Araenè tried to smile. She hoped Trei would do well at his audition; of course she did. But she knew already how much she would miss his company—not just the freedom his escort gave her around the city, but his actual company, too, and who would ever have expected that? Trei met her gaze for a moment, then flushed and looked down at his hands, and Araenè knew he was aware of her conflicted feelings. She felt her own face heat and hastily went to bring in more bread.

Later, after Trei and Father were gone, Mother fluttered around restlessly, hardly beginning one task before forgetting about it and starting something else almost at random. She, too, seemed to have caught the summer cough, though she wasn't yet coughing much. Araenè made her tea with honey and lime.

"Thank you, dear," Mother said gratefully. "Such a nuisance!" But it wasn't really the cough that made her restless, Araenè knew. Mother was worried about Trei, too—worried about how Trei would feel if he failed his audition, but also worried, mother-like, about the possibility that he might be hurt somehow during it. Sometimes that happened. Mother was probably even worrying a little about the dangers Trei would face if everything went beautifully, because being a kajurai wasn't as safe as being a minister or a magistrate.

"You ought to go visit Adeila Hanerè," Araenè told her at last. "She'll be worried for her own son. You can take her some of my bread."

"My dear," Mother said gratefully, "that is such a splendid idea. But surely you would like to come? Teresna Hanerè is just your age—"

"Teresna and I aren't really friends, not as you and Adeila

are. And you'll want to stay all day, won't you? I wouldn't want to stay so long. I have work I'd like to do here. You know that's what will make me feel better, really. . . ." Araenè eased her mother out the door, encouraging her to take Cimè to carry a pot of custard as well as the bread. Then she sent Ti out on an errand that would keep him out all morning and told him to take the afternoon off as well.

Then, after the house was empty, she changed quickly into boys' clothing and slipped out into the alley behind the house. She felt guilty about using Trei's audition to make a free day for herself, but what use would it be to her cousin if she stayed home and fretted? And freedom was going to be so much harder to find now. . . . Araenè realized that she expected Trei to succeed today. She really did, and was surprised to remember her disbelief—all right, even disapproval—when he'd first suggested it. But that was before she'd seen how wind-mad he really was.

There weren't any famous lecturers scheduled for the day, and somehow Araenè didn't really feel like going to the University anyway. She'd automatically turned that way at first, but then she found her steps slowing. The wide Second City streets opened out around her, inviting her to explore inward, toward the center of Canpra and the sea. Instead she headed toward the busy noise of Third City. There were booksellers . . . or she might find another secondhand boy's shirt at a cheap price; she'd need another before too long . . . or she could look for odd spices; strange things from Yngul and other distant places sometimes turned up in Third City shops.

She found herself relaxing as soon as she plunged into the

narrow, angular alleyways of Third City. She hadn't even known she was tense until she felt the knots at the back of her neck dissolve. A trio of girls younger than she hurried by, laughing and talking: Araenè looked after them for a moment, jealous of their assurance and freedom, and of their . . . togetherness, she supposed. None of the girls looked back. Araenè followed them slowly, wishing she was with them, one of them. Or, no, not exactly . . . but maybe wishing that Trei was with her. They could go see a play, even an informal street performance. Or just walk down random alleys and buy bread to feed the birds.

Coming to an awkward intersection of seven alleyways, Araenè chose the one that looked the most interesting. Overhanging rooftops closed out the sky as she made her way down the alley. It was cooler in the shade, where only the occasional glint of sunlight made its way down to the cobblestones. Somebody had put a large tub of flowers where one of those unexpected shafts of light could strike it; the orange and gold flowers blazed like sunlight. A boy sitting on the steps outside one shop was sharing bread and dates with a white monkey, which sat on his knee and gravely accepted each tidbit. Somewhere a woman was singing.

Araenè nodded to the boy, stepped around the flowers, and found herself walking beside a long wall. The wall, two or (in places) three stories high, stretched without a break ahead of her and then turned around a corner. Yellow bricks scattered among the red ones made an odd, angular pattern that somehow drew her eye. Araenè put out a curious hand, tracing the pattern as high as she could, and followed the wall and the pattern around the corner.

Almost as soon as she'd turned the corner, she found a door in the wall. Three times her height, the door was nevertheless so narrow her shoulders would brush its frame if she passed through it. It was made of some dark wood, but with squares of a pale yellow wood inlaid here and there. The inlay wasn't really random, Araenè saw: the inlaid pale squares echoed the broader pattern of the yellow bricks. She touched one of the yellow squares, and the door swung silently open.

All at once, Araenè remembered the other door—the quartered oak door, with behind it the long hallway and cluttered room, and the Yngulin man and the boys and the strange glass sphere that tasted of anise and cumin, ginger and lemon. She hadn't forgotten about any of that, exactly. But the memory of that strange and frightening evening had somehow settled to the back of her mind, never quite noticed or examined. Now it rushed back to her, so that she backed up and sat down abruptly on the step of the ordinary little shop across from the narrow door.

Across from her, the door stood open. Waiting. Araenè wondered what would happen if she simply turned her back on it and started making her way east, toward the Second City and home. Would she find herself lost again, with everyone she asked assuring her that her way lay just a street ahead and around a corner? Maybe every time she left her house, she'd find one strange door or another standing before her? She found herself growing angry: what business of anyone's was it where she went?

At the same time, Araenè found she actually *wanted* to push that door wide, step through it, find out what waited on the other side. She got up, crossed the alley, and stepped warily through the door.

This time she found herself in a warm, richly appointed room. Its walls were oak and ebony, its small tables of carved ebony, its chairs upholstered in white. Lanterns hung from the ceiling by short chains. A long translucent feather hung from the base of one of the lanterns, twisting gently.

A pedestal almost as tall as Araenè occupied each corner of the room. Three of the pedestals were occupied by thick books bound in gold-embossed leather, each chained to its own stand. A fourth pedestal was empty, its chain hanging limp.

On the farthest chair sat the black-skinned Yngulin man. Against the white cloth of the upholstery, his robe and face and hands looked even blacker. A gold-flame marmoset perched on his knee; a slender white lizard with ruby eyes clung to his shoulder. The marmoset turned its head when Araenè entered the room, bounced a little, and chirped. The lizard blinked, slowly.

The book from the empty pedestal lay open on a glass-topped table beside the black man's chair, and he held a long quill in one hand. But he was not writing in the book. He wasn't even looking at it. He was looking at Araenè.

She swallowed. Then, though she thought of ducking back through the door, she moved forward one step. "You're a mage." Her voice sounded thin to her own ears, as though the room absorbed sound and gave little back.

"So are you," the man answered. His voice was just as Araenè remembered: smoky and dark, with a rough undertone. "Or you will be, if you do not strangle the magic as it rises in you. What is your name?"

"Ar—Arei." Araenè hesitated, half expecting the mage to suddenly realize she was a girl and become offended or shocked or angry. But despite his intense scrutiny, he did not seem to see anything unusual. Maybe he was just looking for a mage gift and hadn't thought to look for anything else. Recovering some of her ordinary confidence in her disguise, she asked boldly, "What's yours?"

The Yngulin mage's smile widened. It was a smile with an edge like a knife. "You may call me Master Tnegun."

From the way he put this, it clearly was not his true name. "What does that mean? Tnegun?"

"You wish to learn Ylembai?" The master smiled again at Araenè's startled head shake. "It means 'black.' Few Islanders wish to take the trouble to learn the correct pronunciation of my true name. 'Tnegun' is difficult enough for an Island tongue."

Araenè blinked. She said, trying out the unaccustomed sound of it, "Tnegun."

"Passable," said the master, with a slight, approving tilt of his head. "However, *Master* Tnegun, if you please—as you will be my student."

Araenè took a step back toward the door. "I . . . I can't stay."

The master frowned at her, a frown as edged as his smile. "You can hardly go. Smothering your mage gift as it rises is a sin against the Gods who gave you the gift. But if you are to use it, you will find magecraft requires dedicated study. Students generally board here in the school—ah. Your family?"

"They won't understand," Araenè agreed, grateful for this easy excuse. "Besides . . ." She stopped.

The Yngulin mage waved a hand, dismissing whatever

objection Araenè could produce. "You have my Dannè sphere. I told you to bring it back to me."

"I . . ."

"Next time you come, bring it." Master Tnegun frowned as Araenè shook her head again. He added severely, "You will find you must return or else smother everything you might become—and you will indeed find the effort much like smothering. Once magery begins to rise in the blood, it doesn't care to be dammed up. Your family will become accustomed to the idea." At Araenè's stubborn head shake, he waved an impatient hand and added, "Oh, go, then. Go, if you must. But bring the sphere when you come next!"

Afraid to argue, Araenè nodded awkwardly, backed out through the door, and, as it swung shut, collided with someone who said, "Oof!" Papers and scrolls and feathers exploded through the air all around her.

"Oh!" Araenè whirled around and stared, shocked. She'd left the room through the same door by which she'd entered it, but she wasn't in the Third City alley *at all.* She was in an endless shadowy hallway, the only light coming in through dusty panes of glass in narrow windows. A plump boy about her own age, sand-colored hair falling over his eyes, was sitting in the middle of the hall, gazing in consternation at the scattered papers. They spread out a long way down the hall.

The boy lifted a round face to blink at Araenè. "I'll be late," he told her reproachfully. "*Really* late instead of just a little late."

"I'm sorry—I didn't expect—I thought—" Araenè looked again, in disbelief, at the hallway. She still half expected to see the alley instead.

The boy sighed. "You're new here. Help me pick all this up?" He began, rather slowly, to gather together the scrolls nearest at hand.

Araenè went down the hall to collect the loose papers and feathers that had scattered farthest. "Feathers?" she asked cautiously.

"The long black ones are black gull and raven; those are mostly for auguries. We get raven eggs from Tolounn—some of the mages like ravens for, um, pets. The red ones and these red-tipped gray ones are from macaws and parrots. Those are good for memory; students use a lot of them. The green ones are Quei."

"What are Quei feathers for?"

"Well, luck, of course." The boy finally climbed to his feet. "Thank you." He accepted a pile of loose papers and nodded at another scattering of scrolls. "Can you get those? And the feathers?" He smiled suddenly, reading Araenè's expression. "Yes, I know, it's really too much; I'd probably have dropped everything even if you hadn't knocked into me. Come on—the stairs are usually just up the hall here, and sometimes around the corner."

Araenè fell into step beside the round-faced boy, her arms full of awkward stacks of papers and the wicker box of feathers. "Um . . . I was trying to get back to the street. . . . I thought the door was just here. . . ."

"Was it?" The boy gave her a surprised glance. "The outside doors aren't usually anywhere near here. Look out there—" He indicated one of the dusty windows.

Araenè squinted obediently out through the glass. They were at least four stories up, and the curving wall she could

71

make out was white. The height and the color and the curve all told her they were in a First City tower. She stepped back, blinking. "But—" she began, and stopped. Then she said, almost a wail, "But how am I supposed to get home?"

"Oh," said the boy, surprised. "Are you trying to leave? I thought you were a new student."

"Master Tnegun—I—he said—but I *can't* stay," Araenè explained incoherently. "He said I'd have to come back, but I can't, I *really* can't, he doesn't *understand*—" Her voice rose too high, and she stopped.

But the boy seemed not to have noticed anything amiss. He whistled through his teeth. "Master Tnegun!" He peered at her with a serious air. "If Tnegun says you'll have to come back, then probably you'll have to, you know. He would know! I expect you have a lot of magery waiting to come out. You have to let it come, or it'll die, and what good would that do anybody? But if you've got family things in the way . . . The masters don't always make enough allowance for that. They've been mages too long to remember what it's like, at first. Look, help me get all this to Master Kopapei in the south tower, and I'll get a door to take you home. All right?"

"Yes," Araenè said, a little numbly. "Um . . . my name's Arei. . . ."

The boy nodded, pretending not to notice Araenè's failure to give her father's name. Or maybe he wasn't pretending, because he answered, "I'm Kanii—I'm a fifth year," and he didn't give his father's name, either.

"Fifth year?"

"I started young," Kanii said matter-of-factly. "I'm Master Kopapei's student, you know. All his students come in early. Look, here are the stairs, cooperating for once. That's the Quei feathers, I expect. Up three flights, here we go. Usually there aren't any fledgling basilisks or anything on these stairs; that's why I came out of my way to take them. Here we are—" He guided Araenè into a large, cool chamber whose single window looked out over endless waves. A salt breeze came in through the window, along with the shouts of sailors on a bright-sailed fishing boat: they were now far underground.

"But we went up," Araenè objected, peering out that window. "And now we're down? I thought we were going to the—the south tower?"

"The school's odd that way," Kanii agreed, barely glancing out the window. "Through here, watch your step." He held the door for Araenè, awkwardly because of the scrolls bundled in his arms. There was a step up, and they were standing in a spacious tower room. The room was round, with a high ceiling painted with birds and stars. There were three doors in the room, three tables, three chairs, and nine windows. Every window showed clouds streaming past in a stiff breeze.

Araenè realized that Kanii was watching her with amused appreciation and closed her mouth.

"It takes practice to learn your way about," he said, and unloaded his armload of scrolls on a nearby table, gesturing for Araenè to do the same.

"Kanii!" roared a voice from an adjoining room. "You're late!"

Araenè jumped, but Kanii, completely unruffled, only shouted back, "Yes, sir! Entirely my fault, sir!" He added to

Araenè, rolling his eyes, "I don't think I've ever been on time for anything in three years."

Master Kopapei appeared in the doorway, bringing with him into the room a warm scent of cardamom and, more faintly, cloves. He was an alarmingly large man with shoulders like a laborer and a belly like a chef who loved his own cooking. He was bald as an egg, but he had bristly eyebrows over shrewd dark eyes. He wore clothing of plain dark blue, rather wrinkled. His shirt was slightly too big even for him and had a small rip on the cuff, and his broad leather belt was shiny and thin with age. His rumpled, cheerful air made Araenè guess that he might originally have come from the Third City.

"You're always nearly on time for meals," Master Kopapei told Kanii, but without heat. Though he spoke to Kanii, he was gazing at Araenè. She flushed nervously, afraid of what he might see. But Master Kopapei, like Master Tnegun, seemed as oblivious to Araenè's deception as everyone always had been. He only continued mildly, "A new student, Kanii? Where are your manners? Introduce this young person to me properly."

Kanii bowed, not very gracefully. "Master Kopapei, allow me to make known to you Arei, a new student of Master Tnegun's."

"I'm not!" Araenè said sharply, afraid to let this pass because it sounded oddly like something that might be true. "I am *not* going to be a mage! I'm going to be—" She collected herself and stopped, finishing lamely, "Anyway, I'm not going to be a mage."

"No?" Master Kopapei gazed at her, blinking vaguely. "You

have some other plan for your life? But you know, young Arei, we do need mages rather badly. And chance or life or the Gods do have a way of interfering with even the firmest-set plans. If magery is rising in you, you might consider permitting it to rise. Hmm?"

Araenè stared at him. She did not know what to say. Another plan? The only life available to a girl of decent family was marriage and children. She knew she couldn't be a chef, not really—she couldn't live her whole *life* disguised as a boy, could she? And she knew she didn't want to marry anyone. But how could she possibly be a mage? She said quickly, trying not to think too hard about whether she might actually *want* to be a mage, "I need to go home. Kanii promised he'd show me the way out."

"Did he?" Master Kopapei tilted his head to the side, regarding Araenè with good-humored indulgence. "Well, then, certainly he must. Kanii, you had better make certain young Arei finds a door that will take him properly home. That will make you later still for your lessons with me, but no doubt you will be happy to work after supper to make up for it."

"Certainly," Kanii agreed, not in the least perturbed. "That means you won't want me this afternoon, of course, sir. I thought I'd show Arei around the school before he goes—if you have time," he added to Araenè.

It *was* still early. Araenè nodded, cautiously, to be polite. But then she realized she really was interested, and nodded again with more enthusiasm. "As long as I'm home by seventh bell," she said; then, because Kanii was always late, prudently amended this to half past sixth.

"Of course," Kanii assured her.

"Be sure of it, if you undertake this trust," Master Kopapei commanded him sternly. "It's important to keep promises. Arei . . . family complications have a way of working out. You need to decide whose life you're living: yours? And if not, then whose?"

Araenè looked up at the mage. She found she liked him a great deal—rare for her. She wanted to ask him why Master Tnegun might want her for his apprentice—her particularly. But she didn't quite dare. She asked Kanii, though, once they were out of the tower room and clattering down flights and flights of stairs.

"And why all the stairs now, when we didn't come this way at all on the way up?" she wanted to know, exasperated.

"Would *you* want to climb that many stairs?" Kanii asked reasonably. "Down, it's not so bad. I can't guess why you caught Master Tnegun's eye, except you must have a lot of potential. He's tremendously skilled, and a good teacher. You're lucky to have him for your master."

"I don't!" Araenè said. But this came out rather shrill and uncertain.

"Well, Arei, family things do work themselves out when they have to, you know: Master Kopapei was right about that. I mean, we get this all the time. We've got a new boy, Cesei, lots younger than you; his father's a high court minister. He was just so set on his son following him in the ministry, you know? But the boy'll be a mage now, no question." Kanii lowered his tone, gave Araenè a significant glance. "It is Master Kopapei who has him now, but they say it was Cassameirin *himself* who found him."

"Cassameirin?" It didn't quite seem an Island name. . . .

"*Master* Cassameirin. He's older than anybody, almost; they say he was a master even before the sky dragons cut the Islands free from the earth. I don't know about *that,* but he wrote half the books in the school libraries. If it's true *he* found Cesei, I expect the brat'll prove brilliant." Belying his words, Kanii's tone was one of casual approval. He added, "No doubt Cesei will turn out to be one of those scholar-mages who wander down now and again from their high tower and absentmindedly explain some theoretical principle that's been baffling everybody for a thousand years."

Araenè paused on a landing to catch her breath and consider this easy flow of alarming information. She found herself wondering what it might actually be like to be a mage. But that didn't even matter, of course it didn't, couldn't. Not for a girl. She said fiercely, "Some family things are harder to work out."

"But they do, all the same," Kanii said without heat.

Not mine, Araenè wanted to say, but she couldn't think of a way to say this without explaining why not. She turned her back on Kanii instead so he wouldn't see the angry tears that threatened.

In a corner of the landing, something glittered and seemed to rise up. She leaped back, caught herself, and stared. A large gold and ebony serpent was curled on a bench, head raised and hood spread. Eyes of gold and jet glittered in its slender head. But it wasn't moving after all. "Gods preserve us—that's just a carving, isn't it? Is it?"

"Yes—so far as I know!" answered Kanii. "But be careful! You can't ever trust things like that to stay what they seem to be. What do you want to see? The aviary? The balcony garden? The common workshop? Oh! I know—the hall of spheres and mirrors!"

"The kitchens?" Araenè suggested diffidently.

Kanii grinned. "Wonderful idea! Splendid idea! A boy with a proper sense of priorities! Down all the way, then— let's take a shortcut—" He led the way off the stairway landing and into a room entirely filled, or so it seemed to Araenè, with ornaments of spun glass and crystal. Some hung from the ceiling on fine transparent cords, with others cluttered in haphazard disorder on knee-high tables. "Careful," Kanii advised, ducking underneath a flock of tiny, delicate birds in jewel-colored glass. The birds swayed on their cords, producing a fragile chiming. Araenè held her breath, but nothing shattered.

"But what are these all *for*?" she asked.

"No idea," Kanii admitted cheerfully. "Tichorei swears you can predict the weather by watching the birds, but I don't know; I expect you could fool yourself, don't you think, changeable as the weather is? But they're pretty, aren't they?"

Araenè nodded, edged carefully by the swaying ornaments, and turned to gaze back into the whole amazing room for a moment before following Kanii through the door he was holding open for her.

The hall he led her into proved to be disappointingly ordinary.

"I know," Kanii said, laughing at her expression. "But don't give up hope! Any of these doors"—he gestured broadly at the dozen or so doors in sight down the wide hallway—"might suddenly open, and we'll find before us an animal never seen before outside the illuminations of an ancient manuscript, or a harp of bone strung with the voices of the forgotten dead, or a Quei sitting on a nest of ruby eggs. But *this* door"—and he strode ahead of her and flung one wide with a flourish—"will probably bring us to the kitchens."

The completely nonmagical fragrance of baking bread and syrup and braised lamb with spices rolled out into the hallway. Araenè took a deep breath and smiled, feeling knots of tension undo themselves in her neck and back.

There were two chefs, with three boys to help them. The older and fatter of the chefs scowled good-naturedly at Kanii, but smiled at Araenè and handed over bowls of rice with sweetened coconut milk and slices of mango.

"A new student, ha?" he said to Kanii. "That's your excuse today, is it, young sir? A good one, yes; we must seem welcoming! Mind, don't touch those pastries! Those are for supper."

"What difference would it make if I had mine early?" Kanii wondered wistfully.

Araenè tasted the coconut rice and suggested, "It needs a little more salt to bring out the sweetness, don't you think? What kind of rice is this? It doesn't seem like ordinary rice."

The chef's eyebrows rose high. He snatched up a long-handled tasting spoon and tried the rice himself. "Perspicacious, young sir!" he exclaimed, reaching for a little box of flaky salt. "You are knowledgeable? You possess an educated palate, hmm? This is Yngulin sticky rice, which must be steamed, for it is too heavy if it is boiled. Master Tnegun prefers this rice above all others. We make it for him. Tonight we will serve it with the lamb dish also, though ordinarily the lamb would be served with a lighter rice." He handed Araenè a tasting spoon of her own and gestured permission for her to try the lamb.

It was meltingly tender, in a creamy sauce fragrant with coriander and cardamom, black pepper and cumin. "You used ground hazelnuts to thicken the sauce? Not walnuts?" she asked.

The chef beamed at her. "This school needs more mages with so discriminating a palate!" he told her.

Araenè didn't try to explain that she wasn't going to be a mage. She said, "I always wanted to be a chef. May I see that rice? Oh, what an interesting shape and color! How long does one steam it? Does it pick up the flavors if you steam it over stock instead of water?"

Araenè pulled herself away from the kitchens only reluctantly, when Kanii's sighs grew too dramatic to ignore. The chef pressed a bag of exotic fruit on her—"Apples, from far northern Tolounn," he told her. "They are excellent in tarts with cassia and a touch of cloves, but eat these out of hand."

"They never let me filch more than a taste now and then," Kanii told her when they finally left the kitchens. "Nobody ever offered me an apple." His tone on this last was wistful, and so was the sidelong glance he gave Araenè. She laughed and handed him one of the fruits.

"I didn't think we'd be so long in the kitchens," Kanii said, tossing his apple in the air and catching it with satisfaction. "I wanted to show you, oh, I don't know, the labyrinth in the deepest part of the school, and the balcony where the black gulls nest—sometimes they hatch out basilisks, though, so you have to be careful—and it *is* a shame to miss the hall of spheres and mirrors—"

Araenè found herself wanting to say, *Well, next time,* but didn't. How could she let there be a next time? She could *not* be a mage—anyway, she didn't *want* to be a mage. . . .

"But it's after fifth bell now," Kanii was continuing. "It wouldn't do to delay, not after Master Kopapei made such a fuss about promises and getting you home on time. Let's see: one of the outside doors ought to be just along here. . . ."

He found the door without much trouble: a heavy, abundantly carved door of oak and ebony, the sort of door a First City tower might have.

"You open it," Kanii told her. "It'll most likely take you straight to your home, if that's where you want to go. We call this one the Akhan Bhotounn—that means 'the friendly one' in Guaon."

Araenè thought Guaon was a language of ancient Tolounn, but she wasn't sure. The words sounded more Tolounnese than anything else. When she opened the door, she found herself looking out at the sun-burnished street in front of her house, framed by its graceful flameberry trees and with its door flanked by pots of red flowers. From the angle, she seemed to be standing in the house across the street. That was, of course, impossible, but she was tempted to step out and look over her shoulder just to see.

But she murmured, "The back would be better," then shut the door and opened it again. This time it showed her the alley behind her house.

"See?" Kanii said. "Friendly. Though that was especially quick; maybe you have a knack. Be sure and tell it you're grateful—thank you, Akhan Bhotounn," he said to it himself, and patted the doorframe.

"Yes, thanks," Araenè said distractedly. She looked at Kanii, somehow reluctant, now that it came to it, to actually step out through the door.

The plump boy grinned at her. "A fine afternoon, Arei. You can raid the kitchens with me anytime, but next time I'll definitely show you the hall of spheres and mirrors, all right?"

Araenè opened her mouth, but closed it again without saying anything. She stepped through the door, which seemed to be set directly in a wall she knew was ordinarily blank. It closed behind her with a decisive-sounding click, and then the wall *was* blank. Only Araenè somehow had a feeling that if she should lay her hand on that wall, the door would appear under her hand, open wide to welcome her back.

She didn't touch the wall but quickly turned, gave a cursory glance around, and climbed up to her window.

Her mother was sitting at Araenè's writing desk. Her face was braced against her hand; with her other hand she was slowly turning a polished brooch over and over. Whatever her thoughts, she was too absorbed in them to hear her daughter at the window. Araenè, frozen in place, thought her mother looked sad and tired and, oddly, lonely. She'd never thought of her mother as *lonely* in her life.

And what was Mother doing home? Anger mixed with shock and worry: it wasn't even sixth bell! Mother never came home from visiting so early. It wasn't fair *at all* that she should pick this particular day to return early—unless, Three Gods be generous, she'd had news about Trei? That kind of early notice couldn't be good, could it? She needed to go in, find out—surely Mother wasn't going to sit in Araenè's room *all afternoon?* In a minute, Araenè suspected, her fingers would cramp and she would topple backward into the alley. Absorbed or not, Mother could hardly fail to hear the resulting crash.

From elsewhere in the house, Cimè called. Mother started, set down the brooch, and hesitated. After a moment she got to her feet, ran both her hands across her hair, checked that her dress fell gracefully straight, donned a smile as deliberately as she might don a garment, glanced in Araenè's mirror to check that everything was in order, and swished out of the room.

Relieved, Araenè hauled herself through her window and dashed to change clothing. Then she climbed back out the window—remembering, just, to check that nobody was walking through the alley, and indeed she had to wait a moment for a tradesman to deliver a package to the neighboring house—it was much more difficult climbing in girls' clothing. Especially when she was in a hurry, though come to that, she was already surely too late to bother hurrying.

Araenè made sure she had the bag of apples and went brazenly around to the front entry of the house.

Cimè met her in the front hall, exclaiming with surprise and relief. "Araenè! Where *have* you been? Your poor mother *has* been worried! Oh—you've been to the market, have you? Did Ti go with you?"

"I only just stepped out for a minute," Araenè said, pretending calm. "Really, Cimè, you do fuss. This is a special kind of fruit. No, I'll take it myself. . . ."

"Araenè, dear." Mother swooshed into the kitchen, following the sound of voices. "Did you walk over to Adeila Hanerè's after all, then? I thought we might have gone crosswise of one another, going opposite directions. Where's Ti? Didn't you ask him to accompany you?" She paused to cough, and in the pause her eye was caught by the apples Araenè was carefully transferring to an earthenware bowl. She frowned. "You didn't go unattended to the market, surely?"

"Only for a moment . . ." Araenè had meant to sound firm, but found her voice wavering. She lowered her eyes before her mother's concerned, exasperated gaze.

"Araenè . . ." But Mother's voice trailed off, as though she simply couldn't think what she should say.

"It's not fair, it's *silly*, requiring me to have an escort just to step out to the market for a moment! Third City women aren't treated like they're too stupid to find their way across the street—"

"Araenè. How Third City women behave is hardly relevant to the daughter of a respected minister. They don't have any choice, you know, and their behavior *does* hurt their prospects. But not as much as carelessness with your reputation will hurt yours, my dear. I know you miss Trei's escort, but you mustn't behave like an ill-raised little beggar's child."

If Araenè had tried to answer, she would have said far too much. She borrowed a trick from Trei and didn't say anything at all.

Mother sighed. "I know you think I don't understand how you feel, how propriety chafes at you. But I do, dear, truly. Come and sit with me and we can talk about these things. . . ."

"What is there to talk about?" Araenè found her voice rising. She tried hard to moderate it, with little success. "I know I've less freedom than a child's pet marmoset or the poorest ill-raised beggar children. I know I'm supposed to pretend the walls of this house haven't any doors. I know Trei is going to learn to ride on the winds, when I'm not even allowed to walk on the earth!"

"Araenè, dear . . ."

Araenè fled. If she stayed in the kitchen another moment, she was either going to scream or cry. Probably both. She fled to her room and slammed the door hard. Nobody came after her.

Unable to sit still, Araenè paced. She wanted to curse, and might have if she'd been wearing boys' clothing, but she couldn't while dressed like a girl. She wanted to cry, girls could, but being a girl was the whole problem and she *wouldn't* cry. She wanted desperately to throw things, but didn't quite have the nerve to throw anything breakable and throwing pillows wasn't satisfying. She flung herself across her bed, but then found it impossible to lie still for more than a moment. So she paced.

And all the time she knew eventually she'd have to open her door and go back into the rest of the house and pretend to be calm, only she thought the pretense was getting thinner every day. Mother might even see how thin the bubble of calmness was that overlay all the violence beneath.

Araenè wanted to climb back out her window and disappear into the maze of Third City streets and never come back out. But that was impossible. So many things were impossible.

When she looked for it, Araenè found the Dannè sphere still resting safely in the secret compartment in the back of her drawer. Though until this moment she had made every effort to avoid even thinking about it, she picked it up now and brought it out into the light.

The sphere seemed heavier than she remembered, and

blacker, though translucent where the light caught it just right. It tasted predominantly of ginger, with undertones of anise and lemon; the cumin was almost hidden below the other tastes. Araenè frowned at it. A Dannè sphere. Dannè was the name of a small island at the edge of the Floating Islands, but it was also a person's name. A woman's name. Was this sphere named after the island or a woman? Or did the word have an actual meaning? What meaning?

Why ginger and lemon? Or anise and cumin? Why should it taste like anything at all? Araenè scowled at the sphere. The tastes weren't very well balanced right now: it needed less ginger and more cumin. . . . As she thought about this, the flavors shifted across her palate. As the cumin became more prominent, the sphere took on a more opaque look. It seemed to vibrate against her fingers, a smoky sort of buzz. Araenè dropped the sphere, which rolled across the floor and under the desk.

For a moment, Araenè just stared after it. She didn't want to touch the sphere again; wished, really, that she'd just left it alone, tucked away in the back of her drawer. She was tempted now to leave it where it had rolled, only she could hardly have Cimè finding it when she swept. . . . Reluctantly Araenè crossed the room and knelt to reach after the sphere, but at the last moment she changed her mind and used a cloth to enfold it before she picked it up. The cloth at least muffled the strange taste sensations. Still, she put it down as quickly as she could and rubbed her fingers.

Lying on her desk next to the sphere was the brooch she'd earlier seen her mother holding. It was the special clouds and dragon brooch Mother had given Araenè when she was five. She'd worn it ever since. Of course Araenè always left it behind when she dressed as a boy . . . but now she wondered what Mother might have thought when she'd found this particular brooch discarded on the desk. It was an uncomfortable question.

5

Trei woke in warm darkness. At first he thought he was at home. In his own room, in his own house, in Rounn, with Mother and Father in the room below and Marrè down the hall. He thought that in a moment he would hear his mother stir awake and leave her room. The servants would make breakfast, but Mother herself always made sweetened barley broth for his father and sister and Trei, and brought it to their rooms. She added nutmeg, something no one else ever seemed to do. Trei could smell the nutmeg, but other things were wrong. The room felt too big. . . . He could hear other people breathing in the darkness, too close. . . . There were outlines of light against the darkness. For one horrified moment, Trei thought he was seeing lines of glimmering fire running down the flanks of Mount Ghaonnè; he thought he saw a great dragon of fire rear up in the midst of the darkness, burning wings spreading wide across the smoke-choked sky—the stone itself was burning—the bitter taste of ash was in his mouth—

Biting back a cry, Trei leaped to his feet, staggered, fell to his knees, caught hold of handfuls of cloth, and scrambled back to his feet. There was no dragon; of course there was not—only a dream, it had only been a dream. There was no mountain, no fiery stone, no ash. Not now, not here. But even once he was sure of that, for one terrible, disorienting moment, Trei had no idea at all where he was.

His sight cleared gradually as he stood panting in the dim light, and he slowly understood that he was standing beside a narrow bed, that it was bed linens he was clutching so hard in both his hands, and that the slender lines of light only showed where windows were shuttered. There were far too many windows, each over a bed like his own, in an utterly unfamiliar hall. But at least there was no fire.

Now truly awake, Trei fumbled up along the wall over his bed, feeling for the catch to the window. The window was placed high, almost too high to reach even standing on the bed, but Trei found the catch at last, put back the shutters, and blinked as brilliant light poured in.

For a long moment, though, he still did not understand what he saw when he turned to look at the room. It certainly was not *his* room. A long hall, it had eighteen beds along its length, counting his own, with boys asleep on five of the closest: pale heads, and brown, and dark. Each bed had two shelves on the wall above its headboard and a chest at its foot. Otherwise, the room was plain. It was nothing at all like home.

Memory came back to Trei, sharp as a knife, worse than any dream. Rounn. Mount Ghaonnè, liquid fire running down its flanks. Choking on the ash and smoke in the air, the soldiers stopping him on the road. The pity and horror in their eyes as they turned back the desperate survivors of the Gods-destroyed city. *"You can't go down there.... No, not you, either, boy. They're all dead down there. ... The provincar's closed the road. Where'd you come from, Sicuon? Go back there...."* Then, after that nightmare journey, his uncle in Sicuon, angry and ashamed: *"Trei, Tolounn won't offer much to a half-bred boy. ... You can't stay with us.... You can't stay...."*

Trei sat back down on his bed, braced his elbows on his knees, and pressed his hands over his eyes. He could still see Rounn in his mind's eye, but now only as he'd seen it at the last: buried under ash, with the thin voices of wailing mourners rising like threads of smoke through the cold air.

Someone sat down next to Trei on his bed and put a hand on his arm. Trei couldn't move, much less speak, but the other boy was patient. Trei struggled to remember. The Floating Islands, the bridge—the path up the mountain, and the pool at the top—Trei rubbed his eyes hard.

"A hard day and a long night, and a confused waking," the other boy said quietly. His name occurred to Trei: Ceirfei Feneirè. He was dressed now merely in a simple beige robe with a red cord for a belt. But though he might have lost his white clothing and his violet ribbon, he still had his natural poise. Something else had changed.... His eyes, Trei realized. Trei didn't remember what color they had been. But now they were black and crystal. Kajurai eyes.

Ceirfei took his hand off Trei's arm and stood up, looking serious. "You're the boy from Rounn. I was most grieved to hear about your home. The Gods' purposes are opaque to us, and thus their actions often seem cruel. I pray the earth lies light above the bones of your family."

Trei nodded mutely, unable to speak.

"I thought you would succeed," Ceirfei said. He sounded gravely approving, but Trei understood that he was also deliberately trying to provide a path that would help lead Trei out of memory and back to this hall. "I thought you would find a right thing to do on Kotipa. Well done. Your eyes are kajurai eyes now."

Trei tentatively put a hand up to his eyes. Though he could perceive nothing different about his sight, he knew this must be true. So he was kajurai. He really was. He should have been excited. Yet it did not seem exactly true, not yet. He wanted to look in a mirror, but at the same time he was afraid of how he might appear. He would look like a kajurai. He *was* kajurai, an Islander, and no longer a boy of Tolounn. . . . He must *truly* be an Islander if he had passed the kajurai audition, and yet this knowledge was strangely unsettling.

"It's odd how it feels, when you achieve an important goal," Ceirfei observed. "It's disorienting at first, isn't it?"

Trei nodded. Disoriented. That was exactly how he felt.

"I, also," Ceirfei said. He held out a hand, helping Trei to his feet. "We might find the baths and breakfast before all this crowd wakens, do you think? That will probably help us both feel more like we're actually here. I think the baths are probably this way." He walked away toward the far end of the sleeping hall.

The baths consisted of a stone pool of steaming water and a smaller one of cold, with towels and bowls of soap laid out on one table and folded clothing ready on another. The steaming pool was not as hot as Trei expected, and the cold one was frigid. He washed quickly and dressed in the clothing provided: very plain, by Island standards. Sleeveless gray shirts, black trousers, a red sash.

Ceirfei held a gray shirt up in front of him, eyeing it for fit. If he was dismayed by its lack of color or elegance, he hid his disappointment well. But then, Trei suspected the other boy didn't care what his clothing looked like, so long as it belonged to a novice kajurai.

"Breakfast," Ceirfei said, and led the way out of the bathing room and down a short hall. He seemed again to know which way to go.

Round loaves of wheat bread and plates of figs were laid out along a large table in a room adjoining the bedchamber, and a large pot of sweetened rice cereal was keeping warm over a central fire pit. There was nutmeg in the cereal. The familiar fragrance still made Trei's throat close up, but the bread and figs made him think of his cousin Araenè, of his uncle and aunt. As soon as he thought of them, he missed them. Yet knowing they were probably thinking of him, that they must be aware he'd passed his audition and would be happy for him, made his grief for his lost family less overpowering. When Ceirfei handed Trei two bowls and started slicing bread, Trei found it possible to ladle out the cereal without tears burning in his eyes.

Somewhere close, a door clicked open and then banged closed, and boots rang on the stone floor. Trei set a bowl of cereal aside and looked up. Ceirfei straightened and bowed as Anerii Pencara appeared in the doorway, the second-ranked kajurai Rei Kensenè at his shoulder. Trei echoed the other boy's bow, a little late and not nearly as gracefully.

Anerii Pencara looked at Ceirfei for a moment, shifted his

gaze to Trei, grunted, and walked past them into the sleeping hall. A moment later, they heard his rough voice: "Up, laggards! The morning is well advanced, and here you lie! Up! Baths, bread, and out to have your first look at wind and weather! Up! That means *you*, boy." There was the scraping sound of a bed being upended, the thud of a boy being tipped out onto the stone floor, and a surprised cry. Ceirfei and Trei looked at each other. Trei found himself smiling, and the other boy grinned.

Rather than following the novice-master into the sleeping hall, Rei Kensenè came over to the table. He leaned a hip against the edge of the table and said cheerfully, "I'll have some bread, yes, and those figs. Thanks. Well done, novices; we say it's good luck to wake early and easily after the change."

Trei wouldn't have called his own awakening *easy*. He said nothing.

"It *is* luck, most likely," Ceirfei said, politely deprecating. "After all, someone must always awaken first. Though it was Trei who was up first. He woke me."

"Did he?" said Rei. He didn't look at Trei, but gave Ceirfei a wary sideways glance.

The novice-master, having shooed the last of his charges toward the baths, came back into the breakfast room and dropped heavily into the chair at the head of the long table. Ceirfei passed him a plate of sliced bread and a bowl of figs. Trei wordlessly followed suit with a bowl of rice cereal. Master Anerii took the bread and ignored the cereal. Ceirfei lifted one eyebrow and took the proffered cereal himself with a courteous nod, just as though Trei had meant to offer it to him all along. Trei tried to look blandly polite, realized he was copying Ceirfei's exact manner, and flushed in confusion.

"As you two are up early," the novice-master said gruffly, looking at Ceirfei rather than Trei, "you will both go with Rei Kensenè to make your offering to the Gods and help him lay out the wings."

"Yes, sir," Ceirfei said.

"And we'd best be quick about it," declared the young kaju-rai. "Eat, boys, eat—or you'll wish you had later, I promise you." He spooned honey over his figs, suiting action to words.

There were candles to light at the Gods' three altars, and libations to pour—water for the First God, wine for the Young God, and blood for the Silent God. Ceirfei donated the blood without waiting to be asked, nicking his finger with the wait-ing knife and letting a single drop of blood fall in the basin be-fore the altar.

"That'll stand for all the novices just enrolled," Rei assured them. "Especially as, well, never mind. Here we go. Let's step out, if you please—it won't do to keep the master waiting, and he'll want everything laid out just so. Here we are."

They had arrived at a long underground chamber with a balcony that overlooked the sea and, in the far distance, a shadow that was probably another of the greater Floating Is-lands. There weren't any bridges here, nothing but sea and sky. The sun was brilliant in the morning sky, striking a violent glare from the waves below, and yet the light didn't blind Trei: he found he could look straight out into the blazing light with-out even blinking.

But the view itself was dizzying. Confusing. Because he could *see* the wind on which the kajuraihi rode. Looking out from the balcony was like . . . like looking through layers of glass, completely clear and yet visible because of the way light slid across it. . . . Really, it was not like anything Trei had ever imagined. He could actually *see* the currents of air, the layers of warmer air riding atop cooler, the changes of pressure and density. The long ribbons of cloud looked strange: he could see the layers of air on which the clouds rode and the changes of temperature they both reflected and caused.

And high up at the very edges of Trei's new sight, dragons flew. He could see them plainly, though they were transparent as ice. Their long bodies coiled and uncoiled, rippling almost like streamers of cloud; their great wings spanned the sky; their heads were fine-boned and delicate as birds' heads. Trei could see that they both created and rode the winds that swept over the ocean. He felt his heart rise up in his chest at the sight of them. The whole world seemed to shift and tilt under his feet. He put a hand out blindly, bracing himself against the stone of the wall.

"Never approach them," Rei told them sternly. He reached to grip Trei's shoulder and Ceirfei's, compelling their attention. "Never trouble them. Their magic is what keeps these Islands in the air, you know, and it's their magic we kajuraihi borrow. Always respect the dragons!"

"They don't mind, though," Trei asked, a little doubtfully, "that you—that *we* use their magic?" The dragons in the far reaches of Tolounn were not at *all* like these graceful creatures of air: Tolounnese dragons were huge and rare and very dangerous. He flinched from the images of his nightmare—of the gaping wound in the mountain above Rounn, its edges black and charred, the Gods' furnaces glowing deep within. Of the dragon rearing out of the mountain's molten heart: a dragon made of fire, with fire blazing in its eyes and dripping from its mouth. Maybe there had never been a fire dragon in Mount Ghaonnè, maybe the mountain had just broken on its own, but Trei remembered the wide and level sea of gray ash where Rounn should have stood and was bitterly glad that these Island dragons of wind and air were so different, bitterly envious that they were so different.

Trei blinked hard and stared up into the wind, trying to erase the image of the fire dragon with the beautiful reality of the dragons of air.

Rei grinned, clearly not noticing Trei's moment of distracted grief. "No, novice, they don't mind! Believe me, you use so small a fraction of the dragon magic surrounding the Islands that so long as you keep your distance, they'll notice you no more than they notice gulls or fish eagles. But it's not the dragons that concern us now," Rei added firmly. "Look at the kajuraihi out there. Trei." He touched Trei's shoulder again, recalling his attention. "Look now at the *kajuraihi* out there, not the dragons. No, over there. See them? See how they're lying on the air? How they catch the warmer air as it rises?"

Trei tore his gaze away from the dragons with some difficulty, peered through layers of crystalline air, and nodded uncertainly.

"Kajurai sight is confusing at first. But soon enough you'll grow accustomed to it," Rei assured both Trei and Ceirfei, "and after that you'll forget you ever lacked dragon sight. Now come, let me show you how to lay out these wings. Let's learn to do it properly, yes? Soon enough you'll be doing this on your own."

There were six sets of wings to lay out, each one wider

than a man's outstretched arms. They were like swans' wings, only longer and narrower. The feathers at the tips were longer than Trei's forearm. Those felt stiff and almost hard when Trei ran his hand across them, but the smaller feathers that made up the main body of the wing were softer. All the feathers were dyed a vivid red, except three on each wing, which were a metallic green.

"What are these . . . What birds do you use?" Trei asked Rei Kensenè.

Rei answered cheerfully, "We want white feathers that'll take the dye, of course, or else feathers that come red. We use feathers from the sea eagle for nobility"—he showed Trei which feathers those were—"and here, feathers from the lammergeyer for fierceness and from the swan for steadfastness and loyalty. And we always use Quei feathers for a few of the secondaries, for luck; three on each wing, one for each God. You can see those aren't dyed."

Trei nodded.

Rei brushed his hand across the softer, smaller feathers underneath the wing. "Then here, look, we use white owl here in the underwing, for quiet flight but also for wisdom. Now, on the upper side, the scapulars are white heron, for patience, and sometimes macaw, for cleverness. And here, for these wing bars, we use albatross for endurance; see the black barring? For black wings, we'll use black swan instead of white, and cormorant instead of heron, and raven instead of macaw."

"But still Quei," Ceirfei said, not a question.

"Oh, yes," Rei agreed. "Always three Quei feathers on each wing."

"But these longest feathers, here"—Ceirfei spread a hand

across the longest of the primaries, at the tips of the wings—
"these aren't eagle or lammergeyer. Are they?"

"Oh, well," Rei said vaguely, and ran a finger down one of
those feathers. It was a clear, translucent kind of red, as
though it had been spun out of garnets rather than simply
dyed. "These are for the living magic. Without these, the
wings would be just so many dead feathers."

Ceirfei nodded thoughtfully. Trei cautiously touched one
of these special feathers. Obviously they were dragon feathers,
but Rei clearly didn't intend to come right out and say so.
There were about a dozen on each wing. Trei wondered how
the dragon feathers were collected, and how long it took to get
enough to make a set of wings.

"Now, these straps, you see how they'll fit across your arms
and chest. Lay them out like this, so they're handy. Never lay
out a set of wings and leave the straps tangled. Check nothing's frayed. Any feathers worn? Check like this; see how you
brush the feathers up to look at the ones below? Here's the
framework: is it sound? No, give it a good tug, no need to be
shy. It's whalebone: you can't break it. Or if you can, it's not
safe to fly on. Like that, yes. Good. All right, Trei, do that set,
please. Everyone else will be here soon enough. Ceirfei—yes,
good."

The wings were heavier than they looked, and awkward to
lift and lay straight. They had a tendency to fold up at the
joints when lifted, and whenever they folded up, the straps
tangled. Trei didn't want to drag the tips of the feathers across
the stone, and yet when he tried to lift the wings up so they
wouldn't drag, he found himself staggering under their weight
and trying to see through scarlet waves of feathers.

"Not ready yet?" barked the novice-master's rough voice, and Trei jumped.

"Nearly, Master Anerii," Rei Kensenè answered, his tone easy. "Excuse our tardiness, please—I was showing the novices how the wings are structured."

"Why, when you'll merely have to repeat it all again for the rest?" The novice-master still sounded annoyed. "Get those last sets laid out properly. Don't drop those wings, boy! Lay them down with some respect!"

Trei tried, wordlessly, to lower the wings he carried to the stone and smooth them into some kind of order. They didn't look as tidily laid out as Rei's set. . . . He couldn't help noticing that Ceirfei's set was laid out more neatly.

"Trei, is it?" the novice-master snapped. "You'll learn to do better, I am certain." His tone implied he suspected the opposite. "What are the parts of the wing, then, as you've been having lessons?"

Trei blinked, took a short breath, and identified the primaries, the secondaries, the underwing, the scapulars, and the wing bars. Then he risked a look up.

The novice-master was still looking annoyed . . . more annoyed, maybe, now that Trei had named all the parts of the wing correctly. Spread out in a loose semicircle beside him were the other five novices who had successfully made, Trei assumed, the climb to the top of the mountain. Rekei, the quarrelsome boy from the audition, was one of their number, the only boy other than Ceirfei he was sure he recognized.

"Those are the placements of the feathers, not the parts of the wing," the novice-master snapped, recalling Trei's attention with a jerk. "Where is the wrist? Which is the leading edge and which the trailing edge?"

Rei might not have had time to describe all that, but the leading edge and trailing edge were obvious, and *this* joint had to be the wrist. . . .

"Very well," the novice-master said, still snapping. "Let us see if you know where those straps should lie. Put them on, boy. Go on."

"Like so," Rei Kensenè said quietly, coming forward to show Trei. "Here, these over your shoulders, like so, and then the buckles here and here. Yes, I know the wings are heavy. It's hard for you young ones. Here . . . ah, Ceirfei . . . brace this wing, please. Just so, yes. And you, what's your name? Genrai, yes." Genrai was one of the Third City boys, Trei knew; though everyone was dressed now in gray and black, he thought all three of the other boys who'd succeeded in their auditions were Third City.

"All right, Genrai, brace the wing on this side," Rei was saying, still brisk and cheerful as ever. "Here. No, here; you don't want to bend or crush the feathers. Good, that's right."

Anerii Pencara himself came forward to show the boys how to arrange the straps that wound around the arms and wrists. His touch on Trei's arms was impersonal, with nothing of his disapproval translated to roughness. Trei felt the novice-master's hostility anyway and tried not to flinch from it.

"We fly," Master Anerii said, stepping back and gesturing broadly to the open balcony, "as the birds fly and as dragons fly: by instinct and natural gift. We learn to fly by flying. Go on, boy. As you've got your wings on, you may demonstrate for the rest."

Rei said quickly, "Leap out and *down,* not up, and spread your arms with a snap." He demonstrated, showing the sharp final flick of the wrist. "You won't fall, but if you do, you'll be caught. Understand?"

"Yes," Trei said. He felt a little numb.

"Show us all how to do it," said Ceirfei, giving Trei a brief, direct look.

Trei understood that Ceirfei didn't mean *Show us all how to fly,* but *Show us all how to be brave.* He gave the First City boy a slight nod. Then he braced himself for the weight of the wings and shrugged carefully free of the other boys' support. He turned, walked to the edge of the rail-less balcony—his arms drooped; it was hard to keep the tips of the wings from dragging across the stone. But he gritted his teeth, fought the weight, and finally stood poised for a moment on the edge. The warm sea wind came against his face, glittering with body and substance; he could see the many-layered currents of pressure and warmth beyond the curl of the nearby breeze. When he spread his arms, the feathers of his wings caught the wind with surprising force and he found himself lifted to stand on tiptoe, even found himself struggling, suddenly, to keep his feet on the balcony at all.

Behind him, Anerii Pencara said something brusque. Trei didn't listen. He spread his arms wider. He could feel the feathers lift and open all down his wings and the wind shiver through them; the moving air rustled the long feathers at his wingtips and shoved hard against the softer feathers of the underwing. *You won't fall,* Rei had said. Trei knew that this was true; he couldn't even imagine falling, not really. He turned his wrists and spread his fingers, and felt his feathers shift and flare in response.

There was no need to leap after all; he only let himself tilt forward and fall. Only he didn't fall, but slid down the wind. Now that he was no longer fighting to hold them up, the wings seemed weightless. A turn of his hands tilted their leading edges and he rose; a tilt of one palm sent him curving around in a smooth arc. The red stone of Milendri came back in front of him, a surprising distance away; Trei blinked at the force of wind rushing past his face and wondered if he was supposed to go back to the balcony. He couldn't even *see* the balcony. . . . The curving spiral of his flight carried him around and up and he found himself with the wide sea and empty sky before him. A fierce, bright exultation filled him: his whole body felt weightless and strong. He wanted to fly higher and higher, to drive himself faster, to race the streaming clouds across the sky . . . to climb to the heights and fly with the dragons. . . . He looked for them, but they had gone elsewhere, or else so high even his kajurai eyes couldn't make them out.

A kajurai came past him, circled, came back, and settled into a path barely a wing-length from Trei's own wingtip. The man called, "Well done, youngster! Follow me!" and drew Trei a smooth line to follow, up and out, neither as high nor as fast as Trei wanted to go.

His teacher showed Trei how to drive himself upward with slow wingbeats, and how to slip into a rising column of warm air to rest, and how to spill air out from his wings to drop height, and how to stall midair and swing his legs down as if he was going to land. The easiest way to get your legs up again, Trei found, was actually to let yourself do a complete somersault in the air and then dive a little to pick up some speed. His instructor laughed the first time Trei did this and called, "Good, youngster!"

Trei found distant Islands good marks to use when trying to fly a straight course or judge his own height. The Island of Dragons from the audition, with its cloud-wreathed mountains and the thin ribbon of its floating bridge, came before him once. Dragons were visible to him now, curling around the tips of the mountain heights. Trei wanted to go that way, look more closely at those dragons. But his instructor led him away from that Island at once and began to show him how to land instead.

"Slow, slow. Settle gently," called his instructor, demonstrating. "More gently than that, boy, or you'll break an ankle when you actually land on solid rock! Let's practice stalling. And a few less dramatic ways to recover from a stall—you won't always have room to somersault!"

It seemed very soon that the instructor led Trei back toward Milendri.

"We'll come in gently and aim to stall right at the edge of the balcony," shouted the other kajurai. "Relax! Tuck your chin down before you hit! Let yourself run forward when you land, or if you fall, let yourself fall to your knees! It's best to keep your wings up over your head, but don't worry overmuch, do you hear? You'll be tying a great many feathers into place, a few more are of no moment! Do you hear?"

"Yes!" Trei shouted back, wondering whether dragon feathers could break and, if they could, where you would get more. He reminded himself of the wings' weight and how hard he'd have to fight to keep them up once he was on his feet. He told himself firmly to relax. *Relax, stall out, let yourself run forward—don't fall*—if the novice-master was watching, he didn't want to fall—or drag his wings on the stone—

"Concentrate on the moment!" called his instructor. "I'll be right behind you! You've been doing fine! Trust your wings and your instincts and the Quei feathers, that's what they're for! Go on in! Tuck your chin down if you fall!"

Trei bit his lip and tried to make the smoothest, easiest approach possible. He arched his wings to stall as he approached the edge of the balcony—it was coming up surprisingly fast—his legs swung down as he slowed toward stalling speed—if he stalled too soon, he'd fall, there wasn't room to recover, not this close to the cliffs—the impulse to close his eyes and clench his teeth was almost overwhelming—he landed on the balcony hard enough to jar not just his ankles and knees, but also, it seemed, every bone he owned all the way up his spine. His teeth snapped together hard, and his wings suddenly weighed as though every feather was made of lead. He didn't have to *let* himself fall: he landed on his knees hard enough to bruise. His arms, flinging instinctively forward, raked the primary and most of the secondary feathers hard across the stone. Beside him, his instructor came down with graceful precision and took two steps to catch his balance; Trei found it hard to imagine he'd ever manage to land so neatly.

"A clumsy landing, novice," Master Anerii said somewhere above Trei.

Trei, his arms trembling, found himself too exhausted to get up or even move to help his instructor undo the wings' straps. His chest and back ached, and his stomach. . . . In fact, he ached all over. Trei tried to get to his feet, stifled a groan, and let himself fall back to sitting.

"That's normal," the instructor told him, glancing at Trei with a smile. He'd laid out the wings on the chamber floor and was looking them over with a critical eye. He was an old man, at least ten years older than Uncle Serfei, with a short grizzled beard and a network of fine lines around his crystalline fliers' eyes, but he gave Trei a companionable nod. "And you'll be stiffer still tomorrow morning; there's nothing like the first week of flying for sore muscles! Now, these aren't too badly broken up, for a first landing. You did very well, youngster. Did you bite your tongue when you landed?"

Trei shook his head. His neck seemed to creak when he moved his head.

"Good; that's a wicked way to learn to tuck your chin. Which you will recall, next landing? Yes? I think so. My name's Hiraisi. Hiraisi Tegana, but you'll find we put little emphasis on family names, among ourselves."

"Yes, sir," Trei whispered. It even hurt to speak.

"You'll do, Trei," Hiraisi said, and slapped him lightly on the shoulder. "Need a hand to straighten up?"

Trei shook his head again, though carefully, eased himself back to lean against the wall, and watched the other boys come in. They all looked intense and nervous as they came down to the balcony. Their clumsy landings made Trei wince, painfully aware he'd looked just as inept, but at least no one missed the balcony or broke an ankle. Although Rekei stalled out a little early and only his instructor's firm boot on his back shoved him forward far enough to make the balcony: a frightening sight. Rekei's instructor, unable to land properly after that rescue, somersaulted backward, twisted in midair, snapped his wings wide, and fell smoothly away from the balcony.

"Worse than clumsy, and dangerous for your instructor,"

Master Anerii said witheringly to Rekei. "Err the other way next time, boy, you hear?"

Of all the novices, only Ceirfei Feneirè and the oldest of the Third City boys—Genrai—managed to stay on their feet when they landed, and only Ceirfei didn't drag at least one wingtip on the balcony stone. Trei found himself grinning wryly: if someone could manage a graceful landing his first time, of course it would be Ceirfei.

"An acceptable performance," the novice-master informed them once all the boys were sitting in a ragged semicircle on the balcony. "For a first flight, generally acceptable. You will now rest and eat. At sixth bell, Rei will show you how to mend these wings. You won't fly again until they're repaired, so that will give you reason to learn proper repair techniques quickly." He smiled thinly at their groans. "No complaints. You'll be too stiff to fly for a day or three anyway. Ceirfei, Genrai, you'll help the others mend their wings, since yours need less work."

Genrai ducked his head, looking embarrassed rather than pleased to be singled out.

"You are dismissed. You will find your noon meal waiting in the novitiate. Sixth bell, remember. You are expected to be prompt."

So there was time for the novices to become acquainted, which had been inevitable. Trei did not look forward to it, feeling himself much the natural outsider, for all he was actually curious about the other boys.

Besides Ceirfei, Rekei, and Trei himself, there were the three Third City novices. They were Genrai, Tokabii, and Kojran. Genrai was the oldest of all the novices, a quiet, sober boy with a narrow build and a thin face. He'd wanted to audition at thirteen, he said, but his family had needed him until his brothers were old enough to work and his sister to marry. So he'd had to wait until he was seventeen—old for a successful audition, Trei gathered.

Tokabii was the youngest; he'd turned twelve just in time for this audition. From what Trei had seen of him, he was even more quarrelsome and annoying than Rekei and might have done better to wait for the next audition along; if he'd grown up four more years, he might have had more sense. Kojran was fourteen, dark-skinned, with a flashing grin and careless manner; the grandfather for whom he had been named had been Yngulin, he said proudly. Someday he would fly all the way to Yngul and meet his grandfather's people.

"And you?" Genrai asked Trei. "You're not Third City."

Trei felt his shoulders tighten. He said in his flattest tone, "I'm from Tolounn. My mother was Islander."

There was a pause. Then Ceirfei said easily, "Clearly the dragons thought you Islander enough. Pass the honey, would you?"

Trei wordlessly handed Ceirfei the crock of honey.

The three Third City novices were still staring at Trei, but Ceirfei sent a glance around the table that somehow picked up their attention. "Genrai and I are oldest and tallest; that's why we landed best."

"I'm taller than you, and I still dragged my wing," said Genrai. He didn't quite look the nobly born Ceirfei in the face, but he was clearly trying to make his tone matter-of-fact.

"I've been using weights to strengthen my arms for months. We can all do that. I'll show you how, if you like. Kojran, you turn the tightest; Rekei, you slow and stall faster than the rest of us, that's why you nearly missed the balcony; Trei has this nice somersault trick for coming out of stalls fast."

It hadn't occurred to Trei to watch the others, certainly not closely; he'd been too lost in the pure delight of the rushing wind and then in the practice of flight. But he somehow wasn't surprised that Ceirfei had paid broader attention.

"You didn't say anything about me," Tokabii objected. "Or Genrai."

"Tokabii, you climb very steeply, more steeply than I could," Ceirfei said, smiling. "And you dive fast; my instructor wouldn't let me dive so fast. And Genrai has something better than a steep climb or a tight turn or a good stall: he has sense."

Genrai looked taken aback.

Ceirfei nodded to him, but said to them all, "We all have things we can teach one another. Wouldn't it be nice if we were the fastest novices ever to earn rank and clear the novitiate?"

For a long moment, no one spoke. This didn't signal any protest, however. It was, Trei thought, pure admiration of Ceirfei's audacity.

"I think we will be," Genrai said at last, and Trei understood that he meant that if *Ceirfei* meant for them to be the best, then they would have to be. Ceirfei understood this, too. He inclined his head a little.

"It's quarter till sixth," Genrai added, and they all got to their feet in a rapid clatter.

There were lessons some mornings and every afternoon. Each day was filled from dawn until well after dusk. Trei was grateful there was so little time for homesickness, though he hardly knew which home he should miss. But he found he missed his cousin—her quick wit, her boldness, even her sarcastic tone—more than he'd expected. Sometimes Genrai made one or another bitter comment about evenings spent with a crowd of *boys*. Ceirfei and the others just laughed, but Trei didn't laugh.

But they were so busy there was little opportunity to miss anything. The second-ranked kajurai Linai Terinisai spent days showing the novices how to splice damaged feathers and replace broken ones, all the time murmuring a continual monologue about feather selection and dyes, and how to judge where to place a feather in a wing, and how to collect feathers, and a great deal else about feathers that Trei did not remember properly afterward.

A master named Berinai Cosererè delivered a long and alarmingly detailed discourse on kajurai hierarchy, customs, and law. He also explained the many, many rules that bound novices, and the penalties accruing to any novice sufficiently reckless as to break them. This was also complicated, but seemed of far more practical importance. Even the youngest and most irrepressible novice, Tokabii, was a little subdued after that series of lectures.

And a truly elderly master named Tobei Kensera began to explain the relationship between dragon magic and natural Island magic. That was at least interesting. Master Tobei gave the first explanation Trei had ever heard for why the dragons had cut the Islands free of the earth in the first place. "There are dragons of earth, generally in the far south of Yngul," he reminded them. "And dragons of fire in the far north of Tolounn."

Trei glanced down, not liking to think about fire dragons. But then he looked up again as the master continued, more than a little smugly, "But *our* dragons are creatures of air, and I suspect they want places of their own to roost and nest—places divorced from both earth and fire. So, ages past, they lifted the Islands into the sky."

"And then *we* came to the Islands," Rekei put in. "I wonder what the dragons thought about that?"

"Well," said Master Tobei, rather tartly, "they allow us to live here and build our homes into the stone of their Islands. And even though we kajuraihi are not mages, they grant us the use of their magic. So I believe we may assume they were not greatly offended."

"Well, but—" Rekei began.

Master Tobei waved him silent. "In fact, I believe our dragons find us Islanders useful for keeping Tolounnese mages and artificers from troubling their peace, and I suspect they value the kajuraihi as their liaisons between earth and air."

This sounded very uncertain to Trei: *I believe, I suspect*. But Ceirfei, too, had said something about the dragons approving prospective novices. That implied a closer relationship between dragons and kajuraihi than was immediately apparent. But Trei didn't ask. He was too eager for lessons to be finished so they could fly. And if they used dragon magic to ride the wind, he was only grateful the sky dragons allowed it, whatever their reasons.

Because flying was glorious.

The stiffness had worsened over the first few days, but then it eased. The novices learned to fly high enough to brush the clouds; they learned to dive fast and pull out of dives, to turn "on a wingtip" and somersault both forward and backward. They learned how to judge how much lift a particular current of air would provide, and how the wind changed from morning to evening, and how the air over an island behaved differently from the air over the sea. They learned to coax the wind around from the prevailing north to the east, which wasn't too difficult, or the south, which was hard. Trei and Rekei were hopelessly bad at this; all three of the Third City novices were better. Ceirfei was in between.

"You try too hard," Kojran explained earnestly. "You think about it too much. All you up-city boys think too much."

"Well, if thinking's bad for pulling the winds, no wonder *you're* so good at it," Rekei said bitingly. He was the slowest of them all at the trick.

Tokabii bristled at his rejoinder, but Kojran just laughed. "True words! I never worry about anything; that's why wind-working's easy for me."

Ceirfei laughed, too, and clapped the younger boy on the shoulder. "Tomorrow, if you see me worrying too hard, you give me a whistle, hear? And I'll try it your way, all right?"

So the argument was averted, and in fact Ceirfei and Trei both did get better at coaxing the winds around to different quarters of the sky. Even Rekei improved a little.

In the evenings, there were lessons to review. Plainly neither Tokabii nor Kojran had ever made any effort to learn anything complicated in their lives and they hated studying the lessons. Sometimes Ceirfei and Genrai would go off by themselves; Trei suspected that Ceirfei was teaching the older boy how to read better and maybe how to write. It was a fine idea, but it meant he and Rekei were sometimes left with the two younger Third City novices in the evenings, and then tempers would flare. Those were the times when Trei found the novitiate far too crowded, even while he still felt isolated from the other boys.

That might have been why, a week after entering the kajurai novitiate, Trei felt so relieved to receive letters from his uncle Serfei and his family. They made him feel much less set apart.

The novices were not allowed to venture out of the novitiate during the first quarter of their training, but once every week, on Gods' Day, they were allowed to receive letters. The younger Third City boys didn't get any, not surprisingly, as probably no one in their families could write. But Rekei both flushed and grinned as he accepted the handful of letters his mother had sent him, and to nobody's surprise Ceirfei got a whole pile from various friends and family, tied up with a violet ribbon. These were laid aside to wait for him, along with a note Genrai's sister had paid a scribe to write for her, since neither Ceirfei nor Genrai was in the dining hall when the letters arrived.

But Trei was surprised to find himself receiving not only a letter, but also a flat, rigid package, two hand-lengths long and wide and perhaps two finger-widths thick. At first he thought Araenè might have sent him something separately from her parents, but that wasn't so. Trei's uncle Serfei *had* written, but Araenè had only scribbled a note at the bottom of his letter. The package was from Tolounn.

His aunt Sosa had sent it, his other uncle's wife, from Sicuon. The address was written in her hand: long, graceful slanted letters, full of loops and curls. Trei just held the package for a moment, looking down at it with a kind of numb surprise. His uncle's voice echoed in his memory: *"You can't stay with us, Trei. I'm sorry, but you know I'm only telling you the truth. You can't stay here. Your mother has kin in those Dragon Islands in the south, doesn't she? You'd much better go to them. . . ."*

And after that dismissal, a letter from Aunt Sosa? Trei carried the package away from the others into the sleeping hall and stood by his bed, turning the package slowly over in his hands. He felt odd, as though Tolounn had been fading from the world over the past weeks and now had suddenly reappeared, looming over the novitiate.

With sharp, abrupt movements, Trei broke the wax seal and folded open the package, opened the thin leather envelope within, and slid the papers inside it onto his bed.

The top paper was a letter in Aunt Sosa's writing. He skimmed down the elegant lines:

> *Trei, dear, I hope this finds you well—I hope it finds you at all! It had better: I've paid the man enough—he really ought to carry it to you personally. The least he can do is find a ship pointed the right way.*

Trei could almost hear Aunt Sosa's tart tone in those lines.

> *Your uncle recently came across these sketches and studies, which must be from that summer your poor sister spent with us when she was twelve; you remember the year. Your uncle and*

I thought you should have them . . . at least a
small remembrance . . . hope you don't mind
that we kept back one of your uncle. . . .

The phrases blurred. Trei tossed the letter aside and, his hands trembling, began to lay out the other papers, one at a time.

Charcoal sketches, yes, and studies done in colored chalk: seven altogether, all of them on the coarse, heavy paper his sister had favored for practice work. But to Trei, they did not look like practice work at all.

There were five plain sketches, each of which captured a complicated subject in remarkably few strokes: the first was of a tree, nearly dead, the few remaining leaves clinging to its twisted branches blown by a hard wind; the second of a sparrow perched on a balcony rail, its head tipped sideways, its eyes bright and wary as it contemplated a crumby plate laid on a windowsill; the third of Marrè's own hand, thin and dabbed with streaks of charcoal, holding a stick of charcoal above a sheet of paper. The fourth, larger and folded down the middle to fit in the packet, showed an open door that looked down across the top of an ornate spiral staircase. Light poured through the door to catch every detail of the staircase railing. The last, which Trei looked at longest, showed a sausage vendor surreptitiously dropping a handful of sausages to a thin street mongrel.

None of the sketches were as good as Marrè's later work, but even so Trei thought that he could feel the wind that was ripping at the leaves, that he could almost hear the chirp of the sparrow as it prepared to leave its perch, that in the next moment the sketch of his sister's hand might draw a dark streak across the paper. He remembered the feel of the bobs and whorls of the staircase railing under his own hand as he ran down the stairs. . . . Aunt Sosa had scolded him for running on the stairs. He recognized the sausage vendor, from whom he and Marrè had bought lunch more than once; the man had pretended to be hard-hearted, but Marrè had said she'd caught him throwing sausages at street dogs when he thought no one was watching. She'd caught that embarrassed, covert generosity perfectly in the self-conscious turn of the man's head as he glanced over his shoulder while tossing his wares to the dog.

The chalk studies were more detailed, and one of them was far more precious, because though the first was only of the house in Sicuon, the second was of Trei's parents. Marrè must have either brought this study with her from Rounn or else done it from memory, because it showed their mother seated in her favorite chair, at the kitchen table, with their father, framed by the doorway that led into the rest of the house, standing behind her.

Marrè had done most of the background simply as a vague wash of color. This indistinct background simply called attention to the figures in the foreground: Mother was looking up at Father, smiling, her hand over his where it rested on her shoulder. Father was looking down into her face. He was not smiling, his expression was even somber, and yet even so Marrè had somehow made his deep affection plain in her drawing.

Trei very carefully slid the drawings back into their protective envelope. He laid the envelope aside on his bed—then changed his mind and picked it up again—then put it carefully down once more.

The young Third City novices, neither of whom had gotten any letters, were teasing Rekei about his mother writing him, and his answer that they were just jealous that their mothers hadn't written them was probably a little too true, and suddenly they were all three shouting, and Trei had no patience or tolerance for any of them. He walked out without a word.

He went down a stairway and then along a rough-hewn corridor almost at random, and then along another, and down another stairway, even though he suspected he might by now be out of the bounds of the novitiate. He didn't care. He followed the taste of salt in the air around a corner and found himself on a wide balcony. After a moment, he recognized it: there was the long, low-arched bridge of floating stones, and there in the distance the rugged crags of Kotipa, the Island of Dragons. The faint, insubstantial glitter of wind dragons was perceptible around and above the sharp-edged peaks; the crystalline wind was everywhere streaked and layered with complicated changes of pressure and temperature and movement. Beyond Kotipa was nothing but the sea, stretching endlessly north. Trei stared out into the blue distance.

Trei found he was clenching his fists so tightly his nails were cutting into his palms.

"She's dead! They're all dead! What do I care about seeing the wind *now*?" Trei said, and only realized after he heard his own voice that he'd spoken aloud. He was trembling, but didn't know whether he was furious or frightened or grieved. He couldn't decide what he felt, far less what he *should* feel. Except he wanted very badly to go home, only he was caught in confusion because he did not know what he meant by "home." Except it was not here.

Novices weren't allowed to venture out of the novitiate.

Trei hesitated for a moment, thinking about that—or not really *thinking* about it, but aware of it and also aware that he did not, at the moment, care. Then he headed for the wide stairway that he knew led from this balcony to the open city. From there, he was sure he could find his way back to Uncle Serfei's house. He wasn't sure why he felt so strongly that he had to go there. But he ran up the stairs.

It was late, late enough that he met no one to stop him, or even ask where he was going. But Ceirfei caught up to Trei before he had gone even half a mile through the moonlit streets of First City. Trei heard the rapid footsteps coming up behind him and spun around, then stared in surprise. He didn't know whom he had expected, but not Ceirfei. The other boy was breathing hard. He'd been running. Trei didn't understand how the older boy had even known to look for him, or where.

Then he realized he did know, and flushed.

"Rekei showed us the letter and drawings," Ceirfei admitted. He had stopped some distance back and now stood still, uncharacteristically tentative, as though afraid Trei might bolt.

"Rekei—? He had no right! *You* had no right!"

Ceirfei gave a little nod, not arguing the point. He said instead, "He was worried for you. So were we all. We didn't know whether you might have gone to fly or just someplace to be alone. Rekei and the younger boys went to search the novitiate, Genrai went to look for you on the flight balcony in case you'd gone to get wings. But—" He hesitated. "We also thought if you had a package like that from your Tolounnese kin, you might very well want to go find your Island kin, so I came to look for you out here."

Trei barely listened to this. "Do you know why they sent

me away?" he asked furiously. "They sent me away because they didn't want to pay the tax to register me on my majority! That's why! I thought they *liked* me, and then they—" Trei stopped, swallowing.

Ceirfei didn't say anything, but only nodded. He came forward to sit down on the high marble steps of some fancy white First City tower.

After a moment, Trei joined him. He said in a quieter voice, "I was fond of them, do you understand that? I thought they were fond of me. I liked Aunt Sosa. I think she *was* fond of Marrè. If *Marrè* had been there with me that summer—if she'd been there instead of me—"

Ceirfei nodded again. "Then perhaps you'd both be in Sicuon. You've lost so much. I'm very sorry for your loss and your grief. I know you would never have traded your kin for the wind and the sky. But once you lost your father's kin, I'm glad you came to your mother's kin and to the sky. When we endure loss, the past reaches out to grip us from behind, but it's not wrong to turn your face forward."

Trei listened to this in silence. He could not find any answer, but after a moment, he managed a small nod.

"Trei . . . if you went flying on your own without leave, well, novices do things like that. Even if you were caught, the punishment would only be a whipping, or grounding at worst. But, Trei, leaving the novitiate without permission? The wingmaster could expel you for that."

At the moment, Trei wasn't certain he cared.

"You'd care in the morning," Ceirfei said, watching his face. "So would I. We'd all hate it if you were gone. So I came after you, to tell you so." He got to his feet, took a step back toward the kajurai precincts, looked at Trei in deliberate invitation. "Come back with me? If we slip in quietly, no one need know anything about this. Will you come?"

Trei hesitated. He looked around, finding himself disoriented now amid the moonlight-drenched white towers of First City. Did he even know how to get back to the kajurai tower? Much less find Uncle Serfei's house? He took a step after Ceirfei, then stopped. "Why did you come after me? *You're* venturing out-of-bounds, too. The wingmaster could expel *you* for that, too."

Ceirfei shrugged. "I don't think he would, though. And if we *were* caught, well, if he didn't expel me, he could hardly expel you. That's why we decided that Genrai would go look for you on the flight balcony and I'd come out here. And I did find you, so that worked well. Will you come back with me now?"

If he didn't, Trei knew, he'd wish he had in the morning. Ceirfei was right about that, too. He stood for a moment longer, looking around at the city. But then he turned back toward Ceirfei.

However, after they found the kajurai tower and the stairway that led down toward the novitiate, and descended most of the way to the bottom of the stairs, Ceirfei paused, a hand on Trei's arm to hold him back. Puzzled, Trei followed the direction of Ceirfei's gaze. Then he swallowed. Two men waited for them below. Even from this distance, Trei immediately recognized the novice-master. He thought the other man was Wingmaster Taimenai himself.

The wingmaster wore unornamented kajurai black and an expression of forbidding patience. Novice-master Anerii also wore black, but he had never looked less patient. In addition, he had a riding whip in his left hand, which he was tapping in a slow rhythm against the side of his boot. A whip like that, Trei found, was an even more fraught item in a country where there were so few horses.

Ceirfei and Trei stepped together from the last stair, came out onto the balcony, stopped shoulder to shoulder, and waited.

"As you have both been excellent students," the novice-master said at last, "I am certain you are able flawlessly to recite the penalties for disobedience and venturing without leave into the city." He pointed at Trei with the whip. "Well?"

"Strokes of a whip, or denial of flying privileges, or expulsion from the kajurai novitiate," Trei recited in a whisper. He tried not to glance at the whip the novice-master held. He'd never been beaten in his life, but he was very sure he would rather face the whip than be expelled. Earlier, when Ceirfei had reminded him of the possible penalties, he hadn't thought he really cared about the possibility of expulsion. But that numbness had passed. He cared now. He knew he couldn't bear it.

"Have you any excuse to offer?"

"No, Novice-master," they answered together. Trei added at once, "But Ceirfei only left the novitiate because I—"

"Enough," ordered the novice-master. For a moment his cold stare pierced Trei. Then his attention shifted to Ceirfei. He frowned.

Ceirfei met his eyes for a moment, then deliberately bowed his head.

"Novice-master Anerii," Wingmaster Taimenai said abruptly. "If I may impose."

Master Anerii turned toward the wingmaster.

"I recognize that I am trespassing upon your duty," the wingmaster told him. "However, I will make this decision." He studied the boys, his expression more forbidding than ever. "I shall hold, this once, the penalty of expulsion. Ten strokes apiece, well laid down. And grounding for a senneri. I will wield the whip myself. I will ask you to attend to your other duties, Master Anerii."

The novice-master, his mouth tight, turned on his heel and went out.

"I would *not* complain to my—" Ceirfei began, clearly outraged.

"Silence," Wingmaster Taimenai ordered sharply. "Remove your shirt, Novice Ceirfei. Turn about and set your hands upon the wall."

The riding whip did not draw blood, but it left wicked welts. Ceirfei did not make a sound, but he could not quite keep from jerking as each blow fell. His breath hissed between his teeth. When it was finished, he was trembling. But he bowed properly to the wingmaster, though there were tears in his eyes.

If I do as well, Trei thought, but the thought dissolved unfinished, all thought dissolved; the moment stretched out into an empty, waiting silence.

For all he had braced himself, the whip's first blow was a surprise; Trei jerked and gasped as much in shock as in pain. Indeed, at first he thought the pain not so much, but then he found it actually arrived slowly and then expanded hugely; it was still expanding as the second stroke arrived, and this time Trei did yelp, because, distracted by the unfolding pain of the first blow, he had somehow forgotten a second was on the way. He heard his own cry, though, and was ashamed. *Ceirfei* hadn't made a sound. He clenched his teeth and endured the third stroke in silence, and the next, and the next, and then he lost count, only braced his arms against the wall and pressed his face against the stone . . . and then it was over.

The wingmaster accepted Trei's shaky bow with a curt nod. "I trust neither of you will give me occasion to repeat this exercise. Or reconsider more severe penalties." He ran the whip through his hands, studying them. His expression was unreadable. "You are dismissed to the novitiate. Do you know your way from here?"

They did, though it seemed longer than previously, and with a lot more stairs. Trei and Ceirfei both walked slowly and carefully. Everything hurt, Trei found; every step pulled at his back, and the brush of his shirt against the welts was worse.

"He didn't need to send the novice-master away—as though I would complain to my uncle!" Ceirfei said through his teeth once they were safely out in the hallway. He was furious.

Trei had never seen Ceirfei angry before. It was a cold, rigid fury, exactly as Trei would have expected if he'd thought about it. He stopped, so that Ceirfei had to stop, too, to face him. Trei asked suddenly, not clearly knowing he was going to ask until the words were out between them: "Who *are* you? Who *is* your uncle?"

For a moment Ceirfei only stared back at him. But at

last he gave a self-deprecating shrug—which made him wince—and a wry smile. "Ah, well . . . my mother is Calaspara Naterensei." And then, when Trei only looked baffled, he added, "The king's sister."

Trei stared at him. He knew perfectly well that Ceirfei had liked having a companion who didn't know his rank. His *exalted* rank. Trei had known Ceirfei's rank must be exalted. But— "You're a *prince*," he said, trying to fix the idea in his mind.

Ceirfei shrugged again, more carefully this time. "The least of princes. Don't think too much of it, Trei. There are four cousins and two brothers between me and the throne."

"Or you'd never have been allowed to audition," Trei agreed. He understood *that*. "Still. A *prince*." Trei tried to adjust to this notion. It was, in some ways, remarkably easy. He said after a moment, "That explains a *lot* about you."

A slow flush rose up Ceirfei's neck and face. "It doesn't really."

"Oh, yes, it does. Gods, no wonder the wingmaster wouldn't let Novice-master Anerii whip you. One doesn't trifle with princes."

"I know he had to punish us both! Does he think I don't understand that? He should know I would never complain to my uncle!"

"Ceirfei! How could he be sure? Of course the wingmaster should protect his people. What would you have done in his place?"

Ceirfei stopped, looking startled. And, after a moment, embarrassed. "Well. The same, I suppose."

"Of course you would." Trei hesitated. "I see why you knew they wouldn't expel you. But you knew . . . as you say, you knew they'd have to punish us both, if we were caught. So . . . thank you for coming after me."

Ceirfei shrugged. He didn't say, *That's what friends do,* because that would be trite, nor did he say, *That's what princes do,* because that would be pretentious. But Trei knew he meant that shrug to stand for both statements. Just knowing that made some of the sick feeling finally die away.

Trei, feeling suddenly embarrassed, turned away abruptly, walked forward, and opened the door to the novitiate's dining hall . . . then met the stares of the other boys with as much composure as he could manage.

Rekei sprang up and hurried over, then hovered, looking anxious. Genrai got more slowly to his feet and told Ceirfei apologetically, "Somebody came by to tell us there would be examinations tomorrow and found us scattered all over the novitiate, and, well . . ."

"It's well enough," Ceirfei assured him. He moved slowly toward a chair by the long table. "We got nothing worse than grounding."

"They said you'd be whipped!" Tokabii exclaimed. "Even though—" Genrai caught the younger boy's arm and gave him a shake, but Tokabii pulled away, looking stubborn. "Oh, stop it, Genrai, I'm not a baby!"

"You're a brat!" snapped Rekei, pulling out a chair for Trei. "Everyone knows grounding's worse than whipping!"

Kojran began, "You only say that because you've never—"

"Enough!" said Genrai, so forcefully that all three of the younger boys stared at him and fell silent after all.

Ceirfei settled gingerly into the chair, but he gave Genrai a little nod. "If you kept everyone else out of trouble, then that was well done, and all you could do. Thank you."

Genrai visibly resisted responding with a deferential nod in return. Instead, he said, "Several of the second-ranked kaju-raihi brought these." He indicated the little pots of salve on the table. "For the, um, welts. Rei Kensenè said it's a rare novice who never needs it, but usually just for flying without leave. He said, well, never mind. You can probably imagine."

Trei could. But the salve did help wonderfully: it went on cold, stung like fire—tears came to Trei's eyes, forcing him to duck his head and blink rapidly—but then both the sting and much of the hot ache faded together.

"Rei said—" Genrai began. But then he looked up, star-tled, as the door opened once more.

"Novice Trei." Wingmaster Taimenai stood in the doorway. Where his expression was usually dispassionate and some-times stern, now he looked truly grim. His tone was flat, un-readable. "I must ask you to attend me at once."

For a long moment, Trei found himself unable to move. The wingmaster's grimness terrified him. He was going to be dismissed—someone had decided a half-Tolounnese novice shouldn't be tolerated after all, especially if he was going to break important rules—or else—or else—Trei couldn't think of anything else that seemed likely. He felt numb. He was aware, dimly, of somebody putting a hand under his elbow to help him to his feet. The wingmaster himself took Trei by the shoulder and guided him through the door, along a short hall-way, up a long stair, and at last into a plainly furnished office with a balcony that looked out over the sea.

Wingmaster Taimenai gestured Trei toward a plain chair that stood before the large desk, but he did not sit himself. He knelt in front of Trei, gripped Trei by the arms, and looked searchingly into his face. "Trei—" he began, and stopped.

Trei stared into the wingmaster's face, so close to his own, and waited. His mouth had gone dry, his hands cold. He could feel his own heartbeat, thready and rapid, in his throat, but he couldn't feel the arms of the chair under his own hands. In a moment the wingmaster would say—he would say—

What he said, with a terrible gentleness, was: "Trei, I fear I must give you difficult news about your family."

6

Grief had turned Araenè to stone by the time Trei found her. She didn't notice his arrival. She was tucked away in the shadows behind her largest wardrobe. Her room's shutters were closed; Araenè had refused to let Cimè open them. She felt that it was wrong of the sun to blaze with light and warmth when everything should be dark and cold; it seemed impossible that the whole world should not echo with her loss. So she sat in the shadows, her arms wrapped around her drawn-up knees, her back against the wall, and ignored the light.

Cimè found her there. "Your cousin's come," she told Araenè, speaking gently. "You should get up. Brush your hair, wash your face, put on a clean dress. . . . Araenè? Can you hear me? Your cousin's here. . . ."

Araenè heard her as she heard the sound of monkeys calling or birds singing or the wind rattling the shutters: as sound without meaning. She did not respond. She did not even remember that she might respond. She was only faintly aware of Cimè's retreat.

There were voices in the hall . . . meaningless, but Araenè dimly wished the sounds would go away. She shut her eyes firmly and pressed her forehead against her knees, trying to listen only to the silence within her own heart.

She was aware, dimly, of someone coming to stand in front of her. She knew, dimly, that this was Trei. He moved to sit next to her, his back against the wall, his shoulder touching hers. He didn't say anything. Araenè was grateful for his silence.

After a while, Trei went away. But then he came back. He sat next to Araenè again, took her hand firmly, and put a cup of steaming chocolate into it. The smell was rich and dark. She hadn't been aware that she was hungry. She had forgotten that she wasn't actually stone. The scent of the chocolate made her remember. She sipped it slowly.

Trei took the cup out of her hand when it was empty, replacing it with a soft roll. The roll was filled with cheese and onions, not at all the right thing to follow a cup of chocolate. The cheese wasn't salty enough, and the onions weren't properly caramelized, but Araenè ate the roll anyway. Then she ate another one, this one filled with spicy lamb. It was much better than the first. It seemed so wrong to even notice anything as trivial as the mix of spices in a lamb-stuffed roll, but she couldn't help it. Then she sat and stared at her hands and tried not to think about anything.

"The grief doesn't go away," Trei said after a while. "But you . . . get used to it, you know? It's like carrying a heavy stone, one that's really too heavy for you: you learn to settle the weight properly, and then you get used to it, and then sometimes you can forget you're carrying it."

"Does it get lighter? Do you ever put it down?" Araenè asked him.

"I don't know." Trei put an arm around her shoulders.

Araenè leaned her head against his shoulder. "I'm sorry," she whispered. "I didn't understand."

"I'd never have wanted you to."

"It was just a summer cough. . . ."

"They said it started that way."

"It didn't . . . If we'd only known . . . The fever came on so *fast*, Trei! I sent for a physician, but he didn't come *fast* enough—"

"Shh. I know. It's not your fault." Trei's grip tightened around her shoulders. "Nobody knew at first how hard the fever would take hold. How could anybody know?"

No one had known how serious the illness was until the fever's first victims died. After that, the physicians understood how fast they'd need to move, how aggressively they'd need to treat the illness. Every physician in the city had exhausted himself in that effort. Eventually, after losing a lot of people, they'd begun saving more victims than they lost. Cimè had told her that. Araenè didn't care. She would have traded all the lives saved for just two that were gone. She bowed her face against her knees, shuddering.

"You need to act like you're still alive yourself," Trei advised. "It's a pretense at first. If you pretend as hard as you can, you'll come to half believe it yourself."

"I know," Araenè whispered. "I did pretend. When people came. The physician, and then the magistrate. Then the death handler, and then the king's tax collector . . ."

"I know," Trei said. "You did everything perfectly. Then you let go. Now you need to pick up some of the pieces again."

This sounded impossible to Araenè.

"You don't need to hold them all," Trei added. "Just start with one." He got to his feet and reached down for Araenè's hands, pulling her up as well. She staggered, and he gave her a close look, adding, "The *very* first thing is for you to fix me something to eat."

It was the best thing he could have asked for. And he knew it, too, as Araenè realized perfectly well. But she was glad to lose herself in preparing a complicated pastry she'd invented. Each round of dough had to be rolled out thin, then fried in hot oil, then brushed with clarified butter infused with lavender, then dusted with fine sugar mixed with ground vanilla, and finally assembled in layers with a compote of walnuts and lavender honey. Araenè set the finished confection on the table, scattered dried lavender flowers across the platter, sat down at her customary place, and burst into tears.

She hadn't wept after Father died; there hadn't been time because by then Mother was slipping into the final desperate fever herself. The physician was there at last. He had come too late to save Father. Astonished at what he found, the physician had worked anxiously over Mother. But Araenè had known even then, from the physician's hard-set mouth and hooded eyes, that he had not expected to save her, either. Nor had he.

But Araenè hadn't cried then, either. She'd known there would be a parade of city officials, of neighbors and friends bringing the customary round cakes, the oranges and melons and tiny spherical pastries glittering with pastel sugars . . . everything sweet, to remind mourners that life was still sweet; everything round, to show that life did not end. . . . The smells of sugar and citrus had nauseated Araenè, but she hadn't cried. She had set aside thought and feeling, and smiled stiffly at everyone, and said all the right things, until she could not bear it and fled to the dimness of her room and just waited for everything to go away.

Trei let her cry. He didn't say anything at all. He just let her cry until she was exhausted. Then he led her back to her room, made her lie down on her bed, and left her alone.

When she woke, Araenè felt better. And instantly guilty, because how could she possibly feel *better*? She lay for a while with her eyes shut, but light poured across her bed. . . . Someone had opened her shutters. Even with her eyes closed, she could tell the light was brilliant, and hot. . . . She'd slept through both afternoon and night, she guessed, and well into the next morning, and just what had Trei put in that chocolate? Araenè surrendered at last to the inevitable and opened her eyes. She needed a bath, and proper clothing . . . and to find Trei.

Trei, when she eventually found him, was in Father's office, looking at papers. He held a quill in one hand. He was frowning. He looked tired and . . . sad, Araenè realized, and felt a sudden, sharp grief that was only for Trei, separate from everything else. What must it be like, to lose your family and travel a thousand miles to kin you'd never met, and be welcomed by them, and then lose that family as well?

Then Trei looked up and saw her. He gave her a little nod. "Cousin. I sent Cimè to her mother—her mother has the illness."

"Oh!" Araenè had barely realized Cimè had a mother. She fought down an impulse so appalling she couldn't believe she felt it: a wish for Cimè's mother to die—if Araenè lost *her* mother, why shouldn't Cimè?

From some faint change in Trei's expression, Araenè thought he'd recognized and understood her brief, terrible wish. That he thought it was normal. Somehow that made her feel it might be all right to suffer such a horrible wish; that it was an impulse she might feel and yet recover from.

Trei said, his tone neutral, "I understand you have to have a guardian, Araenè. It's all right. I'm writing a letter to Wingmaster Taimenai, explaining that family matters compel me to quit the kajuraihi. I know sometimes kajuraihi do leave the kajurai precincts. And I've written another letter to the high minister of shipping asking for a position in his ministry—Cimè tells me that's the custom, that he'll give me a place there 'on the books' until I'm sixteen and can really start at the ministry."

"Trei, you can't!"

"It's all right. Cimè says I'll be an assistant minister by the time I'm twenty, probably. Then our position will be good enough for you to marry properly."

"It isn't *all right*!" Araenè was appalled. "You can't go into the ministry, Trei! And give up the sky? Tear up that letter, Trei, and let me write my mother's sisters; I can go to one of my aunts' families—"

"No!"

She stopped, her mouth still open.

Trei said, "You can't leave Canpra!" He sounded really upset. "Araenè, you'd hate it, shut up on some sheep farm in the country!" And when she tried again to protest, he added, his tone strained, "Araenè, I don't want you to go away. Don't you see? I don't want to lose you, too. I'd rather—I'd rather give up the sky. Truly, Araenè."

Araenè stared at her cousin for a long moment. Then she turned, went back into her bedroom, and stared at herself in her mirror. It was like a window, showing her herself: she thought she looked much older, as though she was looking at her future self. The future stretched out and out in front of her, measureless. But was it something to endure, or something to seize hold of?

Araenè changed into her best boys' things. Then she took her sharpest pair of scissors, sat down in front of her mirror, and cut off her hair. It was harder to cut evenly than she'd expected, and much harder to watch the mass of it collect in discarded swaths on the floor and table. Araenè bit her lip and went on: even if she changed her mind—she told herself fiercely she would *never* change her mind—it was too late to stop now. The top was still ragged when she finished, and she was afraid the back was worse. But it was short. When she looked at herself . . . she saw a boy with a bad haircut, not a girl.

So did Trei when she went to show him.

"Araenè!" he exclaimed, eyes going wide.

"Arei," she said sharply. Pretending she had no doubts. She couldn't have doubts now. Or Trei would quit the kajuraihi, and she—well, she would have to explain the shorn hair. She was fierce to hide any trace of doubt from either of them. "You tear up those letters, Trei. Tear them up! You can tell the kajurai masters I've gone to my mother's sister. I'll write to my aunts and tell them you're taking care of me. Then you can go back to the kajuraihi and I can go—*Arei* can go—to the mages' school. Araenè can just disappear. Who will ever know?"

"Araenè—"

"*Arei.*"

"Arei, then," Trei conceded. "The *mages'* school?"

Araenè had forgotten he did not know. She got the Dannè sphere from the back of her drawer and showed it to Trei. It was opaque, featureless. It tasted mainly of cumin, though the other tastes were still faintly perceptible.

"Cumin?" Trei said doubtfully. He touched the sphere with the tip of one finger, cautiously.

"That's just how it seems to me. I don't think other—" Araenè shied off from the presumption of applying the title "mage" to herself. She finished instead, "People taste magic this way."

"Well, if somebody was going to *taste* magic, it would be you, cousin." Trei sat back in his chair and looked at her, still doubtful, as though she had changed shape under his gaze—not just from girl to boy, but from known to unknown. Araenè waited for him to say, *Girls can't be mages,* but he said instead, "There might be a war coming—did you know?"

Father had worried about that. Araenè nodded.

"And you want to go pretend to be a boy at the mages' school—the *mages'* school. I don't think that's very wise, Ar—Arei. You might have fooled other people, but mages? Anyway, I thought . . . You're family, Araenè, you're my only family, and I thought we would live here and"—he gestured vaguely—"manage somehow. I don't think . . ." His voice trailed off. He looked at her doubtfully.

Araenè said fiercely, "The mages didn't see I was a girl before! They say magic—they say it's like a tide rising in your blood. That's what they said: magic rising like a tide. I think . . . I think maybe it is like that. They said you can smother it. I don't want to do that! I don't even know why, but I don't! I didn't want to be a mage—why would I ever think of being a mage? But now . . ." She stopped.

"You want to?" Trei asked her. "*Do* you?"

"I think . . . maybe I want to. Oh, I can't tell anymore!" Araenè cried, and burst into tears. She hadn't expected to. She hadn't even realized tears were threatening. She certainly didn't want to cry, a *boy* wouldn't cry. . . . She turned her back and hid her face in her hands.

But Trei leaped up to take her hands and make her sit in a chair. He said earnestly, "It takes you that way sometimes. Don't worry. Don't worry about it, cousin. Cry if you want. Let me get you a cloth. You don't have to decide right now."

"I've decided," choked Araenè. "I *have*—"

"You *don't* have to decide now. You really don't. Araenè—"

"I can't live here, Trei! I can't live in this house!" It seemed to Araenè that all the rooms were filled with grief and memories, thick as bitter syrup.

"We can move—we could find a smaller house—we could move near the University, we could even move to Third City, wouldn't you like that? And we—"

"I can't ever be a chef," Araenè said, muffled.

Trei didn't say anything.

"I can't! I know that! But maybe—I think I might—I don't know! But, Trei, I *can't* stay closed up in any house and just wait for everything to just happen! War, or *life*, or, or anything! I can't!" Araenè lifted her head and glared at Trei, her eyes hot. "I might be a mage; maybe I *can* do *this*. Anyway, if I get the training, then I *will* be a mage and what can anybody do then?

135

I can make everybody think I'm a boy, I can do it for a long time, years if I have to, I know I can! And you—*you* need to be in the air. You *are* kajurai, you know you are! You have to let me do this!"

Trei stood still for a long time, gazing at her. Araenè, waiting to see what he would say, felt sick and hot and anxious. She said quickly, "It's not that I don't want to be—to be with you, Trei—"

"I know," her cousin said. He held out his hands to her. "I know, Araenè. Arei. It's all right. You write your aunts. And we can send the letter in a day or two, if you haven't changed your mind. But"—and he sounded quite fierce on this last—"but you take some time and you think if you really want this, if you can really *do* this! Because we can think of something else if we have to, Gods weeping, we can go—I don't know—to Cen Periven, if we have to. Clear away from both the Islands *and* Tolounn. Maybe you could be a chef there."

But Trei couldn't be kajurai there. But he didn't say that. Araenè knew she had already decided.

Araenè let Trei persuade her to wait one extra day, until Sun's Day should turn to Gods' Day, for luck. But Araenè was determined she had waited long enough; she felt sick with the need to leave this house.

"So how do we *get* to the hidden school?" Trei asked. "I mean, isn't it, you know, hidden?"

Araenè shook her head. "I don't think it will be hard to find." She weighed the Dannè sphere in her hand for a moment. The lemon was starting to spark through the smoky cumin. Araenè tucked the sphere under her arm, led the way to the front of the house, said, "Master Tnegun?" and opened the door on a wave of bitter fenugreek balanced by fragrant heat.

The door swung back, but it did not open on the Avenue of Flameberry Trees. It opened straight into a familiar shadowy hallway, where the sun gleamed dimly through dusty panes of glass in many high-set, narrow windows. Across from them, a tall door even narrower than the windows led—perhaps—to a room with ebony tables and white chairs and heavy books chained to their pedestals.

"Oh," said Trei, staring along the hallway. "That was easy." He gave Araenè a wary sidelong look.

Araenè knew he was thinking again that this was too dangerous for her, that one of the mages would recognize she was a girl and there would be trouble. She didn't want to think about that, and anyway, she was sure it wouldn't happen. She caught Trei's hand in hers and stepped firmly forward into the dim light of the hallway. Behind them, the door swung quietly shut and disappeared into the paneled wall.

This time, the narrow door opened on a small, luxuriously furnished library. They were high up in a square Second City tower, each wall lined with shelves of books and racks of scrolls. A single chair occupied the center of the room, upholstered in dark cloth. A raven sidled back and forth along the back of this chair. Master Tnegun sat below the raven, a book propped on his knee and a tiny crimson lizard with golden eyes clinging to his wrist.

The master looked up as the door opened. His hooded eyes were fierce and vivid in his dark face, his black hand outlined clean as a flame against the white pages of his book. He regarded Araenè for a moment. Then his gaze shifted to Trei, standing at her right hand. One elegant eyebrow lifted.

Araenè felt herself blushing under that sardonic regard. She said, "This is my cousin—" trying to sound unemotional and finding she only sounded angry. She stopped.

"Ar—Arei's parents died. Of the fever," Trei said. He *did* sound flat and unemotional. Whatever he'd learned in order to manage after his own parents' death, he was using it now. Araenè wondered how long it would take her to sound that indifferent. Never, she thought. She would never manage it. She blinked hard and fixed her gaze on the view out one of Master Tnegun's windows.

Trei was continuing, "So Arei can stay here now. We think sh—he ought to, and he says he wants to. That you said you wanted him as your apprentice." He looked straight at Master Tnegun. Fearlessly.

Araenè had liked her cousin, and pitied him, and been deeply glad of his presence when he'd come to pull her out of grief's heavy undertow. That he'd suffered the same loss that now struck her, and survived it, was comforting. But she hadn't *admired* Trei until he spoke so decisively to Master Tnegun, even though she knew he was filled with doubts about her coming here.

The master's expression lost its edge of mockery. He shut his book, set it aside, and rose to his feet. The raven muttered, tucking its head down into its shoulders and fluffing its black feathers. The lizard clung to his sleeve, not in the least discommoded by his movement. Its tiny head turned as it inspected Araenè and Trei from first one golden eye and then the other. When the master took a step toward them, it ran up his arm to his shoulder and twirled around to watch them from beneath his ear.

"It is a terrible thing, to lose one's family," Master Tnegun said to Araenè, his tone dark and somber. "My people say the high mountains will wear to level ground before grief wears to nothing. That was a wicked fever that little showed what it would do until far too late. I am most grieved to hear of your loss."

Araenè couldn't answer his sympathy. Instead she said stiffly, not looking away from the lizard, "I want . . . I mean, my cousin . . ."

"I want to be able to see Arei," Trei said firmly. "I don't want him to be hidden away here, even if this is the hidden school."

"One should be ashamed to separate kin," Master Tnegun answered gravely. He held out his hand. A crystal lay on his palm, so pure it was almost invisible. Cinnamon and fennel sparkled from it. It was attached to a fine silver chain. The chain, dangling between the master's dark fingers, tasted crisply of lime and ginger.

"Crystal for the young kajurai," Master Tnegun said. "Wear it, if you will. Speak the name of your cousin and open any door, and that door will bring you to him. Or if not, speak my name, and it will assuredly bring you to me. You know my name? It comes smoothly from your tongue?"

Trei nodded. "Yes, Master Tnegun. What about Arei?"

"Our apprentices are not prisoners. Arei may go about the city as he chooses."

Trei nodded again, cautiously reassured.

"You may safely leave your cousin to my care," said Master

Tnegun. He stepped to the door and opened it wide. It looked out upon a flickering, opalescent mist.

"Step through," the master told Trei, "and the door will carry you wherever you choose within the limits of the city. Merely keep clearly in mind which destination you favor."

Trei nodded, came to Araenè, hesitated, and put his hands on her shoulders—more appropriate than an embrace, since she was a boy. He gave her a steady look out of his strange kajurai eyes. "Arei?"

"I'll be fine," Araenè promised him. "I'll be fine. Truly."

But even so, she felt amazingly bereft after her cousin was gone. And frightened. She told herself sharply that she hadn't any reason to be *frightened*—Master Tnegun had *told* her to come—he couldn't be wrong; she must be suited to this school. Even though she was a girl. But doubts crowded into her mind: maybe magecraft was just too hard for girls . . . maybe the reason girls didn't become mages was because they truly, truly couldn't. For a moment Araenè longed to run through the mist-filled doorway after her cousin and back to her own home. Only, the home she wanted to run to was the home with Mother humming popular street tunes over her needlework, with Father working on ministry documents and occasionally adding a whistled phrase to whatever tune Mother was humming.

But that home was gone. Dead. Araenè closed her eyes for a moment, found a strange, dizzy confusion of longed-for past and bitter present assailing her, and opened them quickly.

Master Tnegun shut the door and turned to stand quietly in the middle of the room, his hands clasped before him, regarding Araenè from his hooded, unreadable eyes. Dangerous eyes, Araenè thought; she was afraid of what he might see, looking at her with such intensity. She could imagine just the tone of sardonic disapproval with which he might say, *We do not permit girls in this school.* She held her breath.

But all the master said was, "I am glad you have come, for we have too few mages here. But I am sorry to have you driven to us by such tragedy. I am tolerably acquainted with loss. If you will accept my prescription, it is for an entire change of scene and a course of demanding study of compelling and un-familiar subjects. One may thus forget for a moment and then a day, and in the end make a peace with grief. Does this seem well to you, young Arei?"

Not trusting her voice, Araenè simply nodded.

"It is poor solace to speak of the passing of time and grief," the master said. His quiet voice had gone somehow bleak, though Araenè could not decide where in his unchanging tone the difference lay. "We do not wish our grief to fade, for it marks the love and honor in which we held our lost kinsmen. Nevertheless, permit me to assure you that while you may find peace a barren desert, yet eventually it may bloom."

Araenè wasn't certain she understood what Master Tnegun meant, but she nodded again.

"Well," the Yngulin master said, and sighed. Then he called, "Kanii!"

There was a pause, which lengthened. And lengthened. Master Tnegun first waited without expression, then cast a patient gaze upward, then tapped his foot and sighed again.

At last Kanii burst into the library, panting. He wore green trousers and a shirt of paler green silk, but his sash was askew and ink stains ran down the shirt. A black feather was tucked in his hair above his ear. It was broken a third of the way from the tip. He clutched an immense armful of scrolls; one tumbled from the top of the stack as he skidded to a halt. He caught it with a practiced snatch, juggled the remaining scrolls for a second, succeeded somehow in steadying the pile, and nodded cheerfully to Araenè and more formally to Master Tnegun. "Yes, sir?"

"Kanii . . . ," the Yngulin master began.

"Sir?" Kanii said, the picture of alert helpfulness.

Master Tnegun shook his head, sighed, and said, "Kanii, I believe you have met my new apprentice. You will do me the favor of settling him into the school. Without asking difficult questions, if you please. Arei, I hope you will permit this young fool to acquaint you with our school and its denizens. Yes?"

Araenè nodded.

"However, before you go . . . my sphere, if you please."

Araenè blinked. She had forgotten the sphere she'd tucked under her arm. Now she drew it out, holding it in both hands. Nearly transparent, the black sphere was now filled by light. Strangely, the light seemed to weigh it down, for it became much heavier as she held it. Araenè stared down into it; she was certain that it had never been so transparent before, yet now she could see the outlines of her fingers right through it. The piquant taste of ginger tingled across Araenè's tongue and its fragrance filled the room. Moving light glittered within the sphere.

"Interesting," commented Master Tnegun's deep voice above her.

"Yes," Araenè said distractedly. "The ginger just came out. The flavors change all the time, even though I never *try* to do anything."

"Flavors?" Master Tnegun regarded Araenè with interest. "Many mages perceive magic as brilliant colors or geometric shapes or musical notes, but I don't believe I have ever encountered a mage who *tastes* magic. How interesting. Are the flavors pleasant ones?"

Usually they were. Araenè nodded hesitantly. She could not think of anything to say. She had not actually meant to mention the tastes the sphere sent across her tongue and fingers; now she wondered whether there might be something actually *wrong* with the way she perceived magic.

But the master merely asked, "What do you see in the sphere, Arei?"

Araenè looked down at it. White shapes flickered in the sphere: the wings of birds, of gulls . . . drifting feathers . . . no, she saw at last: sails. White sails, filled with an urgent wind, rising in tiered ranks above great ships that drove up white foam as they rushed through the slate-dark sea. She thought she could feel their speed in her hands, half closed her eyes against the wind of their swift passage.

Then the image in the sphere changed. A great crimson sun slid toward the horizon. Its red light fell across sails and ships and sea all alike, until the fierce wind seemed to fill sails of fire, and the ships raced across a sea of blood. Flames suddenly seemed to fill the sphere: white at the center, then yellow and orange and red. Where the flames washed against the cool glass, they were a color darker than mere red, so dark there should have been another name for it. At the heart of the fire there was something that was not fire. . . . Araenè bent her face low over the sphere, trying to make out what it might be. . . .

Master Tnegun plucked the sphere neatly from Araenè's hands. The smoky taste of cumin rose through the light, overwhelming the ginger. In his grip, the sphere darkened and became opaque.

Araenè stared at him, blinking. She felt strangely charred around the edges, as though she'd stood too close to a powerful stove.

"Hmm." Regarding her with narrow concentration, Master Tnegun tossed the sphere into the air. At the apex of its rise, it vanished. The master said thoughtfully, "I think you may have an affinity for vision and fire, Arei. Those are useful affinities. We shall see if we can bring them out."

Araenè blinked again and nodded, not trying to find words. Her palms felt sensitive and tender, as though she had been holding fire.

The master turned to Kanii. "Take this child away, Kanii, and if Master Kopapei is able to spare you, you might ensure that he finds his way back to me in the morning. Early, if you please."

"Yes, sir," Kanii said earnestly. He tumbled half his load of scrolls into Araenè's hands—startled, she barely caught them—and bumped her shoulder with his. "Come on, then."

The hallway outside Master Tnegun's library wasn't the same hall Araenè remembered, though. This one was much wider and curved across the top, carved directly out of red stone: they were underground. The cool of this deep hall contrasted so sharply with the warmth of Master Tnegun's library that Araenè shivered. Then she could not stop shivering.

Kanii must have noticed this, but he only said, deliberately cheerful, "Let me show you my apartment. We can drop all this clutter there and go find yours. Here we go." Kanii shoved his way through a curtained doorway.

"We each . . . have our own apartment?" Araenè followed Kanii and found herself in a small underground room with three doorways and one window. Through one doorway, Araenè could see a tiny bedchamber; through another, a table covered with scrolls and loose sheets of paper. Books and cushions littered the floor of all three rooms.

"Of course; we have to study, you know," Kanii said over his shoulder, dumping his armful of scrolls on a table. "Meals are common, I'll show you where, but you can go by the kitchens and get a tray if you'd rather. I expect the kitchens would load a tray for *you* with delicacies and deliver it straight to your apartment." He turned to gesture Araenè forward. "Don't worry, just pile them up," he told her. "Here, come along, we'll find your apartment and then go by the dining hall in time for supper and you can meet everyone."

Araenè swallowed.

Kanii picked up on her nervousness and went on immediately in the same cheerful tone, "There are nine apprentices in the school just now, counting you, and six masters—at least, we think there are six. And twelve adjuvants. It's good you're here: nine balances well against six and twelve: all threes."

Araenè gave Kanii a skeptical look, finding her voice at last. "It matters how the numbers balance?"

Kanii seemed surprised that she should question this. "Of

course it does. I hope you're good at mathematics! Here, come on." He brushed a beaded curtain out of their way and led Araenè up a flight of three stairs. As they reached the top of this small stair, the school reordered itself around them and they found themselves walking along a narrow, high-arched gallery of shining white marble.

"Not likely," Kanii muttered, and led the way toward the nearest door, which was of carved wood, with polished brass hinges.

"We . . . Are we actually *looking* for my apartment?" Araenè ventured. "I mean, you don't know where it is?"

"I know more or less where it ought to be," Kanii assured her. "We'll recognize it when we find it. Here, I think this might be it." He shoved open the carved door. It opened upon a trim room with plaster walls and dark wooden furniture: a comfortable, familiar-seeming room. The plaster was painted a blue that matched the sky, visible from a wide window that looked out into a small but wildly overgrown garden surrounded by a high wall of straw-yellow brick. The room was placed so low that anyone even remotely agile could easily jump straight down to the garden below, and a broad white stone below the window provided a convenient step to get back in. An open door on the other side of the room showed a pleasant, roomy bedchamber.

"Nice," Kanii observed, sounding mildly envious. He went over to the window and peered out. "Not much view, though. And you won't pick up a breeze down here. You might be able to get the school to put you up higher—"

"I like the room where it is," Araenè said. She stepped up on the windowsill and jumped down into the garden. Green herbal scents surrounded her, heavy in the hot air: mint and lime, basil and cilantro. A gate in the far wall of the garden gave her a glimpse of a Third City alleyway, though oddly little noise seemed to come into the garden from the city. Araenè took a deep breath of the herb-scented air and found herself smiling easily for the first time since—for the first time in a long time.

"I suppose it suits you after all," allowed Kanii. "Do you want me to leave you here? You can rest if you like, but I really ought to show you how to get around in the school."

"Yes," Araenè agreed reluctantly. She stepped up on the convenient rock and scrambled back through the window, not without a lingering glance over her shoulder.

"All right," Kanii said, rubbing his hands together and smiling at Araenè. "Shall we see how the school's got you placed?" He opened her door with a flourish. It now opened onto what was obviously the dining hall: a wide room with heavy wooden beams across its vaulted ceiling and four long wooden tables set up in a square. There was far more room along those tables than would be needed by nine apprentices, even if all twelve adjuvants—whatever adjuvants might be—and six masters joined them, but two of the tables were cluttered with a great miscellany of books and scrolls and glass spheres and racks of feathers. Only the tables at either end of the hall were cleared for service.

Araenè started to step into the dining hall, but Kanii shook his head and shut the door. She looked at him in surprise.

"You open it," he told her. "Go ahead."

Araenè looked at him for a moment. Then she laid a wary hand on the knob and swung the door wide.

It led now straight to the kitchens. The warm, yeasty smell of baking bread wafted invitingly into Araenè's apartment, and when one of the chefs bellowed for a boy to hurry along with disjointing those geese and get them in the sugar lacquer, she smiled.

"Well," Kanii allowed after a moment, looking over her shoulder, "I suppose we might have expected that, mightn't we?" He reached past her and pushed the door shut again. "Open it again."

Araenè obediently opened the door once more. This time it opened in the familiar dim hall, with its high, narrow windows and tall, narrow door.

"You'd probably find Master Tnegun there," Kanii said, which Araenè already knew. "You've got something of a knack for doors, I think. Once more."

This time, Araenè's door opened to show a wide workroom, all cluttered tables and odd equipment and a swirl of complicated scents and flavors so intense that Araenè instantly shut the door again, coughing, leaving the surprised faces of two boys to gaze after her.

"That was Jenekei and Taobai," Kanii said reproachfully. "We could have gone straight in and met them. . . . Well, it doesn't matter, I suppose. You can meet them later. Now, there are four rules for apprentices in this school. Ready?"

Araenè nodded mutely.

Kanii looked at her seriously. "The first rule is, trust your master, and remember he'll hear you if you call him. If you get into trouble, or if you start something and find you can't finish it, or if you discover something more than usually peculiar in some out-of-the-way corridor or attic—call Master Tnegun."

He added less formally, "You won't do or start or find anything that can surprise the masters, all right?"

Araenè nodded again, though she had her doubts about this last.

"Master Tnegun can daunt the whole court if he tries, but if I had to have some master other than Master Kopapei, I'd want Master Tnegun. Now, the second rule is, don't do any magic until your master says you may, and never touch anything in the school unless you know what it is and what it's likely to do. You won't be able to follow that rule at first, because a new apprentice just never *does* know what anything is or what it's likely to do, so remember the first rule, all right?"

"But—"

"Hush. Third rule: always tell the truth to the masters, and if a master asks you to do something, at least *try* to do it." Kanii grinned. "Even if you have no idea in the world what you're doing, all right?"

Araenè tried to persuade herself, not very successfully, that not mentioning things wasn't the same as lying. This argument didn't seem to have much heft, even to her. She hoped she didn't look guilty.

"And the fourth rule is, never approach a dragon, but if you do, don't make it any promises. But don't approach one in the first place!"

"A dragon," Araenè repeated.

"I know. It doesn't usually come up: dealing with dragons is for kajuraihi, not for us. But the hidden school really does find itself in odd places. I've looked out a window into the heights of Kotipa—twice—and seen wind dragons coiling right around Horera Tower. And there are tales about a fire dragon that dwells somewhere in the depths of the school."

"A *fire* dragon." This didn't seem plausible at all. Fire dragons swam through the molten depths of fiery mountains, and there could hardly be a volcano underneath a *floating* Island.

"I know, I know!" Kanii agreed ruefully, shrugging. "But Master Kopapei says fire dragons and sky dragons are more closely allied than you'd expect; don't ask *me* how. The magic of sky dragons is for kajuraihi; the fire dragon at the heart of the school is something else again. Master Kopapei says the mages built their school over it because they wanted to borrow its power—but he also says magery is distinct from dragon magic and no kajurai has ever been a mage, so don't ask me about the borrowing-its-power part. Anyway, remember the rule. Now, quick, what are the four rules?"

Araenè stared at him for a moment. Then she said, "Trust your master, don't do magic and don't touch things, tell the truth, don't make promises to dragons."

"Right, good." Kanii grinned at her again. "Time for supper! Let's go meet the others. Can you get the dining hall back again?"

Araenè couldn't. But she could get the kitchens and did, on her second try.

"That'll do," Kanii decided. "A knack, see?" He led the way through the door.

The school's chefs were happy to see Araenè, especially the fat one, who roared, "A discriminating palate in this school at last! How do you like your chicken, young sir: in a stew with apricots and olives as they do in southern Tolounn, or gently braised in a sauce of spiced yogurt and ground almonds in the style of Candera?"

"Both ways," Araenè said truthfully, heading across the kitchens to peek into the simmering pots. "Have you tried adding blanched almonds along with the apricots and olives? What kinds of olives do you use? May I stir this sauce?"

The supper was abundant and very good. The kitchen boys served the apprentices at one table and a small group of silent gray-robed adjuvants at the other, but Araenè was the only one who got generous servings of both chicken dishes—far more than she could eat. "Arei's made friends in strategic places," Kanii told the other apprentices when they stared. "Smile, if you please! If *he* asks for more pastries, we might get them."

"Ha!" The oldest of the other apprentices thumped his hand down on the table, making Araenè jump. "Well done, new boy! Arei, is it? My name is Tichorei; I'm Master Camatii's student." He was much older than Araenè: a young man rather than a boy—at least eighteen, Araenè thought. He had a thin, bony face, deep-set eyes, and a sharp accent; she guessed he'd come to Milendri from Bodonè or Tisei. He looked like he was usually serious, but he was smiling now. Araenè felt her face heating and hoped the dim light hid her blush.

Two of the apprentices were apparently still busy with whatever they'd been about earlier in the workroom and weren't present. Araenè was grateful for their absence. There were four other apprentices at the table besides Kanii and Ti-chorei, which seemed crowd enough to her. There was a husky, broad-shouldered boy of fifteen or sixteen, Sayai, who claimed Master Akhai. Two dark-haired, dark-eyed twins of fourteen, exactly alike except that Kebei had a thin scar over his right eye and Kepai did not, both claimed Master Yamatei. The last of the four was a red-haired boy named Cesei, eight or so, much the baby of the group.

Like Kanii, Cesei was Master Kopapei's apprentice. He had entered the school only days earlier, but he seemed startlingly at home already. "Don't you love it here?" he asked Araenè, with sunny confidence that of course she would agree. "There's so much to learn and know and do! It's much better than the library: I'm never bored here." He added with the unconscious arrogance of the very young, "Yet, anyway."

The older apprentices traded indulgent grins above the boy's head.

"Do you . . . like living here?" Araenè asked cautiously. It seemed a boy so young ought to be desperately homesick—surely he could not actually *like* living alone in an apartment? "Don't you miss your . . . family?" She should not have tried to put this question into words; tears pressed at her eyes and she blinked quickly and looked down at the table.

Tichorei and Kanii might have noticed, but the little boy didn't. "Oh," he declared, waving both hands in dramatic dismissal. "No, I don't even remember my mother anyway, so this is much easier, because my father *had* to accept my coming here, and now I *will* be a scholar—only not exactly the kind I thought, or not *only* the kind I thought—but it's fine. Master Kopapei knows a *lot*," he added, with clear admiration.

"So does this brat," Kanii told Araenè, with deliberate lightness. "He's already helping me with my geometry, you know."

Araenè blinked hard and looked up, her heart sinking for a different reason. "We have to know geometry?"

"Well, the angles at which crystals fracture matter—" Kanii began. Cesei said at the same time, just diffidently enough that Araenè guessed not every older boy appreciated such an offer, "I could help you, if you like—"

"Thank you; I'd like that," Araenè said sincerely, and the little redheaded boy grinned, instantly insouciant again.

"Master Tnegun!" Kepai exclaimed when Araenè named her own particular master. The dark boy cocked his head to one side, studying Araenè with undisguised interest. "I thought he didn't take apprentices! Tichorei?"

"Never, that I know," agreed the young man. "And he's been here a long time." He gazed curiously at Araenè.

"How—why did he come here?" she asked. "I mean, to the Islands."

Tichorei shrugged. "He hardly discusses that with any of *us*. I suppose the other masters know. At least Master Kopapei."

"Master Kopapei said something once about Yngulin politics being complicated and dangerous," Kanii volunteered. "I thought Master Tnegun might have been exiled from Yngul—but I don't know."

"I think I saw a book about Yngul in the common library," little Cesei said eagerly. "I'll find it for you, if you like. Can I read it first, though? I don't know anything about Yngul. Master Tnegun is interesting, isn't he? I expect Yngul is really interesting, too."

"You think everything is interesting, brat," Sayai said, with an edge to his tone that suggested he didn't mean it altogether kindly. Cesei flushed.

"Master Tnegun knows a lot," Kebei said quickly to

153

Araenè. "Yngulin as well as Islander magecraft. He's very skilled, they say, and powerful for his age."

"For his age?" Araenè asked, willing to cooperate with Kebei to smooth over the uncomfortable moment. Besides, she was genuinely puzzled.

"Oh, well, mages lose power as they grow older," Kebei explained. "You didn't know? Well, it's true. You'll never be stronger than you are right after your magery comes in. That's what the adjuvants are for—they aren't mages exactly. But they have power. They, well, loan it to the mages, sort of."

Araenè looked across the hall toward the anonymous dark-robed adjuvants. She wondered how they liked being "not mages exactly." "Do they . . . ," she began, but then didn't know exactly what question she wanted to ask.

"Some apprentices develop their magery but lose their power," Tichorei explained, understanding the question she did not know how to ask. "Some of the rest lose their magery but keep their power. Those become adjuvants—if they're willing to. Not everyone is. I mean . . . nobody comes into the hidden school hoping to be an *adjuvant*."

There was a small pause. It was clear to Araenè that all of the apprentices were at least a little worried that they might turn out to be adjuvants and not mages at all—except, she thought, Cesei. *He* looked supremely self-confident.

Master Tnegun hadn't explained any of this to Araenè. . . .

"*You'll* be fine," Kanii said briskly, tapping Araenè on the arm. "I don't think Master Tnegun put himself to the trouble of bringing you in just to gain an adjuvant. Although," he added hastily, "the adjuvants are important."

"I doubt he can tell, any more than any other master," Sayai said, a little sharply.

"Oh, well . . . Master Tnegun . . . ," Kepai began, but then stopped. Everybody glanced with an odd wariness at Araenè.

"He's a little . . . ," Kebei said, but trailed off just as his twin had.

Araenè exclaimed, "It isn't as though I ever *asked* him! I never wanted to be a mage at all! I wanted to be a chef! Only—" She stopped.

A little silence fell. "It's hard, coming in late," Tichorei said at last. "We would all do it like Cesei, if we could: come in when we're little and grow up in the school. You'll do well enough, Arei. Try some of this bread, and do you think the kitchen staff might give us more if you asked?"

The fatter chef, who turned out to be named Horei, was delighted to offer more bread, and then extra pastries, and Araenè found herself the recipient of enthusiastic, expansive approval from all the other apprentices.

"You can borrow my compasses," Kebei offered. "Master Tnegun's a fierce one for getting your figures perfect."

Kepai cuffed his brother. "Those are my compasses, too!" But he added to Araenè, "Not that you can't borrow them, though, if your master sets you figuring."

"I'll show you the upper towers, if you like," Tichorei suggested. He gave her a shy sideways glance. "The Horera Tower, what we call the Tower of the Winds. Sometimes you can see dragons riding the winds from the uppermost chamber."

"Yes, Kanii said—"

"I could show you the black gulls," declared little Cesei, falling over Araenè's answer in his enthusiasm. "They're really interesting! Or the aviary, if you'd rather see the pretty little birds."

Araenè thanked them all, feeling horribly awkward because

somehow it seemed worse to lie to these boys than it had to just wander the streets of Canpra dressed as a boy. She was supposed to be one of them, and how could she be? They were all ready to be her friends, and she was lying to them. . . . She pressed a hand across her mouth, fighting off the tears that had become so easy, far too easy.

"Arei's tired," Kanii said firmly. "And little surprise it is. Arei, what you need is a long, quiet night. Do you want me to show you back to your room? Here, try this: open the door over there, and if it doesn't show your apartment, give out a shout, yes?"

Araenè *was* horribly tired. She felt the day had been a hundred days long, and nothing else in the world sounded as inviting as a long, quiet night in a private apartment all her own. She nodded to all the other boys—trying hard to make it a curt, boy-like nod—and walked across to the door Kanii had pointed out. She opened it cautiously, found to her relief that it did indeed open to show her apartment waiting for her. But even as she looked, the view began to grow misty and opalescent around the edges—she leaped forward quickly, before the door could change its mind.

Araenè jumped forward, the mist rushed inward, and for a long, lingering moment cold fog surrounded her. Then she completed her jump, coming down somewhere utterly unexpected, somewhere dense with brilliant, moving light. Heat came down on her like the blast of a furnace, and the light moved like a live thing—Araenè opened her mouth to gasp, and that terrible heat reached down her throat and tried to char her lungs—flinching, cowering from the heat, she *did something.* She had no idea what she'd done, but *something.*

Coolness surrounded her suddenly, like glass set firmly between herself and the flames. The fragrance of mint became very strong; mint and lemon tingled across her skin. She straightened cautiously, looking around.

She stood in the middle of a vast chamber of stone. . . . Molten stone, in places, ran across the walls and crept in flaming rivulets across the floor. She was surrounded by fire: flames leaped and danced all around her. Drops of fire fell from above, splashing harmlessly against Araenè's arm and hand and running off the cool glass that she seemed to wear like a second set of clothing.

All around the walls of the fiery chamber was looped and coiled a dragon of gold and fire. Its eyes were fire; its mouth was filled with fire; the feathers of its outspread wings glowed like molten gold and dripped fire as they moved. . . . That was the source of the falling fire, Araenè saw, gazing in awe up and up along the curve of one great wing. She fumbled behind her, running shaking hands across the wall, searching for the door.

The dragon coiled its neck suddenly and brought its head down to look at Araenè from one fiery eye. The way it cocked its head was absurdly bird-like. Araenè froze, expecting the dragon to dart its head forward like a bird after an insect. She wondered whether the cool glass-like bubble surrounding her would shatter in the furnace of the dragon's jaws: would she burn to death before it could even bite her?

"Daughter of men," said the dragon. Its voice was strangely delicate, like the chiming of crystals.

Araenè answered, her voice shaking, "Dragon?"

"Daughter of men," repeated the dragon. "I have waited for you, and you have come, just at the tail of time."

It moved, golden coils rising and falling all along the walls of the fiery chamber. It folded and unfolded its wings, restless . . . indecisive? Araenè wondered. One slender foreleg reached into the midst of dense golden flames at the center of the chamber. Then, turning, the dragon offered Araenè a sphere as large as her head. It was gold as the fire, traced with a filigree of flame orange and crimson. Drops of fire scattered from it. Within it, dimly, a shadowy form seemed to move and shift.

"Quicken my child," the dragon commanded.

Horrified but not daring to refuse, Araenè reached, cautiously, toward the sphere . . . the egg. Heat beat against her hands; snatching them back, she looked helplessly at the dragon.

"Quicken my child," said the dragon a second time. "I no longer have the strength to free any fire sufficiently great. You hold the rising wind in one hand and in the other the living fire. Promise me you will take my child, and guard it, and cast it into the furnace of the earth. You will not fail in this. Swear this to me, daughter of men."

There was something in the dragon's tone, audible even in that strange, inhuman voice . . . not fierceness, not exactly command. Grief, Araenè realized at last. She'd had plenty of experience with grief lately. She didn't think she was mistaken. It occurred to her that the dragon was very thin, and that the fire that burned in its eyes seemed . . . dim, perhaps. Or not dim so much as . . . set too deep. Like a fire that was burning lower and lower and would soon go out.

"Quicken my child," the dragon repeated once more, but this time it was less like a command and more like a plea.

Araenè's terror faded in the face of the dragon's grief.

Trying not to think too clearly about what she was doing, Araenè reached out and took the egg. Somehow she folded it into a bubble of protective coolness as it fell into her hands: mint and lemon on the outside, so she could hold it safely; so fiercely clove-hot on the inside that her whole tongue seemed numbed by the heat of it. She cradled the egg with instinctive care. It was amazingly light, as though it contained nothing but fire. "But I—but I don't know how—how do I quicken it?" she asked helplessly. "Wind and, and the living fire? The furnace of the earth? I don't know what you mean! I would, I *will*, but how?"

"Look!" commanded the dragon, and showed her a taloned hand filled with fire.

Araenè stared into the fire, watching visions unfold in the flames like flowers blooming: she saw a silver wind that shredded high streamers of cloud and then somehow blazed into fire. She saw Islands falling out of the sky toward the sea and cried out in shock, but she did not see them fall into the water; though she tried to watch the falling Islands, her vision was wrenched aside and instead she saw three great buildings of black iron standing in a row on a shore of gray shale. She could see not only the flames that burned at the heart of each building, but also the heaving molten fire that rolled, uneasily trapped, below the earth. . . .

"There it waits. Beyond my strength. Promise me," pleaded the dragon. "Daughter of men, cast my child upon the winds and into the furnace of the earth. Call the wind to break open the earth and let out the hidden fire. You must call the wind, and the wind must become fire. Do you understand? Swear it to me!"

"I swear, I *swear* I will," Araenè promised, though she did not understand at all. She was terrified by the dragon's grief and desperation. She would have said anything to ease that desperation, and found herself repeating, "I will. I *will.*"

The dragon opened its wings once more. Araenè stumbled backward and found the door behind her, open, cool air coming through it like the winter rain after a hard summer. Only she fell over the edge of the doorway, or over her own feet as she tried to turn, and sprawled. She cried out as she fell, tucking herself up around the egg, guarding it from harm, and wound up sitting on the floor of her half-familiar apartment, with a bruised shoulder and a knot on her head. But the egg was safe in her lap.

Tears of shock welled in her eyes, but at the same time, Araenè found herself laughing—she could hear the shocked, hysterical edge of her laughter and choked it off. The egg, cradled in her arms, glowed with warmth through the bubble Araenè had put around it—and how had she done that, and would it last? But it seemed safe enough for the moment.

"I don't—" she said aloud, and stopped. "I can't—" and stopped again. For the first time, it occurred to her that she could have, *should* have called Master Tnegun in the first moment, the first *instant* she'd found herself caught within the dragon's furnace. But now . . . "I can't—" she said again. She couldn't call him *now*. She couldn't bring him the egg *now*. Could she? Because she would have to say that the fire dragon had given her its egg and that she'd promised to quicken it, and he'd find out—of course he would—that the dragon had called her "daughter of men," and said it had been waiting for

160

her. He would know that it had been waiting to give its egg to a *girl.*

Araenè wondered, caught again between laughter and tears, whether any apprentice before her had ever broken *all four* of the mages' rules less than a day after arriving at the school.

7

Trei arrived unannounced at the kajurai towers, stepping directly from Master Tnegun's library to the novitiate sleeping hall. This was deserted, which was as well, because Trei did not want to see anyone. He walked slowly through the long sleeping hall, from one slanting rectangle of light to the next where the high windows let the afternoon sun past the thick walls, and sat down rather blankly on his bed. His things were still here, folded on the shelves above his bed. This added somehow to his general sense of unreality, as though he had not really left the kajurai precincts at all. As though Uncle Serfei and Aunt Edona still dwelled in their comfortable house with his cousin. Trei lay back on his bed and laid an arm across his eyes.

It was all the loss. Too much loss, coming so fast—he shied from that thought and tried not to think at all. Exhaustion weighed him down like iron.

He didn't know what to think about Araenè. He was glad she had something she wanted. He could imagine Marrè declaring boldly that she *would be* a mage, only his sister would have laughed as she declared her intention, knowing that whatever the town thought of girl mages, her father would support her. Araenè . . . someone would surely *notice* . . . but she had wanted it so much. Not to be a mage, not even really to be a chef, Trei thought, but to somehow shed herself entirely and take up a new life. Almost any new life. And now she had. Only what would happen when somebody realized she was a girl? Trei should have insisted on . . . But here he ran aground, for what exactly could he have insisted on?

"Trei!" cried a familiar voice, and Rekei bounded forward, but then slowed and stopped, looking uncharacteristically self-conscious. "Trei—I didn't know you were back! It's great, ah, that is, I'm glad to see you, Trei, but . . . are you . . ."

Trei took his arm down and tried to find the energy to sit up. "I guess I'm staying. At least for now."

"Well, good," Rekei said, awkward but touchingly enthusiastic. "It's not the same here without you and Ceirfei—"

"Without Ceirfei?" Trei did sit up at that, letting himself be pulled back to novitiate concerns.

"Oh." Rekei hunched his shoulders, looking suddenly smaller and somehow younger. "You didn't know?"

"Know what?" Trei demanded, trying to be exasperated when really he was frightened. Ceirfei had gotten angry, remembered he was a prince, and stormed out. Wingmaster Taimenai had gotten angry because Ceirfei had acted like a prince, and he had thrown him out. Ceirfei's mother or uncle had found out Ceirfei had been whipped, and *they* had gotten angry and taken him away. . . .

"Ceirfei's brother and two of his cousins died. And the

queen herself is terribly ill," Rekei said in a low voice, as though he could hardly bear to say the words at all. "Of the . . . of the same fever that laid down your uncle and aunt, they say. It's fairly well burned out, and anyway the physicians know how to treat it now, but a lot of people died, I guess. Especially in First and Second Cities. They say it was a new Yngulin ambassador from Tguw. He was ill when he came. It was all people who'd met him who got it first, and their, um. Their families. But then it ran through the city and got . . . pretty bad, I guess."

"You don't think . . . ," Trei began, and paused. But everyone knew Yngul had no sense of honor. He asked, "You don't think Yngul did this on purpose, do you?"

Rekei looked horrified. "Oh, no! Why would they? The senior ambassador is very upset, they say, and they say Yngul's going to pay an indemnity. I guess they don't get so ill with that fever, in Yngul. The ambassador from Tguw wasn't very ill, they say."

Trei thought the other boy was probably right. Yngul might have sent a man to carry illness to the Islands; that was the sort of thing the Yngulin Emperor might think was clever and amusing. He might have done that, if he wanted the Floating Islands weakened for some reason. But why would he want that?

So probably Rekei was right: probably the illness had been an accident. But Trei couldn't decide whether it made it better or worse, that the illness had been a pointless accident. He said nothing.

But he almost thought he could feel the whole city reverberate with the loss it had suffered. Trei closed his eyes, ashamed that he found this thought somehow satisfying. But it only seemed right that everyone in Canpra should understand his grief, Araenè's grief. . . .

Even so, he didn't want to think of the novitiate without Ceirfei.

"Well, you're back now, anyway!" Rekei said, with forced cheer. "So that's one thing better."

The cheerfulness might be forced, but not the sentiment. Trei looked away, blinking. To steady himself, he said, "I should see the wingmaster, I suppose." Trei assured Rekei he did not need company, then found, as he climbed the stairs, that in fact he would have liked the other boy's support. He went more and more slowly, thinking of the wingmaster's piercing kajurai eyes and humorless mouth. He wondered how many novices had ever dared to lie to Taimenai Cenfenisai, and how many had successfully slipped the lie over on the wingmaster.

He did at least remember where the wingmaster's office was: down the hall and up a long stair; he even remembered which of the stair's landings he should take. Every step of the way seemed emblazoned on his nerves. He left the stair and walked down the short hall to the wingmaster's office. The door was solid wood, plain and heavy, with a clapper of black iron. When Trei touched the clapper, he heard its distant, deep note even through the heavy door.

Wingmaster Taimenai opened the door himself, tall and severe as always. But the fierce afternoon light revealed fine lines around his kajurai eyes, and Trei thought he looked tired. "Trei," he said, and formally, "we are glad to find you again in your place among us."

Not knowing what to say, Trei nodded awkwardly.

"Come in." The wingmaster stepped back and held the door wide.

To Trei's surprise and relief, Ceirfei was already in the wingmaster's office.

"Your family affairs?" queried the wingmaster, returning to his place behind his desk.

"Um . . . settled," Trei answered cautiously. "My, um. My cousin has gone to my aunt's sister's family, in the country. And arrangements have been made to sell my uncle's house and effects. So I . . . I was free. To come back."

To Trei's relief, the wingmaster seemed willing to dismiss the topic of his cousin. He said instead, "We do not have so many kajuraihi that we wish to cast our novices back into the world. Once you have learned to see the wind, you will never again be blind."

Trei let himself glance over at Ceirfei.

The wingmaster barely smiled. "Just so."

Ceirfei said to Trei, "I'm required to attend my uncle every third morning, and for a full day every senneri. But I *am* kajurai."

Wingmaster Taimenai gave him a nod. "I shall expect you to keep pace with the other novices. In that regard, I believe I shall waive the remainder of your senneri grounding—" He held up a stern hand to check Ceirfei's surprised nod. "This is not by any means to be construed as acceptance of your disobedience, however."

"No, sir. And Trei?"

"Waiving only your punishment would hardly be just," the wingmaster said coolly, and nodded to Trei. "You have both missed several days' training, however. You must work hard to meet the standards set by Novice-master Anerii."

"Yes, sir," Trei and Ceirfei said together, and received a final dismissal.

"I was grieved to hear of your new loss," Ceirfei told Trei as they went down the stair side by side. "The sea is made of salt tears, we say, and the waves are made of the griefs of men, but I am sorry so many should fall upon you."

Ceirfei sounded sincere, even heartfelt; Trei felt awkward as he returned similar sentiments, for he could not manage such smoothness.

"Your cousin is well? I have a brother remaining, and two sisters, and my parents are well, but I think you now have only your cousin?"

Trei did not want to lie to Ceirfei, even by omission. He said only, "My cousin grieves, of course. But your aunt remains ill?"

Ceirfei bowed his head a little. "The physicians think she may be saved. If she falls from us into the hand of the Silent God, my uncle—" But he cut off unvoiced whatever he'd meant to say about his uncle.

His uncle, the king. Trei still found this a hard belief to hold in the forefront of his mind. Ceirfei certainly never said "the king, my uncle." But even so . . . Trei said, "I'm surprised . . . if I may say so, I'm surprised your uncle didn't hold you at his side."

"Ah, well, he might have done, but Taimenai is right, you know—truly, we do not have so many kajuraihi as we might wish."

"We," as though Ceirfei felt himself already one of the kajuraihi; that was Trei's first impression. But then he thought, *Or "we," as though he spoke for Milendri entire? Or for all the Floating Islands?* Perhaps growing up a prince, one naturally took to a broader view. "Why not?" he asked. "I wondered that before. Why not more kajuraihi? Eighteen beds in the novitiate, and only six novices?"

"Perhaps boys today dream of high court positions, not the heights of the wind." Ceirfei's tone was dry. "They say our dragons of wind and sky accept fewer boys than they used— that our dragons are fewer in number themselves. Though," he added judiciously, "my father says that isn't so, but fewer of the dragons stay close to the Floating Islands than once was true. That by itself is worrisome enough now, though certainly no one can say the Islands have dropped lower in the sky—ah, supper! Our timing is impeccable!"

Then they had to meet the effusion of the other boys; though Trei knew this was directed mainly toward Ceirfei, he felt some of the others' pleasure was for his own return. Since he was not able to meet their words of sympathy gracefully, he turned as quickly as he could to matters of more immediate importance to novice kajuraihi. "What have you been doing? Have you been flying every day?" he asked, and to his surprise found himself genuinely interested in the least details of the other boys' days.

"Rekei took notes for you," Genrai told them both, with a shy duck of his head when he looked at Ceirfei.

"Good ones! Well laid out!" Rekei assured them earnestly. "We're into kajurai history and the history of the Floating Islands, so you probably know all that, Ceirfei, but Trei doesn't. But we're also deep into kajurai hierarchy and law, Gods! I didn't think I'd land here and *still* end by studying law!"

"We're making our own wings," Kojran told them, rolling his eyes at this talk of classes and study. "We make our own, did you know? But it's going to take *forever.*" He sighed dramatically.

"We all practice on little frames, with these ragged old feathers, but yesterday Linai let us start setting up the real frames for our real wings," Tokabii added.

"It's finicky work," Genrai said, glancing at Ceirfei and then away again. "I thought—that is, we hoped you might return. Linai gave us a framework and some gulls' feathers so we could show you. After supper—"

And for the next little while they could all forget everything else in learning the delicate technique of setting feathers in place in a wing. Ceirfei had steadier hands, but Trei was happy to find he seemed to have a natural feel for where in the framework any particular feather should be placed.

Yet, though Trei had hoped . . . had wished . . . to slip back into the kajurai novitiate and pretend he'd never left it, he found himself, through the next few days, watching the other novices without feeling himself one of them. Though he attended classes and took notes alongside Rekei, and let Genrai help him with the demanding art of wingcrafting, and tried to make the resisting Kojran study properly, through it all he felt himself standing almost outside of all this. He almost felt he watched *himself* from the outside, as though he watched himself move and speak in the same way he might watch a street entertainer's puppet going through the motions of life, as though a sheet of impenetrable glass stood between himself and the world.

Trei knew this feeling was born of grief. He had almost forgotten this strange distance and separation, and had not realized he had almost forgotten it, and—worst of all—felt guilty for ever having forgotten, for beginning to feel once more that he belonged to life.

He thought Ceirfei might join him in this dim, distant kind of half-life. Sometimes he saw him standing a little way from the other boys and looking at them with a kind of remote wistfulness, but then, Ceirfei might only be feeling set aside by his royal blood. Ceirfei never spoke of his brother who had died, any more than Trei mentioned his parents or sister, or Uncle Serfei and Aunt Edona.

Only when he flew did Trei feel properly alive.

The sky was filled with complex beauty. There was a clean, uncomplicated joy in flight, in threading a path through pearlescent winds and crystal-bright layers of pressure and temperature. Sometimes violent storms raced across the sea, and then the winds, tossing above iron-dark waves, seemed made of silver and dark pewter. When it was fine, gulls flew in and out of the shadows cast by the Floating Islands, white wings flashing. And sometimes the long forms of sky dragons coiled and rippled high above the Islands, the transparent feathers of their wings seeming as fragile and insubstantial as the wind itself. It was impossible to believe any creatures so beautiful could be related in any way to the terrible dragon of fire that had, in Trei's dream or memory, shattered Mount Ghaonnè and destroyed Rounn.

Their kajurai instructors taught the boys how to land in the tight space provided by the deck of a ship, and what courtesies were owed a ship's captain when they came down, and how to lift themselves from a ship's deck back into the sky by wind magic alone when they had no height from which to leap. Their instructors taught them how to tack across the face of a violent storm, and how much height was enough when unpredictable winds suddenly threw them down toward the raging sea, and how the air above even a quite terrible storm was always calm. Trei wondered what the Island monsoons were truly like and whether they could possibly be worse than the terrible icy storms that locked northern Tolounn into ice and silence every winter.

And the instructors began to teach the boys how to carry heavy stones aloft, and how to cast them down to strike targets bobbing amid the waves. This was harder than seemed plausible.

"You can't get within bow shoot, fool," one instructor roared at Tokabii one morning not long after Trei had returned. "Get some height under you! You'll find it hard to fly arrow-struck!"

Trei shook his head about this later. "Why practice anything of the sort?" he asked. "When no one can attack the Floating Islands anyway. What defense can you possibly need, besides height?"

Ceirfei glanced up. "Oh, well, you don't yet know much Island history. In the reign of Komaonn the Elder, the Yngulin attacked our shipping and blockaded our trade. We might have been forced to become just a province of Yngul, but Tai Tairenaima invented clingfire and we drove them off."

"Trei?" called Rei, putting his head in the door. "There you are! The wingmaster wants you, so shake the iron out of your wings!"

Trei shoved his chair back and stood up. His stomach clenched, remembering the last summons from the wingmaster— but no. This couldn't be the same. Though if the wingmaster had found out about Araenè . . . His stomach clenched harder. He followed Rei, his steps dragging. And found Ceirfei at his elbow, uninvited.

Wingmaster Taimenai wasn't alone in his office, Trei found. Novice-master Anerii was also present, and so were two men Trei didn't recognize. Not kajuraihi. Court nobles, he guessed from the style and fineness of their dress. Araenè— Trei didn't want to think of his cousin, not now; he knew he would only look guilty if he thought of his cousin. He tried hard to think of nothing at all.

But Wingmaster Taimenai's grim expression was not reassuring.

All the men were standing except for one of the strangers. That one was a tall man, neither old nor very young, with a long, expressive face and a tired, worried look in his eyes. He wore a white shirt and a violet sash. He had a narrow violet ribbon woven through his dark hair and a band of woven gold about his neck, another about one wrist. Trei thought he *surely* was a court noble. Trei's heart sank as he tried to imagine what pressing interest could have brought a man like this to kajurai precincts to ask after a mere novice.

"Trei," said the wingmaster, and beckoned.

Rei Kensenè, hovering uncertainly, received a dismissive wave from the novice-master and went away. Trei wished *he* could retreat so easily. But Ceirfei was still a supportive presence at his back. That was reassuring. He took a reluctant step forward.

"If you please," Wingmaster Taimenai said to the strangers, "allow me to make known to you Novice Trei Naseida, lately of Tolounn and now an Island kajurai."

172

Trei found it enormously reassuring to have the wingmaster put the introduction just that way. The seated man—*surely* he must be a court noble?—gave Trei a small nod.

"This is my cousin, Prince Imrei Naterensai," Ceirfei murmured in Trei's ear. "And that is Lord Manasi Teirdana, first minister of finance and my uncle's close advisor."

Trei blinked and tried to collect his scattering wits.

"Trei," said Prince Imrei. His voice was quiet and husky. He studied Trei with careful interest. "Tell me about your journey from Tolounn. Surely you did not leave Tolounn from the harbor at Rounn? That harbor is closed, I believe?"

Trei hesitated. He hadn't expected to be asked about *Rounn,* not now: even after learning who the prince was, he'd braced himself for questions about Araenè. He said at last, "No, sir. Your Highness. From Sicuon."

"You walked from Rounn to Sicuon? You went to Sicuon directly? How long did that take you?"

Trei hardly remembered. That journey had been a dense nightmare of exhaustion and grief. He remembered the dust and ash that had veiled the sun, so all those on the road had traveled through a continual twilight. Ash had fallen like snow; they had all choked on the bitter taste of it. "Days," he managed. But he did not know how many. At the time, it had seemed forever.

"How was it you came to be outside Rounn when the mountain exploded?" asked the prince.

"You can do this," Ceirfei said, gripping Trei's arm hard, and Trei, who had come within a feather's width of turning on his heel and walking out of the room, explained instead about his summer visit to his uncle in Sicuon. He didn't say anything about how it had felt to stand on the mountain road above Rounn and see the plumes of ash in the air, the shattered mountain rearing above, its internal fire glowing through the cracks in the stone. He didn't describe the time he had spent just sitting at the side of the road, staring down at the lake of still-molten stone and billowing ash that had, so small a time before, poured down across the city.

Prince Imrei wanted to know about Rounn, and then all about the journey back to Sicuon and from there to the Floating Islands. Trei didn't tell him his uncle in Sicuon had sent him away. Maybe he knew, or guessed. But Trei wasn't going to say anything about it.

The prince was polite—was that Ceirfei's presence?—but he went on and on. What ship had Trei taken south? Had it gone well out to sea before turning south, or had it hugged the coast? What ports had they touched on the way? Ah, they had landed at Tetouann? Why? To take on supplies, merchandise, passengers, all three? How long had the ship stayed at Tetouann? Oh, Trei had changed ships at Tetouann? Why was that? How many days had he stayed in Tetouann? Had his new ship—what was its name?—put in at Marsosa? At Goenn? At Teraica? How long had it taken to sail from Goenn to Teraica? How many days had they stayed at Teraica?

Trei could give almost none of the answers to these questions. He remembered, dimly, that he had switched ships twice, and he thought that the second time had been at Goenn, but it might have been Teraica. He thought the ship that had carried him from Tetouann to Goenn (or Teraica) might have been called the *Temenann,* or maybe it had been the *Temoinè?* He didn't remember the captains' names. He didn't even remember whether there had *been* other passengers. Most of the time during that long journey he'd felt like a disembodied ghost: one of the thousands of ghosts of Rounn. The taste of bitter ashes had been on his tongue the whole way, until the hammering heat of the southern sun had begun at last to burn out the memory of the dim, ash-ridden chill of the north.

But he didn't know how to tell Prince Imrei that.

"A thin tale," Lord Manasi said to the prince at last, shaking his head.

"Too thin," said Prince Imrei, sitting back in his chair and running his hand thoughtfully back and forth across its arm. "If the boy was a spy, or the agent of spies, he'd have a far better tale prepared."

A spy! Trei stiffened, trying not to show either shock or outrage. He looked quickly at Ceirfei, who touched his shoulder in reassurance and shook his head a little. *Just wait,* Trei thought that meant.

"Every spy for the next forty years will be claiming to be a survivor of Rounn," argued Lord Manasi. "It's a Gods-given excuse to have no records tracing your past movements."

"Trei *is* from Rounn," Ceirfei said quietly, and when his cousin looked at him, he added, "He dreams of it."

Prince Imrei's eyebrows rose, and he nodded thoughtfully.

"Well, but Tolounn's spymasters are clever," said Lord Manasi. "A half-bred boy heading to the Islands would be a gift to them. Perhaps someone picked up this one at Goenn. That would explain those days ashore. It's not plausible to suggest it'd take five days to find a southbound ship out of Goenn."

Prince Imrei held up a hand for silence and said to Trei,

"Surely you hesitated to make so long a journey, and with no certainty of welcome at the end of it? Perhaps someone in Tolounn suggested you should come here? Or perhaps someone along your way suggested you might try for kajurai training? That if you brought any artifacts or knowledge of wind-dragon magic back for Tolounnese mages to examine, you might be well rewarded?"

"No!" Trei exclaimed. He wanted to feel outraged. Furious. Instead he only felt frightened and ill.

"Your uncle was a well-regarded minister," Lord Manasi observed. "You might have had a good place in a ministry in a year or two—you might have looked to become a court minister yourself. Instead you came"—he gestured broadly, indicating not the wingmaster's office but the wider kajurai precincts—"here."

"I wanted to fly!" Trei said, but even to his own ears this protest sounded weak and childish. He could not begin to put into words the deep longing that had struck him the first time he'd seen the kajuraihi soaring above the waves. . . .

Lord Manasi tilted his head skeptically, plainly having no understanding at all of that longing and not really believing in it. "Valuable as Tolounn would find a spy in any of the ministries—and we may be certain there are some— Tolounnese artificers would be even better pleased to have someone bring them a sample of dragon magic. That's something, so far as we know, that Tolounn has never accomplished. If we grow careless, we might find Tolounn far too closely acquainted with all the arts by which we protect the Islands—"

"*We* don't protect the Islands," Wingmaster Taimenai said sharply.

"We do," snapped Lord Manasi, "and we must, as your precious dragons will do nothing more than keep us aloft—"

"If you please." Prince Imrei lifted his hands in a mollifying gesture. "Our height *is* our protection. Nor do we wish to offend the sky dragons who hold us above the waves by allowing any trace of their power to fall into the hands of Tolounnese artificers."

The wingmaster was as sternly expressionless as ever, but his crystalline kajurai eyes glinted with impatience. "Prince Imrei, the boy made the climb up to the heights of Kotipa. Do not mistake the situation. *We* do not decide which boys to accept into the novitiate. That is a judgment the dragons make. Unless you doubt the judgment of the dragons whose magic you so determinedly protect, Lord Manasi's suspicion is untenable."

Novice-master Anerii said harshly, "A half-bred boy might be approached *after* his audition. When he finds himself divided in blood and heart and loyalty, who knows what choices such a boy will make?"

"We are all acquainted with your opinion," the wingmaster said. His tone was absolutely flat, yet somehow conveyed a profound rebuke. Novice-master Anerii crossed his arms over his chest and glowered, but he did not say anything else.

"Trei *is* kajurai," Ceirfei said to his cousin. "Who would know better than I?"

Prince Imrei nodded thoughtfully, seeming to find his cousin's opinion persuasive.

The wingmaster added, taking adroit advantage of Ceirfei's support, "And as this is so, and as you have now met the boy yourself, Prince Imrei, I will be grateful to see you put these suspicions to rest."

For a moment, he and Prince Imrei simply gazed at one another. Then Prince Imrei said to Trei, "You maintain no one approached you—not a Tolounnese mage, nor any Tolounnese official, nor anyone else. No one suggested you should audition on Kotipa."

"No," Trei said faintly. He wanted to lean against the wall—he wanted to sit down on the floor, if he couldn't sit in a chair—he locked his knees and tried not to sway.

"And no one has approached you since your audition. No one has said anything to you about, say, loyalty to Tolounn, or suggested you return to your father's people?"

Trei shook his head.

"Our novices stay in the novitiate," Wingmaster Taimenai said shortly. "We keep them close; we keep them busy."

"But the boy left the novitiate for several days, I believe," observed Lord Manasi.

The wingmaster sighed sharply. He looked at Trei and asked, "Well, Trei, and did anyone approach you in such a manner while you were comforting your bereaved cousin after the tragic loss of your uncle and aunt?"

"No," Trei whispered.

"I will check that this is true," Lord Manasi declared.

"I shall leave you to that," Prince Imrei said to him, but added to Trei in a soothing tone, "Though I'm sure it's true." He gripped the arms of his chair, rose to his feet, and nodded to Ceirfei. "Cousin, thank you. Wingmaster Taimenai, I'm grateful for your assistance. I believe we're satisfied. You have been most helpful."

The wingmaster inclined his head briefly and then glanced around the room, gathering all their attention. "Novices, you are dismissed. Return to the novitiate. Novice-master Anerii, if you will await me here? Prince Imrei, Lord Manasi, I hope you will permit me the honor of escorting you—" He stepped politely over to open the door and ushered his noble guests out and down the hall.

Trei made it most of the way down the stairs before he began to shake.

"Sit down," Ceirfei urged him, and sank down himself on the stair above. "I'm sorry—I *am* sorry, Trei. I couldn't warn you."

"No," Trei managed to agree. He understood that. He tucked his face against his knees and said, muffled, "I—you were—thank you."

"You'll be all right." Ceirfei rested a hand briefly on Trei's shoulder. "Manasi suspects everyone. Imrei doesn't suspect anyone; it's not his nature. That's why my uncle sent them both. You understand we think Tolounn is preparing to invade? Do you see?"

Trei shook his head blankly. "I know people think so. But how *can* they? And why should they?" He heard himself say "they" almost as though someone else were speaking, and wondered if his voice sounded as strained and artificial to Ceirfei as it did to himself.

But Ceirfei only shrugged. "How? We have no idea. But why? If they think they can succeed, then why not?" Ceirfei's tone had taken on an uncharacteristic bite. "They might invade us because they've always resented our independence and think we ought by rights to return to being a Tolounnese province. Or because they're ambitious to add Cen Periven to the Empire, and the Islands are an important base for any such attempt. Or maybe just because it'll make somebody's political career to press a short, successful war."

Trei didn't say anything. He could see that all of those reasons might be true at once, but any of them might be enough alone. If some Tolounnese general or provincar thought he had a way to successfully invade the Islands, it wouldn't be hard to get public opinion in Tolounn to favor the attempt. The Islands were so small: it wouldn't be a very expensive war. The Little Emperor would probably view an invasion almost as a game if he saw a way to invade at all: he would think the effort would be useful and valuable if it succeeded and might be entertaining even if it failed. And all of Tolounn would agree with him. Only the Islands would care passionately about the outcome, because only they had anything important to lose.

It had never occurred to Trei to wonder how, say, Toipakom had felt about being conquered and made a part of the Tolounnese Empire. It was just the natural order of the world for small countries to fall before Tolounn's strength. But even after so short a time in the Islands, he knew the Islanders didn't feel that way at all.

Ceirfei tapped his fingers impatiently on the worn stone of the steps and added, "If they have some way to get *at* us, well . . . we don't really have any soldiers. Not real soldiers, not the kind that might stand against Tolounnese troops. And now, after that illness—"

Trei interrupted him, "Do *you* think Yngul deliberately set the illness loose in the Islands? Rekei said no, but I—" He wanted it to be true, he discovered, because he wanted someone *else* to blame for the tension between Tolounn and the

Islands. Someone he could loathe with a purity he couldn't direct against Tolounn.

"Some people think maybe *Tolounn* did, in such a way as to lay the blame on Yngul—"

"Oh, no!" Trei was horrified. "No one in Tolounn would do anything so dishonorable—and that's dishonorable *twice,* setting the illness and then blaming somebody else! Anyway, no one from Tolounn would think they had to! Why should any Tolounnese general or provincar care whether there's been illness in Canpra? Your people couldn't possibly fight Tolounnese soldiers—if the soldiers got up here at all." He realized after the words were out that he'd said "your people," and stopped, awkward and confused.

"Besides," Trei added after a moment, feeling, despite his confusion, obscurely responsible for defending Tolounn's honor in the face of this unexpected slur, "besides, Ceirfei, if somebody did, and it got out, well, nobody would risk *that,* do you see? Think of what the public opprobrium would do to his reputation! That's why I said maybe Yngul: the Yngulin Emperor might do something like that. Only I don't know *why* he would. . . ."

"Maybe it really was an accident. But, Trei, whatever happens, if it comes to war, the Islands will have to depend on the kajuraihi to throw more than rocks. But there aren't many kajuraihi. A few hundred, not the thousands we might have mustered in my grandfather's day."

"Yes, I've heard that, but why?"

"We don't know. There might be fewer dragons, so then we'd have less dragon magic available to borrow. But then why would there be fewer dragons? Have they found a different island chain elsewhere to their liking, so that their strongest winds no longer surround *our* Islands? Or maybe the dragons still ride the winds around and above our Islands, but they've simply become less willing to share their magic with men. We don't really *know* why they ever chose to allow us to borrow their magic and ride their winds; if they ever choose otherwise, we might not understand that, either. But," he added encouragingly, "they still do make some of us into kajuraihi."

Trei nodded. "The dragons themselves—they don't actually fight, is that right?"

"Never," Ceirfei agreed. "They never fight men, they never have, not in all our common history. Maybe they can't, maybe their nature isn't suited to it; maybe they won't lower themselves to do battle. Maybe they just don't notice the quarrels of men. No one knows. But they keep the Islands high above the sea, and when *we* have to fight to defend the Islands, we do it from the heights. So we borrow their magic to defend the Islands for both ourselves and for them." Ceirfei got slowly to his feet and offered Trei a hand up. "We should get back to the novitiate."

"Gods. Master Anerii—"

"Taimenai will surely pin *his* wings back." Ceirfei sounded uncharacteristically fierce, so that Trei stared at him in surprise.

"Really, Trei. The *master of novices,* speaking out in open suspicion *right in front* of the very novices with whom he's charged? Incredible. He should be removed from his position. If *I* were the wingmaster—well. Well. Can you stand?"

Trei let Ceirfei pull him to his feet. The sick feeling was passing off at last, but he found himself suddenly, violently angry. With Lord Manasi, with himself, with the whole Tolounnese Empire? He hardly knew. He said, "Ceirfei, I *am* kajurai now." But then he wasn't sure. *Divided in blood and heart and loyalty,* Novice-master Anerii had said, and angry and uncomfortable as he was, Trei was aware that, despite Ceirfei's quick defense of him, the novice-master might even be right. He shook his head, trying to dismiss both the anger and the crowding doubts. Said at last, "Anyway, Tolounn hasn't any business invading the Islands. The Empire won't even care whether it wins or loses—not much. But it *matters* to the Islands. If there is war, I'll—I *am* kajurai—"

Ceirfei didn't seem to hear his hesitation. "I know you are. It's all right." He offered a reassuring little nod.

Ceirfei's confidence was heartening, and though he couldn't actually share it, Trei found his confusion and anger easing.

8

Araenè slept through the night with the egg tucked up against her chest, a strange cool-hot presence in the bed; she'd been fearful of breaking it, but unable to rest without it next to her. She'd been afraid that, her first night in the hidden school, she would dream of . . . things, of her mother standing helplessly in the hall while Araenè stormed away to her room, of her father during that last horrible night before he died.

Instead she dreamed all night of fire that rode through the sky on the back of the wind and crawled, molten, through the earth, locked under stone. She dreamed of blocky iron walls that loomed above her: black, but glowing red with contained fire. When she pressed her hands to an iron wall, the heat should have charred through her palms and burned her bones to ash. She felt the heat, yet she did not burn.

These weren't *her* dreams, she knew. They pressed against

her mind from the dragonet right through shell and cool shield alike. She was grateful for those dreams, though, because they blocked her own nightmares. She was grateful even when she woke hot-eyed and headachy and wondering just how far from hatching the egg really was. *Quicken my child.* Yes, and Araenè thought that if she cast it into a hot enough fire, it was ready to quicken *now*. But she did not know where she could find any fire hot *enough*. . . . She had no idea how to find those great iron furnaces. . . .

She found herself reluctant to let the egg out of her sight. But since she could hardly carry it around in her pocket, she hid it at the back of the deepest drawer in her room. Then she slipped into the kitchens, still very early, to help make the day's bread and eat her breakfast with the kitchen staff: warm bread with sheep's milk butter and figs. She almost forgot about the fire dragon's egg hidden in her room until she found her way to Master Tnegun's workroom. Then she suddenly found herself able to think of nothing else.

But Master Tnegun did not seem to see the reflection of fire in her eyes. Or the reflection of the ten thousand rules she'd broken.

His workroom was the big one in which Araenè had first met him, with its enormous, cluttered table and strangely dim light. Three granite spheres lay on the table near the master's hand, and a thin copper plate held upright in a clamp, and a scattering of ravens' feathers. The scent and flavor of cumin filled the room, but there was also something else. . . . Araenè tried to decipher the thin, bitter taste, which was a little like turmeric. She didn't exactly like it, but it seemed . . . powerful.

Not just powerful. Secretive, somehow. Or not exactly secretive, but . . . guarded, maybe.

Araenè stood as Master Tnegun directed, by the table where she could look directly into the dim reflection cast back by the copper plate. The reflection looked alarmingly girlish. Her throat looked too long and smooth, her cheekbones too delicate; her eyes, wide now with nerves, did not look like the eyes of a boy.

But Master Tnegun did not seem to notice anything amiss with Araenè's reflection. "You have settled in well enough? Your apartment pleases you?" he asked. His deep voice seemed to come out of the far reaches of the room rather than from the place near at hand where he stood.

Araenè nodded mutely.

"Good." The master gestured sternly toward a chair near the table. "Sit. We will see what sort of magery your mind and blood contain, young Arei, and discover how and in what form it is emerging. You may find the process disconcerting. Sit down."

Araenè supposed it was too late to declare that she really just wanted to be a chef. But she was frightened, and her fear made her angry. She straightened her shoulders and glared at the master. "What if I don't want to?"

Master Tnegun regarded her in silence for a moment. Long enough that Araenè began to be ashamed of her angry question, though she was still angry. Or frightened; it was hard to tell which.

But he only said at last, with no trace of annoyance, "You will find it impossible to reach the heart of magic unless you permit a master to guide your journey. I am aware that I am asking you to take a long step into trust. I give you my word that I will not harm you, Arei. When you are ready, I must still ask you to sit."

Araenè sat slowly down in the chair Master Tnegun had indicated.

"Good." The master changed the angle of the copper plate by a degree or so and picked up a long black feather. He brushed the feather across the surface of the plate, and the complicated scents in the room were abruptly joined by something almost like crushed coriander, but sweeter. Master Tnegun touched the copper plate with the tips of two fingers, looked up to meet Araenè's eyes, and sent his mind probing suddenly behind her eyes, into her mind and her heart.

Araenè *did something.* She did not make or summon the mint-and-lemon shield that had protected her in the dragon's furnace. This was something else, but . . . it was a little bit the same. It tasted of anise and lemon and pepper, and it stopped Master Tnegun instantly.

The Yngulin master paused, thin eyebrows rising. Yet he looked thoughtful rather than displeased. "Has someone shown you how to do this? No, of course not. Hmm." He sent his mind toward hers again, but his probing thought skidded once more away from her protected heart and mind, and he ceased, frowning.

"I'm not doing it deliberately," Araenè protested.

"Certainly you are, child. If I were to teach you how to yield your mind to mine, would you do so? If I were to break your hard-held protection by force, would you be pleased?"

It seemed impudent to say no, but Araenè certainly could not say yes.

"Of course you would not." The master sat down in an ornate high-backed chair that Araenè was almost certain hadn't been there a moment ago, steepled his hands, and regarded her over his fingertips for a long moment. "Unfortunately, a good deal of magery may only be taught directly. Whatever secret you so urgently conceal, young Arei, I assure you, you may trust it to me."

Araenè didn't answer.

Master Tnegun sighed. "So. We will begin with something less demanding." Reaching out, he collected the smallest of the granite spheres. He tossed this to Araenè, who caught it and stared at him.

"What is that?"

Araenè felt herself growing angry again. "How could I possibly know?"

"You might ask it what it is," Master Tnegun suggested.

Araenè blinked, puzzled. Bending her head, she gazed at the sphere. It was granite, heavy and rough-textured. It tasted of . . . something dark and heavy . . . molasses. Yes, black molasses. And ginger. And something else, something that balanced oddly against the ginger . . . pepper, but not exactly. The heat was sweeter on the tongue than pepper, but in a completely different way than cloves.

"What might it do?"

Though the master spoke softly, his question startled Araenè. She jerked her head up and blinked at him. "Um . . ." Molasses, bright ginger, and that strange hot sweetness. But she had no idea what it *did*. Maybe if she . . . She cautiously tried to bring out the unfamiliar hot flavor. The sphere trembled in her hands, sweet warmth rushed up from her toes right up to the roots of her hair, and she exclaimed wordlessly.

"Well?" asked Master Tnegun.

"I . . . Is it for holding light?" Araenè turned the sphere over in her hands. "But how do you get the light out?"

"You almost released the light yourself just then. Releasing the light is not difficult. If you wish to learn how to hide light away in stone, however, that will require you to allow me to show you directly." Master Tnegun made this last statement in a tone of pointed irony.

Araenè clenched her teeth, refusing to be drawn.

"Well. Granite, born in fire, is well suited to spellwork involving heat and light. You will learn this. Name me other stones born in fire, young Arei."

Araenè had absolutely no idea how granite or any other kind of stone could be "born in fire," far less which stones those might be. She shook her head.

Master Tnegun sighed. "What *do* they teach in those libraries? Anything at all other than parochial Island law and limited classics? Well, Kanii will no doubt be able to direct you to appropriate references. Now, the other aspects of this sphere?"

The dark molasses proved to reflect a powerful kind of magic of making and unmaking, far in advance, Master Tnegun assured Araenè, of anything she should expect to manage. "Unmaking is not as difficult as making, but has costs of its own that are not immediately apparent to the untutored mind," he told her. "When you are ready to truly commence the study of magic, we shall concentrate on making. And the final use to which this stone has been put?"

Araenè bent her head over the sphere, coaxing the molasses to recede into the background so that the ginger could dominate. Ginger turned out to be associated with spells of vision and foretelling. Master Tnegun explained that every kind of stone influenced the sort of visibility and divination to which it was suited, adding offhandedly that three hundred forty-three kinds of stone could be considered relevant to the study of magic.

"Three hundred forty-three?" Araenè repeated, appalled.

Master Tnegun was amused. "Indeed. A most useful and appropriate number, as it divides by seven three times over. But that is not so many. You will learn all those very soon. More complicated is the study of how different forms of spellwork interact when introduced into stone. There are nine hundred eighty-four spheres in the hall of spheres and mirrors. To commence your studies, you may categorize them all for me. As it is impossible to begin your instruction in the heart of magic, you may as well begin that task today."

"Nine hun—what does *that* divide by?" Araenè demanded.

"One might have hoped you had learned mathematics if not geology, young Arei. It divides by two, three, four, six, and eight. A very useful, powerful number." The master lifted an amused, scornful eyebrow. "So many of you young ones don't believe mathematics can possibly be useful because you see no immediate use for it. Mathematical theory, fortunately, is also something you may study at once, so we may rectify any shortcomings you may have in this area." He paused. "Of course, if you find the study tedious, you may admit my mind to yours, and we will proceed with a more applied course of study."

Araenè glared, then jumped to her feet and stalked toward the door. Reaching it, she said over her shoulder, "Nine hundred eighty-four. Very well!" She stepped through the door, closed it hard behind her, and then paused, realizing too late that she had no idea at all where the hall of spheres and mirrors lay. First she found this infuriating—then funny. She choked back giggles. But then, with no transition, as though any random emotion might become a gateway for grief, she found herself abruptly fighting back tears.

Horrified at the idea that anyone might find her in tears in the hall, Araenè fled to her apartment. She did not even realize at once how easily she had *found* her apartment, only flung herself through its door, ran straight across to the window, jumped down into the tangled garden without pausing, tucked herself down among the vines and flowers, and let herself cry in the safe privacy the wild growth afforded her.

The tears, once allowed to storm through her, did not last long; in some strange way, Araenè felt she owned that fierce burst of grief no more than the earlier fit of giggles. As seemed so common since . . . since . . . The strange abrupt storms that shook her did not really feel like her *own* emotions. Araenè rubbed her face on her sleeve, leaned back against the garden wall, and tilted her face up to the sky.

The morning sun, already powerful, somehow made Araenè feel more real, more anchored to the moment and to herself; the fragrance of the flowers rose dizzyingly into the hot air around her. Birds were quiet at this time of the day, but a small troop of mustached brown marmosets bobbed their heads at her and chattered. Calming at last, Araenè lifted her face to the sun and thought hard about safe things: about wheat dough and how differently rice dough behaved, about the different qualities of palm sugar and cane sugar. She knew she ought to be thinking about spheres—nine hundred eighty-four spheres! And how was one supposed to know that nine hundred eighty-four was divisible by three or eight without actually dividing it? And why did it matter?

She knew she ought to go find a book on mathematical theory, or on kinds of stone. Maybe Kanii would be able to explain things to her? More likely he would be shocked at how little she knew: he would probably guess she'd never been schooled at a library. He might even—probably not, but he *might* even guess why.

How long would it take to learn three hundred and whatever kinds of stone? Not long, Master Tnegun said. How long was "not long," and how disgusted would he be when she didn't learn them that fast? And nine hundred eighty-four spheres. And he clearly intended to try to let sheer tedium drive her into letting him into her mind. What would he do when she wouldn't? Or couldn't? Eventually he would send her away, Araenè supposed. Did she care? Her earlier moment of panic at the thought had been . . . exaggerated, maybe. She had money. . . . Well, Trei had money, but she could get all she needed. She could take a room at the University. . . . She could cook at Cesera's and take the next apprentice position a master chef offered. . . .

She was uneasily aware that she could have done that from

the beginning, never mentioning the hidden school to Trei. Instead she had come here. Nor did she want to leave now. She didn't even know exactly *why* she wanted to stay at this school and learn the attributes of nine hundred eighty-four spheres, even if she couldn't let Master Tnegun show her the true heart of magic. . . . In fact, probably she *didn't* really want to stay, she just told herself she *ought* to want that, though, Gods knew, the only thing she *should* want was a suitable marriage and a wealthy household to manage.

Everything was confusing, and thinking about it made her want to cry again, though she didn't know why. Both the threatening tears and the confusion made her angry. Scowling, Araenè rubbed her face again, got to her feet, hesitated for a moment, and then deliberately stalked across the garden and put her hand on the gate.

She'd thought the gate would be locked. But the tastes of fenugreek and fennel and a high note of sweet fragrant heat burned across her tongue and her fingertips, and the gate swung easily open. The noise and dust and sheer commotion of the Third City streets rolled through the gate into her garden.

Araenè half wanted to walk away from the hidden school into the freedom of Third City. She could feel herself relax just standing in her garden, listening to the bustle of the busy streets. She could go anywhere, at whatever pace she chose; she could speak to anyone, browse in any shop. No one would question her—no one would really notice her at all. When they saw her, they would only see Arei. Out in Third City, no one would expect anything of Arei at all.

And she wanted that. Didn't she?

Yet she did not step through the gate. In the end, she swung the gate closed once more, stepped back through the window into her apartment, and went grimly up to the hall of spheres and mirrors to begin examining the nine hundred eighty-four spheres it contained.

9

The kajuraihi were the first to spot the Tolounnese warships, barely a week after Trei's return to the novitiate.

The kajuraihi had been keeping watch on the Tolounnese coast, especially on the harbor at Teraica, and even the one farther north at Goenn. If Tolounn did launch an offensive, those were considered the most likely ports from which to launch it. So the kajuraihi were keeping watch: a distant and sporadic watch, for not every kajurai had the stamina to reach the Tolounnese coast, even with the floating rocks that served as scattered waystations. But, the novices now learned, the Island wingmasters had been sending their strongest kajuraihi on that long journey twice a senneri ever since the previous year's great monsoon storms had ceased.

"And now they've seen unmistakable evidence that Tolounn is planning war," Ceirfei told them. *He* had known from the first, of course. The ignorance novices normally suffered was not for him. But now he passed his knowledge on to the rest of them. "Ships, gathering at Teraica—big but narrow, built for speed, not cargo. Plenty of canvas, but ranks of oars for close-in work. Decks sheathed with metal . . ." Here Ceirfei's tone grew doubtful. "Or so we are told."

"Against clingfire, maybe?" Tokabii asked. "But the sails?"

Ceirfei shrugged. "We're not sure. They may think their mages can protect them from fire. And from dragon winds, and from everything else we can do."

Trei said, "Tolounn wouldn't move against us unless they thought they could win." No one else commented about the "us," but the word rang oddly in his own ears.

"Maybe they're just ambitious?" Tokabii suggested, uncharacteristically diffident. "Maybe they're excited and just forgot about clingfire?"

No one laughed. Genrai said kindly, "The Tolounnese Empire isn't a mean drunk, 'Kabii. It doesn't swing a fist without looking to make sure what it's hitting—and that it's bigger. Of course, it usually *is* bigger."

"So what do we do?" Rekei asked, looking at Ceirfei.

"What we're told, I suppose." Ceirfei hesitated. Then he looked at Trei, drew a piece of paper over from a pile in front of Rekei, and began to sketch. "The Tolounnese have these things at Teraica. Down at the harbor's edge. Big." He carefully drew a tiny human figure at the edge of the paper to show the scale. "They have three, right in a row. They're all like this. They pour coal down this chute here. There must be huge forges within, but we don't know what great fire magic they're meant to invoke."

Trei stared at the sketch.

"What is it?" Kojran wanted to know, craning forward to

examine the drawing. "Some kind of, no, I guess not. All right, what?"

"It's a steam engine," Trei said. He asked Ceirfei, "Are there wheels that turn? Pistons that move up and down?"

Ceirfei looked down at the sketch, as though details he hadn't drawn might suddenly appear in it. "Not that I know."

"What's a piston?" Tokabii asked.

Trei floundered, looking for words. He'd never tried to explain steam power before, and found that it wasn't easy when his audience didn't know the first thing about the principles. "Well, this is obviously a steam engine. It's for making things move. Boats, wagons, mine scoops . . . What you do is, you pour in the coal, and the fire heats water, and the water turns into steam, and the steam pushes and makes a wheel turn or a piston go up. If there aren't any wheels or pistons, then I don't know. . . ."

"Steam *pushes*?" Tokabii said skeptically.

"Well . . ." Trei didn't quite know how to explain this.

"So the Tolounnese provincar at Teraica has built these steam engines. So he's making a lot of power, but he's not using it to turn wheels or lift pistons," Ceirfei said, ignoring the details of how exactly steam power worked. "And if they aren't using the power at Teraica . . . then . . . is it possible for *mages* to gather power from engines like these and channel it into magic?" He paused. "Power, access to power, that always limits what mages can do. They never have enough adjuvants, do they? But if Tolounnese mages have learned how to use *steam engines* for power . . ."

Trei hesitated. He'd never heard of anything like that. But . . . "I can't see why they'd go to the trouble of pouring coal into those furnaces if they weren't getting power out," he said slowly. "Artificers make and use engines; mages don't. Only . . . maybe they've learned they can. I think you're right. I think Tolounn must have mages channeling that power out of Teraica and using it somewhere else."

"Or storing it, to use against us. How, specifically? Can you guess?"

Trei shook his head uncertainly. He felt as though he *should* be able to guess how exactly a Tolounnese warship might use that power, but he couldn't. Warships and furnaces, magecraft and steam power: obviously the Tolounnese planned to use their engines as a source of power when they attacked the Islands. But he had no idea how they might do it.

Across the table, Genrai said tentatively, "If they—"

The door was flung open, and Rei Kensenè burst in. He said sharply—to all of them, but mostly to Ceirfei—"A Tolounnese fleet of warships has set sail. No one knows what they mean to do—at least, *what* is clear, but no one can guess *how* they plan to do it. They're expected to be at Milendri as early as the day after tomorrow."

"Well," said Ceirfei, "I suppose we'll find out what they plan to do, and how."

They found out. "The ships are carrying a tremendous amount of power with them," Ceirfei told the novices, relaying information as he got it. "We know from where, don't we? Each ship has a mage, and they're clearing the dragons right out of the sky as they approach. Pushing them entirely away from the Islands with sheer brute strength."

"They aren't," Rekei said, voicing the general disbelief.

"They are. And as we lose the living wind of the sky dragons, the Islands they pass settle lower and lower. Some of the smallest Islands have fallen right out of the sky into the sea." There was an appalled pause, and Ceirfei added hastily, "It's not that bad! The big Islands don't lose height so quickly or violently, and as the warships pass an Island and leave it behind, the living winds come in behind them and the Island mounts again into the air—that's what our observers see."

"But, of course," said Rekei, "when those ships get to Milendri, they won't just pass by."

"No," agreed Ceirfei.

Trei understood: the Tolounnese force didn't want to drown the Islands; what they wanted was to make the Islands into a good, productive, tax-paying province. So they wouldn't damage any Island if they could avoid it: instead they would head straight for Milendri, invest it with troops, and try for a swift, decisive stroke against the king and his court in Canpra.

"So what are we doing that *works?*" Genrai asked, practical as ever.

"Nothing, so far. We—kajuraihi—can overfly the warships if we stay high enough to avoid their dead air. But that doesn't matter, because nothing we're doing is helping. We've dropped clingfire, but the ships are very difficult to hit from that height." But then Ceirfei fell silent, glancing up as steps sounded. A man put his head through the door. The man wore court white and a badge with a violet dragon; Ceirfei got stiffly to his feet.

"Prince Ceirfei—" said the man.

"I know. I'm coming," said Ceirfei. He gave a distracted

glance around at the rest of them, managed a strained smile, and went out without looking back.

"Do you think he'll come back this time?" Tokabii asked in a hushed tone.

"The man said, '*Prince* Ceirfei,'" Genrai answered. "So I don't think so, 'Kabii."

"He didn't even say goodbye!"

"He probably didn't want to think about not coming back—"

"They may send him back here if they need to hide him," Trei suggested.

Genrai rounded on him at once. "Stop it! Tolounn isn't going to *win*. You think Tolounn is so wonderful, so unbeatable—"

"*You* stop!" snapped Rekei, jumping to his feet. He clenched his fists, leaning forward. "Trei didn't mean anything! What do you think, that he *wants* Tolounn to win?"

Trei stared at them both, taken aback. It seemed obvious to him that Tolounn was going to win. Acknowledging that wasn't a matter of loyalty or disloyalty. This new method Tolounn had, this way to somehow power magic with steam engines . . . Tolounnese artificers and mages must have been very clever to realize they could tie their arts together.

But . . . he couldn't help but be aware that it *was* disloyalty to want Tolounn to fail. But there was no way to be loyal to *everybody*. Uncle Redoenn's voice echoed in his memory: *You can't stay here, Trei. . . .* He had turned Trei away, sent him south. Trei remembered the anger and the fear and, worse than either, the shame. . . . He had listened to Uncle Redoenn's door shut behind him and, for the first time in his life, he had been ashamed of his half-Islander blood. He hadn't really *understood* that at the time, but he'd known, without putting the knowledge into words, that what Uncle Redoenn had meant was, *You're not good enough for Tolounn or for me*.

And then Uncle Serfei, in contrast, had said warmly: *You're not Tolounnese; you're my nephew*. And Araenè, encouraging him before the kajurai audition, had assured him: *You're an Islander now*. And that was true. Wasn't it true? And didn't he *want* it to be true? If he did, was it just because he still felt angry and ashamed?

No. No, it wasn't just what Uncle Redoenn had said. It was more than that. Wasn't it more than that? Tolounn wanted to subjugate the Islands, make them pay taxes and furnish conscripts; they wouldn't want to *destroy* the Islands. Tolounnese provinces benefited from belonging to a great Empire: Trei's father had said that and he was sure it was true. But the Floating Islands didn't *want* to be a Tolounnese province, especially not a subject province. And why should they be forced into the Tolounnese Empire? Just because Tolounn's art was the art of war?

And what about Ceirfei? The *best* that could happen to any captured members of the Island royal family was to be displayed in a triumphal procession in the Great Emperor's city of Rodounnè and then imprisoned.

Suddenly unable to sit still, Trei jumped up, paced, and found himself staring blankly out the windows at the sky. The crystalline winds whirled past, glittering and many-layered. He could see the winds because the sky dragons had given him a little of their magic: he *was* kajurai. He found he was angry, *furious*—and he knew who he should be angry with. Not the dragons. Not the Floating Islands. *Tolounn* had thrown him away; the *Islands* had given him a new family and a new life.

Trei turned back to the other novices, glowering at them all. "I'm going to see the wingmaster," he declared, and walked out while they were all gaping at him.

The wingmaster himself opened his office door. He looked drawn and tired. And surprised. "Trei," he said. "Yes?" He stepped back, inviting Trei to enter with an economical tip of his head.

In the face of the wingmaster's cool interest, Trei's anger faded to nervousness and even embarrassment. He already felt that he had made a mistake in coming. But he obeyed the wingmaster's gesture, crossing the antechamber to the office proper. A map of the Islands was spread out on the desk, along with a glass timer and a crystal sphere. Trei paused to look at the map, delaying the moment when he must look at Wingmaster Taimenai.

"Well?" said the wingmaster. He did not sound impatient. Yet.

Trei took a breath, steeled himself, and turned. He said, "Tolounn is using steam engines."

"Yes," said the wingmaster, and waited.

"Ceirfei drew us a picture. If he drew it right, I don't think . . . I didn't see a damper. At least not a big one. Even if there *are* dampers, if the fires are hot enough—"

"Dampers."

"To damp the fire in case the steam builds up too much. But if the fires are hot enough, even the best damper will fail—"

"Trei. Can you explain what you mean as though I know nothing about steam engines?"

Trei flushed. He tried to collect his thoughts. It was hard; he was nervous. He tried to explain. "Boilers—the part of the engine where you heat the water to steam? The boilers explode when they overheat. It happens when somebody tries to force more power than the engine's built for—but you never really know the limits of an engine until you pass them, and then it's, well, it's too late, you know."

"Yes?"

"Well, they say—Ceirfei says—all the magic is out here, over the ships." He put a hand over the map, about where he supposed the Tolounnese ships might be. "But if the power for that magic is coming from those engines in the harbor at Teraica . . . if someone could reach those engines . . . if someone could do something to force the fires hotter than they should go . . . then the engines would explode, do you see? And then the magic out *here*"—he touched the map again—"would fail."

The wingmaster studied Trei for a long moment. Then he said gently, "It seems to me that if someone made the fires in a Tolounnese engine hotter, the engine would get more powerful, not less. That is how things work generally: if you put more power in, you get more power out. Yes?"

"Yes, but not if you exceed the engine's capacity—"

"Trei."

Trei stopped. He tried to read Wingmaster Taimenai's expression, but he couldn't. It occurred to Trei, belatedly, that the wingmaster might think he was trying to fool the Islands into trying a strategy that would simply boost Tolounnese power. A man who thought he was a spy might think that. He protested, "I'm telling you the truth about how these engines work!"

"I'm sure you are," said the wingmaster. "You did well to come to me."

"Anyone who knows about steam engines would tell you the same!"

"I've no doubt of you," Wingmaster Taimenai said firmly. He laid his hand for a moment on Trei's shoulder. "It's understandable you would wish to prove your loyalty, Trei. But you needn't try quite so hard."

"But—"

"I will pass on what you've told me. I assure you that I will." The wingmaster inexorably turned Trei back toward the door. "Now go back to the novitiate, please, and I will ask you to stay there."

Trei couldn't bring himself to argue. He went out, and back down the long stair, and back into the novitiate. Everyone stared at him. Trei could hardly stand to look back at them. He said, "He doesn't believe me." This was less painful than saying, *He doesn't trust me,* which was what Trei knew was actually the truth. But it was hard enough.

"He should!" Rekei said fiercely. "Uh—*what* doesn't he believe?"

"If somebody could get to Teraica . . . if there was a way to make the engines too hot . . ."

"Wait, wait," objected Rekei. "Don't you put coal in them to *make* them hot? Can they get *too* hot? Isn't heat the whole point?"

Trei flung up his hands. "That's what the wingmaster said."

"Well, then—" said Genrai.

"I know. I'm from Tolounn," Trei said bitterly.

"Oh, yes, and even more importantly, you're a fool," Rekei said vehemently. "*We* all know you're kajurai."

"I *don't* want Tolounn to win!" Trei declared—straight to Genrai. "I would stop them if I could! But I can't—I can't do *anything* if the wingmaster won't believe me!"

"You're Ceirfei's friend," Genrai said slowly. "Ceirfei trusts you." He shrugged, looking uncomfortable as everyone stared at him. "All right. All right, Trei. You're kajurai, and you don't want Tolounn to win. But what are we supposed to do to stop it?"

"If the engines get too hot, they *will* explode."

"That doesn't make sense," Kojran objected. "Well, I'm sorry, but it doesn't! If you burn a great fire to make magic, then making the engines hotter ought to make the magic stronger."

Trei groaned. "That's what the wingmaster said!" He flung himself down on his bed and put an arm over his face. "Never mind, then!"

Genrai said after a moment, "They have steam engines where you're from, do they?"

Trei moved his arm. "My grandfather got rich from boats with steam engines. They're faster going upriver than any keelboat. And my . . . my father's brother in Sicuon, he uses steam engines to lift ore out of his mines. We use steam engines a lot in the north."

"Well, but . . . what can we do? Make the engines too hot, you say. But how could anyone make the engines too hot?"

"I don't—" *know,* Trei meant to say. But he stopped without saying it. He said instead, slowly, "My cousin—" and stopped again.

"Your cousin?" Genrai asked patiently.

"My cousin in the hidden school—"

Tokabii, Kojran, and Rekei all exclaimed simultaneously, "You have a cousin in the *hidden school*?"

"Your cousin is a mage?" Genrai asked with more restraint. His dark eyes held intense thought.

"Studying to be a mage," Trei amended. "If sh—if he could do something, give me something—something small and light and easy to carry, something that would make the Tolounnese engines overheat. If he could give me something like that . . ."

"The wingmaster might really listen to you if you had something like that," Tokabii said, sounding impressed.

"He won't listen to me," Trei said definitely. "But . . ." He looked at Genrai.

The older boy said slowly, "If your cousin knows a way to carry a lot of heat, all bundled up. Like a piece of coal, only . . . more. If he could give you something like that . . . we might keep it for later, do you think? For if things look . . . really bad. Is that what you think?"

"Yes!" Tokabii cried enthusiastically. "We could all have hot coals to carry. If everything is desperate, we could fly to Teraica and make the engines hot—we'd all be heroes—let's do that!"

"Yes, let's!" agreed Kojran, sitting up and looking interested at this talk of desperate circumstances and heroes.

Genrai said with more restraint, "Well. All you need to do is talk to your cousin. Isn't that right? Maybe he won't be able to give you anything like that. But if he can . . . if things don't go badly, you can always just give it back, and then all you've done is talk. Isn't that right?"

Trei was grateful for Genrai's steadiness and good sense. "I think that's right. I really think it is." Then he added, "If Ceirfei does come back . . ."

"We'll tell him everything," said Genrai.

"No. You can't tell him *anything*. Because if you tell him, he'll go straight to Wingmaster Taimenai. Or to his . . . his uncle. You know he will," Trei added when Genrai looked blank. "He'll have to. You *know* that."

"I guess," the older boy said, not looking happy about it.

"Besides," Trei said, realizing something else, "even if that wasn't true, if Ceirfei knew we were going to do something dangerous and against the rules, you know he'd insist on coming with us—*and* on taking the most dangerous part himself."

Genrai held up his hands, conceding the point. "You're right about *that*," he said, this time with conviction.

Trei got to his feet and said, "All I'll do right now is *talk* to my cousin."

Genrai nodded. "Exactly. Just talk. But I think . . . I think maybe you should hurry. We'll wait for you. But I think there're some things we can do while we wait. Rekei, don't we have a map of the waystations between here and the coast somewhere?"

Trei found his crystal pendant, laid his hand on the nearest door—it happened to lead to the bathing room, but when he whispered Araenè's name and opened it, it didn't open to the baths. It opened instead to a spacious twelve-walled hall, with a curving balustrade where a narrow stair came up in the middle of the floor, turned three times in a neat spiral, and disappeared again into the ceiling.

A warm yellow glow fell across an incredible array of spheres. All the walls were lined with them: shelf after shelf. Stone of every kind, glass of every color, polished wood and rough-textured clay and polished metal; some of the spheres were larger than a man's head and some smaller than the tip of a finger. Some of them glittered brilliantly with light; others seemed to *absorb* light; one, near at hand, glowed as though it contained its own internal fire. And mirrors on every wall doubled and redoubled the number of spheres until they seemed as uncountable as stars in the summer sky.

Araenè sat cross-legged in the midst of all these spheres and mirrors. She was holding a small one—brown, swirled with patterns of darker brown and sulfur yellow—in one hand. In her other hand she held a quill. A book lay open beside her, its page half filled with small, cramped writing. Other books lay piled haphazardly across the floor.

Araenè had been gazing intently into the brown sphere, but now at last, perhaps realizing she had heard a door open, she turned to look over her shoulder. Her eyes, wide and distracted, met his. "Trei!" she exclaimed.

Trei, only half aware of the other boys murmuring in surprise behind him, stepped forward and let the door swing shut behind him. "You're thinner," he said, staring at his cousin. "You look . . ." He was unable to put his impression into words, and crouched down instead to take the quill out of Araenè's hand before she could blot her page. "Are you all right?"

"Well, of course!" Araenè said, too quickly. She put the sphere down on the floor and started to get to her feet, but swayed. Trei caught her arm to steady her, but Araenè jerked back and stared at him.

Trei looked around at the many-sided room, the spheres, the spiral stairway. He hadn't asked himself what Araenè might be doing, how she might be spending her days in the mages' school. Now he felt guilty for that thoughtlessness and bewildered at the place in which he had found his cousin.

He looked at her in concern. Her chestnut hair seemed . . . darker than he remembered, rougher, though perhaps that was only because it was so short now. Or because she was pale. Though that might be the quality of the light . . . but he was sure she was thinner than she had been a week ago. Her eyes were huge and dark in her fine-boned face, and they held a new kind of strain that worried him. "Do you always study so late?"

"Sometimes," Araenè answered stiffly. She glanced around, distracted, at the clutter of spheres. "I need to work—"

"This late?" Trei asked her, dismayed. "With the ships coming? Master Tnegun's so hard a taskmaster?"

"Well—"

"We can't talk here." Trei waved a hand to encompass the room. "It's too strange."

Araenè gazed at him for a moment. At last her brow creased and she nodded. "All right. This way." She led the way toward the central stair. Trei, glancing back, found that the door he'd come through had disappeared. Not only that, but there seemed no place for any door in these walls lined with spheres and mirrors.

"What did the door look like from this side?" Trei wondered aloud. "A frameless door set right into the air?"

"Yes, exactly. Doors are untrustworthy," Araenè said over her shoulder. "But here, this might do." They'd descended nine turns of the spiral stair to reach a landing, and Araenè opened a door that seemed made of glass and pewter. It opened onto a cluttered room filled with smoke, light, crashing sounds, and voices shouting.

"No," Araenè said, shutting the door again quickly.

"But were those people all right?" Trei asked, trying to decide whether he should be alarmed.

"Oh, yes. That was Jenekei and Taobai; they're always smashing up the workroom, but they'll clean it up before Tichorei wants it in the morning. Here—" She opened the door again, but this time it opened on a much more ordinary room, lit by round porcelain lamps. Blue walls, dark furniture, and a window open to the humid warmth of the night: this was far more comfortable.

"Yes. My apartment," Araenè said, and stepped through the door with an odd wariness that Trei didn't understand. She kept a foot on the threshold while she waved Trei past her, then followed him into the room and shut the door—and relaxed, suddenly and visibly. She said, as though struck by a sudden thought, "Trei, if you've come to find out if we know anything about how to stop the Tolounnese warships, we don't. Or if the masters do, they haven't told us."

"That's not why I came." Trei explained in a few words about the Teraica engines and what the Tolounnese mages were probably using them for and what he thought might be done about them. For several minutes after he was done, Araenè said nothing at all, and Trei began almost to wonder whether his cousin might think—actually might wonder—

Then Araenè said, "I have this, um. This . . . um." She shook her head, crossed the room, and knelt to dig through one of her drawers. Then, turning, she held out to Trei a large glass sphere filled with fire. "This," she said.

"What is it?" Trei touched the sphere warily with the tip of one finger. To his surprise, it did not feel hot to the touch. It certainly *looked* hot. He looked admiringly at his cousin. "Did you make this?"

"It's nice you think I could. Um. This is, um." Araenè looked embarrassed. "A fire dragon's egg. I, well. I promised to, um, quicken it. That means . . ."

"I think I know what it means." Trei stared at the egg. "You think it would hatch if someone threw it in one of the engines at Teraica? Why would that help? How did you . . . You promised a *dragon*. . . ."

"I wasn't supposed to," Araenè admitted. "You're not supposed to promise dragons anything. But I did. And I saw . . . that is, I think I saw . . . I *did* see your engines. The dragon showed them to me when it gave me the egg. Three iron buildings on a gray shore, with fire inside them and beneath them. Those must be your engines, Trei, what else would they be? I think you ought to take the egg, Trei, I really do. I think I'm *supposed* to give it to you. The dragon said I should, um, 'cast it upon the winds and into the furnace of the earth.' If I give it to you, isn't that casting it upon the wind? And if you throw it into one of the engines at Teraica, isn't *that* casting it into the furnace of the earth?"

Trei looked doubtfully at the egg. "But would an engine get hotter if a young fire dragon hatched inside it? Why?"

Araenè handed the egg to Trei, jumped to her feet, and got

a thick book off the top of a stack piled on the floor. "Look," she said, bringing the book back to show it to Trei. "I got this out of Master Tnegun's library. I'm supposed to be studying about numbers, but this one has a lot about dragons in it; that's why I really got it. I was trying to see how I could quicken the egg, but I couldn't figure out . . . But now look, when it's talking about volcanoes . . . um, something about eggs hatching and violent fires, hmm, oh, here it is—'The cracking of the egg of the fire dragon is attended by violence and raging heat, the very stone shatters, molten stone is forced to the surface. . . .' Oh, and here, all this part is about volcanoes and fire dragons, see?"

Trei looked at the illustration his cousin showed him, a fiery mountain and flaming dragon, done all in vermilion ink and gold leaf. It looked very real. Too real. He thought about Mount Ghaonnè, about the huge cracks torn into the mountain's side, about the living fire within . . . about the dragon he'd dreamed he'd seen within the burning mountain. He shuddered.

"Oh, Trei. I'm sorry. I wasn't thinking." Araenè tried to take the book back.

Trei shook his head, holding on to it. He studied the illuminated image of the volcano, deliberately refusing to look away. "No, it's . . . that's all right. You think that if, um. If someone threw this egg into one of the Tolounnese engines, its hatching would create heat enough to break open the earth underneath the furnace? Or is molten fire only found . . . underneath the mountains of the north?"

"I think there must be fire underneath Teraica, too. I saw . . . I think the dragon showed me that, too. But we do have to be careful not to hurt the egg." Araenè took it back from Trei and examined it worriedly.

Trei nodded, staring at the egg. Flames seemed to crawl over its surface. It looked . . . really powerful. "I don't think . . . It doesn't look very, um. Very breakable."

"I guess it isn't." His cousin hesitated, cradling the egg protectively . . . but then she held it out to him again.

Trei took it. It was absurdly light. He imagined he could still somehow feel the heat it contained even through its cool shell. "You think it will work."

Araenè nodded. "I think it will. I think if you throw this into one of the Tolounnese engines, it will quicken. And I really do think that will create a huge burst of heat, just as you want. That would redeem my promise to the dragon *and* ruin the engine. I *think* it will work. And I . . . honestly, I can't think what else might."

Trei nodded slowly. "All right."

"I wish you could stay here and watch the dawn with me. But we're all supposed to be up in the Tower of the Winds at dawn so we can see the Tolounnese ships come. I think Master Akhai thinks we might be able to do something. . . ." She hesitated.

"You don't think so?" Trei guessed.

"Well . . . I think Master Tnegun doesn't think we can do enough to stop the ships," Araenè said at last. "So I don't suppose we can. They say if Master Cassameirin were here—actually, I'm not sure what they think he could do, but they say he's clever. But, anyway, nobody knows where he is." She nodded with sudden decision toward the egg Trei now held. "So you take that. You take it, and you use it."

"If I can," Trei assured her. He wrapped the egg up in a fold of cloth his cousin gave him. "Araenè—*are* you all right?"

"Of course," his cousin said, too quickly. "It's almost dawn. You'd better go."

She went to the door, and Trei noticed again how cautious she was about the door, even though it opened properly to the novitiate sleeping hall on the first try, and how she kept a foot in the open door until they were through, and he wondered a little about that caution, but then the other novices were crowding forward and he forgot the question that had been in the back of his mind.

The Tolounnese ships arrived at dawn, along with Ceirfei, whose uncle had ordered him back to the kajurai precincts.

"My uncle thinks I'll be safer here," Ceirfei said, in a tone- less voice that made it clear he was ashamed to have been or- dered to safety.

"And so you will be," Genrai said firmly, but gave Trei a raised-eyebrow glance that Trei could answer only with a shrug.

The novices watched the Tolounnese ships from a balcony of a white tower, one of the highest towers within the kajurai precincts, where novices were not normally permitted. Trei was glad for the additional height, for the ships brought an un- natural calm with them: air as heavy and thick as syrup, visible to kajurai eyes as a flat deadness without any of the usual com- plicated structure of wind and pressure. The sea around the ships was pressed out as flat as glass, but the zone of dead air only reached about three times the height of the ships' masts: not nearly as high as their balcony.

The sails of the ships hung limp from their masts, but Trei, leaning to look over the edge of the novices' balcony, saw the long oars reach forward and pull back, reach forward and pull back, and then run in and lock into their resting positions. The ships glided slowly through the quiet water into Milendri's vast shadow, dropped anchors fore and aft, and settled into their positions.

There were fifteen ships: slender shapes with sharp-edged iron prows for ramming and three-tiered ranks of long oars on either side for speed and maneuverability. Not that they needed either to attack the Islands. What they needed for that were men and a way to *reach* the Islands. Trei guessed that each ship might hold hundreds of soldiers—if all the men pulling the oars were soldiers, which seemed likely. And given the reports about Islands falling into the sea, they could all guess how the Tolounnese commanders meant to get their men up to the Islands. Or, more likely, the reverse . . .

Narrow strips of steel had been inlaid from bow to stern down each ship's uppermost deck and similarly down the hull between the banks of oars; the metal blazed in the brilliant light. . . . No, it *wasn't* merely the sunlight that made the metal shine like that: power that was actually visible to Trei's kajurai eyes ran in swift pulses down the steel and curled out like steam around and behind each ship. Trei could see the mages on the nearest ship: a man on the captain's afterdeck, surrounded by clouds of thickly gathered magic.

Though kajuraihi, wings red or gold or white, were soaring in high spirals above the region of dead air, no dragons were visible anywhere. And all those watching from the balcony felt the shudder as Milendri began to settle heavily toward the sea and the waiting ships.

They all flinched; Tokabii let out a little squeak of surprise and then looked embarrassed, but even Rekei didn't tease him about it. "Gods," muttered Ceirfei, catching the balcony railing and peering over. He was pale, but steady: they had known this was going to happen.

The Island settled . . . and steadied. But then it shuddered again and dropped once more, this time falling faster and farther. Both Kojran and Rekei yelped, and Genrai grunted. They jerked to a sharp halt for a moment and then dropped again. Trei clung to the balcony railing with a grip that hurt his hands. He couldn't have made a sound to save his life.

They steadied again at last, much lower in the air. Trei wondered whether the lowermost tips of jagged stone were underwater yet and guessed they probably were. He stared down at the flat air, now hardly a wing-length below their balcony, and realized that even if the Island mages *could* fight the Tolounnese mages, they might not dare: if the Tolounnese mages lost control, or lost too much of their power, then unless the living wind came back right away, Milendri would fall not only into the water, but all the way to the bottom of the sea.

"We're still awfully high for them to reach," Genrai observed shakily.

"Wait," said Ceirfei. They waited tensely. But the Island did not sink lower.

Instead the deck of the nearest ship rose up. No. Not the deck itself, but the strips of metal that sheathed it. Those ratcheted jerkily up off the deck until they tilted upward at an awkward, straining angle. Then the steel boarding ladders, for that was what they were, flung themselves up and out from the ship with roaring screams and bright, hot billows of steam. Their leading edges, lined with glittering hooks, slammed against the Island's side, shattered the outermost walls of Canpra's belowground buildings, scraped down along the red stone, caught on broken stonework, and held.

"Gods!" Genrai said.

Tolounnese soldiers began to climb up the ladders, toward the balconies and wide windows and broken walls of Canpra's underground city. Shouts came from every side. Islanders were running down into the underground parts of the city, hurrying into places where they might meet the entering Tolounnese. Trei imagined the meeting between the Islanders and the Tolounnese soldiers, in the broken towers, among buckling walls and shattered ceilings and falling stones. He swallowed. "Don't you have *any* soldiers?" he asked Ceirfei.

Ceirfei shook his head. "Real soldiers, soldiers meant to do more than keep order in the streets on a wild festival day? Soldiers meant to stand up against the likes of that? No."

"We'll fight," Genrai said. He, too, was grim. "Soldiers or not." He looked around, as though he might find a sword, or at least a club, waiting conveniently close at hand.

Trei could just imagine what professional Tolounnese soldiers would do to a lot of Islanders armed with knives and clubs. Then he tried hard, and unsuccessfully, *not* to imagine it. Maybe it wouldn't happen. Maybe the Islanders would surrender quickly. But Genrai had said, *We'll fight,* and Trei knew they would try. A lot of Islanders would die, and then they'd be defeated anyway, and Trei could hardly stand to think of either the deaths or the defeat. He knew, for the first time with a visceral certainty, that he'd really meant it when he'd insisted to Genrai, *I would stop them if I could.*

Genrai glanced at Ceirfei and suddenly left the balcony.

"Where's he going?" Tokabii asked, astonished.

"I don't know," Ceirfei answered. He looked at Trei, his eyebrows raised, but Trei could only shake his head.

Genrai came back in and said curtly to Ceirfei, "The wingmaster wants you."

Ceirfei stared at the other boy, outraged. "What, you suggested he tuck me away somewhere safer still?"

"Yes," Genrai snapped. He was very pale, but determined. "Though I shouldn't have needed to! You ought to have the sense to know when to step back on your own account! Now, Wingmaster Taimenai expects you: will you keep him waiting?"

For a moment, Trei thought Ceirfei might blaze into a rage none of them had the time—or the ability—to withstand. But then the young prince simply turned on his heel and stalked out. His furious temper was plain from the stiffness of his back. But he went.

"I didn't think of that," Trei said shakily to Genrai.

Genrai gave him a wry look. "The wingmaster had already sent to tell us we're *all* supposed to fly over to Kotipa, quick while we can still reach good air. We haven't much time. Kojran, you and Tokabii lay out the wings. Trei, run get the thing your cousin gave you—you *are* willing to do this? You're quite sure?" He gave Trei a steady look, meaning he'd guessed what Trei already knew: that no one, no matter how skilled in the air, would find it very easy to fly down to a close-guarded

Tolounnese furnace, throw something into it, and then just fly away.

"Yes," Trei whispered. Then he said it more strongly. "Yes, I'll go. But you—"

"We'll all go at least partway. I'll go all the way. In case . . . Well, we should have somebody to . . . to be a second chance." He meant that he would throw the egg into the furnace if, at the last moment, Trei couldn't or just wouldn't.

Trei said, "Someone needs to stay here and explain to . . . explain. In case."

Genrai shook his head. "They'll figure it out if we succeed. And if we fail, what will it matter? We'll get everything else ready. Go. Run!"

Trei did run. He wrapped the dragon's egg up in a blanket, tied the blanket across his chest like a sling, and ran back to the balcony.

All the others were already wearing their wings. Trei made sure the egg was secure and struggled into his. He seemed especially clumsy now, when speed mattered. Genrai helped, his face taut with effort as he struggled to do up Trei's buckles without raking his own wings against the floor or walls. But at last it was done, and they could all let themselves drop off the balcony and catch the wind, working hard to get lift before they could fall into the dead air below.

"Up!" shouted Genrai. "Up and out!" Then an arrow cut through the feathers at the tip of his left wing, and he shouted in startled terror and clawed for height.

There were more arrows—somewhere close by, someone screamed—then a man Trei didn't know, a kajurai with fire-gold wings, cut between him and the ships, perilously close to the region of dead air. The gold-winged kajurai flung something down at the ships below, and the archers stopped shooting at Trei and started aiming at their attacker. The kajurai flung something else and then rose sharply, his wings beating hard as fire bloomed below.

Trei didn't stay to watch. He found Kotipa in the distance, took his bearings, and flew north and east. Someone flew way over to his right: Rekei, he thought at first. But then something about the way that figure flew told him it was not Rekei, but Kojran. He looked for Rekei—found Genrai instead. There was no sign of Rekei. He remembered the arrows, someone screaming; he didn't want to believe it had been his friend, but if it hadn't, where *was* Rekei? Trei looked around once more.

A kajurai dropped out of the heights: the second-ranked kajurai Rei Kensenè. He slid down to balance on the wind next to Trei, their wingtips only a foot apart. "Get over to Kotipa!" he shouted. "Fool! You can't help here: you haven't the strength or the training! Did Ceirfei come out here? *Did you bring Ceirfei out here?*"

Trei shouted, "No! Genrai got him out of the way before we came out!"

"Thank the generous Gods! Get over to Kotipa!"

"Yes, all right! Did you see Rekei?"

Rei hesitated. Then he shouted, "No!" and slipped the wind abruptly through his wings, wheeling back toward Milendri.

Trei let himself slide down a curve of wind, dropping toward Tokabii and Genrai. Kojran closed up on their other side. The trailing edge of his right wing was ragged; more than one arrow had gone through his wing, Trei guessed. It was only by the grace of the Gods none of the arrows had hit somewhere worse. He cried, "Did you see Rekei?"

"No!" shouted Kojran, and Genrai echoed him, "No!"

"He was hit! He fell into the bad air, but I think another kajurai might have caught him!" shouted Tokabii.

They all flew on in silence for a moment. Trei, at least, was thinking about how impossible it would have been for any kajurai, no matter how strong and skilled, to carry a wounded boy through that unnaturally heavy air.

"What did Rei say?" Genrai shouted over at last.

"He said to go to Kotipa!" Trei answered.

"We'll head for Bodonè instead!" Genrai answered. "That way! It's on the way to Teraica! We can land there to get water!"

Trei was surprised that the other boy still seemed to assume they were actually going to head for Teraica. After whatever had happened to Rekei, Trei felt himself almost wanting to just obey orders and head for the Island of Dragons.

But, with Genrai leading, they all climbed instead into a rising spiral. When they turned, they could see Milendri. The Island was far behind them now, yet the flashes of light and fire were still clearly visible. The heavy air was visible, too: from this distance, it looked darker and more solid than any air ought to.

Trei thought they were all hoping someone else would suggest staying safe on Bodonè, but no one did. They only stopped there to rest. Genrai shared out some hard bread he'd brought, gave everybody a flask to fill at a nearby pool, and brought out a sighting glass to measure against the stars as they began to come out. Trei, who hadn't thought to bring any of those things, gave the older boy a respectful look. "Ceirfei was right—you do have sense."

Genrai flushed. "I had time to think about what to bring while you went to visit your cousin."

And he'd tried to live up to Ceirfei's good opinion, yes. Trei understood that perfectly. He gestured toward the sighting glass. "Do you think we should fly at night?"

"No, do we have to?" Tokabii, examining his damaged wing, looked up in dismay. "I'm tired—and look at all these broken feathers! Lucky the arrows missed the primaries. Throw me that pouch of spares, Kojran, will you?"

Genrai looked grim. "We'll get the worst-damaged feathers replaced, 'Kabii, but then I think we'd best press our speed. Don't you?"

The boys all looked at one another. Trei knew they were all thinking about those Tolounnese ships, about the heavy air pressing the dragons away from the Islands and bringing Milendri down where the siege ladders could reach it. Tokabii bent his head over his repairs, but he didn't object again.

"After Rekei, you're the next best at star navigation," Genrai said to Trei. He hesitated, then added deliberately, "Without you, we can't go on at all, you know. None of the rest of us can do the math in our heads. Are you sure—?"

Trei knew Genrai was asking once more: *Are you sure* you *want to take the Islands' side against Tolounn? Now that it comes to this, are you* sure *you're willing to risk your life for the Islands?* His first impulse was toward anger: hadn't he already answered those doubts two and three times over? But his anger died in the face of Genrai's wary concern . . . which left room for all his doubts, which crowded into the forefront of his mind. He turned away from the other boys, staring away in the direction of Milendri.

Tolounn had everything: the artificers who'd made the steam engines, and the mages who'd figured out how to harness the huge power of those engines, and the slender iron-prowed warships, and all the soldiers. And Tolounn had the aggression and the, what, the will to win?

The Islands might share the will to win. But other than that, they had only the kajuraihi, who couldn't even fly through the dead air the Tolounnese ships had brought with them. And the egg a fire dragon had given Araenè, which Araenè had in turn given to him. Had the dragon somehow known its sky kin were going to be forced away from their chosen habitation? Was *that* the reason, or a reason, it had given its egg to his cousin?

But Trei didn't know how to put any of his questions or thoughts or decisions into words. At last he said merely, "I'm sure."

Genrai gave him a slow nod, accepting this. "All right."

Kojran, who'd been standing at the edge of the Island, shading his eyes and staring up into the sky, turned and shouted, "The first stars are out!"

Genrai nodded again. "Then I think we'd better fly."

Trei returned the older boy's nod. But then he hesitated, glancing at the other novices. "Tokabii, Kojran—you could stay here."

"What? No!" said Tokabii, offended.

Kojran, to Trei's surprise, actually seemed to consider this suggestion. "No," he said at last. "Not here." He hesitated for another moment and then added, "Maybe at a waystation. Like Kerii?" He looked at Genrai.

"Maybe," said Genrai.

"What?" asked Trei, confused.

"It's from a play," Genrai said. "Never mind, Kojran, no need to explain it right now. Trei, you go first. Do you have your heading clear? Straight north until, um, would it be half past third bell? Then ten points north-northeast, and we should be just about on top of the first waystation by dawn, if we hold a good pace. We don't want to make it before dawn, though."

Because if they reached the floating rock of the waystation in the dark, he meant, they would probably fly right past it. "If we do miss the first waystation," Trei asked, "how much farther to the second?"

"Too far," Genrai said, and waited, his eyes on Trei's. When Trei slowly nodded, Genrai went on, "We'll go high first, dive to get speed, hold a fast pace. Kojran and Tokabii, you'll fly out to either side of Trei, half a span back. I'll come behind—you boys will have to stay in place because I'll be too far back to see Trei. Hear me?"

The younger Third City boys both looked insulted. "Go on!" Kojran said scornfully. "You think we can't hold a formation?"

"It'll be harder when you're tired," Genrai said. "Ninety miles to the first waystation. You both think you can do that? Don't say yes if you mean no: no one will be able to carry you if you can't make the distance." He looked stern, and much older than seventeen.

Kojran said proudly, "We can make it. We've done ninety miles before."

Not after fighting clear of Milendri while dodging arrows, then flying eighty miles to Bodonè, then resting for only a few bells. But no one pointed this out. Trei helped Tokabii with his wings while Genrai helped Kojran. Next he let Genrai help him with his own. Then he arched his wings, lifted straight up off the surface of the Island, and turned in a tight spiral, waiting for the others to join him.

IO

The mages and adjuvants and apprentices of the Floating Islands—all but the legendary and, as far as Araenè could tell, possibly imaginary Master Cassameirin—watched the arrival of the Tolounnese ships from the highest balcony of the square-sided Horera Tower, the Tower of the Winds. But there were no winds today. Except where the ships' oars splashed, the sea lay as flat and gray as though it had been beaten out of a sheet of pewter.

"Sheer power. No subtlety to it at all," Master Akhai commented. Bearded, handsome, and the youngest of the masters, Master Akhai had intimidated Araenè from the first moment she'd met him: she felt that he looked too closely at things and noticed too much. But he wasn't looking at her now. Nor was he watching the Tolounnese ships. His face was tilted up to the sky, his too-piercing gaze fixed on it. "They've forced the dragons out of the Islands. And if we've lost the dragon winds—" He caught the balcony railing as the whole Island of

Milendri abruptly staggered in the air and dropped, in a series of unsteady lurches, toward the sea.

It felt like the Island was falling right out from under them.

Araenè's sharp cry was disconcertingly high-pitched, but she hoped no one had heard it, lost as it was in the exclamations and shouts of the other apprentices and adjuvants. Master Tnegun closed a powerful hand on her elbow to help her stay on her feet, everyone was grabbing at the railing or the tower wall or each other, one of the adjuvants caught Taobai as he lost his balance, and Master Kopapei caught his little apprentice, Cesei. Jenekei and Sayai braced each other, but Tichorei missed his grab and fell to his knees, swearing in embarrassment and fear. His master, Master Camatii, leaned down to lift him back to his feet, and Araenè realized at last that Milendri was no longer falling. Maybe they weren't all going to drown after all—well, that made sense; why would the Tolounnese have sent warships at all if they just meant to drown the Islands? She shrugged away from her master's grip, embarrassed to have panicked.

Master Yamatei cautiously let go of Kebei and Kepai; he'd steadied one twin with each hand. He said to Master Akhai, "I think subtlety is not the rod by which the Tolounnese mages measure their success." His dry, almost amused tone gave no indication of fear.

Master Yamatei was a bland, even insipid-looking man who, to Araenè, seemed to have exactly the appearance and manner of any midlevel ministry official. But the twins, who were his apprentices, had told her he was actually clever and subtle and very hard to fool about anything, so Araenè had avoided him almost as carefully as she had avoided Master Akhai. But Master Yamatei had other things to think about now and did not even seem to notice Araenè.

The healer mage, Master Camatii, shook his head at Master Yamatei's black humor. "There will be bones broken just from that drop, though no Tolounnese soldier has yet set foot on Milendri. Imagine being on a stair when that happened. Worse: the Island itself won't be the only thing that dropped. With the dragon winds gone, all our floating bridges and stairways will have fallen." He glanced from Master Kopapei to Master Tnegun and back to Kopapei. "I should go. Shall I go? There will be work for me out in the city. If you have no suggestion for how else I should spend my efforts . . ."

"Indeed." Big Master Kopapei looked grimmer than Araenè had ever imagined the good-humored master *could* look. "You must go. Tichorei, if you will?" With a gesture, he invited Camatii's apprentice to join him.

Master Camatii looked at Tichorei, began to speak, closed his mouth again without saying a word, and gave his apprentice a gentle shove toward Kopapei. Then he beckoned to the three adjuvants nearest him and vanished. The three adjuvants vanished as well. The heavy air closed into the space where they'd stood with an audible but strangely flat sound.

Tichorei, his expression strained, joined Kanii and little Cesei near Master Kopapei. Two of the other adjuvants were also standing near Master Kopapei. One or two or three stood close to each of the masters. Araenè didn't really know any of them; apprentices hardly ever spoke to adjuvants, and as far as she could tell, adjuvants put a certain dedication into keeping clear of apprentices. But at least the *adjuvants* knew what role they would play when the masters decided what to do: they would furnish the power the masters needed to act. Though she also knew there couldn't be enough adjuvants in the whole world to match the sheer brute strength those ships carried with them, at least that was a useful—a *crucial*—role. What she wondered was what role the *apprentices* would play. If she was expected to do something herself, she was afraid that whatever it was, she probably would not be able to do it.

"If we were able to call back the winds, the dragons should return as well," Master Akhai said to Master Kopapei. Araenè hadn't really realized that Master Kopapei was in some way the head of the school, but she thought now, from the way the other mages deferred to him, that he must be. "Though I don't know whether that's of any practical importance, as I confess I don't see any possible way we can break *that*." Akhai gestured out over the balcony railing.

That? What? Araenè peered out at the blank air. Whatever Master Akhai was indicating, she couldn't see it. Tichorei and Taobai were both nodding; so were Kanii and Jenekei and the twins. Even little Cesei was nodding; could *everyone* see what Akhai meant except her? If she couldn't, was that because she was so new, or because she hadn't let Master Tnegun see into her mind, or simply because she was a girl? She glanced uncertainly at her master.

Master Tnegun was standing, one hand resting lightly on the railing, studying the Tolounnese ships. His dark face was calm, but there was a tightness around his eyes that told Araenè he was afraid. That frightened her. More. Aware of her gaze on him, he dropped his other hand to rest on her shoulder and smiled down at her. Araenè only wished she saw reassurance in that smile. But she could not pretend, even to herself, that she saw anything of the kind.

"It's futile to set our strength against the augmented power of the Tolounnese mages," Master Tnegun said to the other masters. "On the other hand . . . they must be thoroughly engaged with the necessity of holding Milendri in place. They can't release the Island now: if they do, we might well sink to the bottom of the sea before the dragons could return with their winds to lift us back into the sky."

"Possibly they'll consider that a tactic rather than a problem," Master Yamatei said drily.

"No," Master Kopapei disagreed. "If they wanted to drown Milendri, they'd never have brought fifteen ships. No, Tnegun's correct: they will neither allow the dragons to return nor allow us to drown."

"And thus we may have identified the only two tactics that the Tolounnese will not use," observed Master Tnegun, with a kind of grim amusement.

"Will they not?" Master Yamatei did not look as though he found this optimism persuasive. "The ability to drown Milendri is a threat we can't answer. They must know it."

Master Tnegun shook his head. "The Tolounnese do not by any means wish to make good any such threat. A threat you will not carry out is no threat. Thus the Tolounnese must exercise restraint, which gives us an opportunity. But if we will act at all, we must be swift, and if we are to make our presence felt, we must step sideways around their power, not meet it head-on."

"You have a suggestion?" Master Yamatei asked. To

Araenè's surprise, she thought she heard an almost hostile note in his tone.

At that moment, the first siege ladder smashed against Milendri, maybe a thousand feet from where the mages stood. Then another, directly below the mages' balcony—again, Araenè was not the only one to cry out, but again her cry was lost among the others. Both ladders raked downward, caught, and clung. Steam billowed out across the water. Black gulls wheeled, crying in outrage, as men began to climb upward from the Tolounnese ships. Araenè looked wildly at Master Tnegun. *Aren't we going to do something?* Her master only gave her an absent little calm-down pat. Araenè couldn't imagine why she should be calm, with the Tolounnese soldiers climbing up right toward their balcony—then the Tower of the Winds shivered, twisted itself somehow, and shifted half a mile to the north. From this distance, the Tolounnese ships were barely visible. But Araenè thought she could, even so far removed, hear the shouts of the Tolounnese soldiers and the screams of the people in the besieged part of the city.

"We cannot break the power of the Tolounnese mages!" Master Yamatei said, with a new urgency in his tone. "We dare not even *disrupt* it—unless we do not mind the Island falling into the sea. Some of us might find that outcome objectionable."

Master Tnegun did not appear to notice the edge in the other mage's tone. He merely replied, "We must leave be the mages and attack the men. It will not be enough, but it is what we can do—and perhaps, if we delay the Tolounnese victory, the kajuraihi may find a way to recall the dragon winds." Turning to Master Kopapei, he added, "Kopapei, you are aware, I have more experience with warfare than any other mage in the Islands."

Master Kopapei did not look at all surprised at this statement. He held up one broad hand, stopping Master Yamatei when the other mage seemed to want to protest, and nodded for Master Tnegun to continue.

"If we confront the Tolounnese mages directly, we will find either that they have the strength to crush us while maintaining their hold on Milendri, which would be bad, or else that they do not, which would be worse. I suspect they themselves do not know whether or not they have such strength. If we force them to respond to us, we may *all* discover that the Island has slipped their hold. We cannot afford that risk."

"So, you suggest?" Master Kopapei asked.

"We may have lost the dragon winds, but . . . though the fire at the heart of the school burns low now our dragon has died, we yet have some of its strength contained in stone."

Araenè flinched: she had thought the fire dragon might be ill, she had guessed it might be dying, but she had not known it had actually *died*. For a moment, she could remember nothing but its grief, the way it had pleaded with her: *Quicken my child*. Her throat closed with grief of her own, though she did not know why, and with fear. What if she'd been wrong? Wrong to give the dragon's egg to Trei, wrong about everything? Too late to think again, too late to call it back to her hands—she'd been right, she *had* to have been right—

Then Master Tnegun plucked a sphere out of the air, and Araenè blinked and caught her breath, almost thankful to have been recalled to the immediate danger and terror of the present moment. Not that it was a dramatic sphere. It wasn't brilliant with fire, as Araenè might have expected; it wasn't even red or flame orange. It was a plain sphere of some black-flecked white stone, though with a distinctive greasy luster. Despite its cool, heavy appearance, it tasted of warm spices: nutmeg and cloves and cassia. It was nepheline . . . nepheline something. Nepheline syenite, that was it. Syenite was one of the stones "born in fire," and nepheline . . . she couldn't remember.

"You might introduce the Tolounnese soldiers to Island fire," Master Tnegun said to Master Yamatei. "No matter how courageous, soldiers cannot climb steel heated to forge heat."

Master Yamatei looked irresolute. Then, as another distant, reverberating crash echoed through the Island, he flinched and glanced quickly at Master Kopapei, who gave him a curt wave, *Go on*. Master Yamatei turned back to Master Tnegun with a nod. "Yes," he said, and carefully, as though it might burn him, took the sphere Master Tnegun held out to him. Then he nodded to two of the adjuvants. All three of them disappeared. The air thumped flatly inward where they had stood.

"Akhai." Master Tnegun turned to the youngest mage. "I would imagine Yamatei will be able to block a certain number of siege ladders. Nevertheless, many soldiers will undoubtedly gain access to Canpra's underground areas. They will be most readily resisted if they can be held to the underground corridors rather than allowed to reach the open streets." He offered the mage a sphere of polished granite and a smaller one of tourmaline. The granite sphere tasted of palm sugar and anise, the tourmaline of bitter ash and fenugreek.

Master Akhai looked surprised. "Granite for making and unmaking . . . very well. But tourmaline?"

"The brighter uses of tourmaline are not what I have in mind," Master Tnegun said. "Think of smothering fire . . . smothering light. Think of summoning a heavy darkness into the belowground corridors and rooms of Canpra."

Akhai smiled—rather a fierce smile. "Yes, good. Effective, yet indirect and subtle." He, too, took several adjuvants with him when he vanished.

"Neither Yamatei nor Akhai will find their tasks so simple as you have suggested," Master Kopapei said to Master Tnegun in a low voice. Master Tnegun did not seem surprised by this, but only nodded.

Fire bloomed suddenly, low against the red stone of the Island's flanks, and a deep, cracking *boom* sounded through the air. Araenè whirled to look, along with the other apprentices, nor was she alone in exclaiming aloud as one of the siege ladders broke free from the Island and tumbled through the still air toward the glass-flat sea. Water fountained upward where it struck. Araenè looked quickly at Master Tnegun's face.

He was not looking at her. His gaze was locked with Master Kopapei's.

"No. Not so subtle as we might wish," Master Kopapei said, as though answering a comment Araenè had not heard. "The Tolounnese mages won't allow that to pass." He paused, his head tilted to the side as though listening for a moment. Then he said, "Yes, there they are now. You feel that? They're extending their attention quite far. And if they overextend and drop Milendri, well, they might be annoyed, but the results would be rather worse for us—"

"Yes," agreed Master Tnegun.

Master Kopapei sighed. "I'll do what I can. You will, I hope, protect—" He gestured, his wave taking in the balcony and, by implication, all the apprentices and the entire school.

Master Tnegun inclined his head. "I shall watch and wait," he said. "I shall supervise the apprentices, and conserve my strength, and the strength of what adjuvants you will spare to wait with me." If he was afraid now, Araenè could not see it. His gaze met Kopapei's with calm reserve.

"Just so." Master Kopapei looked around at the remaining adjuvants. "I believe I shall ask . . . Koranai and Meitai to support me." His voice gentled. "And Sayai."

"Me?" Sayai said. He sounded both nervous and uncertain, as though he guessed why Master Kopapei might have singled him out but hoped he was wrong.

"If you will," the master said, still very gently. "I'm sorry, Sayai. You will never be a mage. But you might become a strong adjuvant—if you would. I hope you will. I shall need your strength now."

His face rigid with the effort to hold back anger or disappointment, Sayai moved slowly to stand in front of Master Kopapei, who put a sympathetic hand on his shoulder and said to Master Tnegun, "Tnegun, my friend. Take care, and don't act too hastily—but I hope that if you see something useful to do, you aren't too slow to act, either." He vanished, taking Sayai and two of the adjuvants with him.

Little Cesei took a distracted step toward the balcony's edge, where his master had stood.

Master Tnegun dropped a hand to rest on the boy's shoulder. "No."

235

Cesei's mouth set stubbornly.

Kanii came over and put an arm around the little boy's shoulders. They and all the rest remaining on the balcony stared at Master Tnegun: three adjuvants, and all the apprentices except poor Sayai. And Araenè, a little apart from the others. She wondered why it was *her* master who was left to "supervise the apprentices" and "protect the school." She wanted to ask, but did not dare. She began to ask instead what they would do, and stopped as a sort of huge, echoing, silent crash seemed suddenly to ring noiselessly out across the Island.

"What was that?" Cesei asked, his voice shrill.

Master Tnegun sighed. "That was a backlash. Someone has overextended his strength and lost control of his spellwork, and the sphere he was using has been allowed to crack. What you felt just then was the magic it contained being released in one dangerous burst of undirected power." He turned his head to meet Tichorei's eyes. "I think that was Master Yamatei. Do you agree?"

Tichorei nodded decisively, though with seeming reluctance.

Master Tnegun barely smiled. "You have an affinity for knowing and naming," he observed. "Camatii has trained you to handle backlash and overextension? Yes, good. And you still have considerable strength. Very good. All your skills will be useful now. I will ask you to go to the hall of spheres and mirrors and watch for overextension. It may yet be possible to catch Yamatei and protect him from the full consequences of the backlash."

Tichorei cleared his throat. "Yes, I'll try. Except you—"

236

"I have no affinity for healing," Master Tnegun said gently. "And far less strength than you. I will stay here and wait for the odd chance. Go. Take the youngest apprentices with you. They will be far safer in the hall of spheres. Arei, Cesei, go with Tichorei."

"Maybe we could help you here—" Araenè began.

Master Tnegun cut her off with a lifted hand. "Even less than Cesei do you have the skills I will need," he told her, not unkindly, but with a flat decisiveness that was very lowering.

Even less than Cesei—yes, and that was her fault, even though Master Tnegun wasn't saying so. Araenè wanted very badly to object, but she knew her master was right. She slunk after Tichorei, who was hauling the protesting Cesei by one wrist.

"We should go back," Cesei protested, pulling to a halt almost before they were back inside the hidden school. "Tichorei, we should go back! Arei was right, we might be able to help—" There were tears of frustration and fear in his eyes. He looked far too young to be facing—whatever they were all facing.

"And do what?" snapped Tichorei, hauling the little boy along by plain force. "You're not a baby, Cesei; do as you're told! If the backlash is bad enough, I might need you myself! Or do you think it's beneath you to work on backlash and overextension?"

Araenè had thought Tichorei had simply been detailed to watch them as though they *were* babies. She knew she, at least, was about as helpless as an infant. Trying to steady her racing thoughts, she asked, "*Can* you, we, um, can we . . . handle the backlash, then?"

"I'm Master Camatii's apprentice," Tichorei said grimly. "And Master Camatii is the best there is at bringing an overextended mage back from the edge. I'm not—" He stopped.

Not him, not as good? Araenè could imagine where that comment had been heading. And then, *But I'm the best we may have.* That's what Tichorei meant.

"Why not Master Camatii, then?" Cesei began.

Tichorei gave the boy a little shake, too worried to be patient. "Because they need him where they're fighting, of course. They'll *need* a healing mage. *He'll* overextend himself—of course he will—Arei!" He wheeled suddenly to face Araenè.

Araenè jerked to a halt, startled and alarmed. "Yes?"

"Can you recognize overextension when you see it?"

She couldn't recognize or understand or do *anything*. She shook her head mutely.

Tichorei started down a hall with low arched ceilings, windowless, lit by spell light. He said over his shoulder, "A mage who overextends goes all still and cold—he might look dead, only you can see he isn't, if you look properly. He's extended too far, his mind isn't aware of his body. If he stays like that, he *will* die. What *you* can do—"

"Is bring him back?" Araenè asked cautiously. She doubted very much she could do any such thing. Did Tichorei think *she*—was she *supposed* to be able to—

"No—that's me," the young man said grimly. "What you can do is keep *me* from overextending while I do it! Cesei!"

"What?" Tichorei had released Cesei's wrist at last, and the boy rubbed it, looking at once sullen and scared.

Tichorei stood in the middle of the hallway, his hands on

his hips, glowering at the younger apprentice. "Have you ever seen your master overextend?"

Cesei hesitated. "I don't think so."

"Then you haven't! Kopapei's probably not the sort to let it happen, but I expect it will tonight. Cesei, you can't do anything to help your master if you can't calm down and let me show you how! Right?"

Cesei glowered and muttered that Tichorei should *do* something, then.

"I am!" snapped Tichorei. He caught the younger boy's wrist again, shoved open a door Araenè hadn't even realized was there, and hauled him into the hall of spheres and mirrors.

Araenè stared after them for an instant. Then she ran after Tichorei . . .

. . . and found herself blundering through a place she had heard of repeatedly but had never visited: the balcony where the black gulls nested. The sharp, acrid smell of guano mingled with the salt smell of the sea. "Weeping *Gods*!" Araenè said, with a good deal more force than was seemly for any girl, and stood still, trying not to crush gull eggs under her feet.

It seemed to her that hundreds of gulls wheeled and cried over the sea, the black ones mingling with the ordinary gray and white gulls, but only the black ones came in over this balcony. And what had everyone said about black gulls hatching out basilisks . . . ? Araenè swallowed and shut her eyes. Narrow black wings beat through the air all around her. . . .

Then everything else was suddenly overwhelmed by a terrible smashing, grating noise, a sound so loud that Araenè felt it echo in all her bones. She reeled sideways and back, not even sure whether the vast noise alone had made her stagger or whether some huge blow had actually struck the balcony. All the gulls were in the air, a wild confusion of beating wings. Araenè cried out and covered her face with her arms. A large hand caught her arm and steadied her when she might otherwise have fallen, and the wild torrent of gulls subsided as the birds fled for the open air over the sea.

The sudden quiet after the overwhelming noise was almost like a blow itself, and Araenè flinched from it—but the grip on her arm did not slacken and after a moment she found herself able to straighten and look, dazedly, for the person who held her.

"Well, now," said the man, blinking down at Araenè. "You need to watch your step here. That's a basilisk egg you just now came near sitting on. Fretful creatures, basilisks; you wouldn't want to hatch one out by falling on top of it."

Araenè stared at the man. Then she looked down—or started to look down: the man caught her chin, tilting her face firmly upward, and she blushed hotly—of course she shouldn't look, she knew very well she shouldn't look at a basilisk; she'd never heard that looking at just the egg was dangerous, but what if it hatched while she stared at it?

"Better," agreed her unexpected protector. He was a large, untidy man with a tangled mass of hair spilling around his round, forgettable face. He let go of Araenè's arm, patting her on the shoulder as a man might pat a nervous dog, still peering down at her. A twist of some green vine was caught in his hair. A bitter green scent clung to him, distinguishable even through the smells of the gulls' nests and the sea.

"What *was* that . . . noise?" Araenè asked him.

"Well, let's go look," suggested the man. He turned, clumsy with his bulk, and picked his way among the gulls' nests to lean over the balcony railing. For all his awkwardness, Araenè noticed, he did not disturb a single nest.

In the west, a great red sun was sinking into the sea. The sky was streaked with crimson; the red light turned the still water to a sheet of blood, sheathed the Tolounnese ships with blood, set their limp white sails on fire. Long metal ladders stretched up and out from five of the ships, their upper edges buried in broken rubble where they had shattered the Island towers built into the stone: the closest was so near Araenè could almost have reached out and touched it. Broken shards of stone and brick were still falling from the cliffs where it had struck, but men were starting to climb it. A lot of men.

Araenè turned to stare at the big man. "Are you . . . going to stop them?"

"Well, more or less. I might stop that lot, I suppose," said the man. He leaned his elbows on the railing without regard for the guano that speckled it, peering down toward the ships. "The question is, what's going to stop the ones after that? Determined, those Tolounnese. Once they begin marching, they don't like to turn around. They're carrying a lot of power in their pockets just at the moment. A great lot more than we can raise up, you know."

"But—" Araenè protested, but then didn't know what to say, or ask. She stopped in confusion.

The man squinted down at her. His eyes were a muddy gray-brown-green color. Given their vague expression, Araenè wasn't even certain he saw her. He said absently, "If everyone works at it, the Tolounnese might be held for a day or so, I suppose. Sometimes a day makes a great deal of difference. I'm sure you've found that in your own life. Or you will."

Araenè found herself growing angry as well as uncertain and frightened. "Can you be plain?" she demanded. "Where should I go? What should I do? I don't know how to do anything, you know! What can *I* do?"

"You might try trusting Tnegun," the man suggested, not really as though he was paying much attention.

"I—*what?*"

"You seem to have decided you can't trust him. That does seem a hard judgment on the poor man, as you haven't yet tried."

Araenè stared at him, utterly speechless.

There was no sign that the man noticed anything of her astonishment or anger or terror. He only looked down at the advancing Tolounnese soldiers, then peered around absently. "Let me see. Mm." He wandered away across the balcony, stooping to pick up a black egg here and there. One he squinted at and put back. Then he glanced at Araenè, smiled, and commented, "We mustn't distract the Tolounnese mages, but a basilisk or two in the right place can do wonders to divert even the most dedicated soldiers, don't you find? You might try that door over there." He waved across the balcony. "That might take you somewhere useful." He held another of the eggs up to the red light of the sun and peered at it thoughtfully. "Hmm."

Araenè stared at the man—the mage—could this be Cassameirin?—for a long moment. Then she looked warily at the door he'd pointed out. It was the only door she could see anywhere. Three times her height, the door was still so narrow she would have to turn sideways to step through it.

Turning back toward the big man, Araenè began to ask where this door would lead—though she already knew whatever answer he gave would probably be unhelpful—but it didn't matter what he might have said, because he was gone. Black gulls flew in and out where he had been standing. Araenè stared out at the red sea and the red sky for a long moment. The shouts of men still echoed out there: shouts and then, abruptly, screams that made her wonder if a basilisk had suddenly hatched out at the feet of the advancing soldiers. And if she could do anything more useless than stand here and wait for a basilisk to hatch at her own feet, Araenè could not imagine what that might be.

She wanted to curse. But even disguised as a boy, Araenè could not quite bring herself to swear. Not, at least, as violently as she wanted to.

But she slammed the narrow door behind her, after making sure it led only to the great twelve-walled hall of spheres and mirrors.

"Gods weeping!" Tichorei looked up, startled, from a row of spheres he'd lined up on the floor in front of a long, low mirror. "Do you have to crash things around? Where have you been? At least, I can see from your boots where you've been; why did you visit the gulls?" Then he waved a dismissive hand. "Never mind, just look here. Cesei, what do you think, this little glass one next, or this big basalt?"

"I don't know," Cesei muttered. He was standing on the other side of the hall, on his toes, craning to see out one of the windows. "How should I know? I don't know anything."

The little boy's mood clearly hadn't improved while Araenè had been touring the outskirts of the hidden school. Though she sympathized with his frustration, she also found herself rolling her eyes impatiently. Did *she* ever seem so sullen? Struck by this thought, she stared at the boy for a moment. Then, as Tichorei started to put the basalt sphere in his row, she held up a hand and said hastily, "No, no—the glass one."

"Yes?" Tichorei sat back on his heels and gazed at Araenè. "Why?"

Araenè found herself unable to explain why it seemed obvious to her that glass should come next in the series Tichorei had arranged. Irritated by her own ignorance, she shrugged. "It just seems right."

Tichorei nodded. "Glass, then." He put the sphere in place.

"I met this man," Araenè said diffidently. "Big. Dressed like a Third City man—not even like that, more like a farmer. He said . . ." She hesitated, then finished, "He said he was going to use basilisk eggs against the Tolounnese. I think that's what he meant."

Tichorei had straightened up. He stared at Araenè. "Big, you say? Lots of untidy hair? Was he—" He stopped, then finished in an embarrassed tone, "A little far into his cups?"

"Oh!" Araenè realized where she had met the man the first time: it had been the same man who'd first directed her to the mages' school. Or . . . *had* it been the same? When she tried to think back, she found her image of the man uncertain. "Yes—maybe," she said uncertainly. "Does he smell . . ." She hesitated. "Sort of green and wild, like crushed herbs?"

Tichorei blinked. "Does he smell like *herbs*? Not that I ever noticed. More like ale, I should think! But if you met a big man who was collecting basilisk eggs, I think maybe that was Cassameirin. *Master* Cassameirin," he said hastily. "I met him once. If he's here now, that's good. I think it's good. He's not—he's too old to be powerful, but he makes things happen, you know." He stared down at the spheres he'd lined up, then uncertainly up at the racks of other spheres. "Maybe I should add one for him. I wonder what kind. . . ."

"That green one," Araenè suggested, pointing to a sphere of soapy-looking stone she didn't recognize. It tickled across her tongue with the same complicated herbal flavor that attended Master Cassameirin. "What are you doing?"

"Setting things up so we can see out properly." Tichorei added the green sphere to his row and studied it critically. He glanced over at Cesei. "You know how to do far-seeing?"

"A little." Not quite so sullen now that there was something to do, Cesei skirted the spiral stair in the center of the floor and came over to kneel down across from Tichorei. They both bent their heads over the row of spheres, suddenly looking very much alike despite all the differences between them. The first sphere in the row was obsidian. Then came topaz, amethyst, a smoky gray stone that Araenè didn't recognize, and finally glass and the soapy green stone. The topaz sphere was the largest, the glass one the smallest. The air around the spheres sparkled with ginger and cumin, with undertones of herbs and pepper and cloves.

"Master Kopapei," Tichorei said, pointing to the obsidian sphere. He went down the row. "Tnegun, Akhai, Yamatei, Camatii, and Cassameirin. Now," the young man explained, "I'm

245

going to show you both how to set a sphere so you can catch the first moment of someone's overextension—and then we'll watch in turn, do you see? If one of the masters overextends, I'll try to catch him, put him back together. Arei, if I start to extend too far myself, you'll have to catch me."

"How?" Araenè asked tensely. She knew already that however one stopped an apprentice mage from overextending, she wouldn't be able to do it.

"You'll have to hit me. Hard enough that I feel it." Tichorei demonstrated, slapping Araenè on the arm hard enough to sting. Surprised, she yelped; the young man looked at her, startled, and she put a hand over her mouth. But the other apprentice only shrugged and put a fingertip out to the first of the spheres in the row. "Now, Cesei, watch me. You'll have to do this if I, well. For now, you only watch, yes?"

The boy nodded earnestly.

"Now, Yamatei first, and we'll see if we can still get him back," Tichorei murmured. He bent over the gray sphere.

That night seemed endless to Araenè. Sometimes shouting and the dim clamor of distant trouble were audible from the hall of spheres and mirrors; more often, not. She supposed it depended on exactly where the hidden school actually *was* at any given moment. Neither she nor Tichorei nor even Cesei ever went and looked out a window, not even when dawn approached. The spheres took all their attention.

The spheres sparkled and glittered . . . and sometimes dimmed. Usually there was nothing to actually *see,* at least not anything for Araenè. But Cesei sometimes bent low over one sphere or another and told her something like, "Master

Camatii is way down underneath First City. I think there's a lot of men there. He's very tired."

Tichorei didn't look into the spheres, but sat with his eyes closed. He waited for Cesei to spot trouble for him, then sent his mind sliding after any mage who'd lost himself in the vastness of sea and sky. Over and over, growing more confident of her judgment and yet more tense as the bells passed, Araenè watched the older apprentice's breathing become slow and shallow. Then she would lean forward and shout his name right in his face, slapping him hard. Tichorei would lean forward and shake his head, or stand up and pace around the twelve-sided hall for a few minutes.

"I lost Master Kopapei," he said bleakly, very early in the morning, shortly after the pearl-gray of dawn began to show around the edges of the shutters. "No, Arei, you were right, you had to bring me back! Cesei, don't cry; he's not *dead*. Just, I think he's very badly overextended. Master Camatii will find him eventually." He didn't say anything about the possibility that they might lose Master Camatii next, only put the obsidian sphere carefully aside.

The morning dragged past.

"There's a lot of fighting," Cesei said, looking worriedly into Master Yamatei's gray-green stone. "I thought he'd be all right once we got him back. But there's a lot of, I don't know; I don't like the way Master Yamatei feels now."

Tichorei came over to look, then grunted and went back to pacing. He didn't say, *There's nothing we can do about that,* but Araenè was sure that was what he'd meant.

At fourth bell, Master Yamatei's stone suddenly splintered with a fine lacework of red veins. Tichorei put it beside the obsidian sphere without comment, but he looked sick. "I shouldn't have—" he began, then cut that off. And said harshly to Cesei, "I have to rest. I *have* to, do you see? Do you understand how I catch them back when they go too far?"

"I've been trying to watch." Cesei didn't look sullen anymore. Now he looked frightened. "I haven't, I can't, uh, *exactly* see what you do. . . ."

Too tired to be gentle, Tichorei simply put one hand on the boy's shoulder, cupped his cheek with the other hand, and looked, with a strange kind of forcefulness, into his eyes. Cesei flinched, his face screwing up, suddenly on the verge of tears. He tried once to break Tichorei's grip, but the older apprentice didn't let go and after a moment Cesei steadied again, though his breathing had gone ragged.

"You have that?" Tichorei asked him, his tone still rough. "It's too advanced for you, I know that. You were brave to let me set the pattern. Can you hold it now?"

Cesei didn't look quite sure. "I guess so. . . . It *hurts,* Tichorei. . . ."

"I know it does. Can you hold it anyway?"

"I—" Cesei's expression turned stubborn. "I can keep it for a while. I *can.*"

Tichorei only nodded. "Good boy," he muttered. He looked blurrily at Araenè. "Gotta rest. Wake me up by, by, I don't know, sixth bell? Or if Cesei can't hold that pattern, wake me up when he loses it." He walked across the hall stiffly, as though just walking hurt him, lay down right on the floor, and went instantly to sleep. Except he looked more unconscious than just *asleep.*

Araenè and Cesei looked at each other. Araenè thought

the little boy was even more frightened than she was. She sat down in Tichorei's old place and patted the floor by her side. Cesei came to sit next to her. He leaned against her shoulder like the child he was, too tired and scared and hurt to remember his eight-year-old pride.

Araenè stroked his bright hair. She missed her mother, suddenly and intensely: she wished her mother was here. Not just for her, but for Cesei. He didn't remember his, she recalled. That would be even worse than missing a mother who had died. . . . She put an arm around the little boy. "Does it still hurt?"

"I'm trying not to think about it," Cesei muttered. There was a long silence.

Then Cesei leaned suddenly forward, staring at the spheres. "Oh," he said in a surprised tone, closed his eyes, and was instantly gone after whoever had overextended. Araenè pulled back and watched him, terrified that she would miss the moment Cesei himself overextended and lose the boy— but if she panicked and broke Cesei's extension too early, they might lose whomever he'd gone after. . . . Then the little boy gasped twice like a drowning swimmer coming back into the air and opened his eyes. "That *hurt*," he said accusingly, glowering at the unconscious Tichorei.

"I'm sorry," Araenè said humbly. She was older than Cesei; she knew she should be doing the hard part. But she could only sit and watch the *boys* do the dangerous work.

It was going to be a very long day. And a *very* long night. And at the end . . . what chance did they really have, Araenè wondered, of throwing back the Tolounnese? Everyone knew the Tolounnese never gave up.

For the first time since everything had started, Araenè remembered her cousin. *Trei* was Tolounnese, too. Half. *He* didn't give up, either. Maybe . . . maybe he would actually get her dragon's egg all the way to . . . to wherever he'd said the Tolounnese had their terrible engines. Maybe . . .

II

A dozen times that night, Trei concluded that he must have made a mistake in navigation—that he'd lost sight of the right stars or calculated an angle wrong, and so they'd gone wildly far from their path. Then Kojran, best of them all at keeping track of passing time, would sing out the count and Trei would take careful note of the stars and decide they were probably still on course after all.

The air was good, though: the wind wanted to come from the north, but up in the heights it could more easily be coaxed around to come from the west and south. Genrai was good at pulling the wind around behind them. So was Kojran, and the two of them worked the wind for everyone. They could soar most of the time: easy flying.

The sun came up right where it should, ten points behind Trei's right wingtip. They were flying high, where the air was lightest and the winds easiest to turn. From this height they could see a long way. But all around them stretched out the wide and empty sea. There was no sign of the waystation.

Trei adjusted their course a feather's width more northerly, and they flew on. And on, over the unchanging sea. His shoulders and back ached; his elbows felt strained out of shape from the unrelieved flight. His wings had grown so familiar that he thought he could feel the separate angle of every individual feather. The great white-winged albatrosses could stay aloft for days—for weeks, Trei had heard. But the albatross feathers woven into the kajurai wings didn't seem to be providing quite as much endurance as Trei might have hoped.

A bell past dawn. Half another bell. Trei knew they'd missed the first waystation. If they'd passed the waystation, probably they'd been too far to the west. If they struck back a little more easterly, maybe they could still find it. If they kept their course, they'd never make the second waystation, not if they'd missed the first. Not the younger boys, at least. Trei wasn't sure whether he could fly that far without rest or not. Maybe it was time to think about handing the egg off to Genrai. . . .

Then Tokabii whooped, spun out of formation into a tumbling somersault, spilled air from his wings, and dropped into a steep dive. Trei back-winged in astonishment, but then Kojran shouted, too, and followed Tokabii. After that Trei, too, spotted the elliptical dimple in the wind where the bulk of a floating island disturbed the air—little more than a large pebble, but enough to create telltale spiraling ripples where the moving air spilled into its lee.

"It's the right waystation, right enough," Genrai assured Trei wearily once they were safely down. "A pond, a single tree; look, here's the mark." He nodded toward the jagged sign carved into the high lintel of the pavilion's doorway.

Trei, still adjusting to the idea that his course had been good after all, couldn't think of anything to say. He couldn't stop shaking, although the morning was already warm. Genrai had had to work his own wings off and then strip Trei's off as well; Trei couldn't get his fingers to steady on the buckles. Kojran was almost as badly off, but Tokabii, stunningly resilient, had already dashed down to the pool to try his luck at fishing.

"Kajuraihi stock every pool large enough to come through a hot summer," Genrai said, amused at Trei's expression. "Did you miss Berinai's lecture about that? Can you make a fist? Can you open your hand all the way? I should have thought to bring salve. Kojran, can you go see if there's any salve in the pavilion?"

Kojran went without a word.

"Tokabii doesn't realize how near we came to missing the station," Genrai commented. "But Kojran does. The kajurai he mentioned, Kerii? Kerii was a kajurai in a play. He dropped out of his formation, stayed behind on a floating pebble like this one. In the play, everyone thinks he's a coward. But he makes a fragrant cedar fire that guides all the other kajuraihi to shelter when they'd otherwise have been lost in a blinding fog."

"Oh."

"The thing is . . . Kerii really was a coward. It was just the Gods' grace that redeemed his cowardice."

"Ah."

"Tokabii would be my choice to wait here. But he won't, you know. Kojran isn't so proud." Genrai waited for Trei to think this through, then added, "It's farther on the way back than it is coming. We won't have to coax the wind around: this time of year the low wind is out of the hard north all the way; that'll help. But even so, we don't dare miss this station."

"No, I see that." Trei looked around. Bare red rock, thin soil trapped in the crevice where the single tree grew. The pool. The pavilion. Wood stacked inside the pavilion. "Cedar?"

Genrai nodded. "There'll be coal, too. Black smoke by day, a tall, fragrant fire by night. Enough for a couple days' burning. It's a famous play."

"Can Tokabii make it to Teraica and back?" Trei tried not to wonder whether *he* could. He tried even harder not to wonder whether he wanted to.

"There's one more waystation. And a scattering of random pebbles, so there's less chance of dropping into the sea. But from the second station, it'll be straight in, hit the engines, and straight out—nearly a hundred miles each way. Tokabii will *have* to wait at the second waystation—by the time we reach it, he'll be ready to admit it." Genrai gave Trei a long look.

Trei met the older boy's eyes. "*You* can make the whole round-trip."

"I think so."

Trei nodded. He opened and closed his hands, carefully. He could just about open his fingers all the way, but his hands were too stiff to make tight fists. His wrists hurt, too. And his elbows, and his shoulders, and all the way down his back . . . Genrai didn't look nearly so stiff. Trei wished fervently that *he* was seventeen, with the strength to make little of a two-hundred-mile flight. He said reluctantly, "I suppose we'd better go on soon."

"Lie down," ordered Genrai. "I don't know what's taking Kojran so long—I'll see about the salve. You just rest. Sleep, if you can. I'll wake you by fourth bell." He gave Trei his own vest as a pillow and walked away.

The second waystation was much easier to find; flying during the day was just easier in every possible way. Even the air seemed more buoyant. They found the waystation a little before dusk and spent a night that was almost comfortable. Even so, Genrai proved correct: even by dawn, Tokabii remained exhausted enough to be willing to wait at the waystation.

"I hope you paid attention to your lessons," Genrai told him sternly. "If you don't see us by late this evening, certainly by tomorrow's dawn, you'll know you'd better take word back to the Islands. You have a clear idea of the way?"

Tokabii tried to smile. "Straight south. That's not complicated. But I'll expect you. Today's Gods' Day. That's good luck, anyway." He carefully worked the Quei feathers out of his wings and offered them to Genrai and Trei. "You'll need the luck."

Genrai hesitated—then gestured for Tokabii to give all six of the feathers to Trei. His manner was so uncompromising that Trei gave in without arguing and fixed three of Tokabii's Quei feathers into each of his wings.

"One more hard flight," Genrai said then, laying out the wings for Trei. "You can manage it."

Trei nodded.

"I don't know how," Tokabii muttered. "You're not *that* much bigger than me."

Trei didn't answer.

But Genrai turned and put a hand on the younger boy's shoulder. " 'Kabii . . . Trei doesn't expect to make the return flight. Just the flight in."

Tokabii took this in. He stared at Genrai for a long moment. Then his expression, from petulant, became almost frightened. He turned toward Trei.

Trei found he was feeling a little ill. Having Genrai say it that way, just out like that, plainly . . . Trei knew there was almost no chance he would be able to fly down to the Tolounnese engines, throw in the dragon's egg, and get away again. But to comfort Tokabii, he said quickly, "I'm Tolounnese—I can just slip away into Teraica and work my passage back to the Islands after things have . . . calmed down."

Tokabii looked relieved. Genrai said merely, "Of course you can."

"One last flight," Trei said, and then wished he hadn't. It sounded altogether too final.

"Black smoke by day, fragrant fire by night," Genrai reminded Tokabii. "Get a tall fire burning by dusk tonight, yes?"

The younger boy nodded. He said, "*You'll* come back," confidently.

Genrai shrugged and looked at Trei. "Ready?"

"I wish we had two eggs," Trei admitted. He rubbed the hard shell of the one they did have through the cloth of its sling. "I hope it's all right."

"Your cousin didn't say it needed special care? Then I'm

sure it's fine." Genrai hesitated. "Trei—you're sure you don't want me to take it? You don't even have to go the rest of the way if you, you know . . ."

Trei shook his head. "I'm the one who understands engines. Those drawings weren't very detailed. Are you sure you'd recognize the right place to throw in the egg?"

"How hard can it be?"

"I don't know. But neither do you. We only have one egg. We both know that I have the best chance to use it."

Tokabii stared from one of them to the other. "Besides, you're not Tolounnese!" he said to Genrai. "*You* couldn't hide in Teraica!"

". . . right," said Genrai. He looked at Trei for another moment. "Stay above me," he said. "I'll get the wind round for you, get you proper lift. All right?"

Trei nodded.

Genrai nodded back and said to Tokabii, "Help me with my wings, will you?"

The way was, for the first time, more east than north. Trei was too tired, or maybe too emotionally numb, to pay much attention to their direction. He just rode the wind, trusting Genrai to hold it in the right quarter of the sky. They stayed low, letting the dense, warm air buoy them.

The day was clear and fine, without a trace of cloud. The ordinary islands that guarded the harbor at Teraica became visible from a startling distance: a dark lumpiness on the horizon, with a haze of black smoke in the sky above the town.

As they approached the harbor, Genrai rose suddenly, passed Trei, slid into a spiral, slowed as Trei came up beside him, and eased closer still, until their wingtips all but overlapped.

He turned his head to call, "Engines?" with a jerk of his chin down toward the edge of the harbor.

Trei didn't answer. There, where the sand met the sea, stood the three great steam engines, just as Ceirfei had drawn them. Their scale was clear from the ships docked along the harbor, from the warehouses set back from the tides. Gangs of men, tiny at this distance, labored to pour wagonloads of coal down into each furnace. Billows of white steam mingled with the smoke, visible long before the engines themselves came into sight.

Trei slid down the wind toward the engines. They were so much bigger than he'd expected—so much bigger than he'd ever imagined, and he found himself doubting whether it *was* after all possible to overheat so vast a boiler. When the wind changed suddenly, he found himself flying through choking black smoke—then hot white fog—he beat his wings hard and pulled against the air with dragon magic—it occurred to him that it was lucky the Tolounnese hadn't saved some of the immense power of the furnaces to kill the air around and over Teraica, but maybe they'd need all of that power to use against the Islands.

He broke at last into the clear winds, gasping. He looked for Genrai, couldn't find him. Then did: well away toward the sea. But there was no point in joining Genrai now. There was nothing to say—at least, nothing Trei felt able to say.

He curved around instead, dropping lower, skirting the billowing smoke and steam. The engines roared: a sound that he imagined might be like the roaring of dragons. He had never imagined anything so big! Trei thought suddenly of Uncle Serfei saying, *Tolounn's only art is the art of war,* and found himself wishing that his uncle could have seen these great engines. The art of war, yes, maybe, but how splendid an art sometimes! He struggled against a totally unexpected dismay at the thought of destroying something so great and powerful.

What a wonder Tolounn had made, here at the boundary between engines and magic! How could anything the Floating Islands do match this? If the Islands couldn't defend themselves, then whatever Trei did or failed to do, eventually Tolounn would conquer them—and was that so terrible? Tolounn was generous to territories it conquered. Not like Yngul.

Though . . . it was true that no land Tolounn conquered ever regained its independence. If Tolounn took the Islands, the king and all his family would surely be imprisoned in Tolounn and a Tolounnese provincar would be put in place to rule. *Tolounn's only art is the art of war.* It *was* true, in a way, and in the service of its art, Tolounn always required newly conquered territories to provide conscripts. If the Islands were subjugated, few young men would be allowed to become chefs or, or . . . whatever they might have wanted to become. They would go instead to swell the ranks of Tolounn's armies—especially if the Tolounnese Emperors saw the Islands as a stepping-stone on the way to Cen Periven. Which they would. *My fault,* Trei thought. *My fault if I can't do this and then we lose.* Then he blinked, realizing that for the first time he'd thought "we" and not "they."

"I *am* an Islander," Trei said aloud into the rushing, smoke-filled air, but the wind roared in his ears and swept the words away as though he had never spoken them, and he found himself uncertain whether he'd spoken aloud at all. Yet he *had* chosen to be Islander, and now he had to take the egg down—had to complete this task, or why had he *come*?

Even if probably the dragon egg wouldn't do anything to those engines anyway, not even if the heat quickened it, and there was no guarantee even of that, was there? He was suddenly certain it wouldn't work. Araenè had just been wrong about what she'd thought the dragon wanted—or about what the egg would do if it was thrown into a furnace—even now, at this last moment, if Trei just found a place way out on the edges of Teraica, he really *could* rest there and then, in a day or two, fly back to the Islands. Give the egg back to Araenè, tell her he hadn't been able to use it after all.

If Araenè was still there. The long flight had all blurred in Trei's mind, but Tolounn's attack on the Islands had begun, what, two full days ago? The Islanders hadn't seemed to be mounting any kind of defense. Trei shook his head angrily, trying to think. Any little town in Tolounn would be ashamed to manage so little defense. The Islands had no *business* assuming the simple fact of their height would always be enough to hold back a determined enemy! One thing was becoming clear the more he thought about it: nothing *he* did could possibly make any difference—

A ripple in the smoke gave way to Genrai, swinging in and down to match Trei's course and speed. He shouted, "The middle engine, yes? The place where the coal falls down? Let me take it, Trei! What you said to Tokabii was true: you could land somewhere hidden, rest, make your way back later!"

Trei realized that Genrai thought he'd frozen in terror, here on the edge of success. And, Trei also realized, the older boy was right. It was fear—not anything else—that underlay all his hesitation. He was afraid to try to reach those engines, so he'd just been making up reasons not to try. Even after he'd *promised* Genrai he would do it—after he'd promised *Araenè* he'd do it. Trei shouted, furiously, to himself more than to Genrai, "I *am* kajurai!" This time, he shouted loudly enough: the angry words seemed to echo in the wind.

He tipped sideways and dropped through the smoke. The smoke choked him, but he could see through it—he couldn't *see* the engines, exactly, but he could see the waves of heat they flung out into the air. The smoke was hard to breathe, but it didn't bother his kajurai eyes at all. He could see the intense heat that marked the entrance to the coal furnaces.

The middle engine: yes. Because if the one in the middle exploded, maybe the explosion would destroy both the other engines as well. Trust Genrai to think of things like that.

But of course the middle engine was the hardest one to reach. The gap between that engine and the next was narrow: Trei would have to come in at a steep angle. He thought at first he might come in slowly, but once he was below the worst of the smoke, he found that was impossible: there were too many men all around the engines. Spearheads flashed; they'd seen Trei—they were turning to face him—their shouts reached him, dimly—he did not slow, but instead put everything he had into speed and rushed by the soldiers, so fast they barely knew he was upon them before he was past.

Trei rode that wave of speed through the gap and right up to the middle engine, flung up his legs to take the shock of landing—he felt that shock not only in his legs but all the way up his back, and if he hadn't tucked his chin, the force of the impact might have broken his neck. He flung his arms forward violently, pure reflex against a horrible landing, and felt every primary feather shatter. The force of the blow numbed his arms, and for a long, agonizing moment he was afraid he'd crushed the egg—or that he'd be unable to get it out of its sling—someone was shouting, much too close—Trei got the egg free at last and flung it, a good clean throw, down into the engine's furnace, right along with the pouring coal.

The next moment, strong hands closed on his shoulders and hauled him back, spun him around, and slammed him back against the hot wall of the engine. Trei's head struck the metal wall hard, and he sagged helplessly in his captor's hold. It didn't matter—he didn't need to worry about escape—in a moment the egg would hatch, and the engine would explode, and then it wouldn't matter at all that he'd been caught—

"Gods wept!" exclaimed a harsh voice, and Trei found himself lifted clear off the ground and handed from one man to another, and then another. His arms dragged, heavy—broken?—no, he realized: the weight was simply the weight of the wings. *Those* were broken. He wanted to ask the men to stop, help him with the straps, carry the wings more gently before they were damaged even worse. But he couldn't make himself form words.

It didn't matter. Because soon the engine would overheat and explode.

Blackness expanded and contracted around him—smoke, he was choking on it, or maybe it was steam; it was terribly hot. Trei, dazed, wondered whether the explosion had taken place and he'd missed it. But then they were out in cooler air, and he was no longer moving—oh, he was lying on the ground? But that was wrong: shouldn't he be lying on the wind? With Genrai? No, that was wrong: he was on the ground and Genrai was still in the air. . . . Trei tried to lift his head, looking for Genrai. But all the sky he could see was empty. And the engines, when he turned his head to look for them, were still there.

He was surrounded by soldiers. And the engines were still in place, all three of them, producing billows of smoke and steam and power.

There had been no explosion at all.

All the time he was being freed from the wreck of his wings, and then all the time he was being carried away from the harbor by the soldiers, and even later when he was carried into a tall house and up flights of stairs and put down on a cot in a plain room . . . all that time, Trei expected an explosion to hammer through the town behind him. He waited for the shock of furious destruction. If even just one of the engines exploded . . . an engine that size . . . surely he couldn't miss it?

But there was no explosion. Not in all that time.

Trei's awareness faded in and out, so that while he was being carried, he sometimes knew he was in the grip of Tolounnese soldiers and sometimes thought he was in the air. . . . His arms hurt, though, especially his left arm, worse when he tried to move it. The soldiers spoke over Trei and around him. He thought they sounded rough and angry. Hearing the anger in their deep voices, he began to remember that he should be afraid. But the man who carried him was gentle, so then Trei was confused and wondered whether he might only be imagining the voices he heard. . . . That would explain why they sometimes seemed loud and sometimes faded almost to nothing. He tried to ask whether they could see Genrai in the sky, but could not hear his own voice at all and did not know whether he had made a sound.

The world steadied around him at last once the soldiers brought him to the house and put him down on a cot that did not move. But it faded, too, swathed more and more deeply in billowing black smoke and hot white fog. . . . He thought someone was asking questions, but Trei did not know whether he answered or not. He was falling through the high winds into a white stillness. . . .

He did not know how long he drifted in that blank quiet. But pain pulled him back to violent awareness. Pain shocked through him, from his hands and arms and splintering through his head. Trei shouted, convulsing—or he thought he shouted, he thought he tried to convulse: someone caught him; immense strength pinned him down when he tried to struggle. The pain sharpened; it gritted along his bones and knifed behind his eyes . . . and, unexpectedly, eased. The powerful grip fell away. Trei blinked, finding his sight blurred. Tears, he understood suddenly, and, ashamed, scrubbed his hands quickly across his face.

"There, you see?" said a light, calm voice. The words were heavily accented; it took Trei a moment to understand what he was hearing. The speaker went on, "Quite simple breaks, all of them. The concussion was the only dangerous injury. I expect the boy will have a headache for some time."

"A headache!" said a rougher voice, and laughed. That voice was not so strongly accented, and not accented the same way. . . . It was deeper, too. . . . A soldier, Trei saw, his vision finally resolving. A Tolounnese soldier, a decouan, a squad leader. The man saw Trei looking at him and said, "So you're back with us, are you, boy? Good, good—that was a brave attack you made. Are all Islander boys so brave?" He patted Trei on the shoulder, but his tone had gone angry and scornful on the last words.

Trei, knowing exactly why the decouan sounded that way, flushed. Struggling to sit up, he said quickly, "They didn't *send* me. They wouldn't send a boy my age—I'm just a *novice;* I wasn't supposed to even leave the novitiate!"

The decouan gave Trei a surprised stare. "Well," he said at last, "there's a strange accent for an Islander boy: I'd swear you were from the north, the way you come down on the ends of your words."

Trei flushed. He did not know what to say. He managed at last, "I was born in Tolounn, sir. In Rounn. But I *am* an Islander. I'm kajurai."

"Well, you are that," said the decouan, with another sharp look. "Aye, you are that, and no mistake. But what, by the good Gods, did you think you were *doing?*"

Trei didn't answer.

"Ah, well," said the decouan. He shrugged, stepped back, looked at the other man. "Master Patan?"

Trei followed his gaze. His eyes widened. The other man . . . Master Patan . . . was definitely not a soldier. He was thin, spidery; he had long hands and a narrow, angular face. He wore a plain blue robe, but the cloth was heavy and the dye rich, and he wore a chain of twisted gold links about his throat and a similar ring on his left thumb. His eyes were gray as the stone of the high northern mountains, his gaze neutral and remote as winter. He said, seeing Trei look at him, "You had five broken fingers, three broken bones in your left hand, your left ulna was cracked, and your left elbow was dislocated. You also had broken bones in both your ankles, and your left knee was quite badly wrenched. I gather you struck against the engine with your hands and feet. Surely that is not an approved landing technique?"

Trei had to pay careful attention to understand this man's words. It was not at all a Tolounnese accent, certainly not the Islander accent that was so close to the speech of southern Tolounn. This was something else entirely. He answered at last, "You're supposed to stall when you're going to land. If you stall right, you can just walk out of the air." He'd been so proud, the first time he'd managed that. He'd never have done it without Ceirfei's arm-strengthening exercises. Trei winced away from that thought and added quickly, "I had to get past all the soldiers, so I had to go fast. Then there wasn't time to stop. Are you . . . from Cen Periven, sir?"

Master Patan's gray eyes glinted. "Hardly. I'm from Toipakom. Originally. What would you guess your velocity to have been when you struck the engine? Your injuries suggest you were moving at roughly the speed of a galloping horse. Assuming that you did slow just before you, ah, landed, your highest velocity must have been quite impressive. I gather that your . . . wings . . . provided some degree of protection to your hands and arms. Those are fascinating, ah, mechanisms. It is most unfortunate they were so badly damaged by your landing."

Trei didn't like to think of how badly he must have wrecked his wings. And that was *with* the extra Quei feathers! But he thought it was probably good he hadn't provided a working set to this man. He said nothing.

"How fast can, ah, you flying people—what is the term? Kajura? What velocities can you attain? Greater in diving than in flat flying, I imagine? A mountain falcon can fly much faster than a horse can run. Can you fly so fast?"

"Kajuraihi," Trei said, but then he thought probably he shouldn't tell Master Patan anything about how fast kajuraihi really could fly. He shouldn't tell him anything. But he was afraid simply to refuse to answer questions. He said, "I don't know how fast the fastest kajurai could fly. I'm just a novice."

"Yes, so I understand," the man said. He regarded Trei for a long moment. Then he asked, "Do you know what I am, novice?"

"You're a mage, sir. Aren't you?"

"Not precisely in the Island sense, I believe," answered Master Patan. "I am an artificer. Fortunately for you, I am also a healer. But I am primarily an artificer." He studied Trei for another moment. "I wish to learn how to make wings such as you kajuraihi use to mount to the heavens. You will teach me."

Trei said nothing. He did not precisely wish that he had died in a terrible explosion down at the harbor's edge. But he knew he *should* wish he had. What had Lord Manasi and Prince Imrei said to him during that difficult interview? Something like, *Perhaps someone suggested you might try for kajurai training? Perhaps someone suggested that you should bring dragon magic back to Tolounn?* Something like that.

And now Trei had done exactly what they had accused him of. He knew he should declare that he wouldn't help Master Patan. But he couldn't bring himself to make any such declaration. The memory of pain and black confusion was too near. The decouan had called him brave, but Trei knew now that he wasn't brave at all. The artificer's wintry eyes and calm manner frightened him: he did not doubt the intensity of Master Patan's curiosity. If Master Patan was determined to make him explain kajurai magic, Trei knew, probably he would not be able to refuse for very long at all.

Trei wanted to find his wings and fly so high and far he would never see the world again. He couldn't do that. He wanted to tuck himself down on the cot and pull the blanket over his head and refuse to speak or move until everyone just left him alone. He couldn't do that, either. His captors would do whatever they wished now and he couldn't stop them . . . any more than he'd stopped the engines. . . .

There was a huge, shattering roar, so vast that it was beyond noise. The house rocked and creaked; a jug of water fell from a table and shattered. Outside the window, tiles plummeted from the roof and smashed on the cobbles below. People screamed and shouted; boots pounded across the ceiling and, not as loudly, on the streets outside. At last there was a great shrieking noise that cut through all the other commotion and went on and on above all the other screams, ending in a second crashing roar nearly as terrible as the first.

Then there was quiet. After the tumult, it was a stunning, oddly deafening silence. People were still screaming, but somehow their cries only seemed to counterpoint the great quiet rather than break it. Trei clutched his blanket and stared fearfully at the ceiling, where the plaster had cracked straight across; Master Patan supported himself against a wall; the decouan ran to the window and stared out. Then he turned to stare at Trei. He opened his mouth, and closed it again.

"Stay here!" Master Patan said sharply to the decouan, and went out himself.

"Great generous Gods!" said the decouan, still staring at Trei. "Boy, what did you throw *in* there?"

Trei said nothing.

The provincar of Teraica, who, Trei gathered, had been intended to govern the Floating Islands after they were properly conquered, had a lot to say. He stormed back and forth in his great hall—there were cracks in its plaster and marble, too—and he said a great deal, mostly to the artificers who had built the engines and to the soldiers who had guarded them. Not even Master Patan, who was evidently the master of all the artificers in Teraica, tried to answer the provincar.

Master Patan had come back to collect Trei, eventually. Trei had hoped he might have a chance to slip out into the confusion of the city; there seemed nothing out there *but* confusion now. Only, not at all to Trei's surprise, the decouan had made sure no such chance came. He wasn't unfriendly, but he *was* thoroughly professional.

So Master Patan had brought Trei to the provincar's palace. Evidently the provincar wanted to see with his own eyes the boy who had wrecked one of his beautiful engines.

Trei tried to stand straight and hold his head up proudly before his captors, but he felt very small and young in the provincar's grand palace, with the provincar himself cursing and shouting. Even Master Patan stood with his head bowed in the face of that fury.

"The greatest weapon of the age, you assured me! Assured *us*!" the provincar shouted at the artificer. "Brought down by a brick lobbed in by a *boy*!" He had said this before; he had said a great many things. No one was trying to answer him. "One of my irreplaceable engines! Destroyed!" He gestured broadly in the direction of the harbor and glared murderously at Master Patan, hand half raised, clearly longing to hit him. He had, once. Master Patan had not said anything to that, either, but he had returned so outraged a stare that the provincar apparently hesitated to do it again. Trei wondered who Master Patan's patron was, or who the artificer was related to, and wished he had such a powerful protector himself. Though the provincar hadn't yet struck *him*. But Trei could guess he would. Or worse.

"It isn't irreplaceable at all. Everything that has been lost can be rebuilt," Master Patan said calmly. "Two of the engines remain, and I am informed that most of the ships continue sound. We have experienced a setback, but the method itself has, I believe, proven itself." His calm seemed almost a deliberate insult, set against the provincar's fury. Another artificer standing close behind him put an urgent hand on his arm, and Master Patan, looking faintly surprised, stopped speaking.

"A *setback*!" shouted the provincar. He was a big, florid man, now very red in the face. Veins stood out in his throat. *"Rebuilt?"* He stared at Master Patan, seeming for the moment beyond speech. Then he took a deep, deep breath and said, much more quietly, "You and yours, go out there and look well at what's left of my harbor! And then you come back to me and tell me how long it will take to *rebuild* what we have lost."

Trei had been afraid of the provincar when he shouted. But he found he was more afraid of him when he stopped shouting. Even Master Patan seemed to feel the same; he inclined his head and turned obediently to go, taking all the other artificers with him.

The provincar glared after them for a moment. Then he took in another deep breath and turned to Trei. He gestured sharply toward the soldiers. "And drop this boy down the deepest oubliette in Teraica!"

Master Patan, nearly at the door, whirled back. "No!" he cried, sounding more outraged now than even when the provincar had hit him. "That is an Island flier; where are we to get another? We—"

The provincar seemed to swell up with the force of his fury, until Trei half thought he might explode like one of his furnaces. "Out!" he roared. "*Out! Do as you are told,* or I swear before the *Gods,* I will drop *you* into an oubliette after this brat!"

Trei had no doubt at all that he meant exactly what he said. Even Master Patan seemed to believe it. The master artificer stared at the provincar for a long, suspended moment. But then he bowed his head, backed away, and disappeared out the door.

"Take him out!" the provincar repeated, glaring at the commander of his soldiers. He added viciously, "If the harbor and my engines are beyond you, perhaps you can at least properly guard one Island boy!"

The commander bowed his head stiffly and gestured to his men. The decouan put a hand on Trei's shoulder and guided him out.

Trei walked numbly beside the decouan, surrounded by soldiers, through the hot haze of sunlit dust and smoke that covered the city. He didn't know whether to be glad that he had, after all, destroyed one of the engines—or dismayed that he had destroyed only one of them: had Tolounn's invasion of the Islands been ruined? Or merely inconvenienced?

The smoke-filled air made him hope he'd at least achieved something more than an *inconvenience:* that had been a really powerful explosion. But if two of the engines were left? Master Patan had said the destruction of one engine was just a "setback." He'd said the "method had proven itself."

Trei doubted he'd have been willing to risk imprisonment in an oubliette just to destroy *one* engine—and he knew with great surety that he wouldn't have done so just to *inconvenience* the Tolounnese. Though . . . maybe the technique of throwing dragon eggs into furnaces had *also* been proven. If Genrai told the wingmaster what they'd done . . . maybe they could find more dragons willing to give their eggs to kajuraihi to throw into furnaces?

But he was still terrified of the oubliettes. He told himself he should try to escape, that this walk was surely the last chance he would have—but he knew that it wasn't any chance at all.

And there really wasn't. The walk was not long at all. The oubliettes were not very far removed from the provincar's palace, which was, Trei found, built into the hills on the far side of Teraica from the harbor. They walked uphill all the way, until they came to the place where the oubliettes had been dug down deep into the chalk of the hills. Trei stood beside the commander as the men levered the grating away from the first oubliette in the line. He did not watch their effort, but lifted his head and gazed up, into the wide and empty sky. Nothing moved except smoke. He could not even see any birds.

"How old are you, boy?" the commander asked him abruptly.

Trei flinched, startled. He looked at the commander: a young man with the red-handled knife of a teruann, commander of a whole company. Presumably this man's company had been in charge of guarding the steam engines, but though the teruann looked stern and angry, he did not seem to be angry with Trei. Trei said, "Fourteen, sir."

The teruann looked grimmer than ever. "Fourteen. Gods."

Trei said hastily, "I wasn't—no one *sent* me. They wouldn't send a boy still in the novitiate to do, well, anything! But Master Taimenai, the wingmaster, I told him, but he didn't understand about the engines, and I thought it might work. . . ."

"Huh." The teruann gave Trei a sharp look. "Why would *you* know about engines? What *was* it you threw in there? Something magic, I suppose? Do you people have more where that one came from? We've rearranged our guard, so I hope it doesn't matter, but I confess I'm curious."

Trei swallowed. He didn't answer. He knew he shouldn't have answered even the first question: it only led to another question, and another after that. To his shame, he knew he would answer whatever questions the teruann asked, if the man persisted. The man wouldn't even have to hit him. Trei would answer him just to delay the oubliette.

However, the teruann didn't press for answers. After a moment, when Trei didn't speak, he sighed. Then he looked around and snapped his fingers. The decouan stepped forward and gave the commander a water flask and a cloth-wrapped packet. The teruann passed these to Trei without a word. The teruann's expression was tight. But he only stepped back, gesturing toward the ladder another of his men had lowered.

Trei stepped jerkily toward the ladder, stopped, turned toward the teruann. But the man shook his head quickly, stopping Trei before he could say anything. He was a soldier: that was what the shake of his head meant. He was a professional Tolounnese soldier, and the Tolounnese were the best soldiers in the world. He would carry out his orders whether he approved of them or not. So there was no reason, after all, for Trei to shame himself by pleading. He just turned and walked to the ladder. And climbed down it, carefully, the flask and packet an awkward burden on the ladder.

It was a long way to the bottom of the oubliette. The narrow shaft cut off the light very quickly, so that it almost seemed to be night instead of day. And it was cold in the oubliette. Twenty feet down it was merely pleasantly cool, but after forty feet, it was cold. Trei reached the end of the ladder and hesitated for a moment. But he couldn't cling to the ladder forever. It couldn't be far to the bottom; they wouldn't do that. Trei shut his eyes and jumped awkwardly backward into the dark. He landed hard, after a fall of no more than a foot or two, and fell to his knees. Then he stood up again, peering upward toward the light. After a moment, he shouted, "I'm down."

The ladder rattled upward, and the iron grate fell back into place between Trei and the sky. Then there was nothing. If there were guards up above, they made no sound he could hear.

The oubliette shaft was round, about six feet across, made of white chalk and cold brick. The floor slanted. There was a drain, about as wide as a man's hand was long, on the low side of the oubliette. For . . . necessary functions, Trei supposed, and also to keep prisoners from drowning when the monsoons came. Prisoners weren't supposed to die quickly in the oubliettes. They were supposed to last a long, long time, down in the dark while the world above forgot them.

Trei walked slowly around the perimeter of his prison. There were marks on the walls, lots of marks, only barely visible in the dim light. He ran his fingers across them, reached up, found the marks went higher than he could reach. Words, pictures, but it was difficult, in this darkness, to understand what story they told. Lines laboriously carved with knives, or pebbles, or shards of brick . . . the marks of someone else's long imprisonment. Trei didn't want to think about that.

Instead he found the packet the teruann had given him, undid the oiled cloth . . . sausage and hard bread and salty cheese, and strips of dried fruit. Soldiers' fare, he thought, and tried to be grateful. He had no idea when prisoners were fed. Or what. Or how often. He couldn't imagine eating anything. But he supposed he would be glad of the food eventually. He set it aside and sat down. Leaned against the brick, flinched away from the cold. Maybe it was cold that prisoners died of down here. Unless it was despair.

The light above vanished, flickered, reappeared. . . . There was an odd sound, a little like wings—Trei put his hands out, warding off whatever was falling, and something soft fell across his outstretched arms. He stared at it for a moment, ran his hands across it . . . looked upward in surprise. One of the guards had thrown a blanket down. Trei's throat tightened at the unexpected kindness. He shouted, "Thank you!" up toward the light. There was no response. But it was that small kindness which gave him the courage to endure as even the dim light faded toward night.

12

At noon on the second day of the siege, Cesei's eyes rolled back in his head and he collapsed. He had once again been trying to do Tichorei's work. Second bell had been when Tichorei had either overextended or died: Araenè was not sure which.

Cesei had said he thought the older apprentice was still alive. Tichorei looked dead to Araenè. He was horrifyingly cool and limp, and she couldn't see any flutter in the thread she held in front of his mouth. But Cesei had assured her she just wasn't looking at Tichorei right.

She was still glad to see that when Cesei collapsed, he didn't look dead: he just looked like an exhausted little boy who'd worn himself out trying to do a job too big for him. Araenè picked him up. He was not heavy, but she was too tired herself to carry him more than a step or two. Fortunately, she only had to turn and look to find the ornate oak and ebony "friendly door" in front of her, set right into a wall that ordinarily would have held a lot of spheres and three narrow mirrors. It was standing open, showing her a slice of Cesei's apartment.

"Thank you," Araenè told the door wearily. She carried Cesei into his apartment and put him into his bed. He looked shockingly young. His eyes looked bruised; his whole face looked pinched and thin. She wished suddenly, desperately, that her mother was here . . . to tuck Cesei into his bed, to tuck *Araenè* into hers. . . . She was too tired to cry. She looked around to the door, which still stood where she had left it.

"Well . . . ," she said, and sighed. She would come back later and look in on Cesei. She could bring him soup, at least. In the meantime . . .

In the meantime, Tichorei still looked dead. He was much too heavy for Araenè to carry, or even to drag. In case Cesei was right and he wasn't dead, she fetched a pillow and an extra blanket from Cesei's room and tried to make him more comfortable where he was, tucked against the wall. Then she went down the spiral stairway—down seven turns and then along a hall, up a short flight and a long jump across a narrow gap that should have been bridged by three floating stones. The stones had fallen, of course, when the Tolounnese mages had driven away the dragons; for all Araenè knew, they had fallen all the way down through Milendri and right into the sea.

On the other side of the gap, she found a small, plain door and went through this into the kitchens. No one was here: the kitchens had been deserted since . . . well, since everything had gone wrong. The ovens were cold and dark, all the fires out.

Araenè found some griddle-baked breads, not too stale. She rolled honey and nuts up in the breads, absently adding a shake of pepper and a pinch of cassia, and made up a tray.

Then she left the kitchens and went down a narrow flight of stairs right to the bottom, where she found a door of glass bound with strips of metal. When she stepped through this one, she came out exactly where she'd meant to, on the balcony of Horera Tower. Master Akhai was there again, sorting through spheres and showing Kanii and Taobai how to release the spells in them: he didn't have the strength to use them himself and the adjuvants were all exhausted. Jenekei and the twins had been here the last time Araenè had come: now they were gone. She bit her lip.

Kanii stood up and took the tray out of her hands with a tired nod. "They're all right. Or they will be. Master Akhai sent them to rest."

"Oh." Araenè hesitated. "I don't know if Tichorei is all right or . . . or not."

Another nod, as weary as the first. "I'll tell Master Akhai."

"How are . . . how is . . . everything?"

Kanii rubbed a hand over his face. "Hard to tell. Maybe better than it was? Something happened. . . ." He gestured vaguely. "A little while ago. The Tolounnese lost a lot of the strength they've been pouring at us. Half, maybe? We don't know why. We don't think it was anything we did. . . ."

Araenè stared at him. "What, then?"

Kanii only shrugged. "We think maybe Cassameirin did something? We all hoped . . . but nothing else like that has happened. And Tolounn still has . . . a lot of strength." *Too much,* he did not quite say. But Araenè heard it anyway. He added, "I think there's fighting all the way out to the Second City now."

"Can I . . . do anything?"

Kanii only shook his head, too tired to be kind.

Araenè bit her lip again and slipped away quietly, not to disturb the ones who might do something. She meant to go back to the kitchens, make some broth for Cesei. But this time, knack or not, she couldn't find the door. So instead she looked, a little impatiently, for the "friendly door."

It stood in front of her at once, half open. To show the hall of spheres and mirrors.

"There isn't anything I can do there," Araenè explained to the door. "Not now that I'm by myself. It was Tichorei and Cesei who could actually do things there." And she did not want to look at Tichorei. She closed the door firmly, said, "The kitchens, please," and opened it again. To find the hall of spheres and mirrors.

She rubbed her hands across her eyes. But it did not seem worth arguing over. She went through the door.

One whole wall of spheres was on fire.

It looked that way at first. Then Araenè, squinting through her fingers, could see that the fire was really contained in the spheres, that nothing in the hall was actually *burning*. The scent of cloves was very strong; the taste of ginger and cloves numbed her mouth. She edged forward, staring.

Every sphere on that wall showed the same thing: fire. Every sphere, whether made of black onyx or white-veined quartz or heavy, polished hematite, seemed filled with fire, and the memory of fire, and the promise of fire. Blackness burned at the heart of the fire, and something moved across that blackness: something small and whip-thin and sinuous that was not exactly fire. Araenè did not at once understand what she saw. She lifted the biggest of the spheres off its shelf and carried it away so she could look at it with less distraction . . . then, on impulse, settled cross-legged on the floor near Tichorei and set the sphere down in front of her. She leaned forward, gazing at it intently, concentrating on bringing out the hot, glittering ginger of vision and foretelling.

In the sphere, flames rose high and hot: at the center of the fire, something that was not fire slid toward her, coiled back on itself, tore at the glowing black iron floor beneath it, and twisted back again in a movement that seemed to express terror and despair. A narrow head lifted atop a long, graceful neck garbed in feathers of fire. . . . Araenè leaped to her feet and backed away from the sphere, horrified: she knew, vividly, not only that Trei had succeeded in throwing her dragon's egg into a Tolounnese furnace, which should have been wonderful, but also that something had gone terribly wrong. Then, as the "friendly door" was gone, she turned and fled down the spiral stair to the first door that offered itself. This was a door three times her own height, made of heavy black oak bound with strips of twisted black iron. Araenè didn't know where the black door might ordinarily lead, nor did she care: she knew where she had to go and she was furiously determined that whatever door this was, it would take her there.

The door opened to show her the balcony where the black gulls nested.

"No!" Araenè said fiercely, and slammed it shut again. She slapped her hand down hard on the door and said, "Master Tnegun, or I'll let all that fire out right *here,* Gods curse you, and see how strong your oak is when it's turned to coal, and all your iron glows red!"

This time, when she opened the door, it swung back

meekly to show her Master Tnegun's workroom. When she stepped through it, the door misted around the edges and tried to take her to the gulls' balcony after all, but, consumed by terror and guilt and fury, Araenè scarcely noticed. She only smacked her hand against the frame, jerked the door back to the workroom, and stepped through.

Master Tnegun was sitting alone at the far end of the great room, in a deep chair at the head of his enormous table. Table and chair and mage alike were drowned in shadows; clad in a severe black robe, the master was hardly visible at all. He did not seem to notice Araenè's entrance. She paused for a horrified moment, thinking that he might have gone too far in whatever magery he was working—like Master Kopapei, who had overextended while trying to mislead and distract the Tolounnese mages, or Master Camatii, who had done the same thing trying to heal too many injured men. She tried not to think, *Or he might be dead.* Then she saw her master's hands move and breathed again. She walked forward.

A single sphere of black glass rested on the table, which was otherwise entirely empty. Master Tnegun was not looking at the sphere, however, but at a long black feather, which he was drawing over and over through his fingers. He still did not look up at her—whatever he was doing, he was intent. The bitter scents of cumin and fenugreek filled the room, and something else, something hot and wild, like the scent of fire itself.

Araenè arrived at her master's end of the room, reached out, and touched the black sphere with a fingertip.

The sphere burst into flames.

Master Tnegun blinked. Blinked again. Awareness seeped

back into his face. He lifted his head to look first at the blazing sphere and then at Araenè.

Araenè said furiously, "You asked me if I wanted you to break my—my hard-held protection, you said! By force, you said! Now I do!"

There was a pause. Araenè wanted simultaneously to scream with impatience and run away. She did not move, but her hands clenched hard.

Master Tnegun said softly, "It was a rhetorical question."

"I know it was! Then!" Araenè snapped. "Now it has an answer. The answer is yes. I think I must have done everything wrong, and now I think you'd better hurry—" Her sharp tone wavered toward tears and she stopped quickly.

"Arei . . . I am aware that you would not hold your mind's privacy so hard if you had no cause." Master Tnegun paused, looking carefully at Araenè. "Allow me to speak plainly. If I break that shield by force, young Arei, I must tell you, it will shatter entirely. I will see first what you most desperately wish to conceal: you will yourself fling your secrets at me. Neither you nor I will be able to prevent this."

Araenè swallowed. She felt very cold. Her rage seemed to have deserted her: she only felt frightened and ashamed. But she said anyway, "It doesn't matter. And there's no time! Just . . . hurry."

Master Tnegun did not ask her again if she was sure. He seemed to trust that she had reason for her urgency—in a strange way, Araenè even felt flattered by the smooth speed with which he rose to his feet, took the one step necessary, dropped one hand to her shoulder and the other to rest against her face—she tried not to flinch—

Master Tnegun's mind slid across the borders of hers with that same quickness, probed suddenly inward toward Araenè's mind and heart. Instantly her cool shield stood in his way: anise and lemon and pepper, a barrier smooth and featureless as glass between her mind and his. But this time, Master Tnegun's mind did not sheer away, but closed around hers like a vise. The glass did not merely shatter: it exploded. Master Tnegun's mind sliced into Araenè's with cold precision.

It hurt. She did not know whether she cried out or not; she tried to fight the mage's intrusion, could not keep herself from fighting it. But she met only an iron determination that closed around all her struggles and pressed her mind to stillness. She was aware of the first stutter of surprise when Master Tnegun found her true name, and then the second when he glimpsed the fire dragon that had given her its egg. And then the third when he understood what fire the spheres were showing, and why.

Then he lifted his hand from her face, and Araenè was free. She found herself sitting in a chair that, moments ago, hadn't been there. Bending forward, she pressed her hands hard over her eyes.

"Look at me," Master Tnegun commanded her. His voice was as dark and smoky as the cumin that swirled in the room, as remorseless as the sea.

Araenè blinked hard, clenched her teeth, straightened abruptly, and met the master's eyes. There was nothing she could read in his; his thoughts were hidden behind a wall of cold reserve.

"I've been in these Islands too long when I can't see a girl in front of my eyes merely because she's wearing boys' clothing," the master said softly.

Araenè shook her head, demanded sharply, "Does that matter now?" She did not let herself think about later, when it would probably matter very much.

"Indeed, no. We must indeed act swiftly. I was warned—" Master Tnegun hesitated briefly, then continued, "I was warned to reserve my strength, but now I find I did not hold back as hard as I should. You have a great deal of power, Araenè. I wish you might set your strength willingly behind mine, but you do not have the training to do it freely and there is no time for you to learn. I must take what you do not have the skill to give."

"Yes," Araenè said. She felt odd: not angry. More just . . . uncertain, and yet also desperately relieved that the deception was over. "Can you—you *are* going to save the little dragon?"

"Among other things. I think there may be a way—I hope there may be; the Islands are greatly in need of dragon fire just now. With fortune and the favor of the Gods, perhaps we may save it." Master Tnegun set his hand back on her shoulder, drew her to her feet, and directed her attention wordlessly toward a delicate door of pale wood and pearl and bone. "Let us see what wind rider the Gods will put in my hand."

Under the master's hand, the pale door swung silently back open upon a clean, sweeping height. Before them, jagged stone reached to the sky; behind them, it fell away to the distant sea. Between sky and sea stood a small white tree, with a perfectly round pool of clear water under the tree.

A tall young man sat beside the pool, staring down into

its still water. But he turned when Master Tnegun closed the door behind them. He rose at once and walked quickly to meet them. Araenè did not exactly recognize him, but he looked familiar—he had kajurai eyes, she realized; they caught and refracted the light as he stepped through a shaft of sun.

The young man glanced quickly at Araenè, away—back, with a sudden intensity that made her hesitate. But then Master Tnegun took a step forward, and the young man turned sharply to him and said, with an odd mix of deference and exasperation, "Though I appreciate everyone's concern, I hardly expect—"

"Prince Ceirfei," Master Tnegun overrode him, "I find myself in sudden pressing need of a kajurai. Will you assist me?"

Prince Ceirfei? Araenè thought, shocked. This was *Prince Ceirfei?* Araenè had certainly heard the name, she now recalled she'd even heard he'd auditioned for the kajuraihi, but she certainly hadn't expected to find any *prince* waiting on the other side of Master Tnegun's door.

The young man took a quick, startled moment to reassess the situation. Then he said simply, "Of course. Whatever you require."

Master Tnegun inclined his head. "The Tolounnese have pressed the living winds far out to sea," he told Prince Ceirfei. Out here on this craggy peak, this was more obvious than ever. The air hung heavy and still; it seemed to weigh down upon them. It was impossible to imagine any breeze breaking the brooding quiet. Even the leaves of the white tree drooped limp and still in the heat.

Prince Ceirfei gave a little nod, waiting.

"I believe I can free the winds from the control of the Tolounnese mages," Master Tnegun said then. "The Tolounnese lost some of their strength some time past. I think I can give you . . . perhaps a quarter-bell."

The prince tilted his head attentively.

"So. I will free the living winds. You must bring a sky dragon to this place; I have no affinity for the winds, so if you do not know a way to do this, I cannot advise you. The dragon must go to Teraica. There it will find a hatchling fire dragon, quickened by the heat of the Tolounnese furnaces. But though the heat of the furnace was sufficient to quicken the fire dragon's egg, it is not enough to sustain the young dragon. The fire below the earth must be freed, but it is buried deep there along the Tolounnese coast and the hatchling cannot break the earth above it."

Araenè blinked. So that was what had gone wrong; she had not known exactly what the trouble was, only that there was trouble. How stupid she had been not to ask Master Tnegun in the first place—she should have asked him about dragon eggs and furnaces—only she hadn't thought of a discreet enough way to ask, and she'd been so certain she understood what the dying fire dragon had wanted, and then it had been too late.

Master Tnegun did not seem to notice Araenè's dismay. He continued, still speaking to the prince, "If no adult dragon breaks open the deep rock to let out the fire, the hatchling will die. Do you understand? There is little time, so ask only what questions you must."

Prince Ceirfei said quietly, "Do I understand correctly: this is a young fire dragon in the furnace? All I can bring you—if any dragon at all will answer me, it will be a wind dragon."

Master Tnegun gave him a brief nod. "Wind and fire are more closely allied than you perhaps realize, Prince Ceirfei, and we may be glad this is so, as I have no one to summon a fire dragon for me. Think of the storm winds that bear lightning at their heart: so the wind may bear fire."

"You must call the wind, and the wind must become fire," quoted Araenè, startled, and then blushed as both prince and mage looked at her. "That's what the fire dragon said. When it gave me the egg."

"Then we may indeed hope that fire and wind are close allied," said Master Tnegun. "We shall hope that from the first, our fire dragon intended—or guessed—or hoped—that a wind dragon would favor this call." He turned gravely back to the prince. "Nevertheless, though my knowledge of wind dragons is limited, I believe it must be a great thing to ask the wind to yield to fire, yet this is precisely what you must persuade the dragon to do."

"Very well," the prince said slowly. "Give me a living wind, then, and I shall try to call a dragon down out of the sky."

Master Tnegun turned at once to Araenè. "I will use your strength to do what I must," he told her. "An experienced adjuvant would be better. But all the adjuvants have spent their strength." He paused, then added, "You will inevitably fight me, Araenè—fight what I must do. I cannot support the effort I must make if I must battle you as well as our opponents."

"I won't fight you," Araenè said. She wanted to sound matter-of-fact and assured, like the prince. But to her own ears, though her words were brave, she sounded weak and frightened. She was immediately furious—with herself, but anger of any kind was much better than fear. She jerked her shoulders back and looked Master Tnegun in the face.

The Yngulin mage gave her an approving nod, but he said, "You will. You will not know how to yield your strength to me. I will show you the technique by which you may do this. It is too advanced a technique for you. You must endure it."

Araenè lifted her chin and said fiercely, trying to reassure herself as well as the master, "I will."

Master Tnegun nodded once more. Then he knelt and drew a large sphere of blackish red pyrargyrite out of the air. Pyrargyrite, if Araenè remembered correctly, was closely allied to fire, to vision, and to magics of unmaking. Indeed, at the moment, that sphere seemed to be filled with dark embers and leaping flames. It tasted of cloves and also something harsher, something violent, something that belonged to the darkness and not to the living fire.

Master Tnegun handled this sphere gingerly, as though it actually was hot to the touch. He set it on the stone and beckoned to Araenè.

Now that it came to this moment, Araenè found she was not afraid. Master Tnegun looked so calm and assured and . . . not indifferent . . . detached. Araenè found she had no doubt that he knew exactly what to do and that he would do it. This surety gave her the courage to kneel down as he directed, the sphere in front of her. Prince Ceirfei stood attentively near at hand, watching everything but saying nothing.

"Araenè, I must go into your mind," Master Tnegun told Araenè. "You will find you have recovered your shield; I will break it quickly and teach you the structures I need you to hold. Are you ready?"

Araenè clenched her jaw, but she nodded.

His mind touched hers, and as he had warned, her shield snapped forcefully into place between them. And shattered, under the relentless power of the master's intrusion. *Iron,* Araenè thought: Master Tnegun's mind was smooth and hard and remorseless as iron. Fight him? She could find no way even to begin to fight him . . . and then she did: an echo of what he had inadvertently shown her himself. Her mind hardened to match his, only her mind was something hotter than iron: something molten that burned and flowed and closed around his. She realized, dimly, that she was fighting him and that she shouldn't, but she did not know how to stop.

Master Tnegun caught her attack with ruthless dispatch, crushing it as he had broken her protective shield. Stunned and momentarily helpless, Araenè spiraled toward darkness. But Master Tnegun caught her before the darkness could drown her: he forced her mind into a . . . kind of shape, a structure that she had never imagined. It was a strange and desperately uncomfortable shape: she felt as though he had handed her a complicated edifice made entirely of sharp knife blades; there was no way to hold it that would not cut her. But she saw at once that this pattern was actually a way of holding *herself:* it flattened her own defenses and left the reserves of her strength open.

Once Master Tnegun had forced her to understand this structure, he let her go. Drawing freely on her strength, he cast his own awareness out of her mind and elsewhere. . . . She could not follow what he did; it was too complicated and strange. But she knew that if she let her mind unfold from the pattern he had shown her, he would lose all access to her strength.

She thought of Tichorei, of Sayai, of Kanii, of little Cesei. Of Trei. Of spheres filled with fire and shattering with fine webs of cracks. And though the hot strength poured out of her like blood from a wound, she held the structure Master Tnegun had shown her with rigid determination.

Then—she could not have said whether a quarter of a bell had passed or a day—the terrible draining weakness ceased. Master Tnegun's mind recoiled from unknown distances, striking hers so that she staggered and lost her hold on the pattern to which she had clung; at once a wild, rolling surge of half-controlled power struck against him. This time, his mind did not meet or counter her defense, only gave way and fled— gone, out—Araenè's head jerked up and she would have fallen except she was already sitting. She fought for breath in gasps that were nearly sobs.

Master Tnegun still knelt across from her, darker than ever against the white gravel. He was not looking at her. His eyes were hooded and his head bowed. The light was harsh on his face; it showed lines of exhaustion and pain around his eyes and mouth. He looked older than she had ever guessed, much older than her father. Older than anyone she'd ever known.

Before Araenè, the pyrargyrite sphere had shattered into a pile of delicate, fine shards.

A breeze slid across the mountain, ruffled through Araenè's short hair, scattered shards of black crystal, rippled capriciously along the edges of Master Tnegun's robe. Died away. Returned.

"Did it work?" Araenè whispered.

The Yngulin mage shifted his hands across the stone, braced himself. Lifted his head. Looked up.

Araenè followed his searching glance.

Prince Ceirfei stood near the white tree and its pool. He was speaking, but Araenè could not see the creature to which he spoke.

". . . for which we may pray to the Gods," he was saying, quickly and forcefully. "And is not all our attention bent to that very end? Let come what will, though the city drown in molten fire and iron and the very stone be broken against the sea." He paused, evidently listening to some response. Then he said sharply, "Well, I am a prince of the Floating Islands, and I give you my word before the Silent God and the Young God and the Great God himself that this is my will and the will of the king, my uncle."

Araenè stared up at Master Tnegun. The mage was studying the prince . . . no, she thought. He was studying the creature to which the prince spoke. He glanced down at her, however, as though her unspoken bewilderment had drawn his attention. He touched her hand, then reached to draw a fingertip across her eyelids . . . ginger and anise tingled across her tongue and the palms of her hand, and when Master Tnegun lifted his hand, she could . . . see.

It was as though layers of cloud and glass spiraled through the air: that was her first thought. A half-glimpsed wing, indistinct as mist, shifted across her vision. Once she discovered the wing, as though the immense size and odd shape of it taught her to understand the rest of what she saw, she made out the outlines of a long, graceful head, transparent as glass, and the elegant curve of the neck that arched higher than the head. Light slid, gleaming, through an opalescent eye larger than Araenè's whole head.

And Prince Ceirfei was speaking to that creature. To Araenè, it seemed that he might as well have argued with the wind itself: there was nothing she could find in the great half-seen dragon to which a man might speak. But the prince seemed to have no such doubts. She whispered to Master Tnegun, "Can you hear it?"

The mage's face was tight with weariness. "A word here and there, no more than that," he answered softly. "Here, Cassameirin would do better than I. Even were I not . . ."

He meant were he not tired almost to death. Araenè nodded.

"You will find that magery such as you and I wield is very little like the natural magic the dragons share with their kajuraihi. You and I work out the mathematical framework of the world and form our spells with stylus and ink as well as natural power; we set our spellwork in stone or metal or glass because we must keep our working contained and, hmm, separate from ourselves. Dragon magic is not akin to magery: it is a magic of being, not of knowing. Your cousin would assure you that the kajuraihi do not fly by *understanding* flight, but simply by flying." Master Tnegun paused, then glanced over and up at the vast crystalline dragon that had come down out of the sky to speak with Prince Ceirfei. The master added wryly, "Though I have dwelled here in the Islands for many years, I know little of your dragons of wind and sky."

The dragon spoke: its voice was not at all like a normal voice. It was more like the ringing of chimes, or the notes of a flute. As she saw the dragon only in glimpses, so Araenè heard only scattered notes when it spoke. She could not understand it at all.

But the prince clearly could. He was saying now, "And thus all the winds above the Islands are at peril, yet still it is the fire that must be released in order to free the winds. Is that not so?"

A pause, sprinkled with delicate chiming notes.

"I am aware," said the prince. And then, "If fire is the cost, we must pray you are willing to pay it. Is not the gain commensurate?"

Beside Araenè, Master Tnegun shifted. She looked up and found that his face had gone tight—with pain and exhaustion, she thought at first, but then she saw that it was more than pain; it was a tension born of indecision, maybe, or maybe simply an awareness of peril. His mouth firmed. He shook his head a little. Araenè thought he looked like he was settling himself for renewed effort. He gave her shoulder a little pat—*Stay here*—climbed painfully to his feet, and walked toward the white tree. Araenè dutifully stayed where she was. She was not at all sure she could get to her feet if she tried.

Once he was at the prince's side, Master Tnegun bent to murmur to him. Araenè could not hear him, but she was almost sure he was saying something like, *There is no time left; get this done now.* Whatever he said, Prince Ceirfei listened attentively. His mouth tightened. Turning to the half-visible dragon, he said with flat decision, "For my part, I am not bargaining. Only tell me plainly what you would require. I swear before the Gods, *we* shall not protest to pay what cost we must."

Delicate chiming.

"Even so," said the prince. And then, after a momentary pause, he inclined his head and said in a tone of finality, "So it is all before the Gods, then, and I will pray for your success in all your endeavors."

The dragon frayed into crystalline music and glittering winds and was gone. Araenè was not perfectly certain at first that it *was* gone: she looked for traceries of feathers against the sky, for the shimmer of light along a transparent neck or within a lucent eye. But the winds seemed to have carried it away.

And only barely in time, for just as Araenè reached this tentative conclusion, the wind—all fragile movements of the air, all life and quickness—was pressed out of the air by a huge, heavy, smothering pressure. The Tolounnese mages had at last discovered what Master Tnegun had done, or had finally found the time or the inclination to undo it. Gathering her remaining strength, Araenè came to join the others, looking nervously at her master: *Is this all right?*

"Yes," the Yngulin mage said quietly. "We were in time; the dragon was well away. What it will do—that I cannot say, but it is free to act."

"It will do exactly as you wished," Prince Ceirfei said wearily. He looked almost as tired as Araenè felt. "Or so I believe. Little though I understand how you arranged for a young fire dragon to quicken in the Teraica furnaces." He glanced at Araenè as he added this last.

Master Tnegun glanced at her, too. "I suspect the hands of men provided merely the agency, not the intention, that led to this event," he said, a little drily. "Many wind dragons ride the winds above the Islands, but a fire dragon has long dwelled at their heart. You did not know this? Well, kajurai attention is always directed outward, I suppose, toward the winds and the sky. But as our fire dragon grew old and its fire dimmed, it seems to have sought—and found—an unusual method by which it might yet quicken its last egg. A method not without risks, but one that may yet prove fruitful: Gods grant we shall not merely save this hatchling, but also claim its strength for the Islands! But at what cost did you persuade the dragon to go to Teraica? If I may ask?"

"You may not," the prince said decisively. Straightening his shoulders, he patted the stones beside the pool. "You are worn beyond endurance, Master Tnegun, if you will permit me to say so. Sit before you fall, and tell me what we have wrought."

There was a little silence. Master Tnegun looked taken aback but also, Araenè thought, in a way he looked pleased. She did not understand why. She would have thought even a prince's flat defiance would have angered the mage, but Ceirfei's did not seem to. Indeed, Master Tnegun simply lowered himself to the stones as Prince Ceirfei had bidden him, leaning back against the smooth trunk of the white tree. He looked into the pool for a moment, then passed a hand slowly above the water. A crease appeared between his eyes—pain, or at least effort.

She could get up, after all, when she tried. Araenè made her way forward, gave Prince Ceirfei a cautious nod, and let herself down again beside Master Tnegun. The prince returned her nod. His gaze slid aside from hers, and after a moment she realized Master Tnegun had used her real name in his hearing: he knew she was a girl. She flinched from this realization, but after a moment the prince met her eyes with a directness that surprised her. Blushing, she looked down.

Master Tnegun had cupped water in his hands. He did not drink, however, but only gazed curiously into the water.

"Can we use the pool to see?" Araenè asked him. "Can I . . . Do you need my strength to see?"

Master Tnegun made a low, thoughtful sound. "Crystal would be better than water. Even this water. As we wish to see into fire, obsidian would be better still."

"If you need my strength . . ."

Lifting his gaze at last, the master gave Araenè a sharp look. "Oh, indeed. I have little left, and as I believe you may have a particular gift for vision, you may indeed do this working, young Araenè. If you will kindly permit me to show you the method?"

Araenè stiffened at his sarcasm. "Show me, then," she snapped.

Master Tnegun smiled, a flash of white teeth in his dark face that changed his expression entirely. He looked satisfied and faintly amused.

Araenè understood that he'd deliberately prompted her proud response but was genuinely pleased she'd made it. "You thought I'd be too afraid?" she demanded.

The master made a small, pacifying gesture. "Araenè, apprentices older and far more experienced than you would have found our recent exercise frightening."

Prince Ceirfei glanced back and forth between them, his eyebrows rising, but he did not ask any questions.

Master Tnegun said, "Compared to what you have already

done, child, this is complicated but not difficult. Can you permit me to come into your mind?" His mind slid deftly toward hers, met the shield that flicked into existence between them, skidded away.

But this time, after the first startled moment, Araenè found the trick of holding her protective shield below the outermost layers of her mind, allowing the master to touch the upper part of her mind while protecting the inward layers. It seemed so obvious . . . suspicion dawned in her mind. "Did you *show* me how to do this?"

Yes. It was not a word, but a kind of glittering intrusion that opened delicately into her mind. Aloud, Master Tnegun said drily, "A shame to waste a moment in which you were vulnerable to the most rapid and direct instruction. I suspect you will seldom be sufficiently motivated to allow it. Now, if you will observe—water is seldom suitable for vision, but then, this is not precisely water—" A second glittering intrusion unfolded, this one complicated, a structure that twisted around and folded back on itself, then, as she followed it, opened dizzyingly outward.

Fire filled Araenè's mind, living flames that rose up and then flattened out, a thin glaze of moving brilliance. She tasted fire: cloves and cassia and a sweet, wild heat that she did not quite recognize.

"That is certainly a unique manner of, hmm, perception," Master Tnegun commented. "The fragrances and flavors provide an interesting layer of complication across the magery you perceive. However, at the moment, I believe you might find ordinary senses more useful." A pause, and then, more sardonically, "Araenè, open your eyes."

Araenè hadn't been aware of closing them. She opened them now.

The pool was filled with fire. Flames crept across its width, just below the surface of the water: dark lower down and brighter near the surface. And something else moved there: something long and serpentine that writhed and struggled, crying in a voice like shattering glass because the fire was not enough, never enough. . . .

"I thought it would be all right," Araenè whispered. "I thought once it was . . . was quick, that it would be all right after that." She looked helplessly at Master Tnegun. "Is it going to die? How can a dragon of . . . of wind and air break open the earth to help my little dragon of fire?"

"Ordinarily, a fire dragon's egg would not quicken to hatching without sufficient fire," the Yngulin mage answered. "You . . . cheated. You and your cousin, I should say. When your cousin cast the dragon's egg into the furnace, the egg did indeed quicken, and when the shell cracked at last, the heat within the furnace increased, and increased again, until at last the capacity of the furnace was exceeded. But then the Tolounnese engine exploded, and the heat the furnace contained was released, yes? And then your trick failed, for there is no longer enough fire in that place to sustain the young dragon."

There was no mockery in his voice now. He sounded . . . tired, yes, but that was not what caught Araenè's ear. He also sounded . . . sad, Araenè thought. And something else: he sounded in some way . . . resigned, maybe. Araenè muttered, "I should have told you. . . ."

The master gave her a little nod. "So you should, child. The rules of the hidden school exist for a very good reason. No apprentice actually follows those rules, you understand. But it does work best for us all if you *try*."

Araenè lowered her head.

"Of course, you did tell me, in the end," added Master Tnegun, and put his hand out over the pool, smoothing the flames and sharpening the image of the young dragon. It should have been brilliant with fire; Araenè knew that. But it was now nearly black; the fires that surrounded it had nearly burned out to ash. "Now it merely remains to be seen whether we have, against all probability, managed to persuade a sky dragon to quicken success out of imminent failure."

"When you have a moment . . . ," murmured Prince Ceirfei. His tone was not precisely annoyed. Impatient, maybe.

"Yes," said Master Tnegun. "In fact, it's very simple—"

Araenè bit her lip, but she did not have to suffer through the master's explanation of her foolishness. The mage did not have time to explain anything. Because, in the pool, the fire they were watching was suddenly whipped to a violent frenzy by a rising wind. Startled, Araenè flinched back and the vision in the pool wavered. Master Tnegun put out a hand; she felt him try to steady the vision, but his strength was not equal even to so small a task. She bit her lip again and tried to steady it herself. Cloves and cassia, cumin and ginger . . . everything tasted hot; smoke and burnt sugar rolled across Araenè's tongue and the palms of her hands. But the vision steadied.

Here by the pool, the air was heavy and flat. But they all saw storm winds break across the Tolounnese coast: neither black clouds nor rain, but winds monsoon fierce. The sky dragon rode those winds down from the heights. Araenè could barely see the stooping dragon: she glimpsed the edges of its wings, a filigree of translucent feathers against the sky, the curve of its long neck, talons sharp and transparent as glass. . . . The wind lashed the guttering fire where the Tolounnese engine had been, and she caught her breath, expecting the fire to blow out like a candle flame. But it was fanned high instead and towered, roaring. Within the fire, the tiny dragon flung back its head and cried piteously.

And then, above Teraica, the very wind caught fire.

Feathers that a moment before had been transparent as crystal caught the red light of the late sun and turned to fiery gold; opalescent light slid through pale eyes, and those eyes caught fire and blazed gold and crimson. The dragon fell through a storm of fire and wind. . . . The earth below cracked open to meet its dive: great fissures surging with molten fire opened all along the edges of the harbor. The sea poured into the fissures to meet a rising tide of molten stone: great fountains of white steam blasted upward along the lines of that elemental battle. Each of the remaining engines exploded, enormous blasts of fire and black smoke, and a huge portion of the Teraica harbor disappeared entirely. Farther from the sea, the cobbled streets of Teraica cracked to let out gouts of molten stone, which poured heavily down toward what remained of the harbor. Wooden buildings, never meant to withstand so much as a carelessly dropped candle, went up like torches. Some of them simply exploded. Everywhere, men and horses scattered and fled, or burned where they stood.

The fire dragon that had once been made of wind plunged down into the boiling water and fire where the furnaces had so recently stood, and disappeared. But even that did not end the destruction, for at least a quarter of the city still burned.

Araenè pressed her hands over her mouth, intensely grateful that the images in the pool were silent. Even so, she could not bear to watch; she couldn't even bear to know that those terrible images were real. Covering her eyes, she *did something*, and the pool ceased to blaze with light and became merely water.

A breeze stirred her hair; she could not understand for a moment why the wind was cool. It seemed to her it should burn with the terror and taste of fire. The air was sweet; it should have been bitter with ash. She asked shakily, "The baby dragon?"

"I do not know." Master Tnegun's voice was a weary thread of sound. "I do not know, Araenè. Certainly the dragon broke open the earth—certainly it *tried* to save the hatchling."

She had let the vision go too early. Araenè reached out toward the pool, flinching from the images of fire and destruction and yet still longing to see, to *know*—then she stopped. She felt dizzy—no. It was Kotipa—it was the very air around them—a sharp wind rose, suddenly, driving down from the heights, and the Island shuddered and rose smoothly back to its proper place, high above the sea.

Araenè got to her feet and stood, looking into the sky. She could see, barely, the long, sinuous shapes of the sky dragons riding the winds high above. She said, with a sense of astonishment, "We won." But that wasn't quite right. She said, "*Trei* won." She heard her voice tremble and didn't even care.

"*We* have all won," Prince Ceirfei said. He tilted his face toward the sky. "Tolounn will not readily answer *this* blow. So we have stepped out from the very embrace of failure and defeat."

Master Tnegun gave a small nod of relieved agreement, put a hand out over the pool, began to reach after some working, and instead folded gradually downward in slow-motion collapse as the last of his strength finally, comprehensively, failed.

13

The oubliette was quiet as well as dark and cold. Like a tomb. That was what oubliettes were supposed to be, after all: tombs for the living instead of the dead. Trei had always known that desperate criminals, the sort that were never going to be released, were sometimes imprisoned in deep oubliettes; he had known that most towns had oubliettes close by their ordinary prisons. Not Rounn; it was too cold in the far north to keep prisoners in holes in the ground. He'd never given any thought to the condition of prisoners kept in such confinement.

Now he only wondered how long it would be before a forgotten prisoner would give up all hope of release and come to wish his prison really *was* a tomb. Weeks, months? Years? He did not want to think about *years*. But already he half wished he had flown into the side of Teraica's steam engine a little harder. Though if he had, he wouldn't have been able to throw the egg down into the furnace.

Of course, it seemed now that this failure wouldn't have made much difference.

The light shifted, always dim, but becoming both redder and more muted still. . . . The sun would set soon, Trei thought. And how dark would the oubliette be at night? And how cold? How could it be so cold when there was such steady heat in the air above? But he was glad for the blanket. He sat on part of it and folded part of it behind his shoulders so he could lean back against the bricks, tilted his face up toward the sky, and watched the changing light.

Since he was watching, he saw the exact moment when the fiery wind whipped across the sky and lashed down across Teraica.

Trei could not decide what he had seen. He stood up, craning his neck, wishing for the ladder back—wishing to be able to press close to the grate above and stare out at the sky. He did not know what had flown at the leading edge of that wind, but he thought . . . he almost thought . . . Could that have been a *dragon* in the sky? But a dragon nothing like the delicate creatures of the Islands, a different kind of dragon, the kind that flew through his nightmares: a dragon with fire in its golden eyes, fire dripping from its mouth and falling from its wings . . .

The explosion cracked through the city while he was still trying to decide what he had seen. Only this explosion seemed a hundred times more powerful than the one he had caused by blowing up the engine. The very earth shook: a hard, abrupt shock that cracked the wall all along one side of the oubliette; Trei staggered and caught at the wall, but even so, a second, lesser shock knocked him to his knees. He could hear things falling and crashing above, sharp, percussive crashes like falling stone and then slower, grinding crashes as wood broke and mortared brick cracked and fell. Or so he thought those sounds might indicate. Some of the crashing seemed very close, but he thought some was much farther away—down in the city proper? There were cries of alarm and terror and pain, also near and far: the shouts of men and, somewhere much too close, the piercing screams of a wounded horse.

It was exactly as he'd imagined the destruction of Rounn must have been—exactly as he'd dreamed it—and Trei, trapped, frightened beyond thought, crouched helplessly against the wall of the oubliette, squeezed his eyes shut, and waited for the world to end.

But no other explosion followed, and the crashes and distant shouts died away. After some time, Trei opened his eyes, almost surprised to find himself still alive and still imprisoned in the oubliette. . . . Dust and smoke rolled through the air above him, closing out even the dim light of the late afternoon. Some of it settled down to the bottom of the oubliette, ash bitter at the back of his tongue . . . a bitterness right out of nightmares.

Trei tucked himself down at the edge of the oubliette, closed his eyes, and tried hard to think about the Floating Islands and how relieved and happy everyone would be if the steam engines were gone and the Tolounnese effort failed completely. But the images that pressed against the darkness behind his closed eyes were terrible, and he could not summon up any memories that did not include fire.

*　　*　　*

306

The night seemed endless. Trei didn't think he slept at all. He feared his dreams. So when he could not bear to sit still, he walked in blind, endless circles around the perimeter of the oubliette. The bitterness of the ash coated his mouth and throat. He was not hungry, but he drank most of the water in the flask. Then it occurred to him that the soldiers might well forget their prisoners if the disaster above was as terrible as he suspected; how long would it be before someone threw down another flask? After that he capped the flask and put it aside. Naturally, he at once discovered he was very thirsty.

Distant crashes and shouting continued sporadically all that night. The sounds were empty of meaning, except for the terror and anger they carried. Trei longed to be up riding the high winds so he could *see*. Or even in a tower prison. Anywhere but in this deep tomb.

To distract himself, he ran his hands over the cracks in the wall and tried to imagine that he might somehow use those fingerholds to climb to the top of the oubliette. Probably by daylight, when he could see the fineness of the cracks and the height of the shaft, the idea would seem far less attractive. Anyway, none of the cracks seemed enough to provide a foothold, and he could hardly climb to the top with just his fingertips.

Dawn came at last . . . a slow, gray dawn, hazy with ash and smoke. It was less of an improvement than Trei had hoped. He still could see nothing. The occasional distant shout still told him nothing except that somewhere someone still existed. Sometimes he called out himself during the course of that long day. No one answered. Though he listened, he heard no one moving above. No one came to the oubliettes at all, as far as he could tell. Trei drank most of the rest of his water and finally ate some of the food from the soldier's packet. All the food tasted bitter, like ash.

At noon, when the smoky light was as strong as it was going to get, he wrapped himself in the blanket, lay down against the curving wall, and fell into an exhausted sleep. If he dreamed, he did not remember his dreams.

It was dark again when he woke. He sat for a long time, breathing the bitter air and listening. For the first time since the great explosion and for as long as he listened, he heard nothing. The light told him little about the time of day: he could not tell whether it was morning or afternoon or evening. He paced stiffly around the oubliette shaft for a while, trying to ignore his thirst. At last he drank the last mouthfuls of his water, sipping it slowly to pretend it was more, and lay down again. After a measureless space of time, he slept.

And woke, in darkness. For some time he could not decide whether this marked the second night he'd spent in the oubliette or maybe the third. Eventually he concluded that surely it was only the second night. Then he could not understand why it had seemed so important to figure that out: what difference could one night possibly make? And then he realized that he was beginning to believe that he would be imprisoned in the oubliette for a long time—he shied away from thinking, *The rest of my life*. And he felt himself shy away from that thought, and wondered how many months . . . years . . . would pass before it seemed merely like any natural thought and not like a nightmare worse than fire.

Another dawn, and another long day. Trei measured time

very simply: dawn to noon, noon to dusk. It was too hard to track the bells in between. He began to chip away at the cracked wall with the shard of a brick. It was something to do, until the shard crumbled under the pressure. He wondered what other prisoners might have used to etch their words and drawings on the wall. He tried to read what they had written, understand their pictures, but little could be made out. Months—years?—of effort, and so little that he could even read.

But just before evening, as the light failed, someone called down from above.

Trei leaped to his feet, shouting. No one answered, but a shadow fell across the grate, followed by a clatter, and a rope came down with a narrow bucket of water and a packet of bread. He laid the bread aside on his blanket, poured the water hastily into his flask, and watched the bucket rise out of reach. He found tears in his eyes—he was very glad to have the water, he longed for the man above to stay and shout the news of the city down to him, but even more he was just intensely relieved to know that somewhere there *were* still people, that the whole city hadn't disappeared into ash and ruin, he the only one left amid its bones.

After that, even the air seemed cleaner, less tainted by ash. The oubliette seemed less cold, the blanket thicker, the night less dark and long. . . . Trei even found he was actually looking forward to the next day's dawn, although he knew very well there would be nothing at all to look forward *to* in that day.

But he was wrong. Because the next day . . . the third? Or *could* it already be the fourth? . . . Whatever the day, he heard the sound of voices from the free air above, and muffled cursing, and someone hauled the heavy iron grate away from the top of his oubliette.

Trei rose to his feet and stared upward. Maybe Master Patan had persuaded the provincar to bring him out? Trei did not want to show anyone dragon magic . . . but . . .

The ladder rattled down across the bricks, and Trei, as though moving through a dream, stepped forward and reached up to put his hand on the nearest rung.

Then the light was blocked, and he saw that he was not meant to climb up at all: someone was coming down. The disappointment was intense. Trei took his hand off the ladder and stepped back to give the newcomer room to come down. The man came to the end of the ladder. He twisted around, peering into the dimness and feeling with one foot beneath him for a rung that wasn't there.

Trei swallowed. He knew this must be a prisoner. But he did not know why the Tolounnese were putting this man here with Trei. He was much bigger than Trei. He looked strong. Trei wanted to be glad of the company, but maybe he should be nervous instead. . . .

When the man did not at once jump the small distance remaining, Trei said cautiously, "It's only about two feet. The ladder doesn't come down all the way."

The man grunted and jumped. He landed awkwardly, took one quick step, and put a hand on the wall to steady himself. Then he turned slowly, inspecting the oubliette and finishing by frowning darkly at Trei.

It was Anerii Pencara. The novice-master of Milendri's red-winged kajuraihi stood in the Teraican oubliette, his crystalline eyes glinting even in the dim light, his heavy jaw set in harsh disapproval.

Trei had never been so astonished by anything in his life.

The novice-master sent a summing look around the oubliette shaft and the scowl deepened. "Well," he said heavily. "You're well otherwise, are you, Trei?"

"Yes . . ." Trei's voice trailed off into incredulity. He blurted, "But why—how—why are *you* here, sir?"

"To recover you, of course." The novice-master's gaze returned to Trei's face. "Am I not the master of novices? And are you not a novice? Genrai managed a fairly coherent account of your . . . stunt. I came as soon as I could." He threw another disgusted look around the oubliette. "For what good that seems likely to do. Like to indulge their tempers, these Tolounnese provincars, do they?"

"But . . . ," Trei managed. "You don't even *like* me!"

"I didn't trust you," the novice-master corrected. "That isn't the same thing." He met Trei's eyes. His heavy features could not easily express embarrassment, but Trei thought he was embarrassed. He said formally, "I was wrong. I apologize for my mistrust, Novice Trei, and I acknowledge you are an Islander and an asset to the kajuraihi."

Trei felt heat creep up his face. Taking refuge in his own formality, trying not to let his voice shake, he said, "Please set any error aside, sir, as I assure you I will." Formally correct or not, this answer seemed presumptuous. He added quickly, "Anyway, I know I can't have been, um. Easy to . . . um."

"Easy to manage?" Novice-master Anerii's mouth quirked upward. "No, not notably. All novices bend the rules from time to time. I cannot at the moment recall any novice showing

311

quite your broad enthusiasm for breaking the rule against venturing, however."

Trei laughed, then caught himself. But the novice-master didn't seem offended at all. He even grinned briefly, a flash of teeth in the dimness.

"Come," he said, gesturing an invitation. "Come sit down with me, Trei, and tell me the tale, if you would. I shall be fascinated to hear it."

"Genrai—"

"Yes, I've had it from Genrai. And from your cousin—who is an interesting young woman, and I gather that a disregard for rules runs in your shared blood, so I suppose I can't blame your Tolounnese heritage for your wide actions."

Trei stared at him.

The novice-master lifted an ironic eyebrow. "She seems well enough. Everything considered. She is afraid for you, of course. But tell me how this wind unrolled from your view, Trei, and I—fair trade, you see—will tell you all the news from the Islands." He sat down and patted the floor beside him.

"I have a blanket," Trei offered, and spread it out for both of them.

Master Anerii listened attentively. He asked few questions. At the end, when Trei tried, fumbling for words, to describe his last flight and his struggle to throw the dragon's egg into the furnace, he said quietly, "So we all do what we must. You did well. I see I will need to have you taught the art of using the wind itself to stop your fall so that you won't again need to ruin your wings in cushioning a violent landing. Were the dragon feathers broken, do you know?"

"Yes—all the primaries were destroyed."

Master Anerii nodded. "That's best, if a Tolounnese artificer has the wings."

"I'm sorry, sir. You were right—"

"Huh." Master Anerii caught Trei's arm in a strong grip and shook him gently, giving him a stern look. "No. I said: you did well. Now, go on. After that?"

Trei tried, haltingly, to explain the part with the artificer, and then the explosion, and then the provincar. He didn't try to describe that last walk to the oubliettes. But he asked, "What happened after that, sir? There was a much bigger explosion. Was that . . . Did I do that?"

The sun, high above, glinted in the master's kajurai eyes. He was not exactly smiling; his expression was too grim to be called a smile. "Yes, in a rather convoluted fashion. Or so I gather. You, and your cousin, and the mage Tnegun, and, ah, Ceirfei."

Trei thought Master Anerii had only just stopped himself from saying "Prince Ceirfei." He said, "Ceirfei? What did *he* do?"

"Tell me, Novice Trei." The master sounded stern at last. "Did you and Novice Genrai deliberately leave Ceirfei behind when you conspired to commit this, ah, exploit of yours?"

Trei winced at this question. "Was he very angry with us? We were sorry to do it that way, but we couldn't . . . You must see that we couldn't possibly tell him. . . ."

"Indeed not." The master sounded much less stern. He patted Trei's arm. "No, indeed. That was also well done, Trei. I vow before the Gods, you and Ceirfei between you will turn the rest of my hair dead white. If I understand correctly, he and that mage Tnegun together acted to send one of our own dragons here. Where it turned—don't ask me how—from a dragon of sky and wind into a fire dragon, shattered the earth beneath the Tolounnese engines, released the fire beneath the earth, and rescued the young dragon you left stranded in the, speaking relatively, cold of the failed furnace. Incidentally destroying roughly half of Teraica in the process."

"Oh," Trei said after a moment. His voice sounded odd even to his own ears. *Destroying half of Teraica.* That was . . . that was horrible. He had never intended . . . never thought . . .

"Don't repine," Master Anerii said briskly. "This also left the Tolounnese on Milendri stranded and willing to reach an accommodation. Now: I came here to offer an exchange of prisoners, Trei. The provincar did not seem favorably disposed to my offer, however. So I do not know. . . ."

It was like suddenly getting a perfect wind after struggling in dead air. Trei stared, arrested, at Master Anerii. "You came here as an ambassador?" he asked, and heard his own voice tremble. "You came here as an ambassador and asked to trade for me, and the provincar had you imprisoned in an *oubliette*?"

The master stared back at Trei. "Obviously, yes," he said after a moment. "Does this signify in some way?"

Trei jumped to his feet and strode back and forth across the oubliette shaft. He wanted to laugh. He wanted to shout up the oubliette shaft, call the guards. They might even answer. Probably not, but they *might*. He spun back to Master Anerii, who was still staring at him in astonishment.

"You don't—" Trei broke that off and began again, trying to keep his voice from rising in hope and in the terror that hope might fail. "Novice-master, please. Tell me. Exactly what you did, and what you said, and to whom, and what the provincar answered."

Master Anerii folded his hands across his knees, sternly calm. "Have I failed to understand something important?"

"I don't know," Trei said. "Please tell me—"

"I came down in the courtyard of the provincar's palace. I gave my name and told them I had come from the king of the Floating Islands to discuss matters of mutual concern. I told them there are thousands of Tolounnese soldiers trapped in the Islands and said I wanted to discuss the disposition of the young kajurai they were holding here—"

"Told who? Courtiers? Soldiers?" Trei leaned forward urgently.

Master Anerii blinked in surprise. "Well, a soldier, first. And then an officer of some kind, I suppose, and then the provincar himself. I thought I was polite enough. He has a temper, that one, and he doesn't take reversals well. He put a good deal more bluster than thought into his responses, it seemed to me."

"Did he shout? At you? At the soldiers? There *were* soldiers present, weren't there?"

"As I recall, he shouted at everyone. Certainly there were soldiers, Trei: an officer with a red-hilted dagger and a file of men."

"A teruann. A company commander, and at least some of his men. So *you* said there were a lot of soldiers left on Milendri, and the *provincar* answered, what? That he would redeem them? Did he say that?"

Master Anerii tilted his head in intense curiosity. "No, he did not. He said . . . let me see. He said Tolounn was well rid of any men who would surrender, and he said he would bargain with the Floating Islands when Tolounn itself mounts into the sky, but he'd hear an ambassador if one came as a supplicant to hear terms. He warned me that when engines have been built, they can be rebuilt and said I could carry that word back to my little Island king. So I asked, what about you? And he said, well, a great many unconsidered things, and I wound up demanding you be put into my hands, and . . ." The master shrugged. "Here I am."

"The provincar is a *fool*," Trei said, not really paying attention to this last.

"Well, and?"

Trei stared at him. It seemed incredible anyone would not know—but then, the provincar *himself* seemed blind to the obvious. He said, "Sir, Tolounnese soldiers are the best in the world."

"So they generally declare," the master said drily.

"No, sir—they really *are* the best in the world. Everyone knows that."

"Spoken like a true citizen of Tolounn. No, forgive me for interrupting, Trei, and make me understand what you mean."

Trei paused, trying to gather his thoughts. He said at last, "Tolounnese soldiers are the best in the world. That's because they always obey orders. Even if they hate their commander, even if their orders are to march forward and die, they always obey orders. Except . . ." He tried to think how to put this.

"Except?" Master Anerii prompted quietly. He seemed to understand Trei's excitement now, even if he didn't know whether he should share it.

Well, Trei himself didn't *know* what would happen. But he said, "He's a fool. Because he threw blame on the men when the first engine exploded, even though that wasn't their fault, and then he did it again when the dragon came. And he threw those men away. He said Tolounn was well rid of them? He might as well have accused them all of cowardice! They weren't cowards—were they?"

"No," Master Anerii said fervently. "Not at all. By no means."

"Of course they weren't. They had bad luck, and maybe bad planning, because everything depended on those engines and the provincar didn't plan for what he'd do if Tolounn lost those. He can't have, can he? Even though he ought to have known the Islands would try anything to ruin them. So he put the blame for the first explosion on me and sent me here to die forgotten, which wasn't truly honorable—" He saw Master Anerii didn't understand what he meant, and tried to explain. "I might have ruined his engine, but if your opponent makes a brave counter to your attack, it's not honorable to hold it against him, is it? If you're going to attack people, it's only natural they should fight back. You can execute a brave opponent, but it's not right to punish him, do you see? So the soldiers didn't like the provincar sending me here, but he didn't see that or else he didn't care. I thought then—but Tolounnese soldiers always obey orders. But then you came to negotiate, and he wouldn't hear you and he threw away all those men, and he sent *you* here, which is *very* dishonorable, because you aren't a soldier or a spy, you're an ambassador whom your king sent in good faith—he did, didn't he?"

"Yes, he did. So . . . Trei, am I to understand that you expect the provincar to cause his own men to mutiny?"

"He's not honorable. And when he fails at something, he puts the dishonor on the soldiers. He's a *fool,*" said Trei passionately. "When Tolounnese soldiers decide to throw over a commander, they *all* decide to do it, all at once. They send to the Little Emperor and demand a different commander. Sometimes they send him pieces of their previous commander, too. If the Emperor's wise, he picks somebody much, much better. It's happened four times, and the last time all the armies joined together and unseated the Little Emperor himself and made the Great Emperor put in a man they approved. That was Medraunn enna Gaourr, great-great-grandfather of our Little Emperor now. My tutor taught me that. Did *his* teach him nothing?"

"Some men are not capable of learning anything that does not agree with their own opinions," the master observed quietly. "And what will this mean for us, if the soldiers here overthrow the provincar?"

"Oh, they'll let us go, of course. At least, they'll take us out of here and treat you as an ambassador, but probably they'll just let us go without asking anything at all."

"They'll do that, will they? Even after losing half of Teraica?"

"Well, that's awful," Trei said honestly. "I wish—they'll think—" He caught himself, swallowed, and went on, "They'll be angry, of course they will. But it *was* war. They won't *blame* us for doing that. It's just stupid to *blame* an opponent for fighting back. They think I was brave, and of course you were, sir, to put yourself forward as the Islands' ambassador. And you did it to get me back, which is honorable. The soldiers will like that; they're Tolounnese, after all. Of course they'd let us go without demands. That's exactly what they'd do. They'd expect *your* honor, sir, and the king's, to make you treat your prisoners decently and negotiate in good faith for their return."

After a pause, Master Anerii said in a dry tone, "Well, I'm grateful to have a half-Tolounnese novice kajurai to explain Tolounn to me. I don't think I understood half of that, for all I'm supposed to be an emissary."

"But—" *That's all obvious,* Trei wanted to say. Except clearly it hadn't been. He was still amazed that Master Anerii hadn't seen it all plainly himself, but he could hardly say so.

"Oh, I knew almost everything you said. I remember that tale, about the Little Emperor's overthrow. But I knew it academically. I wouldn't have—didn't—put that all together with our situation the way you just explained it."

Trei nodded. That made more sense. He looked wistfully up toward the light, wishing again, desperately, that they were in some tower prison where they could *see.*

Master Anerii got to his feet at last, stretching. "Cold down here for a man my age," he commented. "Earth-cold, stone-cold; not like the high winds at all, is it? I wonder why that is?" Then he gave Trei a sharp look and asked, almost as though he expected him to be able to answer, "I don't suppose any such mutiny, if it comes, will happen today, however?"

Trei guiltily brought his gaze down from the circle of light above. "No, sir, I don't think so."

The master smiled, a little grimly. "Then perhaps we shall have time to discuss your landing style and the manner in which control of the winds can be used to compensate for overenthusiasm. I must conclude from your report that your skills in that direction are gravely lacking. Even in a pit such as this, the winds are not *absent,*" he added when Trei stared at him. "Merely attenuated. Now, name for me the five principal qualities of the wind and explain, if you please, the nine methods by which a kajurai may influence each of these qualities."

Trei laughed. He couldn't help it. But that was all right, because the master laughed, too.

14

Araenè thought at first that after the unnatural Tolounnese strength was broken and the dragon's magic of sky and wind freed, everything would be *over*. Master Tnegun might have collapsed, but that wouldn't matter; he would rest for a while and then wake, the Tolounnese ships would meanwhile take all the Tolounnese soldiers away, and they could all go *home*.

She knew very well that some of the towers and underground buildings at the edge of Canpra had been damaged; she knew that there had been fighting and that people had died. There would be a lot of work to do to fix everything. She knew that. But that's all she thought it would be: a lot of work, and tears for those lost, and then they could all go on with their lives.

At first, nothing interrupted this hopeful idea. She and Prince Ceirfei together arranged Master Tnegun in reasonable comfort by the edge of the pool.

"He will be well; he passed the edge of his endurance, but I think he needs no more than rest. No place in the Islands is safer than this, and he may perhaps have useful, or at least interesting, dreams," the prince said to Araenè.

She had been kneeling by Master Tnegun, watching his slow breathing and assuring herself that he would be fine. She didn't think he had overextended—he didn't look nearly as dead as Tichorei had. So she looked up at the prince and nodded, hoping this was all true. She let the prince lead her away from the pool to stand at the edge of the cliffs at the top of Kotipa and stare across the sea toward Milendri. So when the power of the Tolounnese mages failed and the kajuraihi led the dragon winds down from the heights, they saw the result plainly.

The winds drove the sea into violence before them, so that the Tolounnese ships staggered where they lay and struggled to turn their prows to the increasingly powerful waves; one ship, still anchored by its boarding ladder to the stone of Milendri above, released its ladder too slowly to come around. A great wave rose across its length, and Araenè put her hands over her mouth as the whole ship rolled over, broached, and went down. She knew she couldn't hear the screams of the men on that ship, not over this distance, not over the roar of the savage wind. But she imagined she could hear them.

A Quei swept between the waves, tiny at this distance, the sun striking its plumage to iridescent emerald fire. The bird rode the violent winds with nonchalant skill. Two kajuraihi, wings crimson as the lowering sun, followed the bird. The men were almost as indifferent as the Quei to the violent winds and surging sea. One of them tilted his wings, skimmed along the leading edge of a wave, and flung something neatly against the side of another ship: fire bloomed, and again Araenè imagined screams.

The remaining Tolounnese ships fled. Kajuraihi pursued them, riding the storm winds, fire in their hands.

"I should be with them," Prince Ceirfei said in a low voice, staring after the kajuraihi. He stood on the sheer edge of the cliffs, perfectly at home with the winds that shredded around the rocks. His dark hair whipped in the wind. Araenè was afraid a particularly fierce gust might blow him right off the edge, but he seemed fearless. He looked exactly like a prince should, she thought. And extravagantly good-looking, though she had no business thinking that. He glanced at her just then, and she blushed and looked down—then up again.

"What are you thinking?" the prince asked curiously.

Araenè could hardly answer that. She asked quickly, before she could blush again, "The dragon wanted something from you, didn't it? You told it that you weren't bargaining, that we wouldn't protest the cost." She paused, added uncertainly, "Isn't that what you told it? But what cost . . . ?"

Prince Ceirfei shook his head, not as though he was refusing to answer, but more as though he simply did not know how to put the answer into words. He said at last, "The destruction of Teraica is a price the Tolounnese paid for their defeat: they might have brought the ruin of their city on themselves, but no one could deserve what happened to Teraica. The wind dragon became fire and gave up the sky; that was the price the wind dragons paid for our victory. But what *our* cost will be, eventually . . . that I do not know. But I know that we will have no choice but to pay it." He looked very serious. "Only, what other choice did I have but to promise anything I must, when your Master Tnegun put a chance of victory, all unlooked for, in my hand?"

"Yes," said Araenè. "I mean, of course there wasn't any other choice."

"No. But I hope the Tolounnese . . . One is never entirely certain what they will consider a legitimate act of war and what an uncivilized act of barbarism."

Araenè was not entirely certain she understood why it mattered what the Tolounnese thought, but she didn't want to ask Prince Ceirfei to explain. She tried to look curious and attentive.

"Hundreds must be dead, hundreds more wounded," the prince told her quietly, which she had known already. But he added, turning his gaze at last toward Milendri, "Thousands of Tolounnese soldiers will have been stranded in Canpra. If they will not surrender, how many more will die before they can be defeated?"

"*Can* they be defeated?" Araenè asked doubtfully.

"It's true we have no soldiers," the prince said, understanding her doubt, "but we have broken their power. Our dragons have returned to our sky. Our mages will recover, and theirs have been driven away. They have no supply, no reserves, no support, no mages. They can achieve only a brief and temporary victory. But . . ."

Araenè nodded. Even a brief, temporary Tolounnese victory could hurt Canpra badly. She bit her lip. "Surely they will surrender? Won't they see what you see, won't they understand they *have* to surrender now?"

"Those are *Tolounnese* soldiers," Prince Ceirfei said grimly. "They are not accustomed to surrender. They may not be able to hold the city for very long. But it would be better for us all if they did not establish that fact through practical experience." He paused. Then he added, "If they are to surrender, they must have someone to surrender *to*. Someone of proper authority who can persuade them of the wisdom of that course."

"Oh," said Araenè, understanding him at last. And then asked doubtfully, "But is it safe for you to go to them?"

"I think so. They *are* Tolounnese. Honor is everything to them. To them, this has been something like a game, to be played according to honorable rules," Prince Ceirfei added, irony edging his tone. "It's important they view us as playing by those rules as well. They prize courage and directness, I believe." He paused. "Your master came to me because he needed a kajurai. Now . . . I think now the need is for a prince." He glanced sidelong at Araenè. "Though perhaps you should remain here, in case I am mistaken. Truly, there are few places safer in all the Islands."

"No!" Araenè glared at the prince. "If Master Tnegun can't help you, then you'll need me!"

"I do," conceded the prince. "Open me a door, Araenè. Something useful. Preferably something that will take us near, but not too near, the ranking Tolounnese officer. A place with a view, ideally, so that we can see what we're stepping into."

Araenè's glare had turned into a stare of surprise at this very specific request. "A door?"

"If you can," said the prince. His eyes met hers, measuring.

Araenè stared at him for another heartbeat. She was afraid she was blushing again. . . . She shut her eyes. A door. Master

Tnegun *said* she had an affinity for doors. There *would be* a door when she opened her eyes. Standing off to one side, set right into the air of the mountain slopes. Not a door to the hidden school. Something helpful. The sort of door that would open to a high balcony near . . . Where would the Tolounnese forces be? She had no idea how to coax a door to find a Tolounnese officer she'd never even met. Where would such an officer be? Near the center of the First City? Near the court ministry? *In* the ministry? Prince Ceirfei said he thought the Tolounnese could take Canpra; maybe they already had?

She opened her eyes. Turned her head.

The Akhan Bhotounn, the "friendly door," stood near at hand. It was not quite where she had meant to put it. It stood instead right at the edge of the cliff, so that it seemed that taking a step through it would surely send you plummeting toward the sea. The ebony wood was carved with dragons, Araenè saw: the abstract swirls hadn't made any sense to her before, but now she could see the hinted curve of the long necks and powerful shoulders, the complicated filigree that barely suggested feathers, the swirl where talons tore through clouds. One of the dragons had its head in the upper left panel of the door, the other in the lower right panel: their tails twined together all across the middle section.

But it showed signs of burning now. It had not been badly damaged, but wisps of smoke were still rising from the edges of the doorframe.

Master Tnegun had also said "an aptitude for fire." Araenè stared at the "friendly door," hoping it would not open into a furnace or burning building. She stepped cautiously forward to the edge of the cliff and touched the knob, which was hot. But when she opened the door a crack, she found it opened merely to her own apartment in the hidden school.

"Where is that?" Prince Ceirfei asked, looking curiously through the open door.

"That's the hidden school," Araenè admitted. "My apartment. Probably it wouldn't be very useful to go there." She closed the door. Opened it again. It opened this time to the hall of spheres and mirrors. The hall was deserted. Tichorei no longer lay against the wall. Araenè hoped that was a good sign.

"A place near the Tolounnese army," prompted Prince Ceirfei. "But not *too* near. Someplace deserted. Someplace with a view."

"I *understand* that," Araenè snapped. She closed the door, opened again. To the balcony where the black gulls nested. She sighed, staring at the squabbling gulls in disgust. "We could go to the hidden school first, I suppose. I can probably get a better door from there than from"—she glanced around uncertainly—"here."

"If you like," the prince agreed.

His tone was too carefully gentle. Araenè glared at him. "I've not *been* an apprentice even one senneri! A boy couldn't do it, either!"

The prince looked at her in surprise for a moment. Then he laughed. "All right," he said, in a much more ordinary tone. "Forgive me, Araenè."

"Arei," Araenè muttered. "It's Arei when I'm supposed to be a boy. I—it's complicated."

The prince tilted his head to the side. "Is it? It seems simple to me. I had to fight very hard for leave to attend the kajurai audition. Very hard. Because princes do not fly. Only, in the end my family gave way, and of course a girl cannot even ask hers for leave to go to the hidden school. So you did not ask, but only became a person who could go . . . his . . . own way."

Araenè stared at him. She had not expected Prince Ceirfei, of all people, to *understand*. She had never before conceived of the idea that being a prince was, in a way, like being a girl. But she saw at once that he was right: it *was* a similar thing. In a way. You were born, and immediately everyone *knew* what kind of person you had to be.

"Shall I call you Arei, then?"

Araenè paused, uncomfortable. "I don't . . . Call me Araenè, if you like. Now that Master Tnegun knows, I suppose . . . call me Araenè."

The prince nodded. "You always wanted to be a mage, I would surmise?"

Araenè gave him a hard stare, but the prince didn't seem to be mocking her. He seemed sincerely interested. She said at last, "The mage gift comes on you like a rising tide. They say. And it's true; it does. They say you can smother it. I . . ." Her voice trailed off.

"Didn't care to smother yours?"

Araenè bit her lip, shook her head. "There was nothing in my life I wanted to keep. Except things I couldn't have anyway. It would have been—I couldn't ask Trei to give up the sky! Especially when I didn't even want the life a girl ought to have. Only a *boy* would at least know about mathematics and rocks and things."

That made the prince smile. But he asked, "Trei?" And, with dawning understanding, "You are his cousin. Of course. He said you had gone to the country."

"Oh," said Araenè, realizing. "You know him, of course."
She lifted a hand to her hair. "He said I would hate the country. He was right. So I cut my hair instead. . . ."

"And that's as well, we find," said the prince. "So, the hidden school? Or will you try again from here?"

Araenè looked at the door once more. She said impulsively, "You open it."

Prince Ceirfei lifted his eyebrows. Then he came forward and opened the door.

The Akhan Bhotounn showed them a high, narrow, windswept balcony. The balcony completely encircled a slender spire of white stone. Araenè could see a small chamber inside the spire, and a narrow, sweeping flight of floating stones that dropped from the balcony to a lower tower nearby, and that was all. She said uncertainly, "It *seems* to be deserted. . . ."

Prince Ceirfei grinned, a swift flash of humor breaking through his usually serious manner. "I know that tower: that's Quei Tower, in my uncle's palace. The only way to that balcony is by floating stairs—and since nobody wants the Quei disturbed, there's no magic on those stairs to keep you from falling. The stones would have fallen when the Tolounnese mages drove the dragons away. Even now, when the stones have likely risen back to their places, well, those are *Tolounnese* soldiers. I can nearly promise you, however firm their grip on the palace, Tolounnese forces will not have crossed a *floating* stairway to occupy Quei Tower."

"Oh. That makes sense. . . ."

The prince put a hand on the door's ebony frame and held his other hand out to Araenè. "I think this will do very well. If you will join me?"

* * *

The room at the top of Quei Tower, round and small, was indeed empty of everything except the wind and a single Quei nest. There were windows all around the room, the sills narrow and rounded, appropriate perches for Quei: half a dozen leaped into the air, crying in their high, wild voices, when their tower was invaded. Aside from the room with the windows, there was nothing but a narrow balcony. That was all. The balcony had no rail. The stairs were small, most of them less than an arm's length across. Though the steps all floated neatly in their places, many of them did indeed show signs of having recently been broken: white chips missing from their edges, or cracks that split one step into two or three pieces. They didn't look at all safe, in fact. Araenè wasn't surprised that the Tolounnese soldiers hadn't stationed men here, even though the tower offered a spectacular view of the palace and the First City.

There were Tolounnese soldiers on the lower tower, though. They spotted Araenè and Prince Ceirfei right away, their attention drawn by the flying Quei. Then they clearly argued about who would have to go up that dangerous flight of floating stairs to deal with the startling appearance of the Islanders.

"There seems no reason for hurry," commented Prince Ceirfei, assessing the general tenor of this argument. "In fact, well. Come here, Araenè. Look there. What do you think?"

The prince was standing on the very edge of the balcony. Araenè stood back a little farther and wished for a railing. But she saw at once what he meant. "They have the whole palace. There's no fighting anywhere." She glanced at Prince Ceirfei, worried. "You don't think they *can* have taken the whole city?"

"They probably pressed to take the palace first," the prince answered calmly. "If they meant to hold Canpra, that would have been important. I wonder if they realize yet that, now they've lost their mages and been cut off from all possible supply and reinforcement, they can't hold the city for long, even if they take it? Or whether they understand how to let it go?"

"Your . . . uncle," Araenè began, and hesitated.

"The king meant to take a position at the Five Towers. One of my cousins was to hold the University, the other to go down to the Deep Run."

"And you . . ."

"I was meant to stay out of the way," agreed Prince Ceirfei. "In case." He didn't say, *In case my uncle and both my cousins die.* He didn't say, *They might be dead right now.* He didn't have to.

Araenè stared downward. "They have bows." At least three of the Tolounnese soldiers below had wicked-looking cross-bows. "Maybe we shouldn't stand here? That's not too far to shoot, is it?"

"They are not shooting."

This was true. One of the soldiers had his bow in his hands, but he didn't have a bolt in place. The other two just had their bows hanging across their backs. Apparently they didn't mean to just solve their dilemma by simply shooting the Islanders.

"I think . . . ," Prince Ceirfei said thoughtfully. "Direct action is indicated here." He glanced at Araenè. "What do you think?"

He seemed to honestly care about her opinion. Araenè hesitated. "Trei is the only citizen of Tolounn I've ever met. . . ."

"True," the prince agreed. "And your cousin is both direct and brave, which I have taken as a measure of Tolounnese character." He studied her. "You, however, could go back to the hidden school. That might be best."

Of course he would suggest that. Araenè said tartly, "If anybody will need a door suddenly open at his back, it will be you."

"Well." The prince's mouth curved in an unwilling smile. "That's true." He glanced down. "Quick, then, before that poor man who lost the toss gets halfway up."

There was indeed a soldier on the stair: only on the second stone from the bottom and already looking unhappy about it. Prince Ceirfei stepped out onto the first stair, then down to the second, and offered a hand back to Araenè. When she hesitated, he said a little sharply, "I'm kajurai. I can coax the winds to support me. Can you say the same? I'd offer the same assistance to a boy, I promise you."

Araenè flushed and then laughed. She didn't say, *That's not why I don't want to take your hand.* She only stepped out onto the first stair and . . . took the prince's hand. His hand was much bigger than hers—broader and longer both, seeming too large for his body. He would grow into his hands, presumably. She wondered how old he was, but couldn't remember. Older than she, obviously. Seventeen, eighteen? He held her hand in a firm, impersonal grip. Araenè could imagine Trei helping her like this. But holding Ceirfei's hand was not at all like holding her cousin's hand. She bit her lip.

The prince descended one step at a time, backward, with only the occasional casual glance over his shoulder to find the next stone. He made it look easy. The winds, still violent with their new freedom, pushed hard against Araenè. But Prince Ceirfei did not seem to feel the wind. He steadied Araenè against even the fiercest gusts.

There were forty-nine stairs between Quei Tower's balcony and the lower tower where the soldiers waited. Araenè counted, and wondered what the significance of the number might be. Forty-nine divided by seven twice. Was that significant somehow? She wondered what Master Tnegun would tell her about that number if he'd been here. That made her wonder if he was all right, and then she tried hard to focus just on the next step and on Ceirfei's hand supporting her.

Then they were down. The soldiers had drawn back to give them room. Ceirfei stepped down onto the roof of the tower and turned, drawing Araenè up beside him.

"Why, they're boys!" exclaimed one of the men. "At least . . ." He gave Araenè a close look, seeing through her boys' clothing to the truth as no Islander ever had. "One boy and a girl?" He started to smile; the others likewise.

"You will respect my companion," Prince Ceirfei said in a cool, impersonal rebuke, and the smiles disappeared instantly. The prince glanced around at the soldiers thoughtfully, and the one who had opened his mouth to say something visibly changed his mind. To the man who'd started to climb up the stairs, Ceirfei added with a slight, gracious nod, "There was no need for us to put you to the trouble. But you owe Lady Araenè your thanks; she might have fallen."

Araenè tried not to blink at her sudden elevation.

The soldier *did* blink. Then he turned to Araenè and said, sincerely, "I do thank you, Lady! I did not look forward to that climb! Forgive us if we offended you."

Araenè didn't have any idea what she ought to say. She returned the nod, trying to match Ceirfei's cool manner.

"Well," said another man, evidently the senior, "but is there anyone else up there?"

"I give you my personal word," the prince answered, "that there is not."

"Your personal word, is it?" said the man. Not exactly skeptically. He studied Ceirfei. "Kajurai, are you?"

"Recently, yes," Ceirfei said, and paused for effect. He *really* did that well, Araenè thought: not a man on the tower was looking anywhere but at him; if she'd pulled a door into place right behind them all, they would never have noticed. It was reassuring just to think she *could*.

"I am Ceirfei Feneirè. My mother is Calaspara Naterensei. Terinai Naterensei is my uncle. I wish to speak to whatever officer commands here, if you please. I am confident," the prince added softly as the soldiers all stared at him, "that he will wish to speak to me."

It was really remarkable, Araenè thought, how respectful the soldiers were after that. They had been respectful before. But it was different after Ceirfei told them who he was. Ceirfei said, "Your commander is in the king's apartment?" and effortlessly took the lead, encountering not the slightest protest from the soldiers. He could not have looked less like a prisoner. Araenè stayed close by his side and hoped she looked half as confident.

They seemed to go a long way. At last a man—an officer, Araenè guessed—came out of a room and frowned at them, and they halted. The soldiers escorting them murmured to the officer, whose eyes widened. He looked closely at Ceirfei. "A kajurai?"

"That also," Ceirfei acknowledged.

"I see. And this . . . young woman?"

"Lady Araenè Naseida will accompany me," Ceirfei said, in a tone that implied there was nothing extraordinary about this.

Araenè tried to look confident and important and noble, the way Ceirfei did just by nature. She felt horribly uncomfortable, in boys' dress but with everyone addressing her as a girl. A lady. Maybe the soldiers would think she'd dressed as a boy because of the war. That would even make sense.

"Of course," the officer said now, making no protest at all. "The general will want to see you, Lord Prince. If I may ask you to wait here for only a moment?" He went back into the room. It was indeed merely a moment before he came back out and held the door for Ceirfei.

Ceirfei graciously inclined his head and offered his hand to Araenè. She was shy of taking it here, in front of everyone, but she stepped up beside him. They went through the door.

The rooms were large, open, and richly appointed and looked out over the city from three huge windows. A large table took up most of the space to one side; a map was unrolled across its surface, held in place by pewter mugs and sheathed daggers. The rest of the room was occupied by a dozen men, all but one of them armed. The man who drew the eye was the one who was not armed: a heavyset man with broad shoulders, a homely, rugged face, and a grim expression. He stood behind an empty chair, his hands resting on its back.

Ceirfei stopped before this man. For a moment they regarded each other in silence. Though Ceirfei looked, in one sense, very young and slight measured against the powerful

Tolounnese commander, in another sense he did not look slight at all.

The Tolounnese commander said, "Prince Ceirfei Feneirè. I am Parron enna Rouharr, commander of all Tolounnese forces remaining on Milendri."

Ceirfei inclined his head courteously. "General Rouharr. I am familiar with your reputation. I am pleased to find you well. I will ask you whether you have recent word of my uncle. Or of my cousins—Prince Imrei? Prince Safei?"

General Rouharr said steadily, "I have no recent word of either the king of the Floating Islands or of Prince Imrei. Your other cousin . . . I regret to inform you that I believe your cousin Prince Safei may have been wounded in the . . . conflict. I had just been discussing with my men my, ah. My *strong* desire to speak to your uncle. However, I did not know where to send a man of mine to find him, nor has he sent me a representative."

"I see." Ceirfei stood in silence for a moment. Then he observed, "General Rouharr, I believe you find yourself in an unusual situation."

There was a little stir around the room. The general held up a hand, and it stilled. He was smiling, but grimly. "Prince Ceirfei, I concede that the situation in which I find myself is indeed unusual. Seldom do the short-term and long-term prospects of a . . . conflict . . . seem more disparate."

"Just so." Ceirfei studied the Tolounnese general for a moment longer. Then he said formally, "General Rouharr, I am prepared to offer terms for your surrender."

For a long moment, no one moved or spoke. Then the general replied, "Prince Ceirfei, I am prepared to hear your terms."

"No!" one of the other men cried. He was a younger man than the general, taller—very distinguished in manner, but clearly furious. "Parron, do you not see what has walked into our hands and offered himself as a hostage to our need? Only send any man anywhere in the city with *this* news, and we may guarantee terms from Terinai Naterensei! Far better terms than *surrender*! We need not hold out longer than—"

Araenè found herself in a towering rage against this man. Against all the Tolounnese, who came here for *no reason* and smashed up Milendri and invaded Canpra, and *killed* people, and then said things about *taking hostages*. She shut her eyes and thought hard about doors: ebony doors with carved dragons, the sort of friendly, cooperative door that might open to . . . open to . . . She opened her eyes, reached out with both hands. The room seemed filled with the over-whelming fragrance of nutmeg and cardamom. The urgent green taste of cilantro filled her mouth and tingled across her palms.

She *did something.*

Before her, the dark bulk of the Akhan Bhotounn loomed suddenly in the room. It was open to a wide and spinning sky—spinning because the "friendly door" was neither level nor set solidly in place: it stood high up on one corner and swung ponderously but smoothly through a wide arc. It did not seem to swing quickly, but no one had time to move. It en-gulfed the young man who had threatened to take Ceirfei hostage. He fell into the empty wind with a sharp cry. The ebony door slammed shut behind him and twirled smoothly into the air: gone.

There was a stunned pause while everyone except Ceirfei

stared at Araenè. She flushed, crossed her arms over her chest, and glowered back at them all.

Ceirfei looked thoughtfully at General Rouharr and lifted one eyebrow. "Well," he said, breaking the silence, "I *thought* I knew your reputation. Perhaps I was mistaken, if you would take hostage a royal emissary of the Islands after he put himself freely into your hands."

The general dropped his eyes. "Prince Ceirfei . . ." His voice trailed off, and he lifted his gaze once more to meet Ceirfei's cool stare. "Prince Ceirfei, as you did not, prior to your arrival, find it convenient to arrange the safe conduct customary for an emissary, permit me to offer it to you now. Also, of course, to your companion, the lady mage Araenè Naseida."

Ceirfei inclined his head graciously. "One would expect no less of Tolounnese honor." He did not glance at the spot where the other man had stood. No one looked that way.

"So," said General Rouharr. He hesitated fractionally, then said, "As I believe I was saying, I am willing to hear your terms, Prince Ceirfei."

Ceirfei said, "I cannot speak directly for my uncle. However, if you put yourself and your men into my hands, I swear he will respect my claim."

This time, no one argued that they should instead take the prince hostage.

The general said to Ceirfei, "Let us be uncomplicated. I will surrender myself and all my men to your authority. The lives of all my men will be spared, and they will be treated honorably, as befits honorable men defeated through no fault of their own. They will be returned to Tolounn for a reasonable ransom as soon as the exchange can be arranged." He stopped. Waited.

Ceirfei nodded. "Acceptable, in principle. Who defines 'honorable treatment'? Who defines 'reasonable ransom'?"

"You, as the victor, define both terms. I will trust you, under the circumstances, to define them with fitting generosity. I will ask you to agree plainly that I may so trust, Prince Ceirfei."

Ceirfei nodded again. "You may: I assure you. I notice that you do not include yourself in these terms, General Rouharr. Is this the Tolounnese custom?"

"It is the custom," agreed the general. "The victor is assumed to have earned a free hand regarding the disposition of the commander of the defeated force." He waited again, his gaze steady on Ceirfei's face.

The Tolounnese, Araenè realized, really *did* think of war almost as a kind of game. Prince Ceirfei had been right: they hedged it about with all kinds of rules of proper conduct. The Tolounnese general was arranging the surrender of his men as he might have tipped over a piece on a game board to concede a match. She wondered if it had occurred to him that the Floating Islands were not at *all* thinking of the Tolounnese invasion as any kind of game. But then she realized what he must mean by "the disposition of the commander of the defeated force," and understood that, indeed, the Tolounnese commander could not consider *that* a game.

But Ceirfei said, gracefully matching his response to Tolounnese expectations, "That is not the Island custom; however, as I have a free hand . . . I guarantee you honorable treatment and release without ransom, General Rouharr, in return for your surrender. I believe that is your due," he added, with a sudden edge to his voice, "for declining to destroy half the male population of Canpra on the way to your eventual defeat."

A murmur went around the room. The general answered graciously, "We are grateful the wisdom of the Islands permits us to avoid both the useless slaughter and the inevitable defeat. We are glad, Prince Ceirfei, to trust the honor of the Floating Islands in your voice and hands."

Ceirfei inclined his head, mollified.

General Rouharr cleared his throat and held out his hand. Somebody drew a sword and put it into his hand, and he stepped forward—Araenè tensed, she couldn't help it, but Ceirfei did not seem concerned, and he was right, because the general only dropped to one knee and laid the sword at Ceirfei's feet.

"Prince Ceirfei," he said formally. "Into your hands I give myself and all my men. Will you accept my surrender?"

"I do accept it," said Ceirfei, remembering to add, "on my own behalf and in the name of Terinai Naterensei, king of the Floating Islands. I will ask you . . . draw your men in close, General Rouharr; keep them in order. You need not yet disarm them, but I will expect you to decline any engagement offered before news of your surrender is widely known. Indeed, I will expect you to decline emphatically."

"I understand, Prince Ceirfei. All that you require will be done." The general paused, then added quietly, "If you will permit me to speak plainly. You need not try to anticipate all eventualities: you may trust me to hold close the spirit of this surrender."

Ceirfei looked down at the older man for a moment. He said, "I do trust you," and offered the general a hand to help him back to his feet.

Then he quirked a brow at Araenè. "A door," he suggested. "And we shall see if we can find my uncle and catch this line from the other end as well."

And proper fools they would both look, Araenè thought, if she couldn't get an acceptable door to appear. But Ceirfei trusted that she could.

So she did.

15

Trei tried not to be too happy about Master Anerii's presence. He knew it was wrong to be so glad another kajurai was trapped here. He knew very well, once the first optimistic blaze of hope had died away, that the greatest likelihood was that nothing would change. Commanders were, after all, sometimes fools. The long sweep of Tolounnese history made that plain. Usually soldiers just endured those commanders. More than a hundred years, after all, had passed since the most recent great mutiny. The provincar of Teraica might be a fool, but so much more so than anyone else in the past age?

No, Trei concluded: he had been too enthusiastic by a wide margin. He wondered if he should say so. But then he decided the novice-master knew it very well. Of course he did. If there was any man in the world less likely than Novice-master Anerii to be swept away on the wild winds of blind optimism, surely there were not two.

But he was very glad, over the next days, to have the distraction of lessons. Master Anerii was right: Trei had never been good at wind magic. Now he learned how to coax the winds around even when there was hardly any moving air at all. It wasn't easy. To his surprise, the novice-master was a patient teacher. He demanded Trei's full attention when he was teaching, but as long as he got that, he didn't seem to *have* a temper, not even when Trei was particularly stupid about learning something.

"And we'll go on with Island history and kajurai law," Master Anerii added, with what seemed to Trei unnecessary enthusiasm. "Nor is there anything to stop you from learning proper navigation, now that we've time to really develop the math. Pity we can't see the stars better, but we shall contrive. Genrai said he thought you barely made it to the first waystation. I'm sure you now really *believe* that every kajurai truly needs to be able to measure angles by eye and calculate accurately in his head."

"Yes, sir," Trei said earnestly. He preferred mathematics to law anyway, and besides, it was true. Though he did fervently hope they wouldn't have *that* much time.

"And you can teach me more about Tolounn's recent history," Master Anerii added. "I suddenly find it a compelling area of study."

Trei only prayed he'd been right, in the conclusions he'd already drawn from Tolounn's history. He looked involuntarily up at the sky, blocked from them by forty feet and the heavy iron grate. He could tell that it was late morning: he had learned to judge the quality of the light and the truncated angle of the sun. He had entirely lost track of the day; Master

Anerii said he'd been brought down here on Moon's Day, but how many days had it been since? Ten days? Twelve? More than that? The sameness of the days made it hard to remember.

More surely than the proper name of the day, Trei knew that this was not the day on which food and water would be lowered to the prisoners. That happened only every other day, almost always in the evening. They should be grateful anybody remembered the prisoners at all, the novice-master had pointed out, what with conditions in the city surely remaining chaotic. Trei knew this was true. He didn't like to think about the earth breaking open underneath Teraica, about the chasms of fire that had battled the sea to reshape the line of the harbor.

That was another reason to be glad of Master Anerii's company. He made sure Trei was too tired at night to dream— or if he dreamed, the master woke him out of his nightmares in such a matter-of-fact manner that Trei could hardly be embarrassed.

"Trei," the master said patiently.

Trei realized that this wasn't the first time he'd said his name. He said, embarrassed, "Sir?"

Master Anerii sighed. "If you—" he began.

The light dimmed, not as clouds or haze or even smoke would have dimmed it, but in the abrupt way that meant someone had bent over the grate. The master fell silent. Both he and Trei stared upward.

The grate clanged as it was hauled away, and the ladder came down.

Without a word, Master Anerii offered Trei his cupped

hands for a step. Trei looked once around the familiar shaft of the oubliette and once, searchingly, into the master's face. He wanted to ask, *Do you think*—? He did not ask. He let the master boost him upward, put his foot on the first rung of the ladder, and climbed up toward the light.

The fierce heat of the world above met him with shocking force; he had forgotten the overpowering southern sun. For those first moments, while a strong hand closed around his and drew him up into the light, Trei found himself stunned and blind. But no one demanded anything of him while he pressed his hands over his tearing eyes and tried, blinking, to see.

"Easy, boy. You don't want to stumble back over the edge!" said a gruff, half-familiar voice, and the hand guided him firmly aside.

Trei cautiously lowered his hands and found himself looking into the face of the same soldier who had carried him away from the engines, right at the beginning. The decouan. Who now looked both grim and pleased, and patted Trei on the shoulder with friendly concern. "You all right, boy? Just stand steady for a moment and get used to the light."

"Thank you," Trei said, and looked around anxiously: surely they were bringing up the novice-master, too? Yes: there were half a dozen soldiers by the oubliette's opening, and one was offering his own hand to Master Anerii. The master, too, was blinking and holding an arm up to block the light. But the soldier steadied him.

Trei let out a breath he hadn't known he was holding and tried to smile.

"This way," the decouan said casually, gesturing down the hill. "Not too stiff? It's a good walk down."

Trei looked to be sure Master Anerii was coming and then obediently went the way the decouan indicated. "To the . . . palace?"

"That's right," the decouan said. He seemed pleased about it. "You and your master. That's right, is it? The ambassador's your own master, is he?"

Trei hesitated and then nodded.

"Yes, that's what he said. When he came right to the palace asking after you." The decouan obviously approved. "Watch your step here, boy."

There were steps down the steepest parts of the climb, worn and awkward. Trei took them carefully, pausing in the middle to look out and down over Teraica. The city . . . was not at all as he remembered it. He did not remember the exact outline of the harbor, but he could see even from this height that there was a lot more harbor and a lot less city than there had been. And a lot of the remaining city had obviously burned. Down near the water, there were no buildings at all, only gray ash. Smoke still rose in thin streams from a deep crevice that stretched right across land that had once held crowded streets; he guessed how big that crevice must be, to be so clearly visible from this distance.

Trei swallowed.

"Hard to look on it," the decouan said, at his shoulder. "Or so it should be. Did you know it would do that? Whatever that thing was you threw in the engine?"

"No," Trei whispered. But he should have. He should have

remembered his nightmares, and guessed what a dragon would do to Teraica. . . .

"Trei," said Master Anerii, coming up beside him and gripping his shoulder. He gave him a little shake. "Trei!"

Trei swallowed, opened his eyes. Whispered, "Yes, sir."

"Look up, not down!"

Trei lifted his gaze to the empty sky. There was still some haze . . . but the wind moved in countless layers of diamond and pearl, shifting with the currents of warm rising air and quiet cooler air . . . and high overhead, a great-winged figure that was not a bird turned in slow, graceful circles. Another. A third . . . Trei swallowed a stab of longing so piercing he thought he might die of it right here on this hillside.

"You'll fly again," Master Anerii said harshly. "Never doubt it, Trei."

"Yes," Trei answered, in a slightly stronger voice. He took the next step, and the next. The stair turned around an outcropping and hid the worst part of the view below. Trei knew it was still there. But the sky was still above, too, and the soaring kajuraihi.

"Amazing," allowed the decouan, following Trei's glance aloft. "But keep your eyes on the path, boy, or you'll break your neck—and not even Master Patan would be able to do much about that! Step carefully."

"If it is not improper to inquire," Master Anerii said to the decouan as they resumed their descent, "may I ask whether you know why the provincar asked to see us?"

The decouan said, with an odd kind of grim good cheer, "Generous Gods, sir, it isn't Provincar Atta called for you! Not likely. The provincar has retired from public life, as they say. No, sir, it's the Little Emperor himself bade us bring you out of the oubliette. Decided you didn't really ought to be forgotten just yet, ha? Arrived in Teraica six days ago, he did. I'm sure he'll find something to say to you about the state of his city."

Master Anerii didn't even blink. "That seems fair enough. I certainly have something to say to him about the state of mine."

For an instant Trei thought the soldiers might be offended. But then the decouan laughed, and he saw he'd been mistaken: all the soldiers were satisfied with the provincar's downfall. They were ready to be tolerant of, even amused by, a foreigner's effrontery.

"Just along here, sir," was all the decouan said. "We'll take you to the blue tower. You can wash and dress properly before you come before the Emperor."

"Well, then, I thank you," Master Anerii said after the barest pause.

"No need, sir: those are my orders." But the decouan seemed pleased with himself and with his orders, and Trei thought that was a good sign.

The blue tower proved to be a prison, but nothing like the oubliette. Each floor held a complete apartment, and though the windows were barred and the doors heavy and guarded, the apartments were appointed as for noble guests. Master Anerii and Trei were led to the lowest tower apartment, where two large basins of hot water already waited, complete with warm towels and bowls of foamy soap. Clothing in proper

Island style was laid out on a bench next to the basins: kajurai black and novice black and gray.

"The Little Emperor wants you at fifth bell," the decouan told them. "So you have plenty of time." He nodded toward a doorway on the opposite side of the room. "If you need anything else, ask the men outside your door, yes?"

"Thank you, ah . . ."

"Decouan Patnaon, sir, and I'm pleased to be of service. I'll call you a bit before fifth bell, sir." The decouan gave a nod both deferential and ironic and left them alone.

Master Anerii and Trei looked at one another. "The Little Emperor, is it?" Master Anerii said. "Tell me how to address an Emperor, Trei. I didn't expect to meet an Emperor, and it's been a long time since I studied high-level Tolounnese protocol. Does one stand or kneel?"

"Oh—one stands." Trei paused, considering this. "At least, citizens of Tolounn stand. You kneel only if you need to, well . . ."

"Impress the Emperor with your earnestness?" Master Anerii began to undo the laces of his shirt. "Ah! I thank the Gods for soap! One wouldn't want to appear before an Emperor looking like a country sheepherder, I'm sure. Worse than a sheepherder. So a Tolounnese citizen stands on his feet before the Emperor? We will, too, then."

"We're not Tolounnese citizens," Trei pointed out.

"All the more, then." Master Anerii stepped into the first basin, sat cautiously down, and reached for the soap. "Put a towel in reach, will you? I won't kneel to that man unless I have to; he's the one who's offended against us, not the other way around."

Trei laid towels over the edge of each basin and stripped quickly, dropping his filthy clothing in a pile by the door. The hot water was wonderful.

And the clean clothing was even better. Trei wrapped the red sash around his waist and pinned it, lingering over the task. It seemed somehow odd to him to wear Island clothing here, to be familiar with the proper way to pin a sash. It seemed somehow a kind of repudiation of Tolounn. And that was strange, because if there had been any clear moment of repudiation, it was surely not this one.

Master Anerii said abruptly, "I suppose we've half a bell, at least. So tell me about this Little Emperor, then."

Trei gathered his thoughts. "Well—he's an enna Gaourr. You know that, of course, sir. Dharoann enna Gaourr. I don't know anything except what everybody knows. His father was a nephew of the last Little Emperor, only he couldn't ever keep his tongue behind his teeth; he argued all the time with the previous Little Emperor and sometimes with the Great Emperor. So he was exiled twice to Patainn and once, for *years,* all the way to Toipakom. Only each time the Great Emperor recalled him eventually. But *nobody* expected the Great Emperor to appoint his son as Little Emperor after his great-uncle died! You knew all that?"

"Go on. Don't worry about what I might know."

"I don't *know* much else," Trei said. "Only, he's been Little Emperor for twelve years, and he's the one who finally conquered Toipakom for the Great Emperor and brought it into Tolounn's Empire. My father—" He stopped.

Master Anerii leaned his hip on the table and waited.

Collecting himself, Trei went on, "My father liked him. He

said, 'He knows how an Emperor ought to handle trade: let it alone.' Every time the provincar of Rounn tried to raise taxes or put tariffs on trade goods or something, the merchants would appeal to the Little Emperor and he'd almost always rule in their favor. My father said, 'He may be overfond of conquest, but at least he's got more sense than to tax honest men just to raise gilded statues to his own glory.' " Trei opened his hands at Master Anerii's snort. "That *is* what he said. He said the enna Gaourr appointment was the best decision the Great Emperor made in sixty years."

"Huh. What else?"

Trei tried to think. "I don't know, sir. I guess . . . the soldiers like him, you see? So he must be a commander they respect, and they must think he's honorable. He'll like an honorable enemy; he'll respect courage and, I don't know, the virtues of soldiers. I think."

"Makes sense," the master conceded. "All right"—as a clap sounded outside their door—"we'll do well enough, Trei." A blank sternness came over his face as he turned.

Decouan Patnaon came in, took in their newly respectable appearance with a nod, and bowed them toward the door.

The blue tower gave straight into the great halls of the provincar's palace. There were a lot more cracks in the fine plaster and stonework than Trei remembered. But neither the decouan nor any of his men gave even the worst of the damage a second glance. They only led the way through one echoing antechamber, up a broad stairway, down a much shorter hallway, and into a large, plain room with an expensive floor of inlaid wood, wide windows curtained against the sun with translucent silk, and a single chair. There, the decouan and all his men took up stations with other soldiers already standing at attention all along the walls.

Tolounn's Little Emperor was already in the room. He was not sitting in the chair, however. He was standing before one of the windows, gazing out through the silken curtains. There were several other men in the room, but Trei had no difficulty picking out the Emperor. Even with his back turned, Dharoann enna Gaourr dominated the room completely. When the Emperor swung around to meet his prisoners, Trei actually swayed with the force of his gaze. If Master Anerii hadn't explicitly said, *We will stand,* he would certainly have gone to his knees.

Master Anerii put a hand on Trei's shoulder, looked for a moment, narrow-eyed, at the Little Emperor's face, and then inclined his head.

The Emperor strode forward, stopped in front of his chair—his throne, Trei supposed—put his fists on his hips, and looked his prisoners up and down. He was not an old man— not as old as Trei had imagined him, anyway. Trei would have guessed him to be younger than, say, Master Anerii—probably over forty, but probably not yet fifty. He had a broad, strong-featured face, familiar to Trei from the profile stamped on Tolounnese coins, but the coins did not show the aggressive power contained in his dark eyes. He *looked* like he'd been a soldier, Trei thought. A general, anyway. And he certainly looked like an Emperor. A circlet of gold oak leaves crowned him; a wide gold ring circled one wrist. He wore no other ornament.

"Kajurai Master Anerii," he said.

Master Anerii bowed. "Emperor of Tolounn."

The Little Emperor smiled, barely. He said, "You are indeed a true ambassador, enabled by Terinai Naterensei, called the king of the Floating Islands, to negotiate in his name?"

Master Anerii bowed a second time. "Yes, O Emperor."

"Good," the Little Emperor said briskly. He sat down in the chair, braced his elbows on its wide arms, and gazed over his tented hands at Master Anerii, ignoring Trei completely.

Trei was very willing to be ignored. He felt extremely young and ignorant—and he had blown up the engine and set things in motion for the destruction of half of the city. Being ignored seemed much the best possibility.

"Well," said the Emperor. "What would the Floating Islands have of me?"

Master Anerii didn't even blink. He said briefly, "We would hope for your personal undertaking, and the Great Emperor's behind yours, that Tolounn will leave the Islands alone, renouncing all claim to our lands and demesnes."

The Emperor leaned back in his chair, smiling. "But the Islands are properly a Tolounnese province, Master Anerii. And the key to any serious ambition we may have toward Cen Periven."

"Two hundred years seems long enough to us to legitimize our independence. And the Islands take no interest in your ambitions toward Cen Periven."

The Emperor said in a very bland tone, "That you have been flouting imperial authority for two hundred years does not legitimize you in our eyes."

"If you wish to bring us under your authority," Master

Anerii said—smoothly, but not quite as smoothly as the Emperor—"you will have to conquer us. My king promises that we shall make any such effort as difficult as possible. He suggests that an amicable relationship between the Islands and Tolounn would be a good deal less difficult."

"Well," said the Emperor softly, "but I don't mind the occasional difficult project."

Master Anerii paused. Then he asked, "Am I to understand, O Emperor, that you decisively reject our request for amity?"

The Emperor half smiled. "What does Terinai Naterensei offer me, Master Anerii, for such an undertaking?"

"We have," the master said precisely, "one thousand six hundred thirty-six Tolounnese soldiers that were stranded on Milendri when your engines failed. They are in our hands. What will you offer us, O Emperor, for all their lives?"

The smile disappeared. Dharoann enna Gaourr sat forward, his hands dropping to grip the arms of his chair. "I will redeem them all," he said flatly. "What will you ask for them? Not an assurance of amity. But name a price in gold and I will pay it."

Master Anerii hesitated, clearly trying to gauge this offer.

Trei caught the master's arm and stretched up to whisper quickly, "Give them all back without ransom!"

Master Anerii blinked down at Trei. He shook his head a little. "Tolounnese honor! You're sure, boy?"

Trei nodded vigorously.

Master Anerii looked up, cleared his throat, and declared, "Justly are Tolounnese soldiers famed for their discipline and honor as well as their courage! In recognition of the courage and honor of Tolounnese soldiers and of your honor, O Emperor, my king has accorded your soldiers generous treatment and will return them all to you without ransom."

All along the walls, and without otherwise moving, the soldiers stamped one foot down on the floor in unison; the wooden floor boomed hollowly. Master Anerii started at the unexpected sound.

The Little Emperor was not startled. But his eyebrows rose. He gave Trei a very thoughtful look. Then he stood up, advanced one precise step, and said formally, "Master Anerii, though I do not acknowledge Terinai Naterensei is a legitimate king, I am glad to acknowledge he is an honorable and generous lord. I accept his generosity on behalf of all my soldiers and freely give you *this* undertaking: I will not send these men again against the Floating Islands."

Master Anerii bowed.

"I will send ships to recover my Tolounnese soldiers," the Emperor added. "In recognition of the generosity of the Floating Islands, I will ask you to permit me to send also an indemnity to cover the cost of rebuilding the damaged portions of your city."

Master Anerii blinked. Then he bowed again.

"Now." Dharoann enna Gaourr resumed his seat. "As to your Islands. I wish you to say this to the so-called king of the Floating Islands: Tolounn is no longer inclined to recognize the autonomy of the Floating Islands. It is far past time the Islands resumed their proper place as a province of Tolounn. Terinai Naterensei would be well advised to consider the terms on which he will yield his autonomy, which will be far more generous if he puts us to less trouble."

The heavy features of Master Anerii did not show the alarm that Trei was sure *his* did. He merely tilted his head to one side and answered, "One might wonder how many Tolounnese cities you wish to sacrifice to this strange ambition, O Emperor. Or do you believe that the dragons that aided the Floating Islands in these past days will decline to do so in the future? Why would you believe that?"

The Little Emperor smiled, if a little grimly. "If this campaign had succeeded, I would have been pleased. But it showed me many things. I see now that it was a mistake to put the steam engines in a city. It was a mistake to guard them against only men—and less well than should have been done; I should have taken better thought for the Island kajuraihi. Next time, I shall build four engines, not three. Three shall press the sky magic away from the path of my ships so that your allies do not threaten them, just as this time. But the fourth—and the fifth, if necessary!—shall guard the first three, so that no dragon or kajurai approaches the place where they stand. And what will you do then?"

Master Anerii said, his tone level, "You are courteous to inform us of your intentions in such detail. I assure you that we will contrive."

"Or you may ask me for terms. I tell you plainly, I am inclined to be generous."

"And this will change, if we put you to such trouble as displeases you. Indeed. I will inform my king. He will give you this answer: we refuse your demand. If you would own the Islands"—here Master Anerii's voice dropped to a harsh growl—"come and take them."

"Proudly declared," acknowledged the Emperor. He sat

back, leaning his chin in his hand for some time, thinking. Then, straightening at last, he turned to Trei. "Trei enna Shiberren, son of Teguinn enna Shiberren, lately of Rounn. Is that so?"

Surprised, Trei bowed. "Yes, O Emperor. How did you—" He flushed, realizing his own temerity, and fell silent.

But the Emperor did not seem offended. He said merely, "You told Decouan Patnaon your provenance, and inquiries yielded the rest. How fortunate for the Islands that they have a half-bred Tolounnese to advise them!"

Trei bowed his head, understanding the condemnation in those words. He had no idea how to answer it, and so said nothing.

"You are from Rounn," the Emperor said. "I regret your loss, then. But you now claim your mother's kin in the Islands, rejecting your father's Tolounnese kin?"

It never got easier to answer that question. Trei said awkwardly, "I did go to my uncle in Sicuon, O Emperor. He wouldn't . . . He didn't . . . It's complicated."

The Little Emperor frowned. He leaned forward, dropping his arms to lie along the arms of the chair. "Perhaps it is not so complicated? Your father meant to pay the half-blood tax to register you on your majority, of course. And your uncle did not care to pay the tax. Is that how it was?"

Trei knew he'd flushed darker still. Lowering his eyes, he admitted, "Yes. I think so."

The Emperor shrugged. "So. That seems simple to me." He glanced at one of the quiet men by the wall. "Make a note, Tibarron. I am displeased by the brother of Teguinn enna

Shiberren, who even in the face of disaster makes so little of the bonds of kinship."

The man inclined his head.

"But—" exclaimed Trei, coming forward an involuntary step.

"I don't intend to put your uncle to death," the Little Emperor said mildly. "I will merely send him a personal rebuke."

"Oh . . ." Trei thought about an imperial messenger arriving at his uncle's house with *that* message and actually smiled. "All right. Good. I mean, thank you, O Emperor."

The Emperor lifted a hand. "I accept your gratitude in this small matter, Trei enna Shiberren. But," he wondered aloud, "what shall I do with you yourself? You are not precisely a foreign agent, are you? You are certainly not a foreign soldier, and thus no ordinary prisoner of war. You seem to me a boy who was so angry at his uncle that he struck at Tolounn entire. A boy of Tolounn who went to a great deal of personal trouble to strike deliberately at war engines of mine. In wartime. In aid of Tolounn's opponent. Shall I take this lightly?"

For a moment, Trei did not understand what the Little Emperor meant. Or no. He understood it at once, but did not want to admit he did. A cold dizziness afflicted him. He thought he might faint—then he thought he might throw up. He said, "I wasn't . . . I didn't . . ." He hadn't decided he was Islander just because he was angry with his uncle. That hadn't been why. Had it? Trei shut his eyes for a moment, trying only to breathe steadily and stay on his feet. Master Anerii put a hand under his elbow to support him.

"Provincar Atta was absolutely wrong to send a foreign

ambassador to the oubliettes," mused the Little Emperor. "He was never intended to hold tactical responsibility for this military stroke, and I think perhaps when ill fortune descended upon him, he became frightened. But . . . imprisoning a Tolounnese traitor in the oubliettes was not unreasonable." He looked thoughtfully at Trei, who met his eyes helplessly but could think of nothing at all to say.

Master Anerii leaned aggressively forward. "Tolounnese honor!" he snapped. "The envy of the world!"

"Islander pride," murmured the Emperor, lifting his eyebrows. "That evidently takes no reasonable account of circumstances. Shall I find this pride presumptuous?"

"Oh," growled Master Anerii. "Is it *pride* that offends you?" He took one step toward the Emperor and dropped heavily to his knees, lifting his hands in forthright entreaty. His manner made the gesture almost an insult . . . but not quite. "Let be the boy, O Emperor. That is an Island boy now and none of yours. According to your own law, he was never a Tolounnese citizen. It's the fault of *Tolounn* he found no place to go in your Empire after Rounn was destroyed. I beg you will thus be gracious and let him go to the place he did find."

The Emperor leaned his chin once more on his palm. "So we find the limits of Islander pride," he observed. "I am pleased to find it is not unbounded."

"I'm more interested in the limits of Tolounnese honor," Master Anerii answered harshly.

The Emperor returned, "The honor of Tolounn is without limit. But what you ask for is generosity. *That* is not unlimited. However"—a dismissive gesture—"I think it may extend so far. As I am in a mood, today, to be generous. Do you understand me, Master Anerii?"

"Yes," growled the master.

"The boy is yours."

Trei shuddered, trying not to fold up where he stood.

Master Anerii inclined his head stiffly. "Thank you, O Emperor. I'm . . . The Floating Islands acknowledge Tolounn's generosity."

"I *wish* to be generous. *Today*. You may stand, Master Anerii."

Master Anerii climbed back to his feet without a word.

Trei took a breath—another—he came forward a step to bow on his own account. Both Master Anerii and the Little Emperor looked at him in surprise.

"I'm sorry," Trei said. He spoke straight to the Emperor. "I don't mean . . . I would do it again if I had to. But I'm sorry. Truly. Maybe I was angry at my uncle. But that's not . . . I don't think that's why . . ." He stopped. Took a breath. Tried to steady himself. "I never meant to betray Tolounn, or you, exactly. Though I see that's exactly what I did." He stopped again. Tried again, more plainly. "There was no way to be loyal to everybody. Not that I could see. But I wish there had been. The Islands are my home now, but I don't hate Tolounn. Or you. At all. My father always . . . Is it insolence to say my father always spoke highly of you, O Emperor? I don't mean to be insolent."

The Emperor gazed at him, a curious expression in his dark, powerful eyes. "I don't find you insolent," he said after a moment. "Or if I do, then I forgive it. Indeed, I'm pleased to know your father spoke well of me. I'm not displeased to see

his son has found a place in the world, Trei enna Shiberren."
He opened one hand. "I release you to that place, and wish you
joy of it. If we meet again, Gods grant it will be with amicabil-
ity between us!"

Trei bowed deeply.

"Can we keep the wings?" asked a quick, light voice. For
the first time, Trei saw that Master Patan was one of the men
in the room. The artificer met Trei's surprised look with an
ironic glint and came a step away from the wall. He said to the
Little Emperor, "If you *must* release the kajuraihi, may we at
least keep their wings? Both sets, preferably?"

"No!" snapped Master Anerii.

Dharoann enna Gaourr made a small palm-down gesture,
amused. "Quietly. Quietly, if you please. Patan, I am devas-
tated to disappoint you, but we cannot blatantly steal the personal property of a foreign ambassador. It is not done. Master
Anerii, your wings are, of course, yours. However, the set used
in commission of an act of war against Tolounn . . . those belong to Tolounn."

Master Anerii hesitated . . . then nodded. Grudgingly, but
he nodded. "I'll have to send for another set for my novice."

"Your kajuraihi will not be molested," the Little Emperor
assured him. "Your novice and others under your authority are
free to come and go. You are not a prisoner here, but a recognized ambassador . . . though I will ask you to permit my soldiers to attend you and yours while you are in Tolounn." He
rose, signaling the end of the interview. "I will anticipate a useful exchange with the Floating Islands. Through your agency,
Master Anerii. I will expect to see you again."

Master Anerii did not comment on any of this. He merely

bowed low. To Trei's surprise—the master clearly remembered *this* piece of high Tolounnese protocol—he held that bow while Tolounn's Little Emperor exchanged a low-voiced comment with one of the waiting men, murmured an order to another, clapped Master Patan on the shoulder in friendly consolation, and finally went out, drawing most of the men and nearly all the personal energy in the room out with him.

Decouan Patnaon came forward as the room emptied and grinned at Trei. "Good for you, boy. Too bad, though. You've got nerve and heart—you might have made a soldier."

Trei laughed, though shakily. "I don't think so! Though I thank you."

The decouan thumped Trei on the shoulder, but he gave Master Anerii a sober, deferential nod. "Thank you, sir. You Islanders may be overconfident, but you're civilized people. That was a generous gesture, returning our soldiers without ransom. *We* will remember it, I promise you."

He meant the soldiers of Tolounn, of course. Master Anerii returned the decouan a reserved nod, for all he was undoubtedly praying the Floating Islands would never have to depend on the goodwill of Tolounnese soldiers. Trei prayed for that, too . . . but if the favor of the Gods failed, then he thought it would be just as well to have the goodwill of the soldiers.

"I'm sure you'd be just as pleased to return to your Islands. We'll get you on your way, sir, no trouble at all. Only tell me what you need. Wings! Gods, give me a solid ship under my feet, if I can't have a decent horse and a good road!"

"There's a spare set of wings waiting at a pebble well over on this side of the second waystation," Master Anerii said to

Trei quietly. "It may take a bell or so to have them brought. But I think we can have you at the waystation by full dark, and back home two days after that."

Home. And Master Anerii said it as though it was a foregone conclusion. Trei couldn't answer. But he nodded.

16

The hidden school was strange in the days after the Tolounnese surrender. Not only the school: there was an odd feel to Canpra itself. The city had sustained some damage, of course, but that was not, Araenè thought, the source of the strangeness. The huge Tolounnese siege ladders had shattered buildings and balconies, and the white marble of the First City was streaked with soot from fires. The damage was troubling, a reminder of danger and fear, but Second City was less damaged, and Third City . . . Third City should by that measure have seemed untouched. The Tolounnese soldiers had not come so far. But the invasion had affected the people of the Third City as it had those of First and Second, even if it had not ruined a single Third City shop or home.

Araenè was not quite able to explain to herself where the difference lay, or whether the change was ill or well, but she knew it was there. She called visions of the city into Master Tnegun's Dannè sphere, and she went out into the Third City twice, dressed once as a boy and once as a Third City girl.

The change in Canpra had to do, she thought, with the raw red earth of the new cemeteries, where men who had been killed in the invasion lay in long rows beside people who had died from the Yngulin illness. She stood for a long time, once everything was over, gazing down from a Second City balcony across the cemetery where her parents lay. There were so many new graves. . . . The cemetery had doubled in size after the coughing illness, but it had doubled again since. Araenè was not the only mourner who had gone to stand silently at the edge of the stripped red earth. But the company of other mourners brought her no comfort, and the grief followed her back to the hidden school; it clung to her no matter how she dressed or what name she called herself.

Too much death too quickly, too much fear, and somehow no part of the city seemed really safe any longer. The mood of the city went beyond that, though: there was a bitterness against Tolounn that had not been there before, but it was mixed with an oddly grim good cheer because, after all, the Islands had defeated Tolounn—and everyone knew that Tolounnese soldiers were the best in the world.

"It's important we be generous and honorable—honorable exactly as Tolounn understands honor," Ceirfei had explained to Araenè before going away to be a prince. "The Tolounnese put such *passion* into their honor. If we are to be opponents, we must ensure they regard us as *honorable* enemies and not barbarians." *In case they come again, and we lose,* he did not say. He did not have to say it. Araenè knew that the triumph running through the streets of Canpra was wrong, though maybe . . . maybe not as dangerous as the bitterness, unchecked, would have been. But she knew Milendri *would* have been taken—the Islands *would* have been conquered—except for Trei. And

no one knew that, except her. And Ceirfei, and Master Tnegun. And the kajuraihi, she supposed.

Everyone should know it. She wanted to go out in the
streets and proclaim it: *My cousin saved you all!* It seemed utterly wrong that so few knew this, even worse that Canpra did
not appreciate her cousin's continuing danger. Even she did
not know what that danger was, precisely. When she tried to
find a vision of Trei in a sphere or in water or fire, she saw
nothing but darkness. He was not *dead;* she knew this and
Master Tnegun confirmed it. Araenè clung to that certainty.
But the darkness and cold she saw in the spheres horrified her.
She knew a kajurai official had gone after Trei; they would get
him back. Master Tnegun would not promise her this, but she
believed it, fiercely. Even though she could not imagine how
the living wind of the kajuraihi could reach into that cold
darkness. She tried not to think about it.

But that left her too much time to think of other things.

She could not go out into Canpra and tell everyone about
Trei. Of course she could not. But after that first visit to the
cemetery, she found herself even more reluctant to go out into
the streets of Canpra for any other reason, either. She did not
know how she should dress if she did; she did not know who
she should be. In a way, the question was like choosing a role
in a play . . . girl, boy, apprentice mage—she did not know what
she should be. It was all roles, and she vacillated between
them. She felt, obscurely but strongly, that when she actually
chose a role, this time it might be the one she would play for
the rest of her life. But she did not know which to choose.

Kajurai or prince . . . those were roles, too, and more in-
tractably separate than even the roles that waited for Araenè's

choice. Ceirfei, she knew, did not exactly get to choose what role he would play, and who would have thought it might be harder to be a prince than a girl?

For the first time in her life, Araenè cared about politics. Everyone in Canpra had a violent opinion about what the Islands should do about Tolounn. Araenè did not, but she wondered what Ceirfei thought. She was sure he would be right. But would his uncle listen to him? She worried about that. She felt intense sympathy for Ceirfei. She also thought Ceirfei would have an easier time managing his various roles if he didn't feel obliged to play every one of them with such *intensity*.

But the hidden school had changed in a different way than the city, and Araenè could not decide whether the change was in the school or in herself, or in some complicated way had emerged from the relationship between herself and the school.

All the mages had recovered from their overextension—or their simple overexhaustion, in Master Tnegun's case—except for Master Yamatei, of course, who had died and left poor Kepai and Kebei with no master of their own. Kanii thought Master Kopapei would take them, or maybe Master Akhai. But Araenè had a faint suspicion that Master Tnegun might do it—to encourage amity between the twins and herself. Because these days, the twins were not really talking to her.

Few of the apprentices were. Tichorei, to be sure, wasn't talking to anybody—he was ill after his exhaustion and overextension during the invasion, and he did not come into the common areas of the school. Araenè was anxious to see him recovered, to tell him how much she admired his committed effort during the invasion. But she was afraid he would be embarrassed and angry, that he would refuse to forgive her deception. And she knew that, Kanii aside, all the younger apprentices would probably follow Tichorei's lead—once he was around to provide one. She hoped Tichorei would recover; of course she did. But she dreaded the lead he might give the other boys.

Of all the apprentices, only Kanii and little Cesei seemed utterly untroubled by the revelation of Araenè's secret. Kanii's manner toward her scarcely changed—though he would not come into her apartment, and did not like for her to visit his. But he did not mind meeting her in the common areas of the school.

"Why should it make any difference? Everyone knows we're terribly short of mages—and worse now." He meant not only *Since Master Yamatei died* but also *Since we know now that Sayai won't ever be a mage*. They did know that now. The masters had known for some time that Sayai was going to be an adjuvant and not a mage, and the invasion had forced them to make it clear to Sayai also. What no one knew, yet, was whether Sayai would refuse to become an adjuvant and instead leave the school entirely. The apprentices didn't discuss it. Araenè thought that in his place, she would let herself become an adjuvant—but Sayai had choices she did not, and she knew he was bitterly disappointed.

In a way, Kanii's acceptance was not a surprise. This was because, as Araenè discovered, Master Kopapei had known she was a girl from the first time he'd seen her—and she'd thought herself so perfectly disguised! But he had known, or so Kanii told her.

"He didn't *tell* me," Kanii assured her. They were in the common library; Kanii was helping Araenè find appropriate introductory books about mathematics and stone lore. "I guess he didn't tell *anyone,* since you say not even Master Tnegun knew! But I knew there was something. I thought—I don't know what I thought! But my master is the best, and if he didn't care, why should I?"

This attitude seemed common to Master Kopapei's apprentices, because Cesei also didn't care. "It's obvious—now," he said, disgusted with himself that he hadn't spotted her secret all by himself. "And it's obvious now why you don't know anything about mathematics or anything. Here." He put a fat little book down on the table in front of Araenè. "This is the best one on geometry. I'll help you with the hard parts, if you like. I don't care you're a girl!"

"You're a little young to notice such things," Kanii told him, amused. "You're the *last* one to have an opinion, brat!" He went on to Araenè, confidently, "Everyone will get used to the idea."

Araenè wished she had his confidence. She said, "I'm sure you're right." But she was not sure, and when she went up to the hall of spheres and mirrors, she went slowly and sadly. Nor could she concentrate on the spheres once she got there. She kept looking into one sphere and then another, hoping for a glimpse of Trei. But she could not find a reflection of her cousin in any sphere, whether of stone or crystal or glass or polished wood.

Master Tnegun found her there, and leaned for a while on the iron railing of the stair, watching her. Araenè was trying to coax the secret of contained magery out of a heavy black-lead sphere the size of her fist. She did not want to speak to her master—she didn't even want to look at him. She never knew how to speak to anyone now, and as soon as she saw Master Tnegun had come up the spiral stair to find her, she was afraid that the masters had after all decided to send her away from the school and that he had come to tell her this. She pretended not to notice him.

"You have been studying that lead sphere for eight minutes," Master Tnegun said at last. "And, lead being unsubtle and single-natured, it holds only one quality. I am confident you identified this some time past. What is it?"

Araenè blushed. "It blocks against vision," she muttered, and put the sphere back on its shelf. She *had* been holding it too long: her wrists, now that she paid attention to them, ached from its weight.

"Indeed. Not a quality I would ordinarily expect you to value."

Araenè did not look up. "I don't want clear vision right now," she admitted in a low tone.

The master did not say, *Your cousin will be well.* He did not say anything at all. But he pushed away from the stair railing and came to kneel down on the floor, facing Araenè across the line of spheres she had been examining. He studied the spheres for a moment. "Tourmaline does not belong in this row," he commented at last. "All the rest you have selected contain spellwork that has to do with shaping and making. That one is not associated with any such magic."

Without a word, Araenè picked up the tourmaline sphere and handed it to him. He took it thoughtfully, but then did not put it back on its shelf, but only held it for a time, studying its rich orange-gold depths. "What does it taste of, to you?" he asked Araenè.

"Fenugreek, and something musty I don't recognize," she said, still not looking at him. "Something with a trace of lime to it, but much more bitter. I don't like it—I tried to bury it behind the fenugreek."

Master Tnegun nodded thoughtfully. "That is the summoning set into it," he murmured. "You submerged that magic underneath a much more polite magic of calling and naming. The summoning is for the smothering dark, the darkness so heavy it puts out fire and crushes light. One understands very well why you should find your hand drawn to this sphere."

Araenè did not say anything.

The master still did not say anything reassuring about Trei. He said instead, "The hidden school would be the poorer without you, Araenè."

Araenè looked up at last. "Does anyone think that, besides you?"

Master Tnegun lifted an eyebrow at her. "Do you value anyone's opinion, except mine?"

Araenè was too taken aback to respond at once. Then she could not help smiling at the trick in that question, where saying yes would be disrespectful of her master's authority and saying no would be simply presumptuous.

"You are too wise to answer," observed the master. He was silent for a moment. Then he said, "You have certainly had an . . . interesting effect on the hidden school. Your affinity for fire and for doors has been and remains beyond price. You have not, I trust, recently stepped through any door into fire?"

Araenè stared at him.

"You might," said Master Tnegun. His unexpected smile startled her, teeth gleaming in his dark face. "The heart of the school once again contains fire, were you aware? No? Then allow me to assure you of it. I would not be astonished to find that the young dragon curled there recalls your name."

Araenè was not at all certain she wanted the baby dragon to remember her name. But she was very glad to know that it was well. She asked hesitantly, "How did it come here? Did you—?"

Master Tnegun tilted his head to the side judiciously: *No.* "We did nothing—indeed, there is nothing we know that we might have done. It merely came there—this morning, we believe. We suspect the great dragon brought it to us: a fire dragon that remembers the sky and wishes, for whatever reason dragons may wish such things, for our Islands to prosper. Master Kopapei assures me the young dragon seems content. If it is not, I suspect you will discover the fact."

"Oh," Araenè said faintly.

Master Tnegun considered her for another moment and then added gravely, "I believe you may not be aware that girls sometimes become mages, in Yngul."

Araenè looked up swiftly.

"It's said a girl's strength fades less swiftly than a boy's. That may be so; I have not tested the question. I believe we will find it does not fade more swiftly, however."

Araenè made a noncommittal sound, though she was listening intently.

"Here, girls look straight ahead down the path their mothers lay down for them, and if power arises in them, they smother it. But Cassameirin . . . When Cassameirin was young, from time to time a girl would come into the hidden school. He had a girl apprentice, once. That girl became Kanora Ireinamei, mage and teacher, who spoke to the wind dragons and coaxed them to settle upon Kotipa."

"I never heard that!" Araenè exclaimed, staring.

"It was long ago. There are accounts in my private library. They are available to you, if you wish. You may find them instructive, if you find yourself speaking to fire dragons on a frequent basis."

"Oh!" said Araenè, and was silent, repressing the urge to leap up at once and go find the master's private library.

"The school put itself in your way. Your cousin abetted you. Master Kopapei knew what you were, and he did not condemn you. Nor do I. What other opinion concerns you?"

"I don't know," Araenè whispered.

"You do your Islands and your city and this school an injustice," Master Tnegun said gently, "if you condemn them out of hand and without trial."

Araenè said, "It was easier—" but stopped without completing the thought.

"It is often easier not to try," agreed the master. "If you wish to leave the hidden school, I cannot prevent you. But if you do not wish to, then no one will cast you forth. I would thus prefer that you cease walking about as though you are afraid of waking a basilisk with every step."

Araenè made herself meet his eyes. It wasn't easy. But she did not look away. She nodded instead, and said, not whispering this time, "All right."

"Good." Master Tnegun rose to his feet, bent, collected a sphere of black iron, and weighed it in his hand. He said, his manner sardonic, "And I believe you may have an unusual chance to bend the opinion of the city in your favor. A visitor has come calling for you, Araenè. You will, I believe, find him waiting for you in your garden."

Trei, Araenè thought at once, but immediately knew that could not be right. Her second guess . . . She knew, once she had thought of him, that her second guess was right. A smile, unfamiliar in these days, tugged at her mouth, and she glanced down at herself. She was wearing a plain dress, as she did these days when she was in the school. Now she wondered whether the dress was too plain. Whether she ought to have found something more . . . more feminine.

"My advice, though you have not asked for it," said her master, "is not to fuss."

"Yes . . . ," Araenè said distractedly. "Excuse me . . . ," and she opened the carved ebony door that stood suddenly at her hand, and stepped through.

17

Trei came back to Milendri less than a senneri after he'd left it. It seemed to him that he'd been away much longer.

Nor was this arrival at all like the first. He'd come like a Tolounnese boy the first time: staring up from below, stunned by his first sight of the winged kajuraihi, amazed by the floating stairway . . . amazed by everything. And dazed with grief and the memory of grief.

The grief was still there. But muted, and . . . not the same. And there was, this time, also an unexpected sense of coming home.

This time, Trei came down from the heights like a proper kajurai: riding the living wind under the inscrutable regard of transparent dragons half visible above. He gazed down through the infinite layers of the air to the white towers of Canpra. And he came in company, surrounded by other kajuraihi: Master Anerii Pencara below and to his right; others, with crimson wings, or white, or gold, flying above and below and all around.

They dropped toward Canpra: the shining towers grew more distinct, and beyond the towers the wide, tree-lined streets of the Second City and the crowded bustle of the Third.

Trei hesitated . . . then slanted his descent toward Master Anerii. He called, "Can we—?"

The novice-master turned his head. He was too far for Trei to read his expression, but after a moment his gruff shout came back: "Why not?" Allowing the other kajuraihi to go on without them, Master Anerii turned out into a wide spiral that would take them well out across the city before bringing them back to the kajurai precincts at the edge of the Island.

At first, Trei thought that surprisingly little damage had been done by the Tolounnese attack. There were large areas, at the edge where Canpra had been built down into the stone, where buildings had been broken and ruined. But there was nothing, of course, of the damage catapults would have done against a recalcitrant grounded city.

Of course, Tolounn had not required artillery to enter Canpra, which had neither walls nor any other defense save its height above the waves. A closer look showed that the people of Canpra had not prevented the Tolounnese from penetrating deeply into their city. There were the marks of fire, where buildings had been put to the torch by either attackers or defenders; there were the remnants of hasty barricades in the streets; there were places where one building or another showed damage from the powder bombs Tolounn had developed according to Yngulin formulae. And, as they passed inland, they overflew a large new cemetery where the red earth was as fresh and raw as a wound.

Master Anerii and Trei turned at last across the city, back toward the sea and kajurai territory. Trei found that the balcony nearest the novitiate had been badly damaged; Master Anerii passed it by and guided Trei to another. This one was smaller and much more difficult to come down on; one had to stall very neatly in order not to rake feathers across the wall. Trei managed it with something approaching grace and tried to look as though he always landed that well.

Master Anerii lifted an amused eyebrow, not fooled at all. But he merely said, "I'm to report to Wingmaster Taimenai at once. So are you," and gestured for Trei to turn so he could help him off with his wings.

The wingmaster was not in his office. He was in the map room, which Trei had previously seen only during lessons. The map posted on the big wall at the moment showed the long sweep of the Tolounnese coast, from Tetouann in the north all the way down past the great island of Toipakom and then past Marsosa and Goenn and Teraica to Emoenn and Gaicana in the far south. Toipakom had only become a part of the great Tolounnese Empire a few years ago. It hadn't actually *wanted* to join the Empire. Either.

Wingmaster Taimenai was not alone in the kajurai map room. Lord Manasi Teirdana was there, standing close by the map with a pointer in his hand; so were two men Trei didn't know. The wingmaster was stepping around a long table cluttered with other maps in order to approach the big one.

Trei hesitated at the door, but Master Anerii went right in. So Trei followed, uncomfortably. Wingmaster Taimenai turned his head and at once all his motion checked. *His* expression wasn't neutral at all: Trei stopped in his tracks, startled at the relief and gladness in the wingmaster's face. The two men he didn't know caught the wingmaster's reaction and turned, glancing first at Master Anerii and then, with obvious surmise, at Trei.

"So Goenn seems to offer the best possible combination of access to resources from the interior and access to shipping down the northern currents," Lord Manasi was saying. Facing the map, his back to the room, he hadn't at once realized no one was attending to his words. But now, finally perceiving the change in the quiet, he swung around. His eyes widened, then narrowed.

"I believe we shall finish this discussion at a later time," Wingmaster Taimenai said.

"Taimenai—" Lord Manasi began.

"We may all hope that after we have had time to consider Master Anerii's detailed report, our discussion will become more fruitful. I hope my lords will not find a brief postponement too inconvenient," the wingmaster said. Firmly.

"Well . . ." Lord Manasi gave Trei an odd look, combining wary approval and simultaneously a kind of suspicious dissatisfaction. "Yes, I suppose so. . . ." He moved toward the door along with the other two men. Master Anerii shut the door behind them.

Wingmaster Taimenai said, "Anerii! Well done!" He crossed the room in two strides and caught Trei by the shoulders, looking at him closely. "Trei. Are you well? Genrai brought us word that you were carried away from the Teraica engines. We believed you injured—imprisoned—possibly close-questioned—" He looked a question at Master Anerii.

"Injured, healed, imprisoned, and released," Master Anerii answered that look. "You will indeed wish to hear my report. Which," he sighed, "I suppose I shall have to put down properly in black ink as soon as possible. Tonight, I suppose."

The wingmaster grinned at the other man, actually grinned, an expression Trei had never imagined breaking through his stern manner. "I fear so." Then he looked back down at Trei. "Trei—"

Trei tried to find words past an unexpected tightness in his throat, but failed.

Wingmaster Taimenai, seeing his difficulty, let him go, stepped back, and drew the familiar reserve across his manner as though he donned a cloak. "We are glad to have you back among us," he said formally. "We had feared worse. You had no need to go to quite such lengths to prove yourself to us, however. Or if you did, I'm sorry for it."

"I didn't do it for that," Trei protested, but then stopped, uncertain.

"Didn't you? Well, it had that effect," the wingmaster answered drily. He reached out, tipped Trei's chin up gently, and looked into his face. "Welcome home, Trei."

Trei had not exactly expected punishment, not after . . . everything. But neither had he expected this welcome. It was as though a weight he'd braced himself to carry had, if not lightened, at least shifted into an easier load to bear. He didn't trust his voice to answer.

The wingmaster let him go, stepped back, and said sternly, "I will ask you to add your own detailed report to Master Anerii's. Write it tonight, if you please. You may begin with a justification of your decision to venture out of the novitiate despite the strictest possible injunction to remain within. Then continue to the moment you departed Tolounn. Is that clear?"

Sternness was much easier to answer than open joy and relief. "Yes, Wingmaster," Trei agreed, though he winced at the thought of the work that report would entail. "Um, Ceirfei? Genrai and the boys? Rekei—he was injured? He didn't . . ." He couldn't make himself say "die." He asked instead, "My cousin? Do you know what . . . Is my cousin all right, do you know, sir? Master Anerii said he didn't wait for much news to come in. Please, may I have leave to visit my cousin?"

"Ah." The wingmaster sounded so serious that Trei was immediately afraid *everyone* had died. But he said instead, "Everyone is well enough, Trei. Rekei was injured, as you say: another kajurai caught him and managed—somehow!—to keep enough height to gain a low balcony. Ceirfei, ah. He and your . . . cousin . . . apparently worked with that Yngulin mage of ours to support your own efforts and thwart the Tolounnese." He paused and then added, "Of course you must visit your cousin as soon as possible. I am confident she will tell you a far more comprehensive tale when you see her."

Trei cleared his throat. "I'm sure she will. Sir. Is she . . . That is, she is still . . ."

"She is, I believe, generally to be found at the hidden school. And Genrai, Kojran, and Tokabii are properly back within the novitiate," Wingmaster Taimenai concluded. "Where you should be, Novice Trei, by dusk, if you please." He gave Trei a dismissive nod. "I expect that report! Clear and direct, novice, and reasonably concise, or I will ask you to rewrite it. I will ask you to have it in my hands by second bell."

"Yes, sir," Trei said. The cool dismissal did not at all blur the warmth of the wingmaster's initial welcome. He added quietly, sincerely, "Thank you, sir."

The wingmaster gave him a nod, then, turning to Master Anerii, said, smiling, "Anerii, if you will stay a moment . . ."

Trei slipped out. But then he hesitated. The wingmaster was one thing, and his cousin was important, but the person he really wanted to find right now was *Ceirfei*. Trei had no way to find him if he wasn't in the novitiate. But then . . . perhaps Araenè knew some way?

He no longer had the little crystal pendant Master Tnegun had given him. But he thought maybe Araenè might be listening for his voice, or at least have done something so he could find her. So he put his hands against a door across from the map room—he had no idea where it led—and whispered his cousin's name. Nor was he surprised when the door swung open under his hands to reveal not whatever room ought to have been there, but a tangled, overgrown garden that smelled of sunlight and herbs, with an iron fence bordering one side and a brick wall on the other. His cousin's voice came clearly from somewhere in the garden: she was laughing. She sounded happy, Trei thought, surprised. His own heart lifted.

He stepped through the door and made his way through the garden toward Araenè's voice, stepping over herbs that had spilled out over pathways and ducking under branches that, as often as not, seemed to have thorns as well as flowers. It seemed a surprisingly large garden when he was actually trying to find someone in it. Araenè laughed again and said something indistinct, and he followed her voice around a small, contorted tree with delicate leaves like lace and red berries like polished garnets.

Araenè was sitting on a low stone by a pool, amid a tangle of vines with small white flowers shaped like trumpets and big-leaved shrubs with purple flowers dangling like bells. She was wearing a plain linen dress with green embroidery around the hem; a narrow green silk cord gathered the dress up around her waist and crossed between her small breasts. Trei paused and frankly stared: she was not exactly pretty, but despite her cropped hair, no one would have mistaken her for a boy. In fact, now that she wore girls' things, her short hair only accented the slender length of her neck and the fineness of her bones; it was hard to see how she had ever looked like a boy.

And an arm's length from Araenè, one foot braced on another stone, stood Ceirfei. He was looking down at her and smiling. Then he looked up and saw Trei, and the smile slipped.

Trei started forward again, more slowly. But no matter the coolness of Ceirfei's reaction, he was glad Araenè looked well—she *did* look well: happy and confident. She hadn't seen him yet. He called, "Cousin!" and held out his hands to her.

"Trei!" Araenè looked up, then jumped to her feet and ran to take his hands, smiling into his face. "I didn't know you were back! It's wonderful to see you!"

"Didn't anyone tell you—?"

"Oh," Araenè said quickly, "yes, Wingmaster Taimenai—isn't he a dear?—told me he was sending a kajurai official after you—and Master Tnegun showed me how to look for you in a glass sphere, because glass is good for visions of wind and sky. So I looked for you every day, and yesterday I saw you in the sky at last! So then I knew you were all right. I was so relieved! And now you're back at last! Can you stay to visit?"

"Yes . . ." Trei found himself laughing, happy in his cousin's enthusiastic welcome. "Or no, not really, not tonight. I'm glad the wingmaster was kind to you, but he expects a long report from me! But I wanted to see you—" *And Ceirfei.* He looked past Araenè to Ceirfei, who was standing stiffly to one side, unsmiling, his arms folded. Trei's happiness faded.

Araenè glanced quickly from one of them to the other and let go of Trei's hands, taking a step back. "You need to talk to each other," she observed. "I'll leave you, all right?" She added to Ceirfei, "When you're ready to leave, the gate will take you wherever you ask. I think!" And to Trei, "But, you, come find me before you leave, all right? Even if you can't stay long. Promise me you won't leave without letting me see you again! I don't want to wonder if I just imagined you were back!"

"I'll find you," Trei promised her.

"Good!" His cousin darted away, down the overgrown path; she stepped up on a white stone outside a window and then onto the windowsill and, ducking her head, through the high window and into the hidden school.

Trei gazed at Ceirfei. The heavy scent of crushed herbs rose around him, so that the heat of the afternoon seemed somehow heavier and more oppressive. The older boy was dressed as he had been when Trei had first seen him: as a prince. All in white, with a violet sash and a violet ribbon threaded through his dark hair. But his eyes were kajurai eyes, and he looked . . . not exactly older. Harder, maybe. The senneri just past had been no easier for Ceirfei, Trei thought, than for himself; he wondered what had happened in the Islands while he had been flying to Tolounn and then imprisoned in the oubliette and then flying back. . . . He said, feeling desperately awkward, "I'm sorry."

"You've no need to be," Ceirfei said at once, and smiled at last. But his shoulders were stiff, and there was a constraint to that smile Trei had never seen before. He continued formally, "By all accounts, you did very well indeed. I am glad to see you well; we were worried. The Islands owe you. . . ."

"Stop it!" Trei cried. He moved a step forward. "Ceirfei . . . I'm sorry we, I didn't tell you. You must see we *couldn't* tell you. You'd have had to go to Wingmaster Taimenai, or your uncle—or else you'd have insisted on coming with us, and you *must* know—"

"Of course," Ceirfei interrupted this incoherent protest. "I understand that perfectly. You were quite right."

Trei stared at him helplessly. Then he took one more step, dropped to his knees, and lifted his hands in supplication. "Prince Ceirfei," he said formally while the other boy was still too startled to stop him, "I'm very sorry for deceiving you and betraying your trust, and I beg you will forgive me."

"Get up!" Ceirfei said sharply. "I've already said I understand you were right!"

"I know that! You know that's not what I mean!"

Ceirfei didn't answer. The heavy stillness of the garden closed in around them.

Trei dropped his hands to rest on his thighs. His eyes burned; his throat felt tight. He said with difficulty, "I'm sorry to trouble you, then," and started to get to his feet.

"I'm jealous of you," Ceirfei said abruptly, and Trei stilled, staring at him.

The prince's voice was sharp, overloud in the quiet. "Of course I am. The meanest Third City beggar has far more freedom than I. Do you see? I know I'm wrong; it's not as though I don't know I'm wrong." He paused, took a hard breath, pressed a hand for a moment over his eyes. Lowered his hand. Stepping forward, he offered Trei his hands. "Forgive me, Trei, and will you please get up?"

Trei wordlessly let the prince take his hands and draw him to his feet. He said, now meaning something quite different, "I'm sorry, Ceirfei. Won't they . . . Surely your uncle hasn't entirely forbidden you the sky?" A thought struck him and he shut his eyes in pity. "Oh, Ceirfei . . . how far are you from the throne now?"

The prince released his hands and turned half away. "You are right: not as far as I was. My cousin Prince Safei died in the fighting. And my brother Mederinai may yet die: he lies unwaking and neither the physicians nor the priests nor the mages can find his wandering soul or guess whether it will return. I don't know . . . I don't know what man struck him down, and that's best, because—did you know?—it was I who guaranteed all the Tolounnese soldiers their lives."

"I didn't know."

"Yes. It was important to be generous, do you see, because, well, for many reasons. So I was generous and spared them all. I am commended on all sides. Because it was"—Ceirfei's mouth twisted—"the sensible thing to do."

Trei said nothing.

"Yes, well," Ceirfei conceded, "I know that is even true.

But . . . I am permitted to fly. As a favorite toy may be given to a petulant child if it behaves well. But I am no longer kajurai." He brushed the tips of his fingers across his eyelids. "Despite the eyes."

"I'm sorry," Trei said once more.

"Yes." Ceirfei's mouth crooked. "As I said . . . I am a fool. I have not wanted . . . Well."

Trei suggested impulsively, "I could teach you everything they teach us about flying, about the sky and wind. I'm sure Genrai would say the same. All the things we learn, all along. The rest of it doesn't matter so much. Does it? I mean, you never meant to be an ambassador, exactly, did you? You'll learn history and protocol and all those things anyway, won't you, as a prince? Does it matter whether you live in the palace or the kajurai novitiate, as long as you can fly?"

Ceirfei was silent for a moment. Then he smiled, this time with something resembling humor. "Less, perhaps, given such generosity. Thank you, Trei. I accept your offer." He hesitated. "Have you seen Genrai since your return?"

Trei understood at once why Ceirfei asked. He shook his head. "Wingmaster Taimenai said he was in the novitiate right now. You might find him there."

". . . and tender him the same apology I gave you. Yes. Only I owe him a stronger apology: I should have gone to see him long since. He will think . . . that is, he will think . . ."

"Yes."

Ceirfei bowed his head. "You would be right to rebuke me."

Trei was slightly shocked. "It's hardly my place."

"Is it not? As Genrai's friend, and mine?"

"Oh." Trei took a breath. "Well, then . . . shall we agree I don't need to? Only, it would be kind of you to assure poor Genrai your silence was not his fault."

"I'll find him," Ceirfei agreed. He turned toward the gate, hesitated, turned back. "Trei—with your permission, I will court your cousin."

Trei stared, taken utterly by surprise.

Ceirfei smiled, a quick flash of genuine amusement. "In fact, I confess, I am courting her already. I've come here often while we waited for your return. She needed the support of a friend. And then, it protects her reputation, you know. I'd do that for her anyway, because she's your cousin and you're my friend."

"Oh," Trei managed. "Well, that's . . . I mean, you . . ."

"And her family's good enough. Anyway, I elevated her when I, ah, well, it was convenient to raise her rank. Earlier. It would hardly be right to degrade her again, you know. And then, as they say, mages always have good blood. So my mother can hardly object. Besides . . . she's young, you know, but anybody can see she'll be pretty in a year or two."

"Ah. Can they?"

This time, it was an outright grin. "Well, anybody besides her cousin. You're too fixed on flying to notice, I suppose. She'll set the most amazing precedent, one we need."

"You think so?" Trei found himself smiling. "Good . . ."

"There's room in the Islands for a lady mage. More than one, I hope. Or there will be. Or if not, we'll deserve to lose our autonomy to Tolounn. Go find Araenè, Trei: she was desperately worried for you, and desperately relieved to glimpse you in the sky again." Ceirfei turned back toward the gate, and this time he pushed it open and stepped through. The novitiate was visible for a moment, and then vanished again as the gate closed. Through its bars, the narrow streets of the Third City sprang back into view.

Trei did not stay to look out at the city, but went to find his cousin. He went smiling, and with a lightness to his step almost as though he were flying, for he felt at last that he had, indeed, come home.

RACHEL NEUMEIER started writing fiction to relax when she was a graduate student. She is also the author of another young adult fantasy, *The City in the Lake,* which *Booklist* called "shimmering" in a starred review, as well as The Griffin Mage series. Rachel lives in rural Missouri with a large garden, a small orchard, and a gradually increasing number of Cavalier King Charles spaniels. You can find out more about Rachel and her books at rachelneumeier.com.

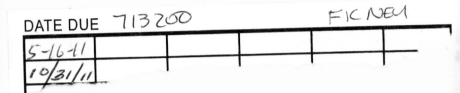